TANGLE

Book Three of the Faceless

RIKKAINE THOMPSON

For Mum and Dad

ACKNOWLEDGMENTS

To Robert, my darling dork, for giving me the world and helping me to chase my dreams. My parents for the constant encouragement. My amazing sister, Felicia, for her ongoing love and support. My brother, Daniel, who still would've loved the puns and the 'bigfoot' joke. My three wonderful children who are growing up too fast. The Frakking mob, my three sisters-of-heart, who I really should've mentioned before.

Katie Luisier, my first reader, best of friends and eternal bouncing board.

Elle Tharp for her love and patience when I said, 'hey, can you do scales?'. You are amazing.

Cheyenne Phakousonh, Haideé T. H, Sabrina Sheldon, Zhanna Postupalyo, Eden Ellis, Karyn Sands, Athiena Eades, Kym Antony and Emily Combs for their comments and support.

CHAPTER 1

The phone rang.

Jonathan Locklear, a deputy in Bellhollow's Sheriff's office, listened to the tone of the ring. Waiting, he leaned back and sighed at the ceiling, hearing the rickety old chair creak beneath his weight.

It had been a long day already and set to get even longer. Bellhollow, the sleepy town nestled in the forests of Northern California, had barely begun to get over one senseless tragedy and had not been prepared for another.

Eighteen-year-old Alyson Gale, barely days after she graduated from high school, had been tragically killed in a shooting at one of the parks near Lake Tahoe in an attack that had stolen ten other lives as well.

It had fallen to Jonathan, as deputy, to inform people what had occurred. The news had been met with various degrees of denial, anger, and grief and it had been hard to control his own feelings about her death.

Penelope and Roger Gale, Aly's parents, had responded in horror. Devastated, Penelope collapsed on the sofa, tearfully sobbing and muttering 'he promised'. Roger, hiding his grief, had tried futilely to console her. Jonathan, dreading telling his own family, stood regretfully to the side and offered what comfort he could and wondered at

1

the suitcases in the Gale's hall.

Aly had been friends with Jonathan's daughter Lijuan, known by the literal translation of her Chinese birth name 'Grace', since the girls were fifteen. Jonathan and Lan, his wife, had moved to Bellhollow several years ago so Lan could open her restaurant, and Aly and her family had been some of their first customers. Jonathan still remembered Aly as the starry-eyed, freckled munchkin with a ponytail and a big heart, who'd been excited when she'd spotted Grace behind the counter serving customers. By the end of the evening, the pair had become fast friends.

Aly and Grace were so similar in many ways and so different in others. Both of them had creative personalities; Aly in art and Grace in music. Grace fit in well with Aly's group of close friends, Fletcher Norman and Delwin Cook, and their extended friendships circles and for once, Grace seemed happy.

Then Fletcher had died. Killed in a motorcycle accident and his death hit the group of friends hard, but Aly especially. She'd been best friends with Fletcher since they were eight, and Penelope had practically raised the boy. He, for all intents and purposes, lived in the Gale household. To lose two children, so close together, Jonathan couldn't hope to understand what Penelope and Roger were going through.

Within hours of Fletcher's death, an FBI agent called Belinda Bell had made herself known to Bellhollow Sheriff's Office, placing herself at their disposal. She wanted everything about Fletcher to be funneled through her. An oddity, considering the way Fletcher had died hadn't been deemed suspicious.

Then Aly had been kidnapped. Taken after she finished her shift at Dirk's Diner. She'd reappeared, injured, drenched, only one shoe and suffering from amnesia, in a forest hundreds of miles from Bellhollow.

Interest in Aly from Belinda Bell had skyrocketed, not

that she would share why. Grace reported that Belinda had accosted Aly outside the town library when the girls had been trying to study for their exams, so Jonathan had asked her to steer clear of the kids from now on. Let Aly heal with the support of her friends.

Which, based on current events, may have been a bad idea.

Grace and Del had been approached by reporters spreading rumors about Fletcher's death and had planted conspiracy theories that Fletcher may have been murdered in Del's head. Del had been adamant something shady was going on, and although he'd done the right thing in coming to Jonathan first, there'd been an eye-witness who said Del and Grace had gone to the reporter's motel room.

And now, at the same time as Aly's death, both Del and Grace had vanished.

Lan was beside herself. She waited by the phone for any news to no avail. Grace hadn't called, hadn't made any effort to contact home and no one knew why. Cassidy Cook, Del's mother, blamed herself for their disappearance because she and Del had fought the last time they'd seen each other. While Jonathan had confirmed that Del and Grace were not among the dead or injured, he couldn't confirm whether or not the pair had actually been *in* Lake Tahoe at the time of Aly's death.

Strange rumors had been coming out of eye-witness reports at Lake Tahoe too, things Jonathan was only privy to because he knew some of the deputies investigating. Men in combat clothing had swept the grounds before the shooting had started. Witnesses claimed to have seen the same combat-clothed people suddenly wearing a different face, even one video had surfaced of someone who appeared to be in the throes of an epileptic seizure with their face rippling. Although the video could be an elaborate hoax, the speed at which it surfaced made people wonder.

Jonathan hadn't been able to locate his beloved

daughter at all. None of the reports or sightings could even give him a clue to her whereabouts.

The discovery of Aly's car abandoned in Sacramento, not Lake Tahoe, amplified the mystery of the situation. Then Roger had left a brief message on Jonathan's phone saying the Gales were going away for a while to grieve, and now wasn't answering at all. Then Lloyd, one of Grace's friends and a reporter-in-training, had mentioned that Aly and Penelope had gone on a trip together to Seattle, so what was she doing in Lake Tahoe without Penelope?

When Jonathan counted in what Del had mentioned about the new person who was becoming friendly with Aly, a young man only known as Noah, who Del believed was connected to Fletcher's death and had subsequently disappeared in the wake of Aly's death, Del's proclamation of a conspiracy was starting to have some merit. Especially when two people matching Aly and Noah's descriptions had been identified in a shootout in Sacramento, then again, renting a car from a small town that was not far north of Lake Tahoe. Aly specifically had been remembered there, because she'd requested the aid of the receptionist—who later logged a wellbeing check—to help her move an unconscious man into the new hire car. That told Jonathan Aly had been there voluntarily.

So many inconsistencies.

Jonathan didn't know what to do. The trail was cold and the longer it remained cold, the harder it would be to find Grace. He'd pulled as many strings as he could, most of the other Sheriff departments were keeping an eye out for Grace as a personal favor to him, but it wasn't enough. He wanted her home. He wanted her safe. And he was willing to do anything to achieve that.

The call answered, "Hello, this is Belinda Bell."

Jonathan sat up. "Ms. Bell, this is Deputy Locklear with the Bellhollow Sheriff's office. I need your help."

Shoes shuffled against tiled floors. Strollers clattered as

they were pushed by exhausted parents, with older children running circles. Rustles of plastic and paper bags as they were clutched in exuberant hands by chatty shoppers. Music echoed over a speaker system and was lost to the rabble of voices.

Walking with determined steps, Alyson Gale navigated her way through the throng of shoppers. So many people going about their everyday business. People talking and laughing without a care in the world. Everything so normal for them.

Not for Aly. Feeling pressure from all sides, she hid the limp in her stride as best she could. Destination in mind, she wove through the crowd. Walking quickly, but not running. Face impassive, offering up an air of unapproachability, but not overly hostile.

Forgettable.

Slipping into people's perceptions long enough that they didn't walk into her, then slipping away just as fast.

Almost everyone's perceptions.

She expected eyes following her. People lurking in shadows and secrets, silently tracking her progress through the mall. She was watched and she knew it.

This particular watcher was a little unexpected.

Not a shapeshifter. No prickles or goose bumps, or warnings of any kind. A regular person.

Short cropped hair, glasses, he seemed several years older than her as he stalked her through the mall too close for comfort. A regular, albeit creepy, guy.

She knew he followed her. His efforts were clumsy and inefficient. Aly suspected he *wanted* her to know he was creeping on her. Irritation filled her. Of all the things she expected to happen today, this wasn't one of them. Fighting a roll of her eyes, she looked for an easy way to ditch him. If his cell came out for photos, she was going to punch him in the face.

Glancing down at her bag, she mentally ran over the things she'd been taught to lose a tail. Change her appearance. Do something unexpected. Stay with a crowd. Don't let herself get trapped.

She didn't deviate from her path, but she switched her shopping bag to her right hand to free her left up to defend herself if necessary. Lifting her head up a little, she loosened the tight, 'don't approach' expression she had and went for one which edged to apprehension.

Spotting a gaggle of girls roughly her age wandering through the mall chatting among themselves, she deviated from her path. "Hi guys!" she said, pouncing on the two stragglers of the group.

The rest of them turned as one of the girls squeaked in fear from Aly's pounce, ready to defend and protect, like Aly had hoped they would.

"I'm really, *really*, sorry," Aly implored quickly. "But I'm being creeped on. Blond dude, green shirt, glasses, about twenty feet behind me. Can I hang with you for a bit?"

Eyes snapped behind Aly and two of them frowned, their eyes zeroing on the yellowed bruise on her face. A third beamed. "Gurl, like, I haven't seen you in *forever*!" she stepped forward, looping her arm around Aly's neck to pull her into a walk, heading away from the man. "How are you?"

And just like that, the protective nature of the group of girls grew to envelop Aly.

"We're heading to the food court," the tallest of them said, casting a subtle glance over her shoulder. She brushed her long, dark braid back over her shoulder as she turned back to smile at Aly. "I'm Aisha. Someone meeting you?"

"No," Aly replied with a shake of her head. "I'm shopping on my own. My mother's waiting back at the hotel."

"Here on holiday? You're welcome to join us for lunch," one of the girls said.

"More the merrier."

"Creepy ass men," the blonde with her arm around Aly

muttered. "We gotcha, gurl. I'm Tiana."

Aly breathed an audible sigh. "I'm Rose, and thanks for the offer but I really just want to get out of here."

"Then we make a pit stop," the smallest of the girls said with a knowing smile. "There's a hallway just before the eatery which goes down to the bathrooms, but it's got a back entrance that leads into the parking lot. We'll loiter in the hall and give you a chance."

"You would?" Aly asked, touched. "Oh, that'd be fantastic."

"We've all been subject to that crap," Aisha said with a sympathetic nod.

"Got his picture," one of the girls from behind said, triumphant as she waved her cell ahead of her. "We'll report him to security. Is he the one who hit you?"

Aly blinked, then lied, "No. I play paintball, took my helmet off and accidentally got brained."

That was met with a wince but no disbelief. "Ooh, ouch."

She laughed sheepishly, "Yeah, won't be doing that again. Learned my lesson, for sure."

The girls chatted as they walked, taking care to include Aly but also keep the conversation neutral. Two of them were recent high school graduates, heading off to college next year, while Aisha was going to visit family in Israel and Tiana was taking an Au Pair position in England for a year. Neutral topics, while still maintaining an airy cheer. The excitable girl with a pixie cut, who said her name was Clover, bounced around them with a manic energy and kept them informed of the stalker's position.

Toying with the hair tie around her wrist as she walked, she joked and laughed with her pseudo friends and tried to ignore the ache in her chest for Grace.

The precision with which the girls spread across the entrance of the hallway was incredible. It looked casual and unorganized, yet they effectively blocked anyone from easy access unless the girls stepped to the side. Their boisterous chatter and loud laughter made it so someone would need to interrupt them to get them to move.

Clover made shooing motions at her, while Tiana winked. Hurrying down the hallway, Aly cast a wave over her shoulder as a thank you.

The moment she turned the corner and walked past the woman's bathroom, Aly shrugged out of her jacket and turned it inside out, changing it from brown to a cream color. After throwing the jacket back on, she looped the shopping bag over her elbow, then gathered her brown hair and made a messy bun out of it. Undoing the blue silk hair scarf she'd disguised as a decorative belt, she wrapped it around her head to use as a headband, making a twisted knot near her forehead.

She was still fiddling with the knot in her scarf when she reached the exit doors so she turned and pushed them open with her back and hurried out into the parking lot. She needed to make as much distance as she could. The girls would keep the visible stalker at bay, but Aly knew she needed to be fast to elude the watchers she couldn't see.

Undercover parking lot with another story of the mall above them. Plenty of places to duck and hide, plus the bonus of several exits, even an escalator that headed back into the mall some distance away.

Returning to the mall, while something her watchers may not expect, was not desirable at present since she wanted to put some distance between them. She had to get out of the line of sight of the exit and start heading in a direction that would lead her to more people.

Pulling out her cell to check the map, she walked briskly through the covered parking lot. Down the street from the mall was another, much smaller and open-aired complex and beyond that, if her memory served her correctly, was Las Vegas' monorail.

With a lighter step, she dug her sunglasses out of her pocket to further hide and hurried toward the station.

Getting onto the monorail was relatively easy and, as she cast a glance around, she couldn't see or feel anyone who set off her sense. Finding an empty seat, she whipped out her cell, ready to gloat.

"Pretty clever," Noah said, flopping into the seat beside her. "Asking that group for help. Really deterred the extra you picked up."

She stared at her best friend and new boyfriend for a heartbeat and then pouted. "Aww."

Laughing, he nudged her. "Had it been anyone else, Als, you would've lost them for sure."

The monorail shuddered as it left the station. Aly pulled a face and reached up to tug the scarf out of her hair. "No fair. Seeing through walls is cheating."

"You lost Bonnie and Ross," he said, mentioning his recently reunited siblings. Part of a genetically-altered shapeshifter group called the Faceless, Noah had grown up in the Institute with eight siblings. Ruth and Boaz, aka Ross and Bonnie, were the first to escape and lose contact with the group. They'd been covertly operating as spies within a group of Purists—people who believe shapeshifters were aberrations and should be destroyed—for Adam, another sibling, and had been tasked to spy on Aly, thus reuniting them with Noah.

With a proud smile, Noah complimented, "That was pretty awesome."

"I was hoping to lose *you*," she said, winding the scarf around her wrist. Huffy, she asked, "Where'd I go wrong?"

"You did a fantastic job and were remarkably clever in using your environment to—"

Aly raised her eyebrows, gave him a blank stare and waited as he faltered.

"Um…you… you didn't do anything—"

She tilted her head.

"Fiiine," he said and his shoulders slumped. "Next time, do all of the change before you enter a new area. You were invisible in the hallway, you should've finished the modifications, then continued. If someone had been watching the exit, they would've noticed you were fiddling with your appearance."

Pressing her lips together, she nodded. "I'll remember."

"But that's *really* nit-picky and I was trying to compliment you," he muttered.

"Compliment accepted but I need to know where I was going wrong."

With a put out noise, he slumped down further in his chair. "Did you feel him at all?"

"Nope," she said, popping the 'p'.

Noah sighed heavily. Extending his feet out before him, he crossed his ankles. "So, he didn't even try."

Today was supposed to be a practice day for all of them. Testing their skills. Aly's at sensing and practicing losing a tail, and Ross' first augmentations to see if he and Bonnie could keep her in their sights. Because Ross and Bonnie escaped before Noah had, they hadn't known augments were possible and were at a disadvantage when compared with the other Faceless. Noah hadn't had any luck getting Ross to try the augments in a practice session, so he'd hoped maybe he could prompt some competitive nature in Ross.

If she was her normal self, she would've been pleased. Bonnie and Ross were trained soldiers and she'd managed to elude them. But there was so much going on recently, she had trouble feeling anything at all.

Noah's fingers pinched the fabric of her jeans at her knee and tugged to get her attention. Repressing a sigh, she half turned on her chair, putting her back to him. Knee up on the seat, ankle tucked beneath her thigh, she rested her chin on the back of the chair so she could stare out the window.

His reflection in the window pressed its lips into a thin line, but he didn't push and Aly appreciated that. His head went down and he folded one arm over his chest, using his cell in his other hand.

She watched him for a breath, then turned her gaze to her own reflection. It told a different story. Dark rings under blue eyes, evidence of the nightmares which haunted her dreams the last few nights. Pain in her chest and her leg as her body worked through the trauma of gunshot wounds hastily fixed with Noah's abilities.

Everything went away when she was distracted, like she had been in the mall. Moments of relief. But here, in the quiet, she remembered.

In the two days they'd been in Las Vegas, waiting for Ross and Bonnie to go through the motions to get Adam on the phone, she'd never felt more isolated from Noah. It wasn't anything he'd done and she knew that he understood that. She was grieving for the life she wanted and could no longer have. Dreams about becoming an animator that couldn't become a reality. Hard work and years of preparation all down the drain.

Friends in Bellhollow who now believed she was dead. Her family... Her mom, her adopted father, her brother Tim.

She wasn't going to see them again.

Throat closing up, she leaned backward, resting her back against Noah's arm for comfort. Sensing her conflicted need to be both left alone and near him, his hand closed around her upper arm and he kissed the nape of her neck, then released her.

He'd gone through this before. He'd given up the life he was trying to build in an attempt to keep her safe. Then he had come back and tried to rebuild what was left of it, only to have to leave everything again.

Noah knew. He knew better than she did. But he'd also gone into the situation knowing he may have to leave at a moment's notice. For Aly, Bellhollow was all she'd known.

He filled the silence between them with chatter.

"Ross and Bonnie are going to meet us at the new hotel for dinner," he said. "We have free time until then."

"Okay."

Noah chuckled. "Ross is complaining you weren't supposed to leave the mall. It's 'unfair', apparently."

"He can deal," Aly said with a shrug. "If he can follow me all the way to Sac, then find my hotel, he can follow me through a stupid mall."

"Absolutely. Did you get what you wanted?"

Glancing down at her bag, she nodded. "Yup." Some toiletries, a shirt, some jeans since her last pair had been destroyed, and sneakers to replace her sandals. And, although she browsed, she didn't buy anything from the art store in the mall. While she was lucky enough to have her artistic laptop, she didn't have her stylus and she didn't want to spend money on something which, in essence, didn't matter anymore.

Noah sighed and seemingly read her mind. "You didn't get a replacement stylus."

She didn't feel like replying to that.

"We can go now and—"

She shook her head. "It's too expensive and—"

"It's a stylus. It's not *that* expensive, even when you're being picky about the type," he countered. "Rex gave us plenty of money, Als. Ross is much better at gambling than I am, so we're up in terms of cash. You need to draw and—"

She resigned and gave him the truth, "There's no point."

Noah made a noise of dismay. "*Please* don't do this to yourself."

Aly sighed, slow and long, and hunched her shoulders. "I know," she murmured and leaned against him. "I'm trying. I just…"

"It's hard."

"*Mmm.*"

Noah said nothing and Aly was grateful he didn't try to console her with 'at least they were together'. That was a given and she was thankful that, out of everything that had gone wrong, he was the one thing that had gone right.

Aly glanced at him in the window reflection. He was looking away from her, down in the direction the monorail headed. "Can I convince you to take a nap?" he asked.

"You can try."

The monorail slowed as they neared the next station and Noah nudged her. "C'mon, lovely, even if you don't nap, it'll be nice to be alone for a while."

Nodding, she got to her feet, held her bag in one hand and took Noah's with the other. Giving her a warm smile, he squeezed her fingers, then lifted her hand to his mouth to kiss the back of it.

The decision to stay in Las Vegas until they'd managed to contact Adam had been a hard one to make. Noah had wanted to move, to get as far away from California as they could, while Ross reasoned that Adam could plausibly be along the West Coast somewhere, and they might have to come back. Tango, Ross' recently escaped clone, was yet to contact them and neither Ross nor Bonnie were willing to go far without him. With all the gambling facilities around Las Vegas and Ross' aptitude with math, they could gather some much-needed currency. In a surprising show of empathy, Ross had delivered the final blow to Noah's argument saying Aly needed rest.

They'd compromised as best they could, staying in different hotels each night and only winning small amounts from the various casinos, and using the downtime to teach Ross and Bonnie augmentations.

As was becoming custom, they didn't enter the hotel straight away. Loitering by a corner a distance away, Noah went through a series of augmented shifts to check the surroundings and see if anyone followed them. Closing her eyes, Aly concentrated on her shifter sense and, except for Noah's shifts, came up empty. Since she could only sense Faceless if they happened to be shifting, her sense wasn't useful in locating them, but it did tell her that no natural shifters in different forms were around.

As Noah's tingles skipped over her, the feeling of being

useless returned. She brought nothing to their partnership. She was a complete liability. Noah had so many skills at his disposal, able to shapeshift and augment his current body to do things no normal person could.

All Aly could do was sense shifters. And, as they had discovered a few days ago, in the face of many shifters all at once, she was doomed.

But then, so were they.

Her biological father, Rex, who was not dead as she'd been told, insisted that Aly was also part of the Faceless. However, instead of being a shifter, she was engineered to be a toxin and strip the abilities from natural shifters, leaving them trapped in their birth forms.

And, for the unlucky ones, outright kill them.

Except that they couldn't be sure she killed them, a hope Aly was desperately clinging to. Everyone was lying to everyone else and they didn't know if the news which had been reported regarding the death toll in Tahoe was the absolute truth or embellished by Rex to hide her 'death'.

It was all so confusing.

Hands thrust into the pockets of her jacket, shopping bag looped around her wrist, Aly stared off into space until the tingles stopped.

"Aly?" he asked softly, vying for her attention. He waited until she looked at him before he suggested, "We don't have to go back to the hotel. We could go for burgers."

"I need to put my leg up," she murmured. "It's starting to ache."

"What about a movie then?" he suggested.

"I'm... not feeling sociable right now," Aly said and looked away again. "I just... I wanna curl up and have the world stop."

"Yeah," he murmured and sighed deeply. "Me too."

CHAPTER 2

Curled up on the armchair and tucked under one of the complimentary blankets from the hotel room, Aly stared out into the Vegas night and tried to ignore the angry, yet hushed conversation of the three Faceless, a feat becoming increasingly difficult since Noah's voice was steadily rising as he became more frustrated with his newly reunited siblings.

Tearing her gaze away from the unassuming beauty of the night, Aly glanced over at the trio.

"I don't see the point," Ross muttered with a scowl. "I've gotten by without augments so far."

Noah scrubbed a hand over his face and did little to hide his annoyance. "You didn't even try."

"I did!"

"Aly can *feel* shifts. You were well within her range, so I *know* you didn't try!"

Ross's glare shot to Aly. "Maybe she's not as good as she says she is."

Noah's tone switched from frustration to fury. "Don't you even dare."

Aly understood Noah's ire. Even Noah's deceased brother Solomon, with the incredible pain he endured while shifting, had still been willing to *try*. Ross gave up, refusing to believe they were even possible for him. And Bonnie...

Aly flicked her eyes from the short, angry, broken-nosed man, to the tall, platinum blonde Amazon of a woman with a jagged scar on her forehead. A bullet to her brain had done more than rob her of speech. In essence, she shared Solomon's fate; incredible pain for even the most simple shifts. She explained, with Noah translating for Aly's benefit, an act as simple as changing the natural scales the Faceless had to skin had been an incredible effort for her. Despite the pain, she was willing to try and, as Solomon had, she wanted to learn the theory of augmenting.

As Aly understood it, Bonnie's pain at shifting was why they'd worn the forms of the twins for so long. If Bonnie couldn't shift, Ross wouldn't either. While that resolve was both noble and commendable, things were different now.

Noah's frustration echoed in his tone, "Even if you don't use them, you should learn the theory behind—"

Throwing up his hands, Ross protested, "*Why*?"

"They *know* Faceless can do this," Noah snapped. "Elaine can do this. So can Adam, if he's even alive. The factions know we can. They assume *all* Faceless can and—"

"We don't register as shifters, let alone Faceless," Ross said, his tone full of scorn. "We've gotten by for this long without them. And besides, you're not a good teacher, the whole process is confusing and—"

"We were able to teach this to Solomon, right under Smith's nose!" Noah growled. "Both through visual aids and verbal instruction. Don't you blame your refusal to try on me."

Bonnie, sitting on the bench, clapped her hands to get Ross' attention, then signed.

Ross glared at her. "I am *not* being a baby!"

"Tell him?" Noah asked Bonnie in response to

something she'd signed. "Tell me what?"

"Fine," Ross snarled at Bonnie. "*Fine*. I'll try again."

Bonnie tossed up her hands, then folded her arms on her chest.

Noah puffed out his breath and prepared to explain, again, the adjustments required to augment ears. There wasn't any point to Aly listening to his explanations since she couldn't shift and most of it involved technical anatomy names.

She tuned them out again, returning to her unending stare across Las Vegas.

She hated feeling this way, but she couldn't seem to break herself free. She felt like... she felt like she did when she thought Fletcher had died. Constantly on the verge of breaking apart. Battling tears in the quiet moments, struggling to keep herself together when surrounded by people. It had been an endeavor to get out of bed in the morning. And now.... she'd lost everything. Her friends. Her life. Her dreams.

But she hadn't lost him. Aly turned her head and rested her cheek on her knees as she watched Noah. Her malaise wasn't fair, not when he was doing everything he could to keep them safe.

"This is useless," Ross snarled.

"It's not useless," Noah snapped. "You're *not* trying."

"I *am* trying."

Noah groaned. He had all the patience of a saint if he liked someone, or he could see they were genuinely trying, so his anger sent a clear message. Since Noah had more patience with Bonnie, Aly was pretty sure Noah's anger was on Aly's—and the fading bruise Ross had caused on her face—behalf. This situation was only going to end up in a screaming match.

Had they been at home, and had it been anyone else other than Ross, she might've tagged in by now to give Noah a chance to calm down. Explained things an alternative way, or changed the subject. But, as she didn't like Ross, she really didn't care if Noah yelled at him.

She did care if Noah yelled, though. He was frustrated and angry and he'd turn sulky if not given a chance to regroup.

Rubbing the aching bruise on her torso, Aly untangled herself from the blanket and stood from the armchair, then she walked to their bag where she rummaged through until she found their uneaten snacks and pulled out a Snickers. "Here," she said, tossing it to Noah.

Turning in surprise, Noah barely managed to catch the chocolate bar. "What?"

"Take a step back," she said.

He lifted an eyebrow in defiance. "Aly—"

"You're grumpy," she said, approaching. Resting her fingertips on Noah's chest, she pushed him back toward the bed until he sat, then gave his shoulder a gentle pat. "Let me have a go."

"Did you really just meme me?" Noah asked, staring at her and wiggling the Snickers.

Ross scoffed and rolled his eyes. "Please don't tell me the non-shifter thinks *she* can teach."

"This non-shifter would really like to break your nose again," she snapped, folding her arms on her chest. She frowned as a thought occurred to her. "Speaking of, why haven't you fixed that?" She glanced at Noah. "Isn't, like, cartilage something you had to build? You could say it's a form of augmentation, right?"

Adjusting his seat on the bed, Noah unwrapped his Snickers. "Yep." Frowning, he looked at Ross. "That's actually a pretty good point. Why haven't you done—"

"We were *pretending* to be Purists," Ross snapped. "Broken noses and all."

"The nose stands out," Aly said. "It was the first thing I noticed about you. It's not good if you're trying to blend in."

Ross glared at her. "Seriously? We're going to complain about my choice of nose?"

"Never comment on someone's appearance unless they can fix it in five minutes," Aly replied. "And since you *can*, why haven't you?"

With another snarl, Ross looked at Bonnie. "You know what? I'm sick of this. You don't get to question or judge me. I'm leaving. Find Adam on your own."

"Good riddance," Noah snapped with a scornful wave of his hand to shoo Ross away faster. "We *don't* need you."

Frowning at Ross, Bonnie shook her head and signed.

"If you want to throw your lot in with them," Ross snapped at Bonnie. "After all we've been through? Go right ahead. I don't care—"

Aly considered him. Bonnie couldn't shift her scar because it caused too much pain. Nevertheless, she had managed to shift away the scales and create a face. Ross had done that at some stage too but maybe he wasn't as adept as they had thought. Maybe he was like Solomon as well, but too proud to admit it. Tactless, Aly blurted out that thought before she had a chance to filter it. "Can you—you *can* shift, right?"

"Of course he can shift," Noah muttered. "He's the one who showed me—"

The look of pure disgust on Ross' face shocked Aly, as did his abrupt storm to the door.

Bonnie made a noise, the first Aly had heard her make. A long sound, made from the back of her throat and it made Ross pause with his hand on the door handle. Clapping her hands, Bonnie made a series of garbled sounds and half-formed words at the same time she signed, while Ross peeked at her over his shoulder.

Frowning, Ross started, "We haven't ignored—" and then he turned around so Bonnie could see his hands as he switched to sign language.

Noah reached out and touched Aly's elbow, coaxing her back to sit on the bed beside him so they could watch. "Bonnie's saying they've ignored their siblings for long enough and it's time for the truth. Ross doesn't want to.

They're arguing about why they joined Adam's cause and what they hoped to achieve. Bonnie's saying... Ross is being a dick about this and... she—" His eyes widened and he cleared his throat. "She wants to talk to Adam about why he's withholding information."

"Talk?" Aly asked, with a shoulder nudge. "Cause that section seemed pretty clear. She wants to shove something—"

"Yeah yeah," Noah muttered, hiding a smile. "Shuddup."

Ross heaved in a sigh. "Fine." Thrusting his hand in his pockets, he moved forward to lean on the wall beside the bathroom door, staring at the floor. Hooking one ankle over the other, he glared at Aly and Noah. "You both need to shut up and let me talk. I don't wanna have to do this again."

Noah raised an eyebrow at him. "Fine."

Ross muttered, "You don't know what it was like for Bonnie and me. After... what happened... I... well... I had to make certain deals to get her help. Faction help. Wasn't Rex's group, but..." He shrugged. "There wasn't time and she was dying and an opportunity fell into my lap..."

"You did what you had to do," Noah said, nodding. "I would've as well."

Ross seemed to accept that. "It was a struggle but she lived. When it became clear she wasn't... healing right, the faction helping us said they could do more, if they had an example of my shifting abilities... a sample of DNA." Ross swallowed. "We were... I was too fresh. Too new. Too *stupid.*"

"Naive," Noah said, with another nod of agreement. "We all made mistakes after we left the Institute."

Ross closed his eyes, tilting his head back until it rested on the wall. "Mine cost me my abilities."

Noah jerked out of his seat. "What?"

Bonnie joined Ross against the wall, standing beside

him without touching him. She put her hands behind her back to cushion her lean and offer silent support. Ross rolled his head against the wall so he could look up at her.

"How?" Noah demanded.

Aly sat perfectly still, a sense of foreboding echoing through her.

Ross shrugged. "They injected me with something and... it was gone and I was stuck in this form."

Noah swore softly under his breath. "Do you know of this happening to anyone else?"

Ross shrugged. "You hear rumors, you know. People vanishing, never to be seen again. Adam mentioned shifters going missing, but between the factions, you can never tell." Ross looked beyond Noah to Aly, still sitting on the bed and trying not to be noticed. "Wasn't like what she did to the shifters at the park. They were forced into their natural forms. I got frozen like this."

Aly curled in on herself.

"Does Adam know?" Noah asked.

"Well, we didn't tell him," Ross said, sour. "And he sure didn't mention anything about those trackers or augmentation. No clue what he knows and what he doesn't. Don't care."

Noah was quiet for a moment, before he said, "Thank you for trusting me."

Ross grunted. "Yeah. Well. Didn't have a choice. Bonnie's got noses to punch."

Noah snorted. "And we don't want to get in the way of that."

"Bro," Ross said and forced a laugh. "You don't know the half of it."

Bonnie shoved Ross with her shoulder and pulled a face at him.

"Yeah, yeah," Ross said with a smile for her, then dropped his eyes to the ground. "So. That's it. Can't shift, so I really don't see the point of learning augmentations. It's... rubbing salt into an open wound."

Aly didn't know why it was such a secret. Bonnie had been so open with the scope of her abilities, why had Ross tried to hide it? Glancing between him and Noah, she suspected pride might have had something to do with it.

"Alright," Noah replied. "I can accept that. But... with your consent, I'd like to tell you the full scope of what I can do, so you can be aware. I'd still like to work with you, Bonnie."

Ross nodded and thrust his hands into his pockets. "Yeah. Fine."

"What happened to the faction?" Aly asked quietly.

Ross looked up and met her eyes with a hard glare. "They don't exist anymore."

Noah nodded and Aly swallowed hard.

With a grimace, Ross said, "Listen, I'm no good at the touchy-feely crap. We're gonna go. See you in the morning."

"Okay," Noah said and got up to follow them out. After making sure he locked the door, he wandered back to the bed, where he flopped on his back and covered his face with his hands.

"Is it even possible?" Aly asked.

"Yeah. I didn't think it was..." he sighed. "But then, you exist, lovely."

"He still... he still *feels* like... um..."

"He still feels like a shifter to me, too." Noah uncovered his face and rested his hands on his chest, staring at the ceiling. "It... *could* be as simple as a mental block or an implanted aversion..."

She waited for him to continue, and after he didn't, she rose and pulled back the bedsheets of the bed enough so it appeared someone had slept in it. She wandered into the bathroom and opened the soap, leaving it on the sink, and dampened the towels like Noah had told her too.

The sliding door to the balcony opened and she poked her head out in time to see Noah leap up onto the railing with their backpack on his back. He twisted and scrambled up to the balcony above them.

Aly ran the shower to dampen the base and made sure to put the hygienic tape sealing the toilet in the bin, then wandered out into the main area to see what else she could do to make it appear as though someone had spent the night here. Taking a few of the complimentary coffee and sugar packets, she ripped them open, poured the coffee in a mug to make it dirty, added water, then tipped the contents down the bathroom sink.

Noah dropped back onto the balcony as Aly looked around to see if anything else needed messing. The room looked rumpled, but not overly messy.

"Looks good," he said and made sure the small, portable spy camera was secure and pointing toward the door.

She smiled. "Thanks."

When they'd booked this room, they had used one of the credit cards Rex had given them. Aly had walked in alone to rent it, while Noah had rented the room directly above it. A test, as he explained, to see if they were being followed, or Rex's card was being tracked and as long as they remembered there were cameras in the hallway and never to leave the wrong room, no one would know unless they were spotted scaling the balcony.

Which, truth be told, terrified her each time. Hanging onto Noah's back as he scurried between balconies, trusting his skill and his abilities, hiding her face in the back of his neck so she didn't have to see the world swimming around her.

After scaling the wall, and wandering into the room they'd be sleeping in, Noah slid the balcony door shut and touched her ankles, trying to get them to uncross. "It's over. You can—"

"Uh-uh," she said and clutched him tighter. "You're now a hunchback. Forever and always."

A mischievous chuckle, then Noah tilted sideways. Aly's squeak was instinctive, but it turned into a giggle as he flopped them both on one of the beds and sprawled. Limbs entangled and he let gravity weigh his body down over hers and squash her against the bedsheets.

"Ow," she complained playfully as she was squished beneath him.

His weight decreased immediately. "Oh! Are you okay?" He rolled, bracing each hand on either side of her so he could check on her. "Did I hurt you?"

"Huh?" she asked, confused. "No."

"Are you sure?" He lifted a hand and hovered it over her side. "I mean, you've gone through a bad trauma and you're favoring it and—"

She plucked at his sleeve. "I'm fine. I was—"

His gaze alternated between her eyes and her side. "Can I see? May I check?"

She frowned. "You're really worried?"

"I've never regenerated a non-shifter before… and someone who's allergic to shifters… I'm… yeah." He puffed out a breath. "I'm worried that it won't take or you'll react or… I dunno."

Studying his expression, she picked up the small subtleties which indicated the worry went a lot deeper than he was willing to admit. "You think I'll burn like Ten did."

Noah swallowed heavily and he couldn't meet her eyes as he nodded.

Even though she was bruised and in an achy sort of pain, but otherwise okay, she knew that Noah's peace of mind mattered. "Okay."

Noah sat back on his ankles and Aly lifted her torso from the bed a little so she could untangle her shirt and lift it up. Tingles rippled over her as Noah focused on her leg first.

Watching his face rather than his hands, Aly asked, "How did you know how to do that, anyway?"

"What? Regenerate others?"

"Yeah."

"Necessity breeds invention," Noah replied. "Adam

and Joseph were gravely injured the night we escaped. After Seth and Solomon, I couldn't lose any more siblings so... I just did it."

"But... shifting hurts... why would you—"

He met her eyes. "And lose you? I'd make the same choice again in a heartbeat."

Lifting her hand, she rested it on his upper arm. "Thank you."

"You don't need to thank me for that," he said. After checking her leg, his fingers tentatively brushed her stomach.

Aly scrunched up her nose and tried not to make a noise.

"Hurts?"

"Well, it is a massive bruise," she mumbled. "It's tender. No pokage."

"I'll be quick."

"Why'd it bruise?" she asked, talking for the sake of it.

"Thought it would be a full heal like mine?" He shook his head. "Not possible. I'm a foreign element invading, your body fought me. The bruising is from all the initial damage and internal bleeding. I can't do much about that. Replacing ripped flesh and closing blood vessels around the point of contact, I can do. Kind of like a surgeon, I guess. Maybe." He hummed. "I can get rid of my own bruising cause I can feel everything, but I'd have to go hunting for your damaged sections, and that'd cause more damage on the way."

"Make sense."

She couldn't see his shifts, but she could see the reactions his shifts had on his eyes. Seeing his pupil's different sizes, each eye focusing separately was odd and disconcerting, so she closed her eyes while he looked. His hands were warm and gentle even if his touch made her ache. He probed her skin and she did her best to hide her winces of pain.

"So what are you looking for?" she asked. "I mean, I

know you can do X-ray, but can you do anything else?"

"Hmm," he said. "It's... tricky to explain. I'm basically altering my eyes to see different light spectrums and trying to piece together a complicated puzzle to make a judgment call."

"Can you see through my clothes?"

"That does come with X-ray vision, Als," he answered somewhat absently, his concentration elsewhere.

"No... I meant, like... just my clothes."

Noah froze. The shifting stopped as he locked onto her eyes for a second and his cheeks went pink. "No. It doesn't work like that."

She narrowed her eyes at him, then smacked his arm. "You little shit! You were literally looking through my pants to check my leg!"

"I don't look!" he protested. "I'm, like... zoomed in, concentrating on the wound. I don't see anything else."

She knew that was probably true, but still felt the need to tease. "I need a fricken lead undershirt. Oh my god, my *panties*?"

"I don't look!" Noah shrilled.

"Uh-huh."

He seemed desperate to make her believe him. "Aly, I promise you—just because I can, doesn't mean I will. I would *never*—"

"Relax," she said, laughing. "I'm teasing."

He stared at her, unwilling to believe her, before he barked out a laugh. "Meanie."

"You're *fun* to tease."

"Glad to be of service," he muttered and returned to his inspection. "Well..." His tingle disappeared as he stopped shifting. "It looks okay at the moment, but it's early days. Let me know if you feel strange or sick or something."

"Okay."

His hand rested on her ribs. "Aly," he said in a serious tone. "Promise me. I know you don't want to talk to me right now, and that's okay, but you need to promise you won't keep stuff like that quiet."

The playful mood disappeared as abruptly has it had arrived. She lifted her hand and rested it on his upper arm. "I wouldn't keep something like that from you."

He studied her, then nodded. "Okay. Good."

Removing her hand from his arm, she threaded the fingers of her hands together and left them to rest on her chest. "I was wondering…"

"Yeah?" he prompted.

"You… you were able to fix me. Do you think you could fix Bonnie?"

Noah blinked at her, then grew thoughtful. After a moment, he flopped down on his back next to her. Head beside hers, he copied her position and stared up at the ceiling. "Brain shifting…" He sighed and tapped his thumbs together. "You know… until recently, I never even considered it would be possible…I guess I'd have to know exactly what was damaged in Bonnie's brain and how… and what it looked like before it was hurt…" He clicked his tongue. "Everyone's brain is different, Als. Different thought patterns, different memories. I'd… for Bonnie's brain, I'd probably do more damage than good."

While that saddened her, she had suspected it would be a long shot. "Oh."

"But, let's talk about the elephant in the room," he said in a matter-of-fact tone. "My brain. You want to know if I could shift my brain."

"No," she protested. "I—"

"Shifting requires a nervous system so we can feel what we're doing. There's no nerve cells in your brain." He waved his hand and scrunched up his face. "I mean, there *are*, but it's not the right ones… neurons, but they're not… gah, this is difficult to explain… I need to be able to *feel* to shift and I can't feel what's going on in my head. The brain's incredibly complicated. I'd have to mess with the neurons and pathways which already existed and… I'd have no way of telling what I was messing with. Memory? Motor functions? It's all one big, confusing mess."

"Oh."

"Which is why Elaine doing it is so… improbable. It could be done, I suppose, with years and years of training, and probably a degree in Neuroscience or something. If I was going to do it, I'd want to find out a way to keep those memories intact, but still… have them not influence my thinking, which… I don't know how I'd do that. The brain self-prunes. It gets rid of unused pathways. How would I separate memories so I couldn't access them, but still have it so my brain didn't just get rid of them since they weren't being used."

"You've thought about this."

"Yeah." He rolled onto his side and propped his head up on his arm so he could look at her. "Here's the thing. *If* I did it, I've also removed the memories of how I did it, which means undoing it would be incredibly risky. Not to mention how incredibly stupid I would've been."

"Not if you never intended to take the memories back."

Reaching over, he tugged her shirt back down her stomach but left his hand there to toy with the hem. "Exactly, and then… what would be the point of worrying about them, if this is who I intended to be. Elaine, on the other hand, she left that flash drive for me to find. It could be a message on how to restore her memories, I don't know, but she'd have to, on some level, realize that she's altered her brain. And if it was a recipe on how to recover them, what would be the point of giving *me* the drive?"

"Plus, I suppose a brain shift is not something you could, like, just experiment with."

"Nope. No way. One wrong move and… you're dead."

Aly nodded.

"There's no gaps in my memories," he said. "At least, not after I left the Institute. I don't think there's been a large change in my personality." He winced. "No. There has, because you've influenced me, but I mean…" He huffed. "I dunno what I mean."

"I get you," she said with a nod.

"And… even if it's possible, why?" He didn't seem to be aware that he ran his fingers up and down the hem of her shirt, brushing over her stomach as he talked. "What'd be the point of it? Why would I do it and not give myself any clues as to how to undo it or why it needed to be done in the first place. There's no missions in Bellhollow."

"No," she said and swallowed heavily. "But there was me."

His hand stilled. "You're not a mission."

"Do you know that for absolute certain, or is that what you choose to believe?"

He blinked at her and his face crumpled. "No. No, don't."

Aly frowned. "Don't what?"

"Don't doubt me now," he said, his voice cracking. He retreated from her, rocking his body backward and pulling his hand away. "You're the one who said—why are you—that's—"

"I said"—she rolled onto her side to face him and propped her head up on her hand—"that we need to discuss things when we're not overly emotional. And certainly not with *him* listening. So, put your hand back and let's entertain the worst-case scenario and work through it together."

"Oh," he said, sheepish.

"Bumble-butt," she said, giving him a little shove.

"Are… are you sure you want to talk worst case now?" Noah asked gently. "You've… there's a lot going on and I know things are so hard right now."

"Yeah," Aly replied, puffing out a breath. She curled her fingers around his shirt and tugged it. "Things are hard. Everything's fallen apart." She dropped her gaze to his throat so she didn't have to watch his reactions. "But… last time my world fell apart, I shut down completely. I can't afford to do that again. We can't afford that."

"Aly, it's okay to take time to—"

"I can't let you do all of this, Fletch," she said and blinked back tears. "This is my life too and this is all the control I have left over it. I need to… participate and we need to discuss things while we have a chance. Cause… if we gotta run, if he's followed or someone's followed… there might not be another chance."

He nodded. "Alright then. Where do you want my hand?"

She rolled her eyes at him, picked his hand up by the wrist and plopped it on her hip. "I meant what I said. Ten years is a long time to pretend you're someone you're not. It's more than half your life. If you changed your brain, it doesn't matter. This is who you are now."

"All right," Noah said and hummed, rubbing his hand across her hip. "Worst case. What if… what if it's not? What if, god forbid, there's some sort of… I dunno… trigger word which changes me back to… whatever I was before?"

Aly sighed and dropped her arm flat on the bed to use as a pillow instead of a prop. "Maybe worst case scenarios aren't a good idea."

He pushed onward. "I'd have to hope that… either I could stop it, or you'd be able to retrigger me… or appeal to the Fletcher part of me somehow."

She smiled. "A mound of Snickers should do the trick."

"I'd like to think so," he said returning the smile. "So, worst case is… I did come to Bellhollow and you were my mission and if, somehow, the old memories get triggered…" he trailed off. "I'd hope to be able to use whatever process I did before cordoning off the memories of being Fletcher so you could activate them later?"

Aly hummed. "Yeah, that sounds a bit far-fetched."

"I… believe that my memories as Fletcher are stronger than any compulsions," Noah told her, trying to sound confident. "You're right in that respect. I have more time spent as Fletcher than anyone else. He is who I want to be. That's gotta be enough."

"Good to know," she said with a nod. "Hypothetically, well, I mean, you hate Rex. So you wouldn't be on a mission for him."

"Right. I'd think, if I was on a mission for him, I'd have made the hate weaker."

"Or non-existent." She pondered. "Do you think Darcy knows about me?"

"Definitely does now," he muttered, looking unhappy about that.

"What about Adam? You said he found you in Bellhollow, right? Did he look surprised to find you there?"

Noah blinked rapidly. "Wow. Never thought of that. You think I could be on a mission from Adam?"

"I dunno. Maybe? I mean, you know him much better than I do."

"Joseph was always the master tactician," he said. "We often deferred to his decisions. Adam was more a follower... but things could've changed. He's always been very charismatic and caring and... You met Adam, you know."

"I did?"

"Mmm-hmm," he said and traced the exposed skin between her shirt and her jeans with the tips of his fingers. "We were... maybe eleven? Twelve? It would've been one of the only times Uncle Lee and I appeared together. Adam stayed a few days and left, but you did meet him."

Frowning, Aly searched her memories. "I... don't..."

"He was... interested in you and wanted to meet you, but I don't remember it being more than idle curiosity. More... you and Penelope were my reasons for staying in Bellhollow and he wanted a chance to see why."

"Huh. Sorry, I can't recall."

"It was a long time ago. He came for dinner," Noah prompted. "Aunt P made veiled comments about neglect all night."

Aly's eyes widened as she remembered that night. "*Oooh*. Mom was *so* angry at him."

Noah chuckled. "Yup. Adam said she spent the night giving him advice on how to be a good parent. It was an excuse for me to have Lee be wary of her"—he snorted—"*aaaand* never come to dinner again."

Aly giggled. "Clever."

"Thanks." His fingers continued to seek out the snatches of exposed skin on her hip, and dared to sneak under the hem. "Doing okay?"

Aly toyed with one of the buttons on his shirt. "Yeah."

"Do you want to keep going?" At Aly's nod, Noah said, "Right. So. Worst case." He sighed. "I suppose the absolute worst case I can think of right now is that one of us is lying to the other."

Unable to help her reaction, Aly tensed in defense. "I'm not lying, how could you even *think* I would lie to you—"

Noah raised his eyebrows at her. "Overreaction much? I don't think you're lying and I hope you don't think I'm lying. We're doing hypotheticals."

Aly cringed. "I guess…" She sighed. "Sorry. Maybe I'm still too emotional for this."

Noah leaned toward her and pressed his lips to her forehead. "Enough for today then," he said and drew back. "There's really only so much we can plan for when we don't have all the information. I'll try again tomorrow to get hold of Adam, but I think we need to move. I don't like sitting still."

With a nod, Aly said, "Yeah. Me too."

Noah used his head to point toward the bathroom. "Go get ready for bed. I'll see what pay-per-view has to offer."

CHAPTER 3

With a cry that was a mix between a yelp and a wail, Aly forced herself awake to flee a nightmare. She sat up, clutching at her chest. Heaving in deep, ragged breaths, she struggled to contain the panic swelling within her.

Eyes drawn to the tiny trickle of light creeping through the closed curtains, Aly scrubbed a hand across her face. The details of her nightmare were already slipping from memory but the panic the dream caused remained.

A peer at the clock told her that though it was still too early to be awake, she'd managed to get a few hours sleep. Glancing over at Noah's bed, she tried to see if she'd woken him. The darkness of the room didn't allow her to see much beyond the fact that it appeared he was still asleep. Which was good. She didn't feel like explaining another nightmare to him.

Bending her knees below the sheets, she pondered whether or not she wanted to try for more sleep or stay awake. With a sigh, Aly reached for her cell. No chance of getting back to sleep, but she could surf the web or catch up on some of her favorite online comics until morning.

It was morbid curiosity that brought her to one of Grace's social media pages. Rex said he was going to make

Aly die and a small and annoying part of her wanted to know how people, how her friends, were reacting to that news. Whether they were okay. What had they said about her. What they'd said to each other. It was attention-seeking and stupid, and Aly called herself all sorts of names and did it anyway.

Instagram was barren. Not a mention of anything, Grace's last post was several days ago; specifically a candid shot of her and Del by the lake. Del's also hadn't been touched for a few days and that concerned Aly. Neither she nor Noah had spoken to Del or Grace before the incident in the park, and really couldn't now, but the last time Aly had spoken to them, the pair had been chasing after Elaine and she'd told them to go home.

Neither of them had been vocal when Fletcher had died either. Del had shut down like she had, closed off his social worlds and spent time grieving in his own way, while Grace had tried to run from it by being there for both of them. So, maybe it was only a matter of time before they tweeted something. Or... maybe they hadn't gone home as she'd told them to.

She didn't know. She *hated* not knowing. She worried and fretted about her friends.

Both Tamara and Kate's most recent post was the same picture of a bee on a flower, which brought tears to Aly's eyes. Lloyd and Ezekiel's pages were empty, but neither of them were particularly vocal on social media. Aly circled around Madison-Lee's name, then decided she wasn't that needy.

Sighing, she rested her head against the wall behind the bed. She wished she could speak to them again. She wanted to hear Grace's voice. She wanted to...

She wanted to talk to her mom. More than anything, she wanted to talk to her mom and say the things she didn't get to say the last time they spoke. But she couldn't talk to Penelope either. For this ruse to work, all contact with everyone had to be terminated.

She might never get to talk to her mom again.

Letting out a deep sigh, Aly turned away from thinking about her past. She had to look forward. To an uncertain future, one where—

Noah made a noise. Deep in his throat, a raspy cry that came with a rustle of fabric and a jerk of his legs. Concerned, Aly tilted her cell to use the light from the screen to illuminate him. It seemed like every muscle in his face was tense, screwed into a tight frown. Eyes clenched shut, hair plastered to his forehead, hands with a death grip on the pillow, he appeared caught in the throes of a nightmare.

Throwing back the blankets, Aly went for the bedside lamp switch first. A soft glow filled the room, not bright enough to scare anyone from sleep, but enough that when he woke, he'd be able to see.

She called his name, soft and gentle, as she cautiously approached his bed. Startling him awake would be bad, she'd learned that from experience when they were much younger. Gingerly sitting beside him, she touched his shoulder.

Noah snapped awake. Tingles engulfed Aly as Noah jerked into a half-seated position, ready for anything.

"It's me," she soothed, taking care to remain still.

He blinked at her like he'd never seen her before, then blinked again and his eyes cleared. "Aly," he said after a long moment. "Hi." The knee-jerk tingles ceased and he scrubbed a hand over his face in an attempt to wake up. He leaned back, supporting his weight on one elbow while his other hand found her arm. "You okay? What's up?"

"I really should be asking that of you," she replied. Nudging him to move over, Aly scooted further onto the bed. "You were moaning. Nightmare?"

Noah blinked at her again, then cringed. "Ahh, shit," he muttered and fell back on his pillow in self-loathing. "Did I wake you?"

"No." She tried to smile and failed. "We're... two peas

in a pod tonight."

Lifting up his blanket, Noah hoisted up, grabbed her, and then dragged her beneath the blankets with him. Squeaking from the suddenness of the attack hug, Aly let herself be bundled up next to him. Snuggling into his side, she used his arm as a pillow.

When she was settled, Noah asked, "Do you want to talk about it?"

She snorted and countered, "Do you?"

Rubbing her back, he laughed and it sounded awkward and forced. "Nope. Nuh-ah. A-okay with ignoring the eff out of this one."

Aly snorted.

With a grumble, he squeezed her, then lazily stroked his fingers along her arm. "What time is it anyway?"

"Um… shy of five."

"Ahh. Sun'll be up soon. I could order room service and we can sit on the balcony and watch it."

"Sounds romantic."

"Or we could just lie here for a while."

"Nah," Aly said, wriggling away to sit up. "There was the promise of food. I heard it. Can't take it back now. Anything with bacon. And a banana. If you could convince them to do bacon-wrapped bananas, I'll love you five-ever."

"Yeah," he scoffed. "Cause *they* go well together. You and your weird foods."

Stretching her arms above her head, she ignored his tease. "Plus, I was thinking, since we're on the move today, we should do a load of laundry first."

Noah wrinkled his nose. "Ugh. Basic hygiene. Next, you'll be asking me to shower on a regular basis."

"Endure," Aly retorted and poked him to get him moving. "Go order. I'll get dressed."

Following a nice breakfast on the balcony, and while Aly was preparing herself for the harrowing jump down to her decoy room by stalling with her shoelaces, Noah called

Ross and asked him if he'd heard any word from Tango. Upon receiving a negative, Noah told him it would be best if they moved on from Las Vegas.

From the sound of Ross' answer, he disagreed.

"You're welcome to stay," Noah said. "But I've got a hunch I need to track down. If you really want to wait for Tango, we can come back tomorrow." He paced across the room as he listened to Ross' reply. "You... huh...really? You sure? ... Yeah, alright." More pacing as he listened. "No, that's actually a good idea, I'll help... okay. Seeya then."

Aly raised an eyebrow as Noah hung up and finished stalling with her shoes.

"They're coming with us, I suspect he's afraid I'll vanish."

Aly snorted. "Wasn't he the one saying he'll disappear?"

"I guess Bonnie talked some sense into him," Noah replied as he rummaged through the rucksack. "And since we can be back tomorrow, Ross suggested we plant some surveillance cameras everywhere we've been, see if we can't shake loose anyone that might be following us."

She tilted her head at him. "I thought you couldn't tell shifters from pictures?"

"We can't," he acknowledged. "What we can tell is people watching. Similar walking patterns, same clothing, people loitering and stuff like that."

Aly nodded. "So, what's the hunch?"

Noah stopped rummaging and ran his hand through his hair until it reached his neck. "There's... a place we used to go... It's about... I dunno. Five hours from here? Maybe a bit more. I'm... half-thinking Elaine left a message for me there. And if she didn't, then taking a picture of it may flush Adam out. Which reminds me," he said, losing the unsure tone. "What'd you find in those pictures Elaine had?"

She hummed. "Not much. There's evidence many of

the photos were cleverly shopped and I found a...word. Could be a name," she pulled a face at him, "but I can't remember it, sorry. I made notes. If I look through the rest of them, I might find more."

Noah nodded. "I'd like to help Ross set up the cameras, would you mind doing the laundry on your own?"

Aly chewed on her lip nervously. "Sight distance?" she asked, seeking reassurance.

"Yup. There's one just around the corner, that way I can keep—" Something chimed, a different ringtone and Noah's whole demeanor brightened in response as he looked at his cell. "Finally!"

"Huh?"

Furiously shoving things into the rucksack, he said, "We need to go. We need some distance from the hotel."

"Why?"

He practically bounced over to her. "Because I'm about to do something potentially dangerous and I don't want it to lead back to the hotel."

His eagerness made her confused and she balked. "Fletch—"

Grabbing her hands, he coaxed her to her feet, then lifted her hands to his mouth to kiss her fingers. "Trust me." With a cheeky eyebrow waggle, he grinned, even wider and brighter than before and Aly's mouth tugged into a smile as she was caught up in his mood.

A quick and terrifying descent to the decoy room, followed by them both awkwardly avoiding drawing attention to themselves and pretending not to know each other as they exited the hotel. Then Aly found herself walking down the main strip of Las Vegas, hand-in-hand with Noah, at seven in the morning. She didn't know where they were going, but she hadn't seen Noah smile like that since this whole thing began and she wanted to know why and how she could keep it on his face.

A good distance from the hotel, Noah dragged a cap

out of his back pocket and threw it on his head. A flurry of tickles along her spine told her Noah was shifting, and she had to stifle a gasp as *Fletcher* turned his head and winked at her.

"What's going on?"

"Wait," he said, his tone full of promise, and put his cap away again.

Eyes darting around, she was certain someone had to have seen it. They were in a public place, and there were people walking by them. No one said anything. No one stared or pointed. No one even seemed to notice.

They reached the fountained plaza outside Caesars Palace, across from the miniature Eiffel Tower, situated on the verge of an intersection. Spinning to face her, Fletcher grabbed Aly's hips and lifted her, setting her down on the raised edge of the fountain, then hopped up to sit beside her. Angling his cell, he lifted it high and pressed his face in beside hers. "Smile."

Still confused, she smiled for the camera. It was a high shot, one that didn't show much in the background beyond the water of the fountain so whoever saw the picture wouldn't have been able to tell much. Their smiling faces took up most of the screen.

Watching him as he hid his screen in a coy, teasing manner, Aly frowned. "I still don't—"

"Aaand sent," he announced, then goofily grinned at her. "Just wait."

"Sent? What?"

"You'll like this," he said and put his hand over his heart. "I swear by the Snickers."

She blinked at him, then squinted. He only used that phrase when he'd been devious and done something he shouldn't have. "What did you do?"

The cell shrilled and Aly felt her heart speed up. Fletcher swiped to answer, then held the screen up ahead of them to initiate video chat.

"I don't understand, what are you—?"

"Hello?" the black square on the screen said, before the picture flickered and illuminated. "Aly?"

Aly's words died in her throat and she gurgled. Staring, she lifted tear-bright eyes to a smug and satisfied Fletcher, who winked at her. "Like I'm going to listen to Rex."

"Aly, are you—" Penelope gasped as the call connected her end. "Oh, my darling girl!"

"*Mom.*" Aly lost the battle with her tears and choked on a sob. "Oh. Mom, I'm so happy to see you. I've been so scared and everything's happened all at once and—" she hiccupped and gulped and covered her face with her hands as she tried to control herself. "I want to go home."

"Oh, honey, I know. I know you do and I want you to be able to," Penelope crooned to soothe her. "I know everything is really hard right now, but you're safe and you're not hurt and we need to get you as far away from those people as we can—"

Scooting over, Fletcher gathered Aly into a one-armed hug, squishing her to his chest. "C'mon Als," he murmured, trying to comfort her. Aly buried her face in his shirt and held on. "I didn't mean to make you cry."

Penelope gasped. "Fletcher," she muffled, as though speaking through her hand.

Rubbing Aly on the back, he said, "Hi, Aunt P. I wish I could've told you everything. If I'd known you knew about my world, I would've."

"Oh, baby boy," Penelope gushed. "I'm just so happy you're *alive*. I thought I'd never see you again."

Desperate to talk to her mother, her uncontrollable burst of tears dried up as fast as they'd arrived. Turning her head so she could see the screen, she didn't release Fletcher as she croaked, "Are you safe? And Roger and Tim?"

"Yes!" Penelope said, wiping a tear away from her cheek. "We're fine. Roger's so concerned about you and Tim's confused about everything but coping well with the sudden holiday. We're up with…" she paused, her eyes widening. "Oh… I can't say, can I?"

"Prefer if you didn't," Fletcher said, still cuddling Aly.

Penelope nodded. "I followed your instructions as best I could."

Tilting her head back, Aly raised an eyebrow at Fletcher, but he shook his head and indicated Penelope with his eyes. She took that to mean he'd tell her later.

Penelope said, "We're… trying to decide what to do. Bellhollow isn't safe anymore." Aly opened her mouth to reply as Penelope waved her hand. "But don't worry about us. Roger and I have contingency plans. We always have. We'll be fine, I promise."

"Always?" Aly asked, surprised.

Penelope nodded. "Honey, there's *so* much I need to tell you. About your birth mother. About everything that's gone on. I wish—"

Fletcher warned, "Aunt P."

With a regretful nod of acknowledgment, Penelope said, "I know, I know. Next time. This time is a test. Aly, do you need anything? Are you eating okay? Do you need money? I can get you your trust fund, just tell me what you need."

A test. Of course. Fletcher would be on the lookout for anyone tracing the call to get to them. Or Penelope. But somehow, it seemed all worth the risk. Aly took a deep breath and let it out slowly. "Honestly, I think I just needed to hear your voice."

Penelope blinked back tears and smiled. "I needed to hear your voice too," she admitted. "It's been a very scary couple of days."

Aly swallowed. "Yeah, it has."

"I wish you'd told me what you were going through," Penelope said.

Aly hunched, feeling guilty. She used to be able to talk to her mother about anything. "Yeah, I know."

"But, I should've told you many things, right from the beginning too," Penelope admitted, her voice soft. "I'd hoped this would never affect you... but wishful thinking."

"Yeah."

"So many things I would've done differently. I should've prepared you better for this, instead, I let those people take you without any knowledge of their world and—"

"You can't... you can't dwell on the past, Mom. It just.... you can't dwell and you can't second guess. We have to..." She ran out of words and shrugged.

With a torn expression, Penelope studied her. "I'm so sorry, honey. This must be so hard for you."

Aly tilted her head and looked up at Fletcher. "It's easier with Fletch here."

Giving her a smile, he pressed his lips to her temple. "We need to go," he said, apologetic.

Aly swallowed the sudden lump in her throat. "Already?"

"Yeah. We need to be really careful right now." Turning to Penelope he asked, "You have a pen and a piece of paper?"

"Of course."

"Write this down," he instructed, then waited until Penelope appeared ready. "First two letters of Aly's middle name, first two letters of the type of fish you gave me when I was eleven, last two letters of your maiden name, then Tim's comfort toy name, at Gmail dot com. All one word, no capitals. The password is capital P underscore, then the name of the character Aly played in Peter Pan, all lowercase and no spaces, then the last two digits of Roger's birth year. Change the password as soon as you can. There's a file in there already, in a draft email, with some instructions on how to clear your laptops of tracers."

"That seems very... convoluted," Penelope said as she jotted down notes.

"It needs to be. We'll contact you through that email. Hide the phone you're using right now at the location you are. I'll be able to tell if it's accessed. Keep the other one for next time."

Penelope nodded. "Whatever it takes if it means I can still talk to both of you."

Aly leaned closer to the screen, desperate to keep her mother with her longer. "I love you, Mom. So much."

Penelope's eyes filled with tears. "I love you too. Both of you. Please be careful."

After signing off, Fletcher lowered the cell to his lap. "I know that this has all been really hard—"

Aly grabbed him by the flannel shirt and pulled him toward her so she could kiss him. He made a muffled noise of surprise against her lips and tensed. "Sorry," she blurted as she backed away. Releasing his shirt, she smoothed it down with nervous fingers and concentrated on her hands rather than his face as she twittered, "Uh, I didn't mean—I just wanted to say thanks. For calling her, I mean. Ah, you didn't have to but you did and it was *wonderful*," she finished, breathing out the last word in a reverent sort of tone.

He puffed out a breath. "*Huh.*"

She peeked at him, surprised to find his expression dazzled. "Fletch?"

Staring into the distance, he said, "You know, I always found it weird when Ethan claimed kissing Madison-Lee could knock the thoughts right out of his head." He pulled a face. "I mean, he did like to describe blood rushing to particular places after that, but... I never understood what he meant. It didn't seem possible someone could make you forget what you were thinking. Like, a society lie, where everyone claims it happens, but it doesn't really, and everyone just contributes by claiming it's true because no one wants to admit it's not. But, just like that—" he simulated an airplane flight with his hand at the same time he made a '*whoosh*' sound. "They're gone." He focused on her, concerned. "Is that normal?"

She blinked at him. "Um... sometimes."

He blinked right back at her. "Really?"

She tried to hold in her laughter and it came out a mixture of a giggle and a snort.

Staring at her, Fletcher asked, "What?"

Smiling, she bopped his nose. "For someone whose mind is supposedly blank, that was a *lot* of thought. Are you going to analyze every kiss?"

"Oh. Ahh. No?" His shoulders hunched and he looked meek. "You... umm... now you probably think I'm weird."

"Oh, bumble-butt," she said affectionately and swung her legs in a child-like manner. "I've *always* thought you were weird. I was just worried cause you tensed."

He cringed. "My bad. You surprised me, that's all. That was..." he puffed out a breath and gave her a silly grin. "...really nice." Jumping off the edge of the fountain, he lifted a finger to hold her in place as he cast a conspiring glance around. "We need to make ourselves scarce." With hunched shoulders and his back to the street, he used the positions of their bodies as a cover to dismantle the cell completely. "Stay here a sec."

She blinked, but nodded.

She watched him wander across to a trash can located at the corner of the street and placed all the pieces of the cell into it. Then he crossed the street and pottered around the other side, weaving in and out of other pedestrians. After doing that with each of the three corners of the intersection, he bounced back to her. "Okay. Let's go."

"Cameras?" she asked, hopping down from her seat on the fountain rims.

"Sneaky ones," he said, taking her hand as they started walking back toward the hotel. "If someone comes here looking and acts suspicious, I'll know. If nothing happens, then I think, *maybe*, we found a way to keep in contact with Penelope."

She was thrilled by that possibility. "Thank you. I thought—"

"I know. I… well, maybe having it as a surprise wasn't the best thing, but I didn't want to get your hopes up in case it didn't work." He smiled and squeezed her fingers. "I know this is really, really hard for you, Als. I get that." He dropped his gaze away from her and his tone saddened. "It's depressing and it sucks and it's absolutely not what you wanted out of life and I know I can't give you your dreams back."

"Fletcher—"

"Just know I'm here for you. When you're ready. I'll do anything to make it easier."

"You lost everything, too," Aly realized. She'd been so selfish about this. Pining away and mourning her life and he'd lost everything as well. In all the mayhem, she'd forgotten that.

"I never had dreams like you have," Fletcher said with a shake of his head. "I knew one day I'd have to go and all I'd have was memories. I was prepared for it. As much as I miss Del and Grace and… and regret all that we had to leave behind, all I wanted was to be a part of your life." He met her eyes with a fondness that turned her insides to goo. "I still have that."

They were in this together, partners and best friends. He could be her pillar of strength while she grieved, while she missed her mother and her family and her friends and the life she wanted. She would keep on missing them, like she had missed Fletcher had when he'd had to leave.

The world didn't stop turning just because things weren't going right and if she was going to survive, she had to make an effort.

"Hey, Fletch?"

"Yeah?"

"Before we go do laundry, can we go get a stylus?"

He smiled at her. "Absolutely."

CHAPTER 4

Washing machines and dryers hummed and clacked as they spun. Rows upon rows of chrome machines lined the laundromat. An older man loaded a dryer by the door, while a green-mohawked man folded his clothes on the bench provided. A mother spoke Spanish to her children as they helped with her load.

Aly sat in a seat near the dryer she'd paid for, away from the main entrance. Tucked away in the back, where she could see everything, but could still hide among the rows of machines if necessary. She alternated between playing with her new stylus and watching the people in the laundromat.

Noah had given her the rest of the images Elaine had sent through to look at while he, along with Bonnie and Ross, peppered the area around the hotel with spy cameras. The laundromat was a few streets from the hotel they spent the previous night and Noah was certain they hadn't been followed.

If she were honest, she was glad of the time to herself and do something as ordinary and mundane as laundry. Even if it was boring, it gave her time to go through the photos Elaine had slipped to Noah. Inserting the flash drive into her laptop, she loaded the images. Eyes narrow, she looked through the new ones. Unlike the last group of photos, which had been selfies, these ones were mostly pictures of landscapes. Street signs. A dog. A sunset. The Grand Canyon. A New York Skyline.

Focusing on the ones which held pictures of people, she started her process of analyzing the images, like checking the metadata for tags or seeing if there was smudging in the background. A few of the images were selfies like the ones Noah had sent her, except that they clearly displayed landmarks. In front of the Statue of Liberty for example. Or in front of the Golden Gate Bridge. Places so easily identified, he hadn't bothered sending them. Definitely a map of Elaine's past which could be plotted, especially since there were date stamps on the images.

Sighing, Aly cupped her chin and rested her elbows on her knee.

A discrepancy appeared in the selfie taken on top of the Empire State building, a picture that was easy to modify by cloning the background, but the edges weren't quite smudged together correctly. It was there again in the one at the Washington Monument. The same kind of smudge she'd identified last time and she found the word 'Isidora' again in the metadata of one of the selfies.

Then, in the one taken at the Lincoln Memorial, a reflection in Elaine's sunglasses appeared.

A woman, her face obscured by the cell phone she held up to take the photo. Aly frowned at the screen as she studied the woman's clothing. She'd seen that beaded top before.

Flipping through the other images of Elaine, she found the same beaded top worn by Elaine in a photograph from Seattle, with the same smudge present in the photo. Across the other side of the country. It wasn't a coincidence. Perhaps this was 'Isidora'. Or someone else. Maybe Noah knew. Still, whoever this woman was, she was connected to Elaine.

The images were a timeline and a map of where Elaine had been, but not why. The last image was dated four years ago and the smudge was absent from that. That might have been the time Elaine returned to Darcy, the creator of the Faceless and leader of the Institute, and the woman who haunted Fletcher even now, years after his escape. *If* that's what Elaine had done, and she wasn't trying to mess up Darcy's plans—another theory that was possible.

It was all so confusing.

Glancing up as the door to the laundromat opened, Aly froze as Fletcher walked through. Fletcher, yet not Fletcher. She knew. She *knew* that wasn't him. No tingles, which meant it had to be a Faceless masquerading as him and not a natural shifter.

The fake Fletcher reminded her of spikes in the same way her Fletcher reminded her of tingles. Not a physical feeling like she got when a Faceless shifted, but a memory of the feeling. She suspected the spike she associated with the Fake-Fletcher was the same feeling she got in the park during the attack. The unknown Faceless with Elaine.

This had to be Jonah then. Joseph. She wasn't sure what name she... he? they went by. Gender changes weren't outside of the Faceless' scope of abilities, so it was hard to know how they identified.

She did know that Fake-Fletcher knew she was here, otherwise, they wouldn't have come in under this guise. Did they want to talk? Or were they trying to test her abilities? She wasn't sure what she should do. Had it been Elaine, she would have bolted and that need still filled her. While Jonah technically hadn't done anything to her, they'd been around when she was shot.

She closed her laptop and packed it in the rucksack, trying to look as nonchalant as she could. No weapon that she could see, but then, if it *was* Jonah, they knew how to augment and that made weapons moot.

Spotting her, Fake-Fletcher offered a smile that looked

more like a grimace than a smile and not at all like her Fletcher's wonderful lopsided one.

Aly hooked her hand through the strap of the rucksack and stood. The clothes should be nearly dry. She would repack and leave as soon as she was able, but, if she had to, she could walk out of here right now. Until she knew what they wanted, she'd keep her distance from the Fake-Fletcher. As they stepped into her row of machines, Aly ducked out the end of the row and into the next one. There were too many people around for Fake-Fletcher to do anything to her without drawing attention.

Noah wouldn't be far. He'd promised he would stay close. She had to wait.

The smile-grimace turned into a smirk. Fake-Fletcher stopped and put their elbows on the closest machine and leaned toward her. "Hello, Alyson."

She kept herself away from their reach. "Aly," she corrected and laid the sarcasm on thick. "Maybe you should, oh, I don't know, *learn* your targets, Jonah."

They snorted. "I prefer Joseph." Leaning on his elbows, Joseph clasped his hands together and then rested his chin on the back. "Elaine said you were good. I had to see for myself."

There were back doors to this place, Noah had shown her before he left, but Joseph's casual approach had her worried. Eyeing the front of the laundromat, she wondered if Elaine was a sniper out there, waiting for her to bolt. She might not survive a second round. They could even be waiting for Noah to ambush *him*. She had to play this through and hope Noah was okay. "Uh-huh. Good for Elaine. How'd you find me?"

"Do you really think you were that hard to find? I know all of Noah's tricks. I taught him most of them."

Trying to be brave, she said, "What do you want?"

"You," he said.

Unsettled, Aly took a step back.

"See"—prying one hand free from his chin, Joseph

gestured at her with his index finger—"that lovely little trick of yours, the one where you remove a shifter's ability, we need that."

Her mouth went dry. "Not happening."

"What makes you think you have a choice?" Joseph asked, mild.

She scowled, taking refuge in anger. "In what demented universe would I ever—"

"I have Grace and Del."

Aly's instinctual, "You're lying," caused Joseph's smirk to widen as he reached for his cell.

"I have proof."

"I am not going to believe any 'proof' unless I see them both. In person," Aly responded, not even looking at the video Joseph offered. "Shifters can't be sensed via screen. That could be any of your gang pretending."

The smirk slipped off his stupid, smug face.

"I am *not* falling for tricks," she snapped at Joseph. "Now leave me alone." She put enough heat into her voice, with a hint of desperation, that some of the other people in the laundromat looked over.

"He really has his claws into you, doesn't he?"

Aly lifted her chin in defiance. She didn't like this, but she wasn't going to allow Joseph to sway her in any way.

"He's not who you think he is. He's been manipulating you for years. Don't trust him."

She told him, quite vehemently, what he could do with that.

Joseph pushed away from the machine and stood straight. "Fine. Don't believe me." He pointed his finger at her. "But you won't tell Noah I was here."

Aly scoffed, "Like I'm going to do *anything* you tell me—"

"Food for thought," Joseph said, mild again and with a hint of smugness which put her on the verge of panic. "What if I *do* have Grace and Del? What if I know every move Noah will make before he makes it? We can follow you anywhere; don't think we can't." His eyes flashed with anger. "I *will* hurt them if you tell him of this encounter. And I'll enjoy it."

Aly swallowed. "You wouldn't—"

"Can you risk that? Not knowing if I'm lying or not, you'll risk them? Some friend you are."

"You haven't got anything to gain by—"

"You underestimate your importance. You are a game-changer and we need you."

Aly balled her hands into fists. "FYI, that is not the way to manipulate me into trusting you. Tell me Fletcher's manipulating me, then turn it on its head and threaten my friends. Some plan that is."

"What makes you think that's what our plan is? We don't need your trust, just your abilities." He drummed the washing machine with his fingers, then pulled a card out of his shirt pocket and left it on the top. "Confirm what I've told you if it makes you feel better. Then call me when you're ready to talk," he said and turned toward the door. "You have twenty-four hours before I do something irreversible to your friends."

A small nugget of doubt formed. Unable to help herself, she blurted. "How did you know?"

Joseph hesitated with a frown. "Know what?"

"That I could do… that I could take…" She shook her head and put a hand on her chest. "*I* didn't even know I could do that. So how did you?"

A shadow crossed Joseph's face before he said, "We have our sources."

Sources. That wasn't an answer at all but she didn't have time to question him as he sauntered from the laundromat.

Puffing out a breath, Aly didn't relax until Joseph disappeared down the street.

How had Joseph even known she was here? Specifically in this particular laundromat, let alone Las Vegas. Were they that close? For that matter, how had they followed her to Lake Tahoe?

Tracking device. It had to be. Was it a coincidence Joseph had come just as Aly was looking through Elaine's pictures, or was it more to it? Trojan horse or some other virus? Had he known she would be alone? Or had he wanted Noah and then improvised?

She didn't know but she knew she had to tell Noah. She couldn't keep this from him. Could she?

Perching on the edge of a vacant chair with the rucksack on her back, she dug her hands into her hair to press her nails against her skull. Doubt and indecision filled her. What if Joseph *did* have Del and Grace? Both their social media pages were suspiciously bare and they had been following Elaine and Joseph. She wanted to call them to find out. She wanted to hear Grace's voice. If they were in danger, she had to help them. Somehow.

First, she had to confirm they were missing. That was the most important part. If they were missing, then *maybe* it could be conceivable that Joseph had them. And she couldn't tell Noah, not until she knew for sure. It would be another worry he didn't need right now. That move from Joseph was intentional. If she told and caused her friends harm, she'd never forgive herself.

She hoped he'd understand.

The dryer which had their clothes in it pinged and Aly surged from her chair. She didn't bother folding the clothes or checking that they were completely dry before she shoved them in the rucksack.

They had to get out of here. That was the important part.

Wildly aware of everything occurring within the laundromat, of the people and the noises, she poised on the edge of panic. Her heartbeat picked up its erratic hammering as Noah appeared outside, casually strolling along the street.

No tingles. He didn't appear anxious or worried. He wasn't checking every corner.

Aly slowed down her frantic packing and stared at him. Was she overreacting?

He smiled at her as he pushed open the laundromat door and walked over. "All done?"

She squeaked out a 'yes'.

With furrowed brow, he touched the small of her back. "I'm ready to go," he said, his easy tone of voice not matching the concerned expression on his face.

Maybe he *did* know. Maybe he was trying to hide it until they were safe. He promised her sight distance the whole time. He had to know.

So... maybe Joseph was still watching? Maybe Noah's hands were as tied as hers were. Aly swallowed and forced herself to smile. "You're just in time to help me fold."

He laughed, and Aly could've sworn it sounded fake, but perhaps that's what she wanted to hear. "Great," he said and reached for one of his shirts to fold. Spotting the piece of paper Joseph left, he reached for it. "What's—"

Aly lunged, snatching it away from him and shoved it in her pocket. "Nothing. Just... some guy..." she improvised and waved her hand around, being over-dramatic. "A dude-bro gave it to me."

Noah raised an eyebrow at her. "Someone trying to pick up in a laundromat? How original."

Feeling sick to her stomach, she went with it. "Pshh, yeah, I know, right? Ridiculous."

Noah chuckled. "Yup."

She wanted to talk, to ask him about the cameras, to warn him of Joseph, but she couldn't find the words. All that came out of her mouth sounded stupid and inane and consisted of more lies. The truth burned at her. They could talk about anything and now she had to keep a secret from him and it hurt. She didn't know if Noah noticed. If he did, he didn't say anything.

This was never going to end. She was never going to feel safe.

***

The moment the door opened, Grace pounced. "Where is she?" she demanded, desperately looking beyond Joseph. Seeing nothing, her eyes snapped to Joseph and she accused, "You didn't bring her!"

"She wouldn't come," he said, wandering into the hotel room. He placed his keys on the bench and sighed. "And she was in a public place. I couldn't make a scene."

Grace gaped at him, unable to believe his words. "But the video! She saw the video, right? You showed it to her?"

Joseph shucked off his jacket and draped it over the seat by the television. "Of course I did. She doesn't care. She didn't even watch it."

"You said that would work!" Grace said, her voice rising until it was shy of a wail.

From his watchful corner, Del growled, low and deep under his breath, a noise of frustration and anger. "We need to get her."

"Agreed," Elaine said, glancing up from her laptop. "And we're working on it, have patience."

"We've *had* patience," Grace snapped. All Elaine seemed to do was be glued to her laptop and Grace was sick of hiding away. They had to be proactive if they ever wanted to see Aly again.

Del had been so quick to believe it was all connected to his conspiracy theory surrounding Fletcher's death and that Noah was somehow involved in or caused it, and the evidence was mounting. Whatever they did, they needed to move on this, rather than playing whatever slow game Elaine thought was necessary. The faster they got to Aly, the better. "My father's in law enforcement and I think I should call home and—"

"We told you, that'll spook Noah and you'll never see your Aly again."

"We're in Vegas," Grace argued, waving her hands around. "He's *already* spooked, so don't give me that bullshit."

"They're moving," Elaine interrupted, effectively

silencing them. Joseph pushed away from the wall he'd been leaning against to join Elaine.

Grumbling, Grace sat down on one of the beds in the room and folded her arms on her chest. "You're sure it's her? Aly, I mean. You're sure it's her they had captive and not one of your people?"

Joseph stilled. Slowly straightening up, he gave Grace a deadpan look. "You people?"

Grace glared at him, daring him to start something. "Your people, not 'you people'. The Aly you saw could be a shifter."

Elaine and Joseph shared a glance before Elaine said, "Shifters can tell each other, that's how we knew about Noah. The Aly we saw captive was not a shifter."

"The one I saw today was," Joseph added. "She's our link to your Aly. We have to be very careful how we play this, or your Aly will pay the price."

Grace narrowed her eyes. Secrets. Lots of them. They clung to Elaine and Joseph, like they'd clung to the Aly-imposter. She knew there was only so much Elaine and Joseph could share with them but still, sometimes it all felt like a lie. Or maybe even a twisted truth, warped and bent to their will.

The world had shapeshifters, people who could change their forms on a whim. Elaine had shown it to them various times and the transformation was *so* quick. That demonstration was the only thing that made Del and Grace believe Elaine and convinced them to go with her and Joseph to rescue Aly.

Aly, who hadn't been returned from the kidnapping like they'd all believed. Aly, who instead had been *replaced*.

According to Elaine, Aly was the estranged non-shifter daughter of some bigwig in the shifter world, who Elaine and Joseph worked for. Her birth father had apparently wanted to visit Aly after he'd found out about the kidnappings and attend her graduation. Grace didn't know anything about Aly's birth father, since Aly only ever talked about Roger being her father after adopting her, so it was plausible at least.

Grace had originally put all the oddities and Aly's recent attitude down to the beginnings of PTSD, or something similar, and had tried to be a supportive friend. Aly was acting out because of trauma and she had every right to.

Now, knowing that Aly had been replaced, Grace replayed events in her mind and viewed them with a whole new light. Not-Aly, whose amnesia of the kidnapping was really a ploy to give people a plausible reason to believe the small, yet noticeable, differences in her personality.

Her artistry. Her smile. All duplicated. Her memories and interactions with her friends were all an act, even her immediate crush on Noah. Ever since Grace had met Aly, she'd always been Fletcher's girl, and that included her other brief crushes, it was always about Fletcher. To see her fall for someone else so hard and fast was something their Aly would never do.

Their Aly—Fletcher's Aly—was still missing. Captured and held prisoner somewhere and their only link to her was to follow this imposter.

As for Fletcher, Grace didn't believe that Fletcher didn't 'exist', as Elaine had said. Fletcher and Aly's friendship had been so old, so entangled, there was no way that had been faked. Even if Fletcher was a shifter and his *identity* was fake, Aly had pictures of her and Fletcher from when they were eight and, from what Grace had garnered listening to Elaine and Joseph's conversations, that age couldn't be faked. Aly and Fletcher's friendship was practically ingrained.

Joseph explained Noah's arrival—and the Not-Aly's apparent infatuation with him—was timed so that he could be her backup when Aly's real father arrived. Aly's birth father had discovered Not-Aly masquerading as his daughter, and something had gone wrong, causing the Not-Aly to flee, whereupon Joseph and Elaine were called in. The word was she reunited with Noah in Sacramento, which explained some of the Not-Aly's incoherent phone call, and now she was being tracked by Joseph and Elaine, who were tasked with Aly's recovery by any means necessary. Those means now included Grace and Del, to gather information regarding the Not-Aly and how she behaved.

What Noah and the Not-Aly were after, Elaine couldn't—or wouldn't—say, except that Noah was extremely dangerous and it was imperative that they rescue Aly from the pair's nefarious clutches and take them into custody.

Grace felt they played into Del's conspiracy theories about Noah, which was why Del had been so quick to agree. Del had been enamored by the idea of the supernatural and hidden worlds, but Grace, sensing Del's decisions were partly made because of the argument with his mother over college, had been more skeptical and only agreed to come along so she could keep Del out of trouble. At the time, neither of them understood what they were getting themselves into and the more they knew, the more dangerous this shifter world seemed.

It made Grace wonder what else lay out there. What other creatures from myth and magic might exist. Werewolves and vampires? Fairies and spirits? What about Bigfoot? Or the Flying Spaghetti Monster?

She didn't know.

Just hours after agreeing to help Elaine and Joseph, there'd been a shooting at a park by Lake Tahoe—a shooting Grace was fairly certain Elaine and Joseph were involved in—wherein the Not-Aly was supposedly killed. A lie, a ruse so that Not-Aly could flee without repercussions.

But, it meant Grace's parents possibly believed Aly to be dead. Since Grace couldn't prove that Aly wasn't dead, not until they found her, she'd adhered to Joseph and Elaine's request for communication blackout and handed over her cell. If she'd known then what she knew now, she never would have done that, and perhaps that's what the pair were banking on.

She missed her parents, she really did, but this was so much more important. Her parents would forgive her, and be overjoyed on her return with Aly in tow.

But the longer they spent away from Bellhollow, the more Elaine and Joseph dropped hints about a war, and the longer Grace was asked not to contact her family, the more Grace had begun to believe what they were doing was dangerous.

There wasn't anything else they could do, not if they wanted to help Aly.

It hurt Grace deeply that she hadn't noticed such a big change in personality between Aly and the Not-Aly. She blamed herself. She was supposed to be Aly's best friend and she hadn't noticed, effectively leaving Aly wherever she was imprisoned. Grace had endured nightmares over the past few nights, worrying about what Aly must be going through.

She knew one thing, with absolute certainty. Grace would do anything to get Aly back and the Not-Aly would pay for hurting her.

CHAPTER 5

Being stuck in a car, traveling to someplace only Noah knew, with three Faceless who were in that weird, overly-polite/awkward stage with each other, was not Aly's idea of fun. Especially now she harbored a secret.

The time was spent in almost silence. A silence broken only by the radio, seemingly set louder to discourage talking. Aly tingled intermittently as Noah checked on something, but she couldn't ask what.

Aly couldn't speak, not without wanting to blurt out what happened in the laundromat and get Noah's take on it. She didn't trust Bonnie completely, and disliked Ross so much she found it difficult to be in a room with him, and that helped her keep her tongue. She needed to get Noah alone and gently gauge whether or not he knew what had happened in the laundromat, and that wasn't going to be possible for a while.

She curled up in the front passenger seat, stared out the window and fought to keep her worries from consuming her. Anxious, she tried to remember her tells, like chewing her nails or nervous fidgeting, because she knew, if Noah asked what was wrong, she'd blurt it all out.

As the road started to stretch, traffic lessened and Las

Vegas was barely a memory, Ross asked, "So, where are we going?"

Noah adjusted in his seat, getting more comfortable. Using one hand to steer, he rested the other on his thigh. "Do you know where the Institute was?"

"Vaguely," Ross replied. He shuffled in the back, banging his knees against Aly's seat for the umpteenth time and she raised her head, wondering how far she could lean back her seat in retaliation. "Somewhere in Utah. We... never found the location. Not much we could do."

"Yeah," Noah said. "Me either, not really. Didn't look for it. Thought if I did, I'd have to... confront demons, or blow the place sky high."

"Or both," Ross said.

"Or that." Staring at the road ahead, Noah wriggled again. His jitters caught Aly's attention and she watched him in her peripherals, concerned why he was so jumpy. Did he know? Or was it something else? "What did Adam tell you about the night we escaped?"

"Not much," Ross replied, exchanging a glance with Bonnie. "Most of our conversations have been mission based..." He paused. "Yeah. Bonnie says 'He's our brother, but we don't really *know* him'."

"We didn't really know each other in the first place," Noah said. "Not really."

"True." Ross sighed. "Bonnie says... yeah... 'It's hard for us to become close. There was a level of distrust from Adam because we escaped earlier, we never could get over that hurdle. We thought maybe we could if we did more missions, we could prove ourselves'."

Noah hummed. "But it just became more and more and you never got anywhere. Plus, you never saw him other than on video. Hard to reach out."

"Yeah."

"But you kept trying."

"Yeah... well... it's what we knew."

"It's hard to trust people on the outside," Noah said.

He swapped his hands over, driving with one and using his other arm to rest on the door frame and cupped his head.

"Yeah."

Aly looked between them, wondering at the subtext of the conversation. There seemed to be a lot more being said than she understood. Tucking herself up tighter, she told herself that if Noah wanted her to know, he'd explain it later.

Noah took a deep breath in and let it out slowly. "When I discovered augmentation, I knew I'd want to share it with the others if I could. I didn't want Smith to get his hands on the knowledge, but, for someone like Solomon, it was a lifesaver. Except that, the first time I tried, I screwed it all up. Got too much information at once, so I didn't share until I got it right. As a result, while I was practicing, I overheard a lot of conversations that occurred outside the room. About Darcy. About Smith. About a breeding program between me and Elijah."

Ross hissed out a sharp breath and Aly snapped her head toward Noah to stare at him.

He wouldn't look at her. "We couldn't stay there. So, we made plans to get out, without leaving anyone behind. What I didn't know at the time was that Elijah had already met Rex and had planned an escape. I still don't really know if that escape included all of us. While Darcy was distracted by our escape, Rex snuck in and wiped their files." He heaved in a large sigh which discouraged questions. "Another thing I'd overheard was that one of us was a traitor and was giving information to Darcy. During the escape, that traitor attacked."

"Moses," Ross ground out.

Noah glanced back. "How...?"

"He was the only one Aly didn't mention," Ross said and then his voice turned sour. "You know. Besides us."

Noah nodded to confirm. "Hmm... We were all shot, but Seth and Solomon were lost to us. We're..." He shuffled again and tilted his body away from Aly. "We're going to their grave."

A flurry of activity and guttural noises from the back seat and Aly peered over her shoulder to see Bonnie furiously signing in among the wordless sounds.

Ross frowned as he watched Bonnie's hands. "We don't *know* that—well because—slow down—yes, I—I know!"

"What's going on?" Noah asked, trying to concentrate on the road and see the pair in the rear-view mirror at the same time.

Ross flung Noah a glance, then looked back at Bonnie. "He's got no reason to lie and Adam has—I know, Bonnie, I don't want that either—"

"Ross?" Noah prompted, vying for attention.

Bonnie thumped the back of Noah's chair twice while glaring at Ross.

Ross heaved in a heavy sigh. "According to Adam, Seth and Solomon aren't dead."

The car jerked and Aly's first instinct was to yelp and grab the door handle to hold on.

"You *saw* them?" Noah blurted, keeping control of the car. "In person. Both of them."

"No," Ross said. "That's the point of contention right now. We saw Seth via screen and we haven't seen Solomon."

"So, it might not be her." Noah's voice cracked halfway through his sentence.

"Maybe," Ross replied, unsure.

Bewildered, Noah mumbled, "I don't get it. Why would Adam say they were alive?"

"Don't know," Ross said with a shrug. "Not sure if I care anymore. Just shows us how much he lied to us, I guess."

Noah's knuckles were white from his hands clenched tightly around the steering wheel. His eyes were so wide Aly could see the whites all the way around his irises. Aly swallowed hard, knowing what was probably going through his head right now.

What if Seth and Solomon *weren't* dead? What if whatever horrors Noah had endured was all an implanted memory? What if Rex was right? What if, what if, *what if*?

She wanted to touch him, but the forced-upon secret burned her and kept her still.

"Bonnie," Ross soothed and his voice dropped low as he reached out and stopped Bonnie's babbling hands with his. "If there's a grave, we need to face that."

The 'if' seemed to hang heavy on Noah's shoulders as they slipped into silence.

After an eternity of silence and music listening, they stopped at a small town north of Las Vegas for lunch and to switch rental cars.

Aly didn't get an opportunity to talk to Noah alone, and there was no way she was doing it in front of Ross and Bonnie. Noah's sullen mood was catching. She picked at her food and watched Bonnie and Ross have signed conversations while Noah and Aly sat awkwardly beside each other and tried to pretend nothing was bothering either of them.

After lunch, while Noah and Ross organized a jeep for off-road travel, Bonnie and Aly went looking for snacks and drinks in the grocery store.

Worry ate at Aly. So many things at once. Worry about Noah. Worry about where they were headed, and what they would find when they got there. Worry for Grace and Del. She needed to find out if they were missing. If that was why their social media was so empty. She needed to know and the feeling had been bubbling inside her all day until it was unbearable.

Wandering down the candy aisle, Aly found herself alone and that in itself was a surprise. Raising up onto her tiptoes, she peered across the top of the aisle to see Bonnie with her back to Aly, flipping through magazines at the back of the store.

Aly didn't even think. She placed her basket on the

ground and abandoned it, striding through the sliding doors at the front of the store where she ducked around the corner and into the alleyway beside the store where she pulled out her cell.

Opening the burner application Noah had installed which allowed her to make untraceable calls, she selected one of the burner numbers and used it to call Grace's cell. Getting message bank, Aly hung up and called Del's cell. Again, nothing, which worried her. Chewing on her bottom lip, she took a massive risk and dialed Grace's home number.

She had to know. If Joseph was telling the truth about Grace and Del, then... she didn't know. If Joseph lied, then it would at least take one worry off the table and she wouldn't need to bother Noah.

Grace's mother, Lan, answered, "Hello?"

Aly's throat clogged as she realized she didn't think this through. She couldn't talk to Lan; Lan knew her voice and they'd know she wasn't dead and that might put her in danger. But it was *Lan,* and Aly loved her and the thought that this woman could believe she was dead caused a terrible ache in her chest.

"Lijuan? Is that you?" Lan asked, her voice bursting with hopefulness.

Aly swallowed and squeaked.

"Lijuan!" Lan blurted and erupted into a stream of Chinese.

Aly didn't understand what Lan said, but she knew the tone of voice. Panic and desperation; the same tone appeared in Penelope's voice when she went missing. Covering her mouth with a hand, she muffled a sob.

Grace was missing. Joseph spoke the truth. He had them. What was she going to do now?

"She's missing?" Aly asked through her hand.

Lan paused mid-word. "Who is this?"

Aly blinked, not realizing she'd spoken. Now she'd done it. She should hang up. She should. But... she might not get another opportunity and she needed to know for sure.

"Who are you?" Lan demanded.

Flustered, Aly kept her hand over her mouth in an attempt to muffle her voice. "I'm... a friend. From band. We were supposed to meet today but... Is Grace... she's not home?"

"Which band?" Lan demanded. "Which friend?"

Aly scrambled, "I... er... My name is Rose and I—"

"I do not know of any Rose's among Grace's—"

A commotion on the other side of the phone. Voices, a startled cry and a snatch, then, "Rose? Rose Ward?"

Aly's jaw dropped as she recognized the voice.

"Rose, this is Belinda Bell. I can help you."

"*Shit.*"

"Tell me where—"

Hands came from nowhere and snatched the cell away from Aly's ear. She whirled in both fear and horror, an instinctual cower seizing her body.

Stiff-backed and red-faced, Noah hung up her cell, angrier than she'd ever seen him. "What the hell are you thinking?" he snarled, glowering.

Panic gave way to relief that it was him and Aly uncurled. "What?"

The cell practically shredded in his hands as he dismantled it to get to the SIM. "Of all the *stupid* things you could do."

Taken aback by what she'd learned on the phone and bewildered in the face of Noah's anger, she couldn't think. "I—"

"I warned you they can *find* us if you connect with one of the old numbers. You just *told* Belinda where we are." Taking the SIM card out, he snapped it in half.

She stared at the broken card in shock. "But—I used the burner—"

"We're on the run!" he said, thrusting the broken remnants of her phone into his pockets. Fingers to his temple, he gestured widely as he glared at her. "You *can't* be stupid like this."

Aly frowned. "Hey!"

"They have more technology, more people, more resources than I do." Tossing up his hands, he ranted, "I'm doing everything I can to keep us safe and you're working against me and screwing things up. How am I supposed to—"

"Stop it!" Aly snapped and she grabbed his arm to try to get him to listen to her. "Grace and Del are missing."

"—keep you safe if you fight me at every turn!"

Being insistent, she grabbed his other arm and pulled him down to get his attention. "Listen to me!"

"I thought I could trust you!" he yelled, scathingly. "Obviously not."

"Del and Grace are missing!" she repeated, trying to ignore how much he was hurting her in his anger.

Shrugging out of her grip, his expression darkened even more. "And?"

Didn't he understand? "They're our friends! We need to—"

"We can't help them. I don't even know where they are! Where would you like me to start, hmm? What is it that you think *I* could possibly do?"

Aly's eyes blew wide and her mouth went dry. One hand crept up to cover her mouth as she realized what he said. "Did you know?"

With a wild glance around and a spluttering tingle, Noah grabbed her wrist and tugged to get her moving. "We need to get out of here."

He walked fast and she couldn't seem to get her legs to work, so she was practically dragged behind him. "You knew," she breathed, appalled by this revelation. "You *knew* and you kept it from me."

"Like you haven't been keeping things from me," he scoffed, staring straight ahead. "Or do you expect me to believe you were going to tell me about Joseph."

"There wasn't time!" she protested, trying to defend herself. "I was following your cues and—"

"There's been plenty of time!" Noah told her. "You've been plotting this whole time—"

"Not to get you alone!" she retorted and planted her feet to offer some resistance. She could see the green jeep he'd hired ahead of them, his destination, and she wanted to talk to him without Bonnie and Ross being there, especially since Ross waited by the jeep, peering at them with curiosity. "Not with Bonnie and Ross. I don't trust them and—"

"Right now, as I see it, *you're* the one who can't be trusted to do the right—"

Affronted and hurt, Aly wrestled her hand from Noah's grip and shoved him in the back to get him away from her. "How dare you? Do you even hear yourself right now?" she asked, taking a step away from him to glower as he spun around to face her. "You knew Del and Grace were missing and you didn't tell me. You let Joseph come up on me, and you *promised* you were watching, and you let me face him without any knowledge my friends could be in danger."

"I did *not*—"

"And you're accusing me of secrets?" She wrapped her arms around herself. "I was trying to confirm where they were, so I didn't have to add to any worries!"

"You should've talked to me first!"

"And would you have actually told me you knew they were missing?"

He didn't answer that. "You put us all in danger by being stupid and reckless. You were told we couldn't contact anyone or we'd put them at risk and now—"

She shook her head at him. "No. I'm not doing this with you. You're being an ass. You need to stop. Right now."

"I am *not*—"

"I knew the second Lan answered, I'd screwed up. I do

not need you to call me stupid for it," she snapped. "I wouldn't have done it if I'd known. So if you want to be angry at someone, be angry at yourself. How *dare* you keep that from me!"

"Don't you blame me. I didn't—"

Scowling, she dragged her eyes away from him and stalked past him to head to the jeep. "Back off."

"I didn't know about Del and Grace, but it's—"

"Don't talk to me."

"—a reasonable assump—Aly!"

"Back the frick off!" She got two steps before she about-faced and marched back toward the grocery store. "I need my stuff," she told him to waylay any conversation.

Stalking back inside the store, she struggled to lock away the tears and the hurt behind a wall of anger. Intellectually, she understood he was probably stressed about the brain shift, added with the possibility that Seth might not be dead, which only led to more questions. Like, if she was alive, why did he implant such a horrible memory of her death and why did Elaine seem to have the same one. She knew he was under a lot of pressure, but that didn't mean he was allowed to take it out on her. Yes, she'd screwed up, but she wouldn't have done it if he'd told her Del and Grace were missing. Even if he hadn't known for sure, why wasn't he reacting to it?

Bonnie eyed her curiously as Aly stalked through the grocery store, shoving items into her small basket. She appeared to not even have noticed that Aly had left the store, or if she had, she didn't mention it.

What was Aly going to do about Del and Grace? Joseph's number was heavy in her pocket, but since Noah had destroyed her cell, there was little chance of using it now. What would she say anyway? Despite his faults. Noah was trying so hard to keep them safe, and Joseph. whatever his game was, wasn't safe.

Joseph had said that they needed her and her ability to remove shifters abilities. So, logically, they wouldn't hur their only bargaining chip until they had her. That didn't make her feel any better, since technically, they needed her body. They didn't need her permission.

"You alright there, hon?" the clerk asked as Aly put her purchases up on the counter.

Aly blinked, and a mild vindictive thought rose up. She could get Noah into a world of trouble if she let her lips quiver a little and played the victim. Not that it would do any good, because he was right. She messed up by calling and they had to get out of here.

She forced a smile as she pulled some cash from her pocket. "Yeah. Long day."

Noah and Ross waited by the jeep and Aly glared at both of them. Noah watched her in a way that reminded her of a skittish rabbit, while Ross looked confused.

Instead of taking the front seat, she forced herself in front of Ross to climb into the back with Bonnie.

Noah murmured, "Aly…"

Perched on the seat with her bag of purchases by her feet, Aly clicked the seatbelt on, then clasped her hands together on her knees and stared at him.

He sighed and closed the door. "Fine."

CHAPTER 6

Choosing to sulk in the back seat and pretend to read the romance book she'd bought for a dollar in the last town, Aly had not been paying attention to where they were. The sudden change in road texture as they turned onto a dirt road startled her and she lifted her head to stare out the window.

She'd been so focused on her fake reading, and passive-aggressively ignoring Noah, she hadn't seen that they were in the middle of a mountainous region. There were a lot more ranges in Nevada than Aly expected, but she'd never visited before. She'd been all over California, up and down the West Coast, even over to England to visit Roger's family, but never visited much farther inland than Reno. While she'd known that there were ranges, there were a lot more scraggly, water-deprived trees than she'd expected in a desert region.

With this amount of foliage, and the fact there didn't seem to be fences, she guessed this was probably one of the national parks littered around Nevada.

She peered out the window, taking in the landscape and feeling much like a little kid spotting their destination and preparing to stretch their legs. As much as landscapes weren't her thing to draw, she still marveled at rolling hills, forests, or starlit desert skies, and the creatures that her imagination created lurking within. There was a certain enthrallment in exploration.

Forgetting that she was giving Noah the silent treatment, she leaned forward and asked, "Is that where we're headed?"

"Yeah," Noah replied with a flicking glance to the rearview mirror to look at her. "There's a trail ahead. We'll go off-path to get to the grave." He sighed and his tone took on a wistful note. "Seth loved the outdoors, but she never got to spend much time outside. We promised Solomon we'd bury them somewhere they could see the sky." He coughed and cleared his throat. "Originally, there wasn't much choice, and, um—well, carting around, um— would've been bad and we had to make do. The four of us came back and reburied them. So I know for sure Rex doesn't know this place, and Adam does."

She sat back and stared out the window again, watching the hilly landscape drift by. She worried her bottom lip with her teeth and resting one hand on her injured leg as she studied the terrain and how fast it had turned rocky and mountainous. "How far is the walk?" She nodded at the sheer cliff face as they drove past it. "Up that?"

Noah gave an exasperated sigh.

"You're going to grumble over a hike?" Ross asked, peering around the front passenger seat. Aly glared at him, almost certain he was gloating.

"You can stay in the car if you want," Noah suggested.

She bit back an angry retort. They both seemed to have forgotten the fact that only a few days ago, she'd been shot in the leg and the stomach and *still* hadn't fully recovered. And they wanted her to take a hike through rocky hills. A part of her wanted to play the brat and complain, but there wasn't a solution. She couldn't stay with the car, in case Joseph had pre-empted Noah and lurked somewhere close, waiting to get her alone to strike. She didn't want to be alone.

She'd have to endure. Fortify, as Grace would say.

Her heart twanged at the thought of Grace and Aly suppressed the impulse to sigh. Or scream. One of them.

Noah parked the jeep in a small dirt bay beside some wooden railings which indicated the start of an obscure trail. His tingles washed over Aly's skin as he checked on something she couldn't see. They loitered around the jeep, collecting their gear since they couldn't leave anything in the car that they wouldn't part with, in case it had to be abandoned.

Noah picked up their rucksack and Ross and Bonnie took their gear. Adjusting her hat on her head, Aly fell into step behind Bonnie, bringing up the rear as the three of them followed Noah down the path.

Aly had to admit it was pretty countryside. She could see herself sitting on any number of the rocks and boulders beside the path and doodling. She ambled behind, taking in the landscape as she walked.

It was hard, especially once the incline became sharper and the path started to weave around rocks and dip up and down. Aly endured as best she could. Between stopping for mini breaks that only served to make her further behind the other three and using the surroundings to lean against, she managed to make it a decent way before pain niggled its way in.

Noah's tingles hit her intermittently as he checked on the surroundings. It was strange, but she could almost tell what he was shifting now. The short, bursting shifts meant he was probably doing muscles, or a longer tingle followed by another, coupled with a look around in between the shifts indicated it was probably one of his senses.

It grated at her that he could shift the fatigue away and had forgotten that she couldn't. Glancing over her shoulder, she peered down the way they'd come and tried to judge how far they'd walked. She couldn't see the jeep anymore, they'd twisted around the side of a hill and headed a lot farther away from the road.

Resting her hand against a boulder, she looked out onto the landscape and took her weight off her injured leg. She hurt and she hated that it made her feel weak, especially since on any other day, this would be an amazing hike. Even in pain, she had to continue pushing forward. It was a matter of stubborn pride now.

Although she tried her best, the fifth stumble made her hiss in pain. Noah's immediate tingle told her he'd noticed, even as she tried to play it off.

Peering at her over his shoulder, Noah said, "We should stop for a bit."

"Already?" Ross complained and Aly grit her teeth. Maybe she should find a big stick to smack him with.

"Yep," Noah retorted. "I need to check on some things."

Aly ducked her head to hide her tears of frustration behind the brim of her hat. Picking the closest boulder beside the path, she used it for a seat and propped her leg up as much as she could. As she took a mouthful of water from her bottle, Noah dumped his bag on the dirt at the base of the boulder and reached for her leg.

She moved her leg away. Not far, because there wasn't room, but it was a clear signal she didn't want him to look.

"Let me see," he said, hunkering down in front of her.

She made a noise of denial, then swallowed her mouthful of water. "No. It's fine."

"It's not fine," he said and augmented to check on her anyway. "Why didn't you tell me?"

Turning her head away to give the impression she was going to ignore him, she said, "Would you have listened?"

"You should've stayed in the car."

"Yeah," she scoffed. "Because Joseph hasn't already pre-empted you once today. I'll just wrap a huge bow around my neck and present myself to him. That should make you happy."

"Stop it," Noah snapped. Casting a glance at Ross and

Bonnie, he lowered his voice and Aly could tell how hard he struggled to keep calm. "You know that wouldn't make me happy."

Aly huffed.

This time, as he reached for her leg, she let him touch it and didn't bother to hide the wince his touch caused. He cupped her thigh as he checked, his thumb stroking her leg. "I can't see any extra damage," he said and the tingles stopped. "I'll carry you—"

Her head whipped back and she bared her teeth at him. "You even try and I will back-slap you into your natural form so hard you won't walk straight for a year, *then* I'll kick your ass so you won't be able to sit either and no amount of Snickers or doe eyes will save your bumble-butt."

Shocked, Noah stared at her. Aly stared back, her resolve steel.

Noah's resolve wasn't as steely. Snorting, his lips twitched into a smothered smile. "Even when you're trying to be threatening, you're cute."

His laugh and compliment blind-sided her and the anger flopped like a flailing fish frantically trying to escape. Indignant, she crossed her arms over her chest. "Don't laugh at me."

"Look at us," Noah said, his voice still laced with laughter. "We shouldn't be fighting."

"It's not *my* fault that—" Noah tilted his head at her and raised his eyebrows and Aly closed her mouth. "Fine," she muttered, reconsidering. "It is partly my fault." She sighed, closed her eyes and relented. "I know that being here probably drags up a lot of memories you don't want to deal with."

Noah looked away. "Yeah."

She tried not to huff. "So, I will be the bigger person and suck it up and apologize."

He laughed again. "Does it really count if you make it sound like you're doing me a favor?"

Now, she did huff. "If you're going to be an ass about it, I won't bother."

With effort, he swallowed the laughter. "I wasn't laughing at you."

"Yeah," she conceded. "I know. Nervous laughter."

He placed his hand over hers and dropped his eyes. By his fidgets, and the fact he opened and closed his mouth several times, Aly knew he was searching for the right words and waited until he did "I didn't know about Del and Grace. But... I knew there was a possibility. I've been trying to confirm it. Without worrying you. Which," he acknowledged with a sigh, "is what you were trying to do."

Aly pressed her lips together. "Hmm... and Joseph?"

"I was... distracted and out of position. I thought..."

"You thought what?"

He hung his head. "Doesn't matter. I shouldn't have left you in danger like that."

"You thought you could get info out of him, that's what you thought," she told him, making an effort to keep any bite from her tone. "Don't worry. I thought the same thing."

He met her eyes with a firm promise of, "It won't happen again."

She believed him, even if she was still angry about it. "I see."

"You handled it, though, that was—"

"Heads up would've been nice."

He sighed. "Will the world end if I apologize?"

Aly snorted. Noah rarely uttered the phrase 'I'm sorry', and when he did, he said it in other ways. She'd once joked that the world would end if he actually said the words. "Better not risk it, not with all the shit that's been going on—"

He swooped on her. With his arms looped over her shoulders, Aly was smothered by his chest as he hugged her. "I am, though."

She clung to him. "I know. I am, too. We're the

dumbiest dumb-dumbs in Dumbsilvania."

"And we owe each other a truckload of Snickers. Enough to melt down and bathe in."

She giggled. "Yup."

"I shouldn't be taking this out on you. It was wrong of me."

"I get it, Fletch. I do. This is an incredibly stressful situation and we've had no time to breathe or—"

Pulling back, he cupped her face and his expression made Aly swallow the rest of her words. With a gentle whisper of her name, his lips sought hers. A surprise, in that he both initiated the kiss and it was in full view of his siblings, but a welcome one. Resting her hands on his chest, Aly leaned into his embrace.

He lingered. Leisurely and sweet, he moved his mouth against hers. Longer than their previous kisses, longer than she had hoped for with his first self-initiated kiss, his lips held the promise of something deeper.

And bittersweet. She couldn't put it into words, but there was something sad about the way he kissed her too.

Hearing Ross' muted complaining, Aly pulled back, only to be chased for one final kiss before she was allowed to retreat. Cheeks flaming, but completely happy, she fought not to break into a beaming smile and failed.

Huffing out a laugh, Noah couldn't take his eyes from Aly as he replied to Ross' complaining with a "Shuddup." He reached down and scooped up the bag to offer it to her. "Shall we?"

She sighed and threw it on. "You're seriously gonna carry me?" she complained for the sake of it. "I'm fine."

"Sure," he said with a disarming smile and a shrug. "It'll be like old times."

"You just want my legs wrapped around you," she muttered, then gasped, clapping her hands over her mouth.

Noah's frozen stare might've been comical had it happened under different circumstances. He blinked several times and flapped his mouth but no words came out.

"I'm sorry," she squeaked, appalled. "That just slipped out."

"I…"

With cheeks flaming from embarrassment, she wanted to hide. "Can we just forget I said that?"

His brow furrowed as he watched her. It was clear he was trying to figure something out, but Aly couldn't tell what. Dragging his gaze away, he turned his back on her and waited, his hands lifted in preparation to help her clamber onto his back. A brief tingle buzzed through her as he augmented, she guessed, his legs and arms muscles to make carrying her easier. And his hands, by the look. His fingers seemed longer and his palms wider, probably to make carrying her more comfortable for them both.

Worrying that she may have somehow offended him, she warily climbed on. When her arms were around his neck, he slid his hands under her thighs for support and hoisted up.

"You're gonna carry her?" Ross teased, with a dramatic back of his hand to his forehead and mock faint. "Can you carry me, too?"

"You weren't shot in the leg," Noah said, setting into an easy walk along the path. "It's not far. Next bit is hard, we go off trail."

His gait was easy and calm, nothing like the last time he'd carried her like this; sprinting through the forest with one of Darcy's creations on their heels. It was nice, after a day of anger and worry, to be touching him, cuddled up against his back with her head beside his. It grounded her, gave her something to hold onto. There was still anger and worry, but maybe they could talk about it now and figure something out.

Draping her arms around his neck, Aly settled so she was comfortable. "So—"

"Did you mean it?" Noah asked softly.

She blinked. "Mean what?"

"The 'legs' thing."

She should've known he wasn't going to drop that. "Um…" She swallowed. "I…"

"If I was anyone else… if I was a different sort of boyfriend, would you have said it?"

Evading, she replied, "I'm tired and I'm sore and everything's muddled up and it sort of slipped out."

"Which means it's something you've thought about," he replied. "I don't want you to censor yourself because of me."

She dropped her face to hide in the back of his neck. "If I loved and trusted someone as much as I do you, then yeah. But… like…" She breathed out through her nose and decided to go for it. Honesty was the best policy. "Okay, here's the thing. If I said that to, like, Carter, he would've taken it as a green light."

Noah snorted. "Yep. Then pushed for more."

"Yes. Exactly. Saying it to *you*… well, it's more like a test of boundaries. An… idea—well, yeah, it's still an invitation," she admitted, heat flooding her face. "But it's more—it's something for you to think about and see if you're comfortable."

"So it's something you'd like to do?"

"Well… yeah. Eventually. It would always be your choice."

"Good to know," he said. "Nice insight into the inner workings of Aly's mind."

She pulled a face. "It's a bit of a maze."

"Do you have a map?"

"Nope. But I have a ball of string so you can find your way out."

He laughed. "You know you're my favorite person, don't you?"

She nuzzled her face against his cheek. "Oh, good. I was worried there for a moment."

He took a moment to return her nuzzle, then gestured ahead with his chin. "See that rock up there? Almost looks like a turtle's shell?"

Aly peered ahead. "No?"

"It's... sort of waist height. Right on the side of the path. Looks like a 'c', with the top of it shell-like."

"I... really can't see it. Are your eyes shifted?"

"No." He paused, then muttered, "Yes," which cause Aly to giggle.

"It's second nature to you isn't it?" she teased.

"Shuddup. You'll see it in a minute. We picked it cause it's big enough that no one's likely to move it, but small enough that most people won't use it as a landmark. We head straight east from there."

She looked to the east and up the rocky mountain. "Bit steep."

"We'll be fine."

Noticing the slight hitch in his voice, she whispered, "You're really worried."

He huffed out a sarcastic sort of laugh. "Yeah. I mean, the fact that the rock is there is a relief but... it's... things aren't making sense, and I always... I can't explain it."

She tightened her arms around his shoulders and put her face beside his. "You think they'll make more sense if you've somehow shifted your brain?"

"No... yes... maybe. I don't know."

"You've been out a long time, Fletch. Things have changed."

"No kidding," he replied.

"I'll still love you no matter what," she told him, trying to be soothing.

His voice was tight and he felt stiff against her. "Thanks. But that also worries me."

Taken aback, she asked, "How so?"

"That kind of loyalty, while... it's wonderful, don't get me wrong, but it... it might bite you in the ass if..." he trailed off, unable to fully voice his concern.

"Oh..." she breathed, realizing what he was getting at. "You don't know if you could protect me from *you*."

"Yeah. Essentially."

She gave that serious consideration. As much as she didn't like the notion she had to be protected, she also knew that she couldn't do this on her own. He was right, in a way. If he had shifted his brain and everything was a lie and his mission had been all about getting close to her, that loyalty, while hard-earned, would be detrimental. On the other hand, if he couldn't shift his brain, what they had was genuine.

She didn't have a solution and she didn't like it hanging over their heads.

Noah cleared his throat. "If I ever do something which scares you or hurts you, or you think I'm not myself anymore, I want you to run. Go somewhere you think I won't expect you to go."

She pulled a face, not liking that idea at all. A part of her wondered if that's why he'd kissed her before, because he thought he might not get to again. Tightening her arms around him, she mumbled, "I guess... we'll know soon, right?"

"Yeah." He reached the turtle-shelled, sweeping sort of rock he mentioned, and turned to look back at Ross and Bonnie following behind. "We go east from here until we reach the next marker." He slid down a small incline away from the path, and bounced over a ditch to the other side and up an incline.

She moved with his gait as much as she could. "I can walk—"

"I'm fine. Honest."

She fell silent as he walked, taking in the scenery. Noah pointed out several markers as he walked, changing direction at each marker. It was like a maze. The landscape looked the same, each valley looked like the last, with only the markers to guide them, there would be no way she'd ever find this place on her own. She guessed that was the way they wanted it to be.

They'd been walking along a valley for the most part,

still plenty of ups and downs, but the last marker had pointed them directly up a steep incline. Green, bushy shrubs which barely came up to her waist clumped together on the rocky ground. Wind-shaped sandstone boulders jutted out of the ground and broke up the uneven terrain. The whole hike felt lonely. There didn't seem to be another soul around except for them.

"It's pretty here."

Nodding, he glanced around. "Yeah. Seth would've liked it. She loved the sky and the sun and this place has plenty of both. It's why we"—he grunted as he scrambled up a steeper incline, sending a cascade of small rocks and pebbles water falling down behind him—"chose it."

"And Solomon?"

He paused to check Bonnie and Ross' progress. "Solomon wanted to be wherever she was."

"How much further?" Ross complained from the bottom of the incline Noah had scaled.

"Not long."

"All right for some," Ross muttered, crawling up the incline. "No free ride, or secret shifts."

Aly pressed her lips into a thin line as she watched Ross stumble and almost lose his footing on the slope. "I don't like him."

"I know." Noah adjusted his stance as he watched Ross and Bonnie help each other. "Not sure I do either, if I'm honest." He sighed. "We... didn't have defined personalities in the Institute, not for a long time. So, I never had a chance to know him."

"Making up for lost time?"

"Yeah," Noah said and turned to continue up the incline. "I guess."

Since the climb was becoming a lot steeper, every step he took was careful now, testing each stone before he moved to the next one. He charged his grip on her several times and she found herself leaning away from him to act as a counterbalance while he climbed. "Fletch, I can walk—"

"I got this. Trust me. It's not far now. There should be a group of rocks on the other side of that hill. We'll see them soon."

She went quiet, considering her words, before she made herself ask, "Fletch?"

"Yeah?"

She lowered her voice, as if saying it aloud somehow made it worse. "What are we gonna do about Del and Grace?"

Noah puffed out a breath and changed his grip on her so it was almost like he was trying to hug her. "I don't know. We don't even know for sure if they are missing, or just not going home for whatever reason. Del and his mom were… there was a bit of tension about him going to college, remember? There could be many reasons for him not to go home that we don't know about."

"And if Joseph has them?"

"*If*—and it's a big if—if he does, then they're probably leverage. Whatever it is," he said, lifting his head and, with a brief tingle, he changed his eyesight. "We have to do it togeth—" He broke off and froze mid-step. Tingles engulfed Aly as Noah changed many things at once.

"What?" Yelping, she slid off his back as he dropped her. She landed awkwardly on the rocky ground, but managed to keep her footing. "Fl—?"

"No," he breathed, then bolted up the incline. Like an antelope, he leaped and bounded upward. Gravity had little meaning to him as he took strides and steps not possible for a normal person.

Aly blinked, then gaped at him. She'd never seen such agile, goat-like movements from him, but as cool as it was, it was also concerning. What had made him react like that? She could think of one thing, and it wasn't a pleasant thought at all.

"What's wrong?" Ross called from behind.

"I don't…" Aly shook her head. Readjusting the

backpack on her back, she cast her own sense around. The rapidly disappearing Noah was the only one shifting in her vicinity, and she couldn't feel anything out of place. Worried, she started crawl-climbing after Noah.

She wasn't fast. Burdened with a heavy backpack and an injured leg, she turtled up the incline and was quickly overtaken by Ross, an action that had her glaring at his back.

As Bonnie reached Aly, she took Aly's elbow to offer her assistance in climbing and gestured for Aly's backpack. As much as Aly didn't want to relinquish the backpack, since Noah said that it always had to be within sight of one of them, she couldn't make it up the incline with it on. Bonnie was an Amazon of a woman and even without augments, she was still physically strong.

The two of them helped each other scramble up the hill, although it was more Bonnie climbing and Aly clinging to her. Glancing up, Aly was in time to see Ross disappear over the top. Aly wasn't sure where Noah had gone, but since she could still feel him shifting, he wouldn't be far. His shifts felt... odd. Kind of sputtering, instead of a steady stream. Like he was changing his mind about what he wanted to augment and how.

Ross yelled for Bonnie, who released Aly and scrambled up the hill ahead of her, pulling a gun from a holster.

Gritting her teeth, Aly hurried after Bonnie as fast as she could go.

Bonnie inched toward the top, gun extended and ready for anything, checking each new angle with military precision. When she reached the top, the gun fell slack and she stared.

Close to panic, Aly scrambled up as fast as she could. When she reached the top, she grabbed onto Bonnie to steady herself and peered around.

The cluster of small rocks, no taller than her knees, sat at the top of a small cliff, beyond which Aly could see for miles and miles. Mountains in the distance, valley, long flat stretches of land and dips in the landscape. But that wasn't what commanded her attention.

Noah clawed dirt in the middle of a makeshift hole at the base of the rocks. Around him, he'd already dug gouges out of the earth. Dirt streaked his face and his fingers bled and he didn't stop trying to dig.

Ross stared at Noah, then looked at Aly as though he expected her to have the answer.

Inching forward, Aly dared to ask, "Fletcher?"

He appeared to ignore her, hunched over so he could shovel dirt with his bare hands. He scrambled, throwing dirt away as fast as he could, turning in a tight circle.

Dropping down to kneel beside him, Aly put her hand on his shoulder and he froze under her touch. "Fletcher?" He couldn't look at her and she knew why. Heart in her throat, Aly asked, "They're not here, are they?"

Head bowed, Noah choked on a sob. His hands clawed against the dirt as he clenched them into fists. "I don't understand," he mumbled, sounding thoroughly broken. "All the signs are here, all the markers and the memories and—and…" He let out a strangled sound and started digging frantically again.

Appalled, Aly covered her mouth with a hand.

"They're not?" Ross asked, stepping forward. "What do you mean 'they're not here'?"

Ignoring him, Aly focused on Noah. She hunkered over beside him, trying to get a look at his face. "Maybe they've, like, already decomposed?" she asked carefully, trying to be considerate. "How long does it take to—"

Ross was not as considerate. Red-faced and hands clenched, he demanded, "Did you seriously bring us all the way here for nothing?"

Noah spoke to Aly, not Ross. "No, that's not—the head stone's gone and—we had a stone for them! A special one, with a fossil, we buried it so that even when the bones decomposed, we'd still know and… and there's nothing but rock here and I was here! Four years ago! And they weren't gone then and... but what if I *wasn't*. What if—"

"Could Elaine have moved them?" Aly asked.

Noah stopped digging again and looked at her. "Huh?"

"Stop and really look," Aly suggested, trying to keep a level head. "Does the dirt look displaced? Roots cut when they shouldn't be? I mean, you can see that, right?" She frowned. "Maybe you can't. X-ray and wood, but... I dunno. Take a breath and try to calm down and then really—"

"Aren't you listening?" Noah blurted. "There's rock. *Solid* rock. No grave. No dirt. Rock! They're not here. They've *never* been here."

CHAPTER 7

Leaning on the railing, Grace clasped her hands together
and crossed one ankle over the other, and stared out into
the twilight desert. They were staying in a small cabin for
the night, rented from a caravan park in one of the towns
scattered through Nevada, equipped with a tiny bathroom,
a living area and two bedrooms.

Despite Elaine saying that Noah had started moving
within minutes of Joseph returning to the hotel this
morning, they'd waited until two in the afternoon to leave
Las Vegas, seemingly following in Noah's footsteps. The
delay, as Elaine explained, was to circumvent Noah and
Not-Aly knowing about a tail. They could take a more
direct route to the pair, once the weaving and backtracking
was done. Noah was careful and overly cautious, Joseph
said, and there would be a lot of backtracking and side
ventures before he reached his true destination. There was
no point in wasting gas in pursuing them, not when they
had a tracker in play.

After a few hours of driving the more direct route
instead of twisting and turning like Noah was apparently
doing, Elaine announced that they would stop for the
night and monitor progress.

Sighing, Grace idly itched her aching hip while she watched Joseph pace in the parking lot ahead as he argued with someone on his cell. While she couldn't make out the words, the angry tone and snarled expression soured the chiseled good looks of his face.

There was something about Joseph that Grace found unnerving. Perhaps it was because he appeared to be too perfect. Not a blemish on that face. No scars or freckles or moles of any kind. His hair was that shiny, golden-blond often seen in magazines or movies that Grace had always assumed was a cinematic trick. Elaine's forms were flawed. Wrinkles and teeth that weren't perfectly aligned. Joseph had no flaws and he should have if he was attempting to hide. Right?

But he was definitely pretty to look at, even if he was raging. That kept things interesting at least.

Joseph hung up the cell and stared at it for a moment, before swearing vehemently.

"Something wrong?" Grace called.

He flicked his head up toward her, anger still prevalent on his face. Taking a controlled breath, he tucked his cell into his shirt pocket. "You could say that," he said as he joined her, leaning on the railing on the other side of the porch. "It'd be nice if people were where they said they'd be."

He didn't seem to want to elaborate, so Grace asked, "Was that Russian?"

"Yeah," Joseph replied, then snorted. "The couple who parked next to us are probably logging a call crying terrorist."

Grace snickered. "You're white *and* blond. They won't be."

"Alas," he said with a dramatic sigh. "That is true. Such is the state of the world." He lightened his tone to curious. "Do you speak anything else?"

"Chinese, though I'm not as fluent as my mom is."

"First-gen?"

Grace smiled at the frequently asked question, "Second."

"Ahh. Ever been?"

Were they having an actual conversation? After their initial conversations, Joseph seemed content to let Elaine do the talking, preferring to lurk ominously in the background. Desperate for civilized conversation, and one that didn't involve Del and her asking each other questions neither of them had answers to, she replied, "A few times. My grandparents are here, but several cousins and second cousins live there."

"Must be nice," Joseph said and reached into his pants pocket. "I've never left the country."

"And yet you speak Russian."

"Uh-huh. Not just Russian, either. Languages come easily to me." Extracting a cigarette packet, he asked, "Would you mind?"

Grace wrinkled her nose. "Rather you didn't."

Joseph nodded and put the packet back without taking one. "Fair enough." He gestured her and said, "Realizing that I'm asking from a purely shapeshifter-born curiosity and not from underlying racism, because I know this can be taken the wrong way, but it's not just Chinese, is it? There's a few features that aren't genetically prevalent with parents of the same ethnic background."

"You can tell that?" Grace asked, then answered his question. "My dad is Native American."

Joseph nodded. "I can tell a lot of things by looking at a person. Which tribe?"

Grace shrugged and looked away. "Your guess is as good as mine. He lost his history."

"Ahh. Shame. Still, good mix of genes."

She turned to face him, planted a hand on her good hip and smirked. "Is that a shapeshifter equivalent of a pick-up line? Good genes?"

Joseph raised an eyebrow at her. "Do you want it to be?"

Eyes flaring wide, Grace's smile faded and was replaced with uncertainty. Turning away, she leaned against the railing again. "I don't suppose a shapeshifter can be racist."

Joseph snorted. "Oh, no, they *can*. Anyone has that potential, I think. Shifters, even more so. Bunch of fucking elitist bast—" he cleared his throat several times. "But just because we can change the color of our skin, doesn't mean we belong to the culture we pretend to be. White and blond, good way to blend in."

Grace nodded. "That makes sense. No one looks twice."

"Exactly." Joseph gestured himself. "This isn't me. Not really. Elaine likes to stand out, I prefer to blend."

She resisted the urge to snort. Blending in, with that handsome face? He was bound to attract a lot of attention, but it wasn't her place to tell him that. "What ethnicity do you belong to?"

Joseph shrugged. "Your guess is as good as mine," he said, parroting her earlier dismissal and changed the subject. "What can you tell me about Fletcher?"

Grace's eyebrow shot up. "What about him?"

"What was he like? What did he tell you of his family?"

With a frown, Grace considered. "He never really talked about his family. He had an uncle, but he died before I met Fletcher." She glanced over her shoulder and idly scratched her hip. "Del would know more about his uncle. Fletcher's family always seemed to be Penelope and Aly. That's all he really needed."

"I see."

"He was… nice. Funny. A great guy. Good with math. Liked to run, always a great guy to have on your team."

"Hmm."

"He had this laugh," Grace said, staring off into the distance as she let melancholy take her. "When he *really* laughed it rose in increments, getting higher and louder. Used to set us all off." Leaning down, she cupped her face in her hands and rested her elbows on the railing. "He was… adventurous. Fletcher could always be counted on to be the first to try things out. First to dive-bomb off a cliff at the lake. First to try my mom's chili dishes. He met life head-on and didn't hesitate."

"Huh."

"Didn't do emotions so well, though. Don't know how Aly managed sometimes. But… yeah. He was great." Tears pricked her eyes. "Can't imagine why someone would want him dead."

"We're still working on why Noah's doing what he's doing," Joseph said. "Originally we thought he was going to replace Fletcher, now…"

"Why would he want to replace Fletcher? That's what I don't get. Fletcher wasn't—there's nothing to gain by replacing him. He was important only to his friends."

Lifting his shoulders in a shrug, Joseph replied, "That's what we are trying to figure out."

Grace stared at her hands. "Not-Aly said Belinda Bell killed Fletcher. She's an FBI agent and—"

"Not-Aly?" Joseph questioned, raising his eyebrows.

"Well, what would you call her?" Grace said, slightly miffed from the humor prevalent on his face. "It's as good a name as any, and you haven't given us her real name."

"That is true. We don't know her name. Not yet. But you're right, we should call her something, like…" he scrunched up his face and thought hard. "Fake-Aly."

With a giggle, Grace teased, "You're not very good at thinking up names, are you?"

"And 'Not-Aly' is the height of your genius?" he asked, teasing in return.

Grace considered. "We could call her 'Alike'."

Joseph stared at her. "Is that a pun?"

"Absolutely."

"Fascinating."

Grace laughed. "Whatever you say, Mr. Spock."

His laugh was free and easy and Grace beamed, happy at his response.

"That's probably what Noah told her," he replied, returning to the original conversation. "Alike also said we were dangerous, didn't she?"

Feeling humor slip away, she made her tone as non-committal as she could, "Hmm."

"And has anything we've done thus far scared you or made you think she was right?"

Pressing her lips into a thin line, Grace shrugged. "I still think you're keeping stuff from us."

"That's a given," Joseph said with a nod. "If we told you everything, you wouldn't be able to go home with Aly at the end of all this. You'd be a liability. Right now, you have no physical evidence beyond your own experiences that shapeshifters exist."

Grace glared at her hands and said in a tone full of sarcasm, "Cause you took our phones."

"A necessary evil," he replied mildly. "We're not the bad guys. All we're asking for is a few more days. There's more at stake than just Aly right now."

"Except that it sounded like you just made the threat 'if you knew more, then we'd have to kill you'."

With a scoff, he shook his head. "You're reading too much into it."

"Am I?" she challenged.

"You're free to leave at any time," Joseph said. "We can drop you off at the next bus interchange if you want."

"Not if I want to get Aly back," Grace responded.

"And if that's what you want, you need to do things our way. Sometimes that might not sit right with you."

"A lot of this doesn't sit right with me," Grace said, feeling tart. "My father is a deputy. I *know* some of the things you're doing are against the law."

He smirked at her. "You're very suspicious by nature, aren't you?"

With a toss of her head, Grace lifted her chin. "When I have to be."

"Prudent." Straightening from his lean, Joseph

stretched his arms over his head and stifled a yawn. "Are you hungry? We could wander down to the store and see what they have on offer. Elaine wants to order delivery soon, but I could go for a beer right now."

Grace nodded. "Sure."

The RV park which housed their cabin was dusty. Dried shrubs bordered the cabins, no large trees, dirt roads leading in and out of the park. Mountains carved a horizon to the north of them. There was music in the wind and poetry in the heat against her face. "Never been to this part of Nevada before."

"There's not much here," Joseph said, hands thrust into his pockets as he walked.

"Sometimes there doesn't need to be," she replied. "Very different to California, but in a good way." Sweeping her long hair over her shoulder, she ran her fingers through it to comb it as she walked.

"You have a nice voice," Joseph remarked.

Grace blinked at him and realized she'd been humming under her breath. "Thanks."

"Heard you the night of the bonfire," he continued. "Impressive. Have you been training long?"

"Since I learned to walk," Grace commented.

Joseph lifted his eyebrows at that. "By choice?"

"Yes. My dad wanted me to have opportunities and choices, so he enrolled me in a different sport and art every year so I could try it out. Music stayed with me. It's what I'm going to study in college."

"Very cool. Good luck with that."

Since she didn't detect any sarcasm, she replied, "Thanks. What did you study?"

He smirked, not necessarily at her, but Grace got the feeling a smirk was his natural resting face. "Lots of things. But I never went to college."

"Why not?"

"Well, I have a lot of identities," Joseph replied. "Which one would be the one to get credentials? The amount of work that has to be dedicated to getting that little, useless piece of paper is something I can't afford. Easier to be a jack-of-all-trades than specialize. It's better for me if I can slip into a town, get a job that nobody wants, notices, or will miss if I'm gone, then slip out."

That made a sort of sense. "I guess. Must be a lonely life, that's all."

"That's what family is for," Joseph replied with a shrug.

Stepping forward, he held the door open to the small store attached to the office of the RV park and let Grace enter before him. Nothing much, the basic essentials. Breakfast cereals, toiletries, bread, milk, an assortment of dried foods, a freezer full of frozen goods, a good stock of candy and a supply of magazines. A clerk appeared from a back room in response to the bell on the door, smiling brightly at them.

Grace wandered through to look at what was on offer, wondering what sort of snack Del would prefer to eat. Knowing Del's preference for sugar, she selected a pack of sour gummy worms and a packet of twizzles, then went toward the fridge full of fresh fruit.

Seeing a postcard rack, she stopped to look at the touristy things they had. There was a pretty postcard of the mountain range in the distance, so she picked that one up, intending to pen her family a quick note to say she was okay. She knew they would be worried, especially since the news had falsely reported Aly's death, and she needed her parents to know she was okay.

"No," Joseph said, without even looking at her. "Put it back."

"It'll take days to reach them," Grace protested.

"No," Joseph repeated.

"They're going to think something bad's happened to all of us."

With an exasperated noise, Joseph's eyes rolled as he turned to face her. "Of course they think something's bad has happened."

Not sure why this was such an issue, Grace pressed, "So, if I could just tell them Del, Aly and I are okay—"

"No. It doesn't work like that."

"Why are you being so resistant?" Grace retorted.

"We told you before," Joseph snapped, his anger biting. "No contact with anyone until we catch up with 'Alike' and Noah. It puts too much at risk. We need to keep a low profile and—" Blood drained away from his face as Joseph cocked his head. A far-away look appeared in his eyes, like he was listening to something Grace couldn't hear. Then, without a word, he dropped the items he was holding and strode out of the store.

"Hey!" the clerk called.

Embarrassed and startled by Joseph's sudden departure, Grace stopped one of the bottles Joseph dropped from rolling under a shelf. "Sorry," she said, ducking her head. "I'll clean it." She couldn't purchase the alcohol, but she could get the rest of what he dropped.

"Is he alright?" the clerk asked, as Grace put her purchases on the bench. "He left in such a hurry."

"Not sure," Grace replied, frowning in the direction of the door.

The clerk quickly tallied Grace's purchases, and, with full knowledge that her father would get an alert, Grace pulled out her emergency credit card.

CHAPTER 8

Aly stared out the window of the motel and watched the cars zip by.

Noah had effectively shut down after his announcement that it was rock. Solid rock. Nothing else. No graves, no bones, only rock that hadn't been there before.

She knew why he wouldn't talk or look at her. It seemed that the irrefutable evidence he'd shifted his brain was now staring at them both.

She tried to find cracks in that argument. What if Elaine had dug a huge hole, removed Seth and Solomon and buried a rock? What if someone had moved the markers, rather than the grave? What if—?

Noah wouldn't listen to her. Nor would he do a thorough, augmented search of the area. He seemed lost in his turmoil and nothing Aly said or did seemed to get through to him. Especially not with Ross yelling at them about this wild goose chase.

After seeing she wasn't getting anywhere, Aly had marched the almost catatonic Noah down the mountaintop and to the jeep. Ross wanted to return to Las Vegas straight away, but Aly wouldn't hear of it. Once

Noah could think again, she was sure he'd want to check the mountains more thoroughly. So, they had to stay close. While Aly and Noah were going to hole up in a motel for the night, Ross was quite welcome to head back to Las Vegas. On his own. Because Aly had the keys to the jeep and she wasn't giving them up.

When the four of them booked in, Noah had come to life long enough to demand separate rooms, then proceeded to lock himself in and away from Aly.

She'd tried to talk to him many times. Knocking on the door, or talking through the wall, but he didn't respond. Not even a reassuring tingle. There wasn't much she could do if he wasn't willing to let her help. She'd seen this kind of coping mechanism from him before, in the rare times he was upset, like when he'd been told Adam had died, but that didn't make things easier. She had to wait until he was ready.

Not that they had time for that.

If he'd talk to her, she was sure they could figure things out. Formulate a plan. Cry together. Anything would be better than this stony silence.

The door to the next room opened with a loud creaking noise. Aly rushed for the window, lifting the curtains to peek through. Noah appeared on the balcony outside the room, astutely ignoring her. He was dressed in a red tank and shorts and Aly immediately knew why.

He was going running. As Fletcher, Noah had been in the track team in Bellhollow, and whenever something troubled him, he always went running. It was his way of cleansing, so it was no surprise that he'd be going today.

Except that he was going to leave her alone when he promised he wouldn't. She had no defense if Joseph came up on them.

She bolted for the door, flung it open with a bellow of his name, but he was already halfway down the stairs. He didn't even glance her way as he broke into a run, sprinting across the parking lot of the motel they were staying at.

Tears pricking her eyes, Aly watched him go and wrapped her arms around herself.

She hated this. Loathed it with every fiber of her being. The stress of the last few days were taking their toll on everyone and the worst was yet to come, she was sure of that. She wanted to yell and scream and break things. She wanted to have an epic tantrum so she could find the cathartic relief that came after. She wanted control back, and the only real thing she had any control over was herself.

A gust of wind raced along the balcony and tossed Aly's hair into her face. Angrily, she yanked it to the side and behind her ear hard enough to make her skull ache. Then, without really thinking about it, she strode back into her room and went for her small art supplies bag she'd purchased in Las Vegas and the small pair of scissors it held.

She was halfway through hacking her hair when she was interrupted by a knock on the door. Thinking it was Noah, she ignored it. He could wait for her this time.

The knock came again, followed by a female voice that sounded computerized. "Aly. I would like to talk to you."

Frowning, Aly put the scissors on the bathroom bench and headed for the door. She peered through the peephole and was surprised to see Bonnie waiting on the other side. Opening the door a crack, she peeked through and said, "Now's not a good time."

Frowning at her, Bonnie lifted her cell and typed, and a few moments later, the voice said, "Are you cutting your hair?"

Aly's hand went to her head, wondering how much it showed and how badly she'd made a mess of it. "Yeah. How are you doing that?"

Bonnie took a moment to reply. "It is an app that translates the ASL alphabet into speech. I am a hairdresser. Would you like help?"

Aly rocked back in surprise. "Really? Um... sure."

Bonnie flashed her a smile, and lifted a finger to indicate she'd be back, then bounced off toward the room she shared with Ross. When she came back out, she was carrying a small black satchel.

Aly let her in, locking the door behind her and Bonnie bustled straight into the bathroom, grabbing the wooden chair in the corner on the way. She poked her head back out of the bathroom and gestured for Aly.

"Why didn't you use that app before?" Aly asked as she walked into the bathroom.

Having opened the satchel and spread her gear out, Bonnie stopped fiddling with her combs and scissors to reply. "I did not need it." She gestured to Aly to sit as she typed one-handed. "What were you trying to do? You cut it short."

Aly shrugged. "I don't know. I just…" She sighed and her shoulders slumped. "I needed something I could control, I guess. Did I ruin it completely?"

Bonnie lifted strands of hair, moving around behind Aly to inspect the damage before she reached for her cell. "I can do a layered bob. The curl in your hair will make it shorter, but it will look nice and will not draw attention."

Aly nodded. She never usually went that short, preferring to keep it below her shoulders, but at least she hadn't destroyed her hair to the point it was unrecoverable. "That'll be okay. Hairdressing?"

Bonnie laughed, and fluffed her own platinum blonde pixie cut. "Not something a bounty hunter would do, right?"

Aly gave a small smile. "Not exactly the image I had of you."

"Ross and I have had many odd jobs over the years. I have worked as a hairdresser and electrician. Ross has been a plumber, a cook, and welder."

"Jobs that are always in demand," Aly concluded. It was odd hearing Bonnie talk without Ross around, even though she was using a computerized voice. The two of them never really had a conversation before that went beyond a few words and gestures.

"It is one of the better ways to hide," Bonnie replied. "Jack-of-all-trades kind of deal. We can move from one town to the next and switch up what job we do. Harder to track."

Putting the cell down, Bonnie wet her hands, then ran them through Aly's hair to make it damp. When she was satisfied with that, Bonne picked up her cell again. "I wanted to ask you about Noah."

Aly held still as Bonnie began to cut her hair. "I figured." Since Bonnie didn't elaborate on what exactly it was she wanted to ask, Aly made a guess. "You're concerned about his reaction to the grave not being there. Especially cause you're certain Seth's alive. You think he's been lying to you."

Bonnie narrowed her eyes at Aly in the mirror, then wobbled her hand, palm down.

"Part of it?" Aly guessed.

Bonnie nodded and bent over so she could check the length at the back of Aly's head.

Aly sighed. "You have to know I don't exactly trust you and Ross." She snorted. "Even if you *are* standing behind me with a pair of scissors right now."

Bonnie smiled at her in the mirror, her expression understanding and nodded.

"I can't... no... I won't explain his reaction," Aly said. "That's for him to decide if he wants to explain."

Bonnie picked up her cell. "Both sides are keeping secrets."

"Yeah. I trusted Elaine because Noah did, and that... bit us in the ass so hard."

Bonnie typed and Aly waited politely for her response. "It is not as though Ross inspires trust."

Aly was glad Bonnie was aware of the failings of her brother. "Yeah. Honestly, I don't know who I can trust anymore. It's..." She swallowed and stopped talking. As

Bonnie picked up her cell again, Aly said, "Can... can I be really rude and ask that we just don't talk. It's been a really long day and I suspect it's not over yet."

Bonnie nodded. "I fell into the cliché hairdresser chatter real fast."

"Well," Aly replied, lifting a shoulder. "You didn't ask me what I'm going to study in college, so you're one up in that respect."

With a mischievous twinkle in her eye, Bonnie quickly typed back, "So, what are you studying in college?"

Aly giggled and it didn't feel forced.

Bonnie typed, "Artist, yes? I saw some of your online works. You are very good."

"Thanks," Aly replied and her mood about-faced. "I suppose there's not going to be much call for that now. If we're on the run."

Bonnie finished the section of the hair she was doing, then typed, "Not necessarily. If you have a strong online presence, you can make a decent living. You can carry your clients with you. Fake personas are easy online, especially with electronic payments and such. You can still draw."

"I suppose," Aly replied. "But I really wanted to get into animation, and that's not really possible now."

Bonnie hummed, gave Aly a sad look and patted her shoulder in sympathy.

Aly studied Bonnie in the bathroom mirror as she worked. "How long were you watching me?"

Bonnie made a noise of consideration and raised her hand showing one finger.

"One day?"

Shaking her head, Bonnie put her finger and her thumb together and then made them wider.

"One week?"

Bonnie nodded.

Aly pressed her lips into a line. One week of someone watching her, without Noah realizing. He'd been wrong. The people watching her hadn't given up. They'd been biding their time. Maybe he was right when he said he wasn't good at this anymore. Or maybe he'd known they were watching and hadn't told her. Maybe he'd known *everything* that was going on and chose not to tell her. Because, if he had told her, maybe she wouldn't have run to Sacramento after encountering Rex, and then maybe they wouldn't be in this mess right now. Maybe he wanted to be in this mess.

Maybe he *had* shifted his brain. Maybe *her* Fletcher, her wonderful Fletcher who she'd shared ten years with, full of life and memory, was already dead and gone and—

That moment of doubt broke her. Tears pricked and threatened to fall and she closed her eyes as she struggled with her emotions. She didn't want to doubt. Didn't want it, didn't like it, why did it have to be so hard? Things were breaking all around her and no one was safe anymore. *Everyone* was lying.

Even Noah. Maybe. Probably. She wasn't sure anymore.

What was she going to do?

Bonnie said nothing as she continued to cut Aly's hair, giving Aly time to compose herself.

She tried to think logically about it all. Follow her head and not her heart, no matter how much it felt like it was breaking.

Noah's reaction was still in-line with her Fletcher's. He hated the idea of hurting her, and he'd rather run from his problems, or at least, run *off* his problems until he could face them. Their communication was still as strong as it ever was, when they actually talked instead of ignoring each other. They were trying, in among many setbacks and all the stress.

The knowledge that he had possibly shifted his brain had devastated him. Surely, had he remembered and lied about it, he wouldn't be as hurt as he was right now. Hiding from her and running away to deal with his problems. Fletcher had never been that good of an actor.

He could keep secrets, but he couldn't hide his emotions from her.

She'd told him that it didn't matter to her if he *had* shifted his brain. If he'd talk to her, she'd probably tell him the same thing again. This was what mattered right now. This moment, right now. How they chose to live, how they interacted.

Ten years of friendship couldn't be a lie.

Was she being an idiot in choosing to believe in him? In them? Possibly. But what other choice was there? Alienate herself completely? Go off on her own and do what?

Call Rex?

She dismissed that thought even before it had time to fully form. She trusted Rex even less.

No. She and Noah had gone through so much together, there was no way she was giving up on him now.

Aly sighed and cleared her throat. Wiping the tears which had leaked from her eyes, she said, "Sorry."

Bonnie didn't reply, instead offering a tissue for Aly to mop her face with, before concentrating on Aly's hair. After a time, she put the scissors down and stepped back, reaching for her cell. "Done."

Aly turned her head from side to side, inspecting the cut. At her jawline, with a little more length at the back, she suspected it would fluff up and curl easily, especially with the layers Bonnie added. "Cute!" she said and meant it. "You did an amazing job, thank you."

Bonnie put her scissors away and unclipped an object from one of the pouches on her satchel to hold it out to Aly. It looked like it was a cross between a tool and a metal hair clip. One of the edges was serrated, with a ruler marked into the opposite edge, and a hexagon-shaped gem was set into the head of the clip.

As Aly studied it, Bonnie typed, then pointed out the parts as the cell explained, "It is a multi-use tool. Knife, screwdriver, wrench, ruler. Looks unassuming, but is really handy. I always have one on me at all times. Most people overlook a hair clip as a means of escape. You can have this one."

"It's awesome," Aly said as she clipped it into her hair. "Thank you."

Lacking a broom or dustpan, Aly took the chair outside the bathroom and dusted the fallen hair toward a corner with a towel while Bonnie typed.

When she was ready, Bonnie held the cell out, "Ross wants to leave. He thinks we will have more of a chance to find Adam without you and that what happened proves that Noah has been lying to us."

Aly wasn't surprised about that at all. "Yeah, I figured."

"He has been looking for a way to leave since Noah said he had to call in Rex. There is a lot of bad blood there."

"And you?"

Bonnie pulled a face and considered, then started to type.

By the time Bonnie was done typing, Aly had the bathroom floor mostly free of cut hair and the bench wiped down. "Not sure. I think there is a lot going on here we do not know, and I am curious where you fit into everything. Rex is interested in you. Welcher was interested. Darcy seems to be after you and I think it has to do with what occurred at the park. I have never seen anything like that. I know the shifter world has been building up to something for a long time and I think you may be a part of it. There is no place better, or more dangerous, than by your side, but I also think answers are coming too."

Listening to Bonnie's message seemed to double the weight on Aly's shoulders. She leaned against the bathroom bench, arms folded on her chest and her shoulders hunched to make her smaller. Bonnie was right, everyone was looking for her, but her presence also made it dangerous for others to be near her. Yet, Aly knew she wouldn't survive on her own. There was still so much that she didn't know.

"I am also worried about Tango," Bonnie said. "He has never been out of contact for so long."

Raising her head, Aly hesitated, and then decided she may as well ask. "Noah said the… I mean, Tango's Ross'… clone, right?" At Bonnie's nod, she continued, "Noah said they… don't live long?"

Bonnie sighed and her expression crumbled. "Yes. That is true, but that does not mean the time he has left cannot be wonderful. They got out, they deserve a small chance at freedom and happiness with those who accept them for what they are."

"Do you take them all in?"

Bonnie considered that. "It is usually Ross'. Sometimes we get both, but never just mine. They come from Adam. He would send us a date and time for a rendezvous and the new one would be there, lost and bewildered. Ross used to think that they were spying on us, but Adam never asked for them to return before they passed. Each one is different and brings different challenges, but they are family and we grieve."

"I'm sorry," Aly whispered. "That must be hard."

Bonnie nodded.

Walking out of the bathroom, Aly went to sit on the bed. She scooted across to the middle and crossed her legs. "Can you tell me what you know about this war? About Rex and Adam and why Adam's now in charge? Noah's told me some stuff, but… it all seems to be old and he's not sure it's current information. You've had a different experience."

Bonnie regarded her, then nodded. "May I sit?"

Aly gestured the bed ahead of her. "Be my guest."

It took time for Bonnie to talk since she had to type it all, but gradually it all filtered through. Five years ago there had been an event which had shaken a lot of the factions of shifters to their foundations. Around the same time the first dysplasia affected Faceless had appeared, the head of the Welcher faction, who believed in the purity of shifter lineage, had been assassinated. There were many who believed it wasn't a coincidence, and the Faceless were responsible for both Welcher's assassination and the dysplasia Faceless.

When Aly asked what people thought about Darcy, Bonnie replied that most shifters either didn't know or didn't believe the Faceless were created. Some believed them to be immortal shifters who had been forced to come out of hiding, others believed they were a genetic mutation.

Bonnie explained that Welcher's faction was the largest, wealthiest, and held the most political weight of all the factions. Money ran deep, and there were Welcher-funded shifters in all forms of government. They believed that shifter society should be kept separate and hidden, shifters should only breed with other shifters to remain pure, but that normal humans had their uses and could be controlled and influenced.

When the head of the Welcher faction was assassinated, Bonnie said a lot of in-fighting occurred as to who would take over. The conflict was mainly between the sons of the previous head, Nicholas and Alistair, and their cousin Lorelai. It seemed that Lorelai had eventually sided with Alistair to consolidate the faction under his leadership, but that Nicholas was still causing problems and trying to incite people to rebel.

In the chaos, Rex had vanished, completely abandoning close followers without explanation. Databases of shifter details were lost, many shifters were exposed to Welcher or other factions and vanished themselves. He restricted access between shifters by closing down methods of communication without warning, so unless shifters were already friends and exchanged details, they had no way of contacting each other and no way to gather information or keep each other safe.

The idea of shifter message boards and online communities was somehow comical to Aly and she wasn't sure why. She knew the internet had hidden areas, but it was hard to believe some conspiracy theorists hadn't stumbled upon them. Or, thinking about the odd videos and websites she'd encountered, perhaps they had. The boards were important to the shifters, because it meant they could keep in contact with others who could also do what they could do. Even if they wanted to live normally, they deserved the right to feel safe and have access to people who could understand.

Rex's abrupt absence had left the renegade faction in an absolute mess. Full of outcast shifters and offspring who were unable to shift, Adam took on the responsibility to keep them safe and reopened as many lines of communication as he could. Adam was the only reason Bonnie and Ross joined and he was the only reason they allowed themselves to be drawn into Welcher's faction as spies. She said there were many reasons why a shifter might join Adam's faction, mostly it was because they had family who weren't shifters they needed to keep safe.

Bonnie didn't know any more about Adam or his ultimate goal for the faction.

It was clear Rex was no longer a safe refuge for Faceless. Aly found this odd, especially when coupled with the knowledge that *all* of them had worked for Rex at some stage. Why would Rex turn against all Faceless so viciously? Bonnie didn't have an answer for that and Aly couldn't help the egotistical part of her wondering if she was part of the reason.

Bonnie slipped into silence and Aly wrapped her arms around her knees and hugged her legs to her chest as she tried to process everything.

"How does your sensing power work?" Bonnie asked. "How close do you need to be?"

Aly raised her head and blinked at Bonnie. "Oh," she said, and unfurled until she could rest her hands on her lap. After how nice Bonnie had been and everything she'd told her, it was only fair Aly shared a little of what she knew. "Two hundred feet is my limit. I don't need to see a shifter, I just... know they're around. Except for Faceless. I can only sense you when you're shifting." She tilted her head. "Except... the new ones, like Tango. Tango felt wrong somehow, but... it wasn't until I looked at him that I felt that."

"Ahh. That is why you did not feel us coming."

Aly nodded. "Rex said... he said he could feel me, but he had to be within a few feet. So, it's not like I can sneak past a pack of shifters. They'd feel me too if I got close. If too many get close... then I guess what happened in the park will happen again."

Bonnie seemed pensive as she typed. "Interesting. Perhaps this is why Rex is so curious about you?"

Aly shrugged, unwilling to answer that. "Do you have any photos of Nicholas or Alistair?" she asked. "I mean, I know you can't tell from a photo, but if I knew some of their aliases, I can watch for that. I'm... decent at memorizing faces."

Bonnie typed out her response before she started swiping through her cell. "I never met them personally. It was too dangerous. But we did get files from Adam on some of their aliases." Offering her cell to Aly, she gestured for Aly to swipe through.

Lots of men, all of them with similar faces and hair color. Aly supposed not all of them could regrow their hair to change their color like Noah could. Nicholas had blond hair and seemed the younger of the two of them. Alistair had brown and somewhat curly hair when it wasn't slicked down and sometimes sported a beard.

Swiping one more time, Aly's heart jumped to her throat and she almost dropped the cell. Scrambling from the bed, she grabbed her room key and bolted for the door.

Bonnie made a loud noise and Aly paused enough in

the door frame to gesture for Bonnie to follow, then rushed to Noah's door and thumped on it. She hadn't sensed his shift, but the door had slammed shut a while ago, indicating he was back.

"Noah!" she yelled between thumps. "Open up!"

Dimly, a "Go away" resounded through the door.

"Fletcher Gertrude Norman! You open this door right now or I will have Bonnie shoot the handle!"

"Gertrude?" he asked, and she could hear him moving closer to the door. "What kind of name is that?" The door creaked opened a crack, enough that Noah could peek through, but not enough so she could stick anything through the gap to keep it open. "I really don't—what did you do to your hair?" he asked, sounding flabbergasted.

"Open the door!" She shoved the wood hard to try to get in.

He held it fast and refused to budge. "Aly—"

She was so full of nervous energy she didn't care who heard anymore. "Alistair Welcher," she said and held up Bonnie's cell. "A.K.A, Rex Braddock."

CHAPTER 9

The first thing Aly noticed when Noah allowed her into his motel room was the bottle of alcohol on the bench beside the television. The second thing was while the bottle was open, there didn't seem to be any missing.

"What the hell?" she blurted, rounding on him.

He ignored that. "What do you mean he's Alistair Welcher?"

"You've been ignoring me and now I find this—"

"Either you tell me, or leave," Noah snapped, his arms folded on his chest. "Or was this a ploy to get in here?"

Bonnie lingered in the doorway, staring at them with watchful eyes as Aly shoved the cell at Noah. "You *know* who that is. You know where I've seen him before. Rex is Alistair Welcher. Who's now in charge of the Welcher faction."

"How do you know he's—" Noah stopped, and glanced at Bonnie. "Ahh." Looking back at the picture, he said, "All this proves is that Alistair knows Rex's natural form. And has reason to copy him."

"No. Don't you see? This is why he tried so hard to get me to go with him," Aly said and paced around the small room. "Remember what he said? What if we could choose who was a shifter and who wasn't? Imagine if he had his own secret weapon, ready to use for the Welcher faction whenever. He'd stop these uprisings or whatever with his precious weapon-dau—"

Noah's eyes widened in panic. "Aly!" he yelped, drowning out the rest of the word.

She dug her fingers into her skull. "He must've *loved* that idea. His little ace in the hole."

"Aly," Noah repeated, with a warning glance at Bonnie. "Stop."

She felt so lost, words tumbling from her as fast as she could think them. "God, he even *named*—"

Noah grabbed her upper arms and spun her to face him in an attempt to make her stop talking. "*Stop.*"

Aly stared blankly at the ferocity in his face, strength draining from her limbs. "I don't care anymore."

"I do," Noah said. Releasing her, he turned to Bonnie. "Can you give us a few?" he asked and approached her to usher her out the door. Looking utterly confused, Bonnie signed something and Noah turned around to look at Aly. "Can she have her cell? Or was there more you wanted to show me?"

Aly shook her head.

Noah took the cell from Aly and handed it to Bonnie. "I'll come talk to you soon, okay?"

Bonnie looked like she wanted to argue or stay as Noah coaxed her from the room, locking the door behind her. With a deep sigh, Noah rested his head against the door. "I think you're jumping to conclusions."

"Oh, and you haven't been?" she scoffed.

He rolled, keeping his head on the door until his back was against it too, and stared up at the ceiling. He clearly didn't want her here and was trying hard to disengage. "You can't tell a shifter from a picture—"

Aly wasn't about to let him blow her off. "No one knows Rex's natural form, remember?" she argued. "You'd never seen it before and you thought that form *was* his natural one. So how would Alistair know?"

Noah frowned. "I…"

"He said his natural form would cause problems. Could you imagine? The head of Welcher has a non-shifter daughter who happens to be able to take away shifting abilities. That would be absolutely perfect."

Noah sighed deeply and scrubbed a hand over his face. "I don't want to do this right now."

"I don't want to do any of it," Aly snapped. "I'd much rather ignore everything and go home and forget about any of this. But I can't. And neither can you. So deal with it." Her eyes settled on the bottle of alcohol. It seemed moot at this point to remind him he was underage. "In a way that's not being stupid. Seriously, what were you thinking?"

Lifting his head from the door, he followed her gaze. "Wasn't." Hands thrust into the pockets of his jeans, he pushed away from the door and walked over to the bottle. "Just wanted everything to stop."

Folding her arms on her chest, she cocked a hip. "That is not the way to do it."

He tilted the bottle so he could pretend to read the label. "It… doesn't affect me in the way it would someone else."

Aly closed her eyes and her arms slithered back down to her sides. "Of course it doesn't." Since he didn't really want to talk, or even listen to her, there was no point staying to watch this. "Well. Fine. I'll just leave you to it then. You obviously don't need me."

He caught her wrist with his index finger and thumb as she brushed past him. Still looking at the bottle, he said, "I don't want to lose you."

She allowed him to stop her from leaving and fixed her eyes on the door. "Shutting me out isn't winning you any favors."

Letting his head fall back, he looked at the ceiling. "And I don't want to hurt you."

"I don't care if you shifted your brain. What matters is—"

"*I* care. Don't make this harder than it is." He released her wrist. "Please... I just need some time."

She studied him, then decided this couldn't wait and he was going to do something stupid if she didn't do something. "Has it occurred to you that maybe Elaine moved the markers?"

He lifted his head. "What?"

"Everything looked exactly the same," she explained. "Mounds and rocks and shrubs, the whole place was nondescript. One valley looked like the next. You made a point of saying that you picked those markers *specifically* because you thought no one would move them. Could you move them?"

He frowned. "I guess."

"So, who's to say *she* didn't?" Aly replied. "All she would have to do is move a marker slightly forward or back along the path, and that would lead you to a different set of rocks. I did try to tell you to do a sweep while we were there, but you weren't listening."

He sighed and turned so he could lean against the bench the television sat on. Crossing his arms on his chest, he hunkered defensively. "You can't explain everything away. I recognized the rock formation they were buried by."

"Yes. I can," she insisted. "She could've moved the whole thing for all we know. Which is why I want to go back tomorrow and have a proper look around. I want you to use those amazing abilities of yours to find their *real* grave instead of giving up so quick. And don't tell me you looked. I know you didn't."

He stared at her in disbelief. "Can you even hear yourself right now? Why would she move the markers?"

"I don't know," Aly yelled, frustrated and hurt by his attitude. "I'm not a mind reader! I don't know what's going on." She pointed a finger at him and pressed on.

"But everyone seems to think you're working for Rex, what if *she* thinks so, too? She worked for Rex for ages, what if he convinced her brain shifts were possible and that you'd done one. She might want to hide them from you. Or Adam! Maybe *he* moved them because of Elaine!"

Noah shook his head. "That's a stretch."

"Stretches are all we have," Aly told him.

"I think…" He took a deep breath and squared his shoulders. "I think we need to separate."

Thinking he was joking, she pulled a face. "Don't be stupid."

"You shouldn't trust me. I don't know anything anymore. Seth and Solomon aren't there. Ross said Seth was alive and I'm… what if he's right? What if all my memories of escaping the Institute are wrong. Elaine and Joseph are with *Darcy*, whether by choice or not, Darcy's the Institute. Rex says I can shift my brain and I'm starting to believe he's right."

"If Rex *is* Alistair Welcher, we really can't take anything he says at face value."

"Nothing is making sense anymore and, Aly, I don't think you're safe with me. I need to go. I need to—"

She grabbed his arm to stop him before he could get too far down that train of thought. "No. I *do* know who to trust. I trust me. If you're being manipulated, and honestly, it's pretty obvious that you are—"

He made an angry face. "I told you that blind loyalty would—"

She interrupted, "It means the gut instincts you have right now, right this second"—she emphasized her words by shaking his arm—"shouldn't be trusted. You want to run, but what if that's what you programmed yourself to do. Or what Elaine and Joseph expect you to do."

He stared at her. "What do you mean?"

"I think you're being railroaded. We know they're watching. Somehow," she said, following that train of thought with a frown, "and we need to figure out how, but anyway"—she released his arm—"we're going to do what *I* think from now on. And I think we should go back tomorrow and do a proper sweep."

He narrowed his eyes. "Do you know how risky it is to go back? It's a rookie move and—"

She gave him a shit-eating grin. "And we're doing it anyway. Think about it. All your planning and countering and whatnot, what's the one thing you can't plan for?" She pushed on, answering the question before he'd had a chance to think about it. "You can't plan for me. Elaine and Joseph might able to predict you. You might be able to predict you."

His jaw went slack. "But I can't predict you. You don't have our training. You're going to see ways out of the situation we can't."

She snapped her fingers, then poked him in the chest. "Exactly. I'm a wildcard. They can pre-empt you all they like, but they can't do that with me." She lost her ferocity and gripped his shirt instead of poking him. "Just don't run. Please. I won't survive on my own."

"Aly—"

She blinked back a sudden influx of tears. "I know you're in a panic about it all, and I'm really trying not to be dismissive of it—but I don't care if you shifted your brain. I really don't. *This* is who you are." She gave his shirt a shake to illustrate her point. "I can't imagine you any other way. This is you. I won't believe otherwise."

He stood up from his lean against the bench and stepped closer to her. "Yeah. You're right."

"You need to tell me what you're thinking, even if it hurts me. We can figure this out. Stop doubting yourself."

"Promise," he said as he lifted a hand to cup her cheek. "You're amazing. I don't know how you do it."

"I know," she said and read the look in his eyes. "I'm still angry. Kiss me now and I'll probably bite you. Just saying."

"Fair enough," he said, caressing her cheek with his

thumb.

"You can hug me though."

He didn't need to be told twice. Chin dropped on her shoulder, arms crossed over on her back, he cuddled close. Returning the hug, she hummed comfortingly and breathed in the scent of hotel soap.

Touching his fingers to the back of her neck, he said, "I like this look on you. Very cute."

"Thanks. I like it," she said, drawing back to fluff her hair. "Bonnie did a nice job, she's a hairdresser, you know."

He ran both hands through her shortened locks. "I didn't. You've got this furious munchkin look going. I'm afraid for my ankles."

She glared at him playfully and bared her teeth. "Watch yourself," she threatened, while Noah laughed. Feeling better and pleased he was laughing, she smiled and leaned into his hand as he toyed with her hair. "Can I go get my stuff? I really don't want to be alone tonight."

Noah hesitated and threw a wild glance to the side. "There's only one bed," he blurted and his voice cracked.

She giggled and rolled her eyes. "Oh no. Whatever will we do."

With a gulp, Noah fumbled, "Aly, I-I'm not ready for... um..."

"For pillow forts and movie night?"

Snorting, Noah relaxed. "That's what you want to do?"

"Of course," she teased. "What else?"

"Minx. Grab the pillows from your bed too, then," he suggested.

Aly tapped the side of her nose. "Absolutely." She dragged her fingers across his chest and then squeezed his upper arm, before heading for the door.

As she reached for the handle, goose bumps swept over her and Aly froze. Natural shifters. More than one.

"Aly?" Noah asked, concerned with her pause.

She tilted her head, trying to get a gauge on the

direction. "Shifters," she said and pointed. "That way."

Noah's tingles burst through her at the same time his hands wrapped around her shoulders and he drew her against his chest, an action that was both for comfort and protection. "Can you tell how many?"

Her eyes were locked on the door, but somehow she wasn't seeing with them anymore. Instead, inside her head, she could see flames dancing against the black. She was strangely detached from everything but those flickers. "There's five," she breathed. "They're bunched together. Two front, three behind... car? They're not moving."

"Anything else?" he asked, sounding urgent. "Can you sense more?"

"I can see their flames," she whispered.

"Aly?" Noah asked. "Flames?" He released her, bounding forward to peer through a crack in the curtain.

Aly blinked and focused on Noah. "Do we run?"

"Yup." Noah kept changing the angle of his head, moving around as he tried to get a better look. He even went as far as to rise up on his toes and jump. "The car... it's... gah, odd angle, there's stuff in the way. Too much noise."

Aly cast a wild look around. The only real exit was the front door, but she rushed to check the bathroom window. No go, she doubted she could wiggle through there, and even if she could, it was a straight drop down to the ground from the second floor. He'd left the sweaty clothes from his run there, so she grabbed them to shove in his rucksack. Seeing his shoes on the ground, she picked them up and tossed them by his feet.

Still looking outside, he shoved his feet into them. "Thanks. They're outside your range."

Aly swallowed hard. "It must be growing again."

"Like, almost exactly. There's no reason for them to stop there. There's a better place to watch for us closer... it's like they knew."

Horror filled her and she covered her mouth with her

hands to gasp.

Noah jerked his head to her. "What?"

She could feel the blood draining from her face. "I told Bonnie my range. She said Ross' been looking for a way out since we met with Rex. Do you think—?"

"Shit," he said, and then uttered a long string of swear words. Lifting his hands, he clutched at his head and turned in a tight circle, augmenting the whole way around. "It makes sense. The implants they had, what if they were voluntary? Ross wanted me to stay in one place, then he didn't want to let us go by ourselves. Why do I trust so blindly? I keep doing that, why—"

Trying to help, Aly watched the flames again. "We don't know anything yet. The shifters are just sitting there. Wait. No. One of them just got out of the car."

Noah swiveled his head back toward the car. "There's—a truck just pulled up. Difficult to make out from this distance with all the interference, but... I can see a couple of people getting out...You're not sensing more shifters?"

One flame moved away from the other four, but she couldn't sense any others nearby. "No."

"Mercenaries then. They're probably getting orders."

"Can you hear what's being said?"

"Not from this distance. Too much ambient noise."

Aly cringed. "The valuables bag is in my room. I'm so sorry," she blurted, feeling awful. "I swear, I just didn't think."

"No. It's okay." Noah scrunched up his face in thought. "Okay, so... we're gonna have to make a break for it, and hope that they're not in position yet. Once they're ready, they're going to rush us."

"How long do we have?"

He turned and did a full three hundred and sixty-degree sweep again. "I can't see anyone acting suspicious, yet at least. Bonnie and Ross are..." He swore again, more viciously this time. "Ross is walking toward them. Can't see Bonnie."

"Ahh, fuck that," Aly snapped, not really speaking to Noah anymore. "I am *done* being betrayed. We need to go on the offensive." She planted her hands on her hips and looked around the room for something that she could use as a weapon. "Take them out before they get to us."

Noah spared her one of his lopsided smiles. "While I appreciate the sentiment, we don't know what kind of resources they have right now. It's safer to run. I don't want you to have to go through that seizure you went through before." Attention back on the window, he continued, "I'm only one person. I might be able to take them on enough to thin the numbers, but... are you okay with me killing them?" He hesitated, then ventured, "Or killing one of them yourself? It might be necessary."

Aly wrinkled her nose and sighed. "Logic. Yeah. You're right. Safer to run."

"They haven't started spreading out, but they will. And soon. Once we move, so will they."

He went for the guns in his rucksack while Aly scoured the room and made sure they had all his gear. As she did so, her eyes landed on the bottle of alcohol. "I have an idea," she blurted.

He tucked a loaded gun into the belt of his jeans and then covered it with his shirt. "Do share."

Aly smiled and picked up the bottle of alcohol. "We walk out the front door, with this half empty—"

Noah's eyes widened and he followed her train of thought with ease. "—arguing because Bonnie knows we're probably yelling at each other."

"—you act drunk and dawdle around, then you can get a good look at them while I get the valuables bag."

"I'll check if they're weapons hot. If not, I'll signal with two taps."

"—and we bolt for the car and get out of Dodge."

He grinned at her. "Good plan."

"If they're weapons hot?" she asked.

"I'll drop the keys by your door, and go and give them a target to shoot at. If you hear gunfire, make for the car and pick me up."

She swallowed her nerves and zipped up the rucksack. "I don't like that idea." Grabbing the bottle, she rushed for the bathroom to tip half of it down the sink.

"Yeah, I know," Noah called and started augmenting a lot of things at once. "But we don't have time for anything else. How long will it take you to get the valuables bag?"

She came out of the bathroom to shrug at him. "Like ten seconds." Picking up the rucksack, she went to wait by the door as he did one last sweep. "I wasn't comfortable here. Didn't unpack or do much."

"Yeah…" he said, the word slow and regretful. "Aly…" His arms wrapped around her shoulders until he hugged her to his chest.

She rested her hand on his arm and took a deep, calming breath.

It was odd. She should be panicked right now. A few months ago, the thought of heading out the door with a dozen or more possibly armed men on the other side would have terrified her. She was scared, but it didn't overpower her. Noah seemed calm and sure of himself, so Aly drew on that. She knew what needed to be done and she was prepared to do it. Later, she would contemplate on what that meant, but right now, she focused on the task at hand. Adjusting her grip on the clothes rucksack, she asked, "Ready?"

"FYI, I'm gonna snatch this bag off you. Put up a fight and then let me have it."

She saw the logic in that and didn't argue. "Okay."

With one final squeeze, he released her. "Let's go."

CHAPTER 10

Getting back into her hotel room was the easy part. The people watching weren't ready for them. With Noah bellowing drunkenly at the door and playing distraction, Aly raced through the room and made sure she had everything.

Their valuables bag was still completely packed, but she rechecked it anyway as she shoved her wallet into her pocket. Once she was sure she had everything, she went to the door and held onto the handle. "Ready."

"C'mon, babe, please, I didn't mean it," Noah called, loudly. "You know it didn't mean anything."

Recognizing the catchphrase of Ethan, Bellhollow High quarterback, and his habit of cheating on Madison-Lee, Aly couldn't contain the burst of laughter. "Really?"

"Ahh, who needs you!" Noah shouted, moving away from the door. "Plenty of other fish in the sea! I'll find one that doesn't whine so much!"

"Ooh, you owe me a Snickers for that one." Rising up on her tiptoes, she peered through the peephole and watched the fuzzy, distorted view of Noah as he staggered down the stairs until he disappeared from sight. He yell-muttered loudly outside and the back door of the jeep slammed.

Taking a deep breath, she waited for his signal and reached out with her senses. Still only five shifters within her range, but they were no longer seated in the car. They'd spread out. Pillars of flame against the black of her mind, a group of three and two single flames. The two singles were a distance from each other, one of them moved closer while the other circled at the edge of her range, a move that was most likely going to end in an ambush from behind.

"One shifter circling to flank," she told the air. "Ten bucks says they have a group of mercenaries with them. They're… um… I forget which way's north. Behind me to the left."

She bounced on her toes, keeping herself tense as she waited. Filled with nervous energy, all she wanted was to get this over with, but she forced herself to hold. If she went out too early, she put them both at risk.

Two deliberate tingle-taps from Noah.

Aly heaved in a breath and surged from the room. She hit the staircase at a full run, leaping down to the landing in the middle of the stairs to land on her good leg, then grabbed onto the railing to propel her down the rest of the stairs.

Noah stood in the middle of the parking lot, bottle of alcohol in one hand and a lighter in the other. When she hit the bottom of the stairs, he lit the makeshift Molotov and tossed it in the direction of the truck.

It burst open in the middle of the road, spreading flames. Beyond the flames, people scrambled. Several ran for one of the three cars parked beside the truck, while others ran toward the flame. Ross was among those standing and staring at them, but Aly couldn't see Bonnie at all.

Diving into the passenger side, Aly threw the backpack onto the back seat and slammed her door shut. As she clicked her seatbelt, Noah slid into the driver side and dropped his gun into her lap. "Seatbelt," he said, jamming the car into reverse before he'd even closed his door. Tires spun and spat dirt, and the engine roared as the jeep accelerated backward.

"It's on," she said, gripping the belt with one hand and the gun with the other. "Follow your own advice."

One hand crossed to the belt, the other on the wheel, he yanked down the seat belt and spun the wheel to turn the car, holding the seat belt in a way that offered it to her, "Could you—?"

"Yup," she said and reached for the belt.

Braking in the middle of the turn, the momentum of the sudden stop shut Noah's door. It threw her to the side as she struggled to get Noah's seatbelt in and not get in his way while driving.

A crack of gunfire and Aly instinctively hunched her shoulders. Clicking Noah's belt in, she grabbed onto her belt and the door frame as the jeep bounced across a pothole in the parking lot. Forced against the back of the seat as Noah floored the jeep, she tried to see what was going on outside the car.

People ran toward cars, or ran after the jeep as it bounced onto the main road. One car, a silver one, was already pulling away from the curb to chase after them. Twisting in her seat so she could look behind them, she tried to keep an eye on things, but so much was happening. "Car coming," she told Noah. "Shifter driver, one maybe back seat. Can't see Ross or Bonnie."

"Ross got into the silver car," Noah said, his tone clipped. The engine roared as he changed gears, then bounced forward as it increased speed. "Not sure about Bonnie."

"Guess that answers which side Ross' on. Who do you think these guys are?"

"No clue. Hold on. Corner."

Aly gripped the door handle tighter as Noah took the corner fast. The tires screeched against the road and the momentum slammed her into the door. Another series of goose bumps alerted Aly and she jerked her head forward. "Shifter," she blurted, her eyes darting around as she tried to give Noah some reference. "Red pickup ahead. Not driving, but I can't tell if its passenger or back seat."

"Thanks," Noah said. "Corner."

Aly clutched the seatbelt so hard that her knuckles whitened and tried to remain in her seat as the jeep slid around a corner. "Where are they coming from?" she asked once they were round. Glancing back, she saw the silver car holding pace with them, and shortly after, the red pickup turned the corner to continue chasing.

Noah pressed his lips into a line. His eyes darted around, snapping between the rear-view mirror and the two side mirrors as he tried to keep track of everything. He seemed to be in a constant state of shifting, sliding from one augmentation to the next with ease as he wove through the light traffic.

"This would be harder if we were in Salt Lake," Aly said, mostly talking to herself.

"No," Noah replied, tension making his tone short. "It'd be easier. More places to hide. Better chance to pick up cops. Here, we're exposed."

"Oh."

"If we make it to Salt Lake, I'll be happy."

He seemed uncertain that they would, and that worried Aly. Prying her hand away from her seatbelt, she rested it on his knee and squeezed.

Noah threw her a smile. "We'll be okay." Another fleeting glance at the mirror. "There's a bounty though, and that's going to make things hard."

"A bounty?"

"Overheard Ross," Noah said and zoomed around a car so fast it felt like the car was parked.

As much as she trusted Noah's driving, he didn't have time to make it smooth and safe, so being thrown around like she was in the car made her anxious. Her heart pounded in her chest, threatening to burst through. Sweat dotted her brow and slicked her shirt against her back. "We're gonna pick up cops."

"Hopefully."

"We expected—"

Noah's sudden curse was the only warning Aly got as a white sedan veered out of an adjacent road and tried to side-swipe them. Noah over-compensated for the sudden obstacle and sent the car into a spin. The back of the jeep clipped a parked car, hard enough that it set off its blaring alarm, and brought them to a halt. Ahead of them, the white sedan screeched to a stop.

Burned rubber stung her nose as she tried to get her bearings. One hand clutched the door, the other gripped her seatbelt.

Wasting no time, Noah jammed the jeep back into gear to send them roaring away from the white sedan. He locked the wheel and whirled them in a complete one-hundred-and-eighty-degree turn to avoid colliding with the red pickup truck, and slamming Aly against the door.

As they ducked around the white sedan, it accelerated until it matched their pace whereupon it wove toward them in an attempt to drive them from the road.

Aly stared into the white sedan. The driver wasn't a shifter, but he looked like a hardened man, someone Aly certainly wouldn't want to meet in a dark alleyway. A mercenary of some sort, all the men in the car seemed to be. Except Bonnie, who met Aly's gaze from the back seat of the sedan. She signed, her mouth moving as she tried to convey something, but Aly didn't understand.

Noah struggled, trying to stay far enough away from the adjacent car that they didn't get swiped, as well as trying to keep oncoming traffic from causing an accident. "Gun!" he yelled, snatching the gun from her lap. "Get down!"

Aly instantly hunkered. She pressed her chest to her knees, stuck her fingers in her ears and squeezed shut her eyes. It made the rocking motion of the car so much worse since she was unable to anticipate the turns Noah took, but the pillars of flame in her mind grew stronger.

Noah fired twice. A screech of wheels, shattered glass, and their car jerked forward. Noah's arm bumped against her as he lowered it.

The flames burned brighter. Five shifters behind them now, all at various distances. Two were close in the silver car, while one was in the red pickup and the other two were in later cars, with the goose bumps on her skin flaring the closer they came. A sixth shifter moved in and out of her range and Aly guessed there were probably more than that out there. "I think one's circling," she said.

"Which way?"

"Behind and to the left of us," Aly said, and reached out to brace against the door as Noah took the next right.

Since he was no longer shooting, Aly uncurled and looked between the front seats to the back at the cars chasing. White sedan, a red pickup, a silver sedan, plus some others behind that could be part of the group, but she wasn't sure. Hard to see what was going on, all three cars were weaving across the road and Aly got the distinct impression the red pickup was trying to keep the white sedan from overtaking them.

All her senses were heightened as they rushed through the town. Her heart pounded, the engine roared in her ears and her eyes zeroed in on every panicked pedestrian they passed. She whipped her head around, trying to see and hear everything, and she was unaugmented. She could only imagine what Noah was going through as he tried to keep them ahead of the people chasing them while his tingles worked overtime across her skin.

The goose bumps the shifters caused were morphing into a sharp pain in her belly and Aly didn't like it. It wasn't like the intense feeling when there were so many shifters close and touching her, but it was becoming uncomfortable. Swiveling back to face the front, she gripped the seat and struggled to hang on and squash the growing panic in her.

The town emptied onto a highway and, mostly free of traffic, Noah sucked in a breath as he floored the jeep.

Throwing a glance back, Aly checked on the cars behind them. Red pickup and white sedan were vying for a position behind them, while the silver sedan followed at a more controlled pace.

"You okay?" Noah asked.

Aly's nervous burst of laughter at the absurdity of his question bordered on hysteria.

"Easy now," Noah told her and reached over to squeeze her hand.

Closing her eyes, she took several deep breaths and let them out slowly. "They're still coming."

"Yeah. I know," Noah replied and the car picked up speed again. "Trying to put some distance."

"What if we can't?" Aly asked, twisting around to peer behind them. "What if they keep chasing us?"

Balancing the gun on his lap, Noah checked the cartridge, then reloaded. "I have a plan."

Goose bumps crawled across Aly's skin and while she tried to take comfort in Noah's gentle tingle, the intensity of the goose bumps was overpowering. The flames in her mind were glowing brighter and a need slowly built in her chest. It was different than it had in the park, which had been a wild, ferocious and overwhelming feeling. Now, she felt like if she reached out her hand, she could touch the flames.

"Where are the cops?" she muttered, watching behind them again. "Why aren't there sirens?"

"They may have already been dealt with," Noah muttered.

Aly pulled a face. "Think they've been paid off?"

"Maybe. Or detained. It only takes one shifter pretending to be a sheriff to get the rest to ignore something is happening."

"Ah."

"We need some distance," Noah said. "Then... I'll have to stop and deal with them." He wriggled in his seat, glancing behind. "I won't do anything until we're closer to Salt Lake if I can help it. There's a chance they'll try and roadblock us."

"Why Salt Lake?" she asked, and picked several pieces of shattered glass from the seam in the seat and dropped them on the floor.

"Bigger city in the region, besides Las Vegas, lots of streets, and it's farther away from where we know Rex is. Plus, gateway to America, we can go anywhere from there."

Aly pressed her lips into a thin line. "Where are *we* going?"

Noah frowned at the road ahead, then reached over to take Aly's hand, taking or offering comfort, Aly wasn't sure which. "You tell me. My gut is telling me to run as far as I can, but we can't trust that right now. What do you think we should do?"

She played with his fingers and tried to keep herself from obsessing about what lay behind them. "What's stopping us from leaving the country? Roger's got obscure family in England we could bunk with for a while."

"Del and Grace for one," Noah said. "Plus, it's a little more difficult to forge a passport than it is to forge a high school enrolment... Mexico might be do-able though. Or Canada. But I still think finding Adam is our best bet."

Looking over her shoulder, she wrinkled her nose at the line of vehicles following them. "Let's just concentrate on getting away first."

There was a limited amount of time a body could maintain a state of heightened awareness before it succumbed to exhaustion and Aly didn't have the benefit of being able to alter her blood chemistry like Noah could. Their pursuers wouldn't let them get too far ahead. Every time Noah tried to pull away, they kept pace. On the straight stretches of road, and there were a lot of them, the vehicles behind would vie for the coveted position directly behind Noah.

If they fought against each other, that might thin the numbers chasing them. Somewhere behind them, Ross and Bonnie lurked. In separate cars, so did that mean they'd joined separate factions? It did seem that the white sedan, where Bonnie sat, cut off the silver car, with Ross in it, more than once.

The shifters skipped in and out of her range, depending on how far ahead they allowed the jeep to get, but being on constant alert from the goose bumps was draining. It was like holding her stomach in for hours, scarcely able to breathe. She didn't want to know what would happen when she couldn't do it any longer.

"Don't they ever get tired?" she complained, scowling at the convoy of cars behind them. "What are they doing?"

"Just keeping track of us. Giving us a bit of a breather before they make their next move. We'll be in trouble if they start falling back."

"Because they've planned something up ahead."

"Yeah."

She rubbed her arms as goose bumps crawled across her skin. "Don't you get tired?"

"Of running?"

"Shapeshifting all the time."

"Not the same sort of tiredness you experience. I'm... using up a lot of energy, I'll have to eat a lot to replace it later. What about you?" he asked, his eyes skipping over her goose bump riddled arms.

She sighed and studied her arms. "It's... like being in a constant flight-or-fight mode. It's getting real old."

"Hang in there," he said and stroked his hand along her arm. "I have a plan. Are you willing to switch?"

Aly turned toward him. "Drive? I can't drive a stick."

"You don't need to do anything fancy. Straight bit, it should be pretty easy right now."

Aly swallowed. "Okay."

The switch took some maneuvering. Noah clicked off his seatbelt and slid back the driver's chair, driving one-handed while Aly slid onto his lap. They wriggled until she could get her foot on the pedal and held the steering wheel, then, while she drove, she lifted up so Noah could slip out from beneath her. Aly readjusted the chair and put on her seatbelt while Noah climbed into the back.

She tried to watch in the mirror as Noah rummaged around in the back of the jeep, but with his back concealing his activities, she couldn't make out what he was doing.

"Okay," he said, kneeling on the back seat and facing out the back window. "I'm going to shoot out the back window."

Aly swallowed hard. Shifting her grip on the wheel, she braced herself. "Ready when you are."

Noah's first shot shattered the glass on the back of the jeep, with Noah lunging over the seat to kick the remains of the window out so he could see. The black car directly behind them swerved in order to avoid the shrapnel of the window. Noah's next shot blew the front tire of the black car and Aly watched the plume of dust it created as it veered from the road.

The next shot sent the red pickup truck into a spin.

"Speed up!" Noah bellowed to her.

Aly realized she'd been too busy paying attention to what he was doing to look ahead. Snapping her eyes ahead of her, she called. "Sorry!"

Four more shots went off, two cars veering away behind them, then Noah called, "Hunch!"

Aly hunched her shoulders, making herself as small as possible. She flicked her eyes to the mirror, catching Noah ducking behind the seat to use it as a shield. Bullets thumped against the back of the jeep.

"They're aiming for the tires!" he called. "Go!"

Aly floored it. She gripped the steering wheel hard,

trying to heighten her senses and look for any pothole in the road ahead which might be detrimental to them. A part of her wanted to weave the car across the road so that those behind them had a harder target to hit, but she knew that she'd be more inclined to lose control that way.

Noah was directly behind her seat, offering up his body as a shield from any stray bullets and her heart skipped as he cried out in pain. His tingles changed from the start-stop that meant his senses, to a sustained shift.

She twisted in her seat, trying to get a look at him, one hand flailing backward in an attempt to reach him. "Fletcher!"

"Drive!" he said, his voice catching.

"But—"

She lifted her eyes to peer out the back. The white car which held Bonnie was still several cars away, but directly behind them was Ross' silver car, with a shifter driver.

"You're drifting!" he told her, catching her arm and pushing it back to indicate she should pay attention to the road. "I'm fine."

She might have believed him if he hadn't left a smear of blood on her arm. Gripping the steering wheel tight, she tilted her arm to look at the blood and its eerie twinkle. She kept forgetting to tell him about that strange glitter in his blood.

His blood.

Anger filled her. White-hot, blinding anger. They hurt him, *again*. He was hurt because of her and because of those bastards chasing them and he didn't deserve this at all. She wanted to lash out. She wanted to hurt them as much as they hurt him. But mostly, she just wanted to protect him over everyone else.

It was Ross' fault. He'd betrayed them. Ross said there was a bounty on her head that would set him up for life, so perhaps that was too tempting. They'd blindly trusted one of Noah's siblings, *again*, and been betrayed.

It wasn't going to happen again.

The constant flames in her mind flared brighter and became so clear, she felt as though she could touch them. Fiery red flames, tall and bright... and... and three tiny yellow ones, small flickers, completely overshadowed by the red ones, so soft and dim and yet...

One was Noah. Sparkling warmth in the crushing darkness. Tiny stars danced among the flame. Friendship and family and hope.

One was Bonnie. Confusion and frustration, a budding trust broken.

One was Ross. Hatred, anger, betrayal, and pain.

Not really knowing what she was doing, Aly reached for the Ross flame.

The silver car behind them swerved, hit the edge of the road too fast and flipped. It slammed upside down in the middle of the road and slid on its roof. It caused a cascade effect, cars knocking into each other as they tried to avoid the accident.

"Whoa," Noah said.

Aly blinked and the flames in her mind vanished. "What happened?"

"Not sure," he replied, sounding bewildered. "Moment of inattention? Maybe someone behind shot the tires."

"Are they okay?"

"There's airbags, but I really can't tell more."

Aly flicked her gaze through the mirrors again. Not many cars left following them now. Those who made their way past the accident were hit with a volley of bullets as Noah took the advantage until there was no one left coming after them.

Aly breathed a sigh of relief as all goose bumps except for Noah's tingle subsided.

Instead of coming straight back to the front seat, Noah fussed around in the back. Wind rushed in through the broken back window, muffling other sounds, but Aly still heard his concealed grunts of pain.

"You were hit, weren't you?"

Hauling their clothing bag from the back, he evaded, "We need to stop at the next gas station and—"

"Fletcher."

She could almost see the hunch in his shoulders and hear the heartfelt sigh. "Yeah. It's not bad. Nearly closed up. Honestly thought they weren't going to risk hitting you, but… well…"

She swallowed and groped back to find him. Noah took her seeking hand and gave it a squeeze.

"I'm okay," he said, ducking his head down to kiss the back of her hand. "I promise."

Swallowing again, she nodded. "Okay."

"We're in the clear for now," he told her, fabric rustling and she glanced back to see him removing his shirt. "I'll gas up and keep watch. You grab whatever food you can, preferably snacks high in sugar. If we make it to Salt Lake, hopefully we'll be good, but after that… well…we'll be driving through the night. I want to get as far from here as possible."

"I thought I was supposed to make the decisions?"

"Okay," he said after a moment's hesitation, then put on a lofty tone of voice. "Oh, great Aly, what do you think we should do?"

"You forgot wise."

"Oh, great, wise and cute Aly, beloved to the bees and Queen of Snickers, what do you think we should do?"

Aly pretended to consider. "Gas up at the next station. Grab food. Make it to Salt Lake. Profit."

With a snicker, Noah said, "Sounds great."

"Then, I think we should double back and check Seth's grave again."

"I was with you until that last step," he said. "Then you lost me."

"I think it's important. For you. For peace of mind. You need to—"

She could hear the moment in his voice when he realized she wasn't joking. "Aly, that's a bad idea."

"Not if we switch cars in Salt Lake. They won't expect us to double back."

"It's a compromised place."

She smiled. "Only that particular entrance. And the markers were wrong anyway. Ross and Bonnie aren't going to think we'll go back."

"We never, ever go back," Noah replied. "It's a rule, never—"

"You did," she said simply. "You came back for me. Don't tell me you thought that was wrong."

Noah sighed. "Point taken."

"You left those cameras in Vegas, too. Don't you want a chance to check them?"

"I can do that online."

"But you can't find their graves online. This is important," she insisted. "For you. We need to know for sure, one way or the other, or we're not going to be able to put this whole 'brain shift' to rest. We need to really look. It's the only proof we have."

"It's risky, especially now," Noah said and crawled into the front with her. He flopped in the passenger chair with a huffy noise. "There's a lot that could go wrong. And we don't know if we're clear of them yet."

"So make it work," Aly replied. "Even if we loop back in a couple of days. I feel it's important." She cleared her throat and squared her shoulders and put on an authoritative tone. "So, I'm not asking."

Noah snorted. "Yes, boss."

She reached over and patted his head. "Good boy."

"Shuddup," he said, catching her hand before she could put it back on the steering wheel. "Road's pretty clear up ahead. Can you drive for a few? I'll look at some maps and see what we can do."

Aly smiled. "Absolutely. As long as we switch before I have to change gear."

He laughed. "I'll keep that in mind."

CHAPTER 11

Dozing in a car was not Aly's idea of comfort, or even a particularly good sleep, but Noah insisted that she at least try. The events of the day, as well as over an hour of constant goose bumps and flight-or-fight mode, made her absolutely exhausted. And if she was this tired, she knew Noah must be exhausted as well, even if he could recharge better than she could.

They couldn't stop. Not yet. Not when they knew they were only a small way ahead of those who followed. The resources that their followers had meant there were probably more shifters moving into positions to stop them and Noah and Aly's only real option was to be unpredictable.

Rex had warned them they only had a small window of opportunity to flee and Noah was so angry at himself because he'd wasted that time trusting Ross and staying close to California. Now, it seemed many of the factions were alerted to the fact she was still alive and wanted her ability.

Noah thought it was likely that Ross had managed to hide a tracking device on the jeep or worse, in their belongings. So while Aly had been driving, he'd ordered a replacement car and had it waiting for them at Salt Lake. He was rather specific about the details; what kind of car he wanted, compensating for her lack of stick abilities, plus an area nearby to dump their current car, and the ability to use a credit card late at night without questions. Their best option to rent a car turned out to be the airport, which led Aly to ask why they didn't jump on a plane, fly to Reno or Carson City and drive back to the gravesite. Noah explained that as tempting as that was, they'd be trapped in a plane with no control over anything, and therefore more at risk at being cornered when they landed. While he could alter his appearance on a whim, it would take a while to disguise her and leave them at a disadvantage.

Which made a world of sense to her. Right now, they could pull off the road and hide, or even ditch the car if they needed to. They had a certain amount of control over everything, but on a plane, they would be trapped in their seats. While trains or buses were inherently slower, they would give them both a much-needed breather to sleep, if it came to that.

There were so many things she had to remember. Danger lurking around every corner. How could anyone live like this?

"How did you ever feel safe enough to settle down?" she asked.

Noah wriggled his back and rolled his shoulders in an effort to ease aching muscles. "It's not going to be like this all the time. Once we get some distance, they'll lose us. Plus, there comes a point where you just say 'fuck it. If they catch me then they catch me, but that girl over there has a pretty cool book and I wanna know more.'"

She giggled.

Grinning, he winked at her. "I'm not talking about you, by the way."

Banter. Something easy and normal and she wanted to play. "Oh, I see. Girl in every port."

"Or a guy. I don't discriminate. Love is love." He

rubbed his chin. "Let's see. There was Baly. And Daly and E-aly, then came Faly—"

"Don't forget Caly."

"Who could?" he teased.

"I was first, I see."

"Always."

Reaching across, she shoved him in the shoulder. "Dork."

"Yes, but I'm your dork."

"You are." Smiling, she used her arm as a pillow against the door and stared out into the blackness of the night.

"Traffic's picking up. We'll hit the city soon."

Having nothing better to do, and nothing to look at, Aly closed her eyes. "Good."

She must have slept because the next thing she knew was being jerked awake by a sharp pain in her belly and her skin covered in goose bumps.

"What?" Noah blurted, alarmed by her sudden yelp and flailing. "What's wrong?"

She bent forward and hugged herself as she struggled to control her fear. "Shifters. Pretty close. Lots of them."

"Ahh. That explains it."

"Explains what?"

"There's been two cars behaving erratically behind me for the past few minutes, but they stopped gaining on me and held pace. And now I'm spotting what looks to be a roadblock up ahead."

She peered ahead into the darkness but was unable to see what he was talking about. "They have a tracking device on us, don't they?"

"Either that, or they just covered every road possible." He shifted his grip on the steering wheel and clicked off the cruise control. "Seat belt on?"

Noting that Noah had started augmenting, Aly replied, "Of course."

With a glance and a sheepish smile, he asked, "I only ask this because I'm being considerate, but how's the bladder?"

"We off-roading?" she asked, trying to follow his train of thought.

"Yup."

She sat so she was no longer slouching, one hand gripped her seat belt and the other went for the door frame. "It's fine," she said, trying to feel more confident than she was. "Go."

"Trust me?"

She smiled at him. "Always."

With a decisive nod, Noah hit the brakes and swerved. Even with her grip, Aly was thrown sideways from the force of the turn. The jeep bounced from the road and slammed through the flimsy wire fence barrier between the highways and into the direct path of traffic coming the opposite direction. He swerved again, ignoring the shrill horns of those cars he'd nearly plowed into and headed back the way they'd come from.

The goose bumps from the cars following them grew stronger and Aly held her breath.

"Here we go," he said and switched off his headlights.

Turning, he slammed back through the flimsy wire fence barrier between the highways, straight across the road. Aly yelped and gripped her seat belt tighter as the jeep shuddered across train tracks, then hit a sharp incline.

"So many salt beds and small pools," Noah muttered to himself when they hit the top of the hill and he turned to drive along the summit. "Right, I think that's a big bag of nope right there."

Aly squinted as she tried to see what he was seeing, but she lacked the night vision he was most likely augmented for. By the small amount of moonlight ahead of her, it seemed like a white bed of something. Probably a salt deposit but there did seem to be water glistening in the middle of it. "Huh?"

"Don't know this area," Noah said. "And… I'm not sure what that is to the right of us."

Aly looked over her shoulder, seeing headlights pierce the sky behind them as the cars climbed the hill. Down the bottom of the hill, two cars raced parallel along a dirt track. Looking ahead, she saw the sudden flash of the lights from cars moving onto the highway, possibly in pursuit.

Noah clicked his tongue. "Have to brave the lake."

Aly didn't like that idea at all. From what she knew, the lake's water levels tended to fluctuate all year round, and the edges of it could be rough or full of pools and potholes. "Wouldn't that be worse—"

Noah turned, bouncing the jeep down the hill and Aly flung a glance backward to see the two cars at the bottom pick up speed in an attempt to cut them off.

Aly grit her teeth as the jeep shuddered over the train tracks again. She didn't like the speed Noah was traveling on dirt, or the amount of bouncing the jeep was doing, but she couldn't complain about it. Bracing, she squeezed shut her eyes as Noah turned toward the highway again.

It didn't help and her eyes forced themselves open from the screech of metal as Noah crashed through the fence in the middle of the highway. The jeep skidded, narrowly missing a horn-blaring truck, before it shot across the highway and into the scrub surrounding the Great Salt Lake.

Realizing she'd been subconsciously mashing an imaginary brake pedal with her foot, she tried to relax as the jeep skittered and bounced across the bush littered plain. Dried branches cracked and tore beneath the wheels and clawed at the underbelly of the jeep. It was not a pleasant ride at all, the jeep careened over ditches and potholes.

Noah swore, swerving to avoid something and the jeep skidded sideways as it tore up dirt. Lifting her hand away from the door, she braced it against the ceiling and held on. She didn't like this. She didn't like the panicky feeling bubbling in her chest, she didn't like being jerked around, the seatbelt squeezing her tight, she didn't like how out of control she was. Combined with the shifter presence pain and Noah's tingles, it was more than enough for nausea to rise.

Then, the pain felt like it doubled. She glanced over her shoulder and, among the bouncing and skidding of the car, she counted more headlights. More had joined the chase, possibly those who had been waiting in the shadows along the road.

"They must know what I am," she told Noah, her stomach lurching as the jeep became airborne over a large ditch. "Right? They know what I can do! Why are they risking it?"

"Maybe they don't believe the rumors," Noah said. "I have no idea. Is it bad?"

Her skin was beginning to burn. "There's a lot of them."

"Just hang on."

Her hands were clenched tight, but she could still feel the tremors. "I... I don't know if I can stop this. I don't want to hurt anyone!"

"Hey," Noah soothed. "I know you don't. This is their choice, not yours. You can't control it."

"What if they don't know?"

"Still not your fault."

She grit her teeth and hunched over, staring at her knees as she tried to contain the pain. "C'mon Aly," she told herself. "Fortify."

Flames flickered. The fiery red of a natural shifter, and the muted yellow sparks of Noah... and Ross. Ross' flame, but not Bonnie. What did that mean?

"Ross is back there," she said, staring at her shoes.

"What? How—is he augmenting?" Noah blurted, throwing her a wild glance, followed by a hiss of pain and a shying wince as a beam of light from the cars behind reflected in the rear-view mirror and hit his eyes.

Aly stared at nothing and everything. "I can see his

flame."

"His flame? You mentioned—*shit*—" he yelped, hitting a ditch at a wrong angle. The jeep lurched, bounced sideways and teetered on two wheels before it righted itself, but in trying to wrestle control of the careening vehicle, they'd lost their momentum and were now at a right angle to the oncoming cars.

Noah struggled with the jeep, dropping back to first gear and flooring it to try to get it moving again. Wheels spun, kicking up a plume of dust behind them, and the jeep sank. Aly stared at the oncoming lights in horror as they grew closer and still the jeep didn't do much more than bunny-hop forward. "Fletcher!"

Noah flung an arm across her chest. Metal shrieked and everything lurched. The jeep was thrown as one of the cars clipped their tail. Aly screamed and held on while the jeep whirled.

She didn't know how, but during the spin, Noah managed to get the car moving again. The jeep sprung forward and picked up its pace, still careening dangerously as the back tires tried to get traction.

So many lights around them, revving cars and salted dust clouds blooming against headlights. Noah swore as he weaved, trying to avoid them and he fumbled for the headlights. Light poured ahead of them, giving Aly a view of the land she never wanted to see. She guessed that with all the lights, he wasn't able to switch between night vision and normal vision fast enough to prevent light blindness.

It was so loud. Loud and scary and everything was moving so fast, and the flames revolved around her, tangling her up in a web of fire and twirling rivers in their wake, leaving echoes in her mind. A deep pain twisted in her belly. Her arms shook. Her chest gulped in every breath.

She felt taut and ready to snap. Closing her eyes, she concentrated on her breathing, a feat that was easier said than done. Too much noise and too much movement and control that was perilous.

Noah did his best. He always did his best.

The flames burned brighter. Noah's steady sparkle at her side, Ross's yellow flame zipping around her, and so many red flares. She...

She wanted to touch them. Wanted to taste. Wanted the flame for herself. If she could touch it, run her fingers through the flame—

A loud horn, a terrifying crunch, but the expected jolt didn't come. Lights spun wildly behind them, another crash resounded as several of the cars chasing them collided, or spun out of control while trying to avoid a collision.

Noah whooped. "They're slamming into each other. That'll teach them for following so close."

Aly curled up tight, pressing her forehead to her knees. "I don't feel good."

"Hang on"—the car jolted forward as Noah floored it—"Yeah. They're dropping back."

She hung on, trying not to whimper.

"Getting some distance now. Still have... hmm... maybe... one—maybe two—cars. Can deal with that." He hesitated and shifted gears as the jeep picked up speed along the dirt. "Can... I hate to ask cause I can see this is hurting you..."

She tried to get a read on the car, but the flares were fading as fast as the shakes were. "Two," she mumbled. "I think."

"Thank you," he said.

Aly grit her teeth and hung on for dear life. The sound of the tires changed, from scratchy, broken underbrush and dirt clumps hitting the underside of the jeep, to the gravel of a make-shift road.

The nausea and shakes from being in close vicinity of the shifters dimmed back to a mild discomfort, but now, since she couldn't see their flames, she couldn't give Noah any information. She could see street lights in the distance, and proper roads, so she assumed they were heading toward Salt Lake City again.

Seeing Aly unfurl, Noah said, "One car. The other one stopped but this one seems content to follow at a distance. Either it is tracking us until the rest have a chance to catch up, or..." he shrugged. "They have a tracker on us."

"Somehow I wouldn't be surprised."

"It's probably in or on the car itself," he said. "Easier to hide one there than risk me seeing it if it's on our person."

Aly made a noise to show she understood. She stretched and wriggled, feeling more comfortable. "So, how do we lose them?"

"Well, they're pretty far behind. We'll play cat and mouse for a while through the back streets, then I'm hoping to find a place we can pull a fast one. Up for a bit of deception?" he asked, smiling at her. "It may mean ditching the car early and legging it to the airport."

Aly nodded. "Ready for anything."

With the car tailing them lingering at a distance Noah found comical, it wasn't long before he found a place in Salt Lake to ditch them. They'd been weaving through what looked to be a mixture of residential and commercial buildings, and there were enough cars on the road to offer a small amount of protection, except their jeep looked like it'd been through a warzone, commandeering odd looks from other people in their cars. Aly hoped they wouldn't pick up police but maybe that would actually help if they did. Two teens being pursued by grownups? The police might save them.

By the expression on his face, Noah was formulating a plan, which was confirmed when he asked her to scramble into the back seat and make sure all their gear was together.

"Also," Noah said, turning right. "Can I borrow your jacket?"

She didn't question at all, pulling out the reversible

jacket they'd bought in Sacramento and placed it on the front seat beside him.

"Okay, I think…" Noah said, turning another right. He checked behind him and nodded to himself. "Yeah, this'll work. When I say, I want you to take the bags, get out, and hide behind the dumpsters directly ahead of you."

Seeing he was circling the block, she readied herself by weaving her arms through the backpack and sitting close to the door. "What then?"

"There'll be a group of stores near you. One's an all-night diner. Hide for ten minutes, then go inside. I'll make my way back."

Aly gulped. "Split up?"

"It's not desirable," Noah said. "But if you're quick at hiding, they won't even know you're gone."

"I… I don't… that's not… What about you?"

"*I*," he began sounding lofty and self-important, "can change my shape."

Reaching across, she shoved him in the shoulder, then left her hand there, needing contact with him.

"I'll be fine," he promised. "Done this part loads of times."

"I haven't got a phone," she mumbled, looking for excuses to stay together.

"I know."

"I really don't think—"

"We don't have time to discuss it," Noah told her. "We have to make a move or I'll need to find another spot. This *will* work."

Swallowing hard, she retreated. Putting her hand on the handle, she tried to banish the thought that he would abandon her, especially since this was the second time today he'd suggested splitting up.

"You can still feel them, right?"

"Yup. What if they have a tracker in our gear?"

"If they stop, whistle for me. I'll do another loop and grab you. If they don't stop, the tracker's on the car somewhere."

"Okay," she mumbled, wishing she had his confidence.

"You'll be fine," he said. "I'll find you. Promise. Trust me."

Taking a deep breath, she waited for his signal. It came with a sudden zoom around the corner and a fast stop. The storefront of the building on the corner came up to the edge, effectively blocking the next street from view and giving her a clear run.

Aly bolted from the jeep and took refuge behind two large dumpsters in the empty parking lot which belonged to the building on the corner, cowering behind as Noah roared away. The dumpsters were pushed together in a wide L-shape and the lamppost they were beneath had a broken light, which effectively let her hide in the darkness.

Aly held her breath as the car—and the shifters—following them screeched around the corner. For several heartbeats, the world seemed to slow down as she waited for the car to stop. Any second, they would spot her, they would see through his ruse and come for her. The tracker was on her, not the car. The alternative was as terrifying, the tracker was on Noah, not her, and he was in danger.

The car didn't stop. Instead, it raced after Noah and the jeep as it disappeared around down the road.

"Be safe," she whispered and curled up to stay hidden. The shifter sense died as the shifters left her range, but that feeling of safety felt fake to her and she refused to be drawn out of her hiding place.

Cars went by, taking no notice of her huddling in the dark by the stinking dumpsters. Flies buzzed and she could see a rat haunting the wall of the building, watching her with sharp eyes as it waited for her to move. The night air was chilly, so Aly rummaged around for one of Noah's long-sleeved shirts to wear.

Her shifter sense didn't flare. A car or two pulled into a small street not far, disappearing behind a closed store and the same cars exited a few minutes later. Aly guessed it was most likely a fast food place, or some other late night store, which was probably where Noah asked her to go.

Peeking around the edges of the dumpster, she took note of parked cars along the road Noah had disappeared, seeing if any were new, or had people loitering in them. She waited and watched for approximately fifteen anxious filled minutes before moving from the dumpsters.

As skittish as a deer, Aly edged out from behind the dumpsters and made sure their gear was firmly strapped to her back. She couldn't lose it now. Trying to look like she knew where she was going, she strode down the street.

The nest of stores held the late-night diner Noah spoke of. Not feeling like eating, she still went in and ordered something to nibble on while she waited. She perched on the edge of a booth, the backpack on the seat beside her and her arm looped through the strap and waited.

She tried to console herself that at least it wasn't a bar, but even so, there were several people inside the store who looked like they'd survived a night on the town. She hoped, with her large backpack and tired eyes, she looked touristy enough to only draw curiosity and not much else.

She didn't like this. She didn't like this at all. She was exposed and alone even among the scattered people in the diner.

She watched the entrance. Where was he? He was coming back, wasn't he? He wasn't going to use this as an excuse to split up.

Negative thoughts swirling in her mind and she hated their presence, but the longer she sat there, staring at the door, the more the negative thoughts accumulated.

"Here you go, doll," the waitress said, sliding a basket of fries and two milkshakes onto the table ahead of her. "Expecting company?"

Aly nodded and wrapped her hands around the milkshake, drawing the glass toward her. She really didn't feel like eating at the moment, but she knew Noah would be hungry when he arrived. If he arrived. Looking up at the waitress, she faked a smile. "Thank you."

Returning Aly's smile, the waitress said, "I'm sure they won't be much longer."

The bell to the door tinkled and Aly flicked her eyes to the door, then stared. "I'm sure she won't be."

Noah turned her head, brushed her long dark hair over her shoulder and gave Aly her best-lopsided smile.

CHAPTER 12

Lying in the back seat of the new hire car, Aly watched Noah drive. It was quite unnerving for her to see her—boyfriend?—girlfriend?—to see Noah in feminine form.

Noah had led those following on a wild goose chase through Salt Lake, which ended at the airport, where Noah had dumped the jeep and sauntered off in this new form. Those shifters following had been looking for an eighteen-year-old girl and a nineteen-year-old guy, not a woman in her late thirties by herself.

From a shifter perspective, no one could change that fast. No one could grow their hair that fast. So Noah's feminine form didn't even ring any alarm bells with them.

Noah had said that, upon exiting the airport with new car keys and a new hire car, the shifters, and mercenaries with them, were clustered around the jeep looking confused. Internally laughing, Noah had driven back to get Aly from the diner, and asked her to hide in the backseat while Noah drove, so it appeared that there was only one person in the car.

Noah drove, still in the woman's form.

It was so confusing. And weird. Aly didn't know what to make of it.

"Okay," Noah said, glancing back. "What?"

"Huh?" Aly replied, still stunned by the pitch of the voice.

"You're staring."

"Am not."

Noah scoffed. "You knew I could do this."

"Knowing and seeing are two... like... um... things."

"Say what you want to say."

Aly stared at Noah. "What?"

Focusing on the road, Noah rested an arm on the door. "I can see you're bursting with questions. Out with it."

"Why'd you have to make yourself so pretty?" she blurted.

Noah blinked and flicked her a glance and a smirk. "Questioning your sexuality, lovely?"

"It's unfair," she complained. "I'd have to work so hard to get long flowing locks like that, and you just... just grow it."

"I wanted to attract the right sort of attention. Guys notice pretty girls, but obviously, I can't be the pretty girl they're looking for, right?"

"And what about your boobs?" she complained.

"What?"

"Do they, like, do anything for you? Is that why they're so big?"

"Aly, what are you on about?"

She waved her hand in the air, then gestured her chest. "Cause, like, guys are always saying that if they got turned into a girl, that would be the first thing they'd check out and—"

Noah lifted an eyebrow and shot her an incredulous glance. "Do you really want to watch me grope myself?"

"No, but—"

"Boobs don't do anything for me. And what do you mean they're big? They're proportional to my body size." Noah peered down at her-his chest. "Are they big?"

"Do you change everything? Or is there... um..." her

eyes widened as she realized what she was asking. "Okay, no, don't answer that. I don't wanna know."

Noah snickered.

"Just let me know if you start craving chocolate. Or having mood swings. Or—"

That caused Noah to splutter. "I'm not going to be in this form long enough for that!"

"How am I supposed to know!" she complained. "I wasn't expecting you to do this!"

"You're the one making it weird!"

"No, I'm not!" she protested. "Change back."

"I can't, we're still too close to Salt Lake."

She groaned and covered her face with her hands. "It's not fair."

Noah let out a long-suffering sigh. "What's not fair?"

"You're too damn pretty."

"So?"

She huffed and stared up at the ceiling. "I think I may be bi." She tapped her fingers against her chest as she thought about that. "No. No, that can't be it. I'm... Fletcher-sexual. My handsome, dork of a boyfriend, who... happens to be able to turn into a very sexy girl."

"Looking to experiment?" Noah teased.

"Bite me."

"If it helps, I'm Aly-ace."

She rolled her eyes. "Oh. Ha-ha. You're enjoying this. Making me all confused."

"I'm really not." Noah hesitated and turned uncertain. "Is it really making you that uncomfortable?"

Aly sighed. "It's weird," she replied. "But no. I'm not uncomfortable."

"Weird how?"

She considered, lifting her hand to watch the headlights of other cars dance over her fingers. "You... you don't care what I look like," she said, after thoughtfully chewing her bottom lip.

"You're gorgeous."

She flushed. "Yeah, okay, but it doesn't matter. You're attracted to my personality."

"Yeah."

"Apparently, I… well… I mean it's not the right word? I guess? But I think I'm vain."

Noah glanced back. "You care about what I look like."

"Yeah. I think so… I mean, my fave form is Fletcher for sure. I prefer you in that one."

"Not surprised, really. That form feels like home to me."

Trying to be reassuring, she fumbled, "The other variants are cute, but this… Don't get me wrong, you're cute like this, but—gah, I don't know how to say it without being, like… insulting! Which is absolutely not what I'm trying to do, I'm trying to—"

"You prefer me as a guy."

She curled in on herself. "Is… is that okay? It feels like it should be wrong."

"If I chose to stay this way forever, you'd totally support me."

"Of course."

"But you couldn't date me."

"It's still you. No matter what form you take. I love you, boobs and all. It would… just take some getting used to, I think. I'm sorry, I'm not making much sense."

Noah smiled. "I think it is okay to prefer me as the sex I identify as."

She puffed out a breath.

"Political correctness can take a hike where shapeshifters are concerned," Noah reassured.

"For sure."

"But, if you want to experiment while I'm a girl, I'm open to it."

She kicked the back of Noah's seat. "You would tease me, Nina."

Noah laughed. "I thought it was Gertrude."

"I'm going to make sure that name sticks now, you

realize."

"Sure you will."

"Can you change back?"

"Not yet, but, if you close your eyes"—tingles spread across Aly's skin and Noah's voice changed, becoming deeper—"you can totally pretend."

Aly breathed a sigh and relaxed into the seat. "Thank you."

"Hey, since we have a bit of a breather, I was wondering if you'd explain something to me."

"Hmm?"

"Those 'flames' you mentioned? With the shifters?"

"Oh!" she said, almost sitting up before she remembered she was supposed to be hiding. "Yeah. It's like... I could see a flare inside them. A flame or something, that I can reach out and... touch. I can't see them when there's only one or two, but a group, they're pretty clear." She chewed her lip. "You... have one too. It's yellow and covered in sparkles, while a natural shifter's flame is red. And... Bonnie's and Ross' flames don't have sparkles. Just yours."

"Yellow, huh?" Noah said, taking the opportunity to tease. "There's a kind of poetry in that."

"I guess. I... I remember touching the flames before... you know when Rex said I took their abilities away. I think. It's confusing."

"Yeah." Noah made a noise of consideration. "I suppose, if you can see the flames, you might be able to control whose abilities you take away. Eventually. If that's the way it works."

"I don't know if I want to learn. It feels... wrong?" She scrunched up her nose. "When that car flipped before... I think I was reaching for a flame."

Noah made a noise in consideration. "That makes sense."

"Ross' flame," she clarified. "Maybe I brushed the driver's on the way. I don't know. It all feels pretty instinctual. Like... it's me doing it, but it's not me at the same time. I don't... it doesn't feel like I have a choice about it, it just happens."

"Ahh."

"Which means..." She hesitated, not wanting to voice it.

Noah shifted uncomfortably. "You could possibly take away my abilities if you felt so inclined."

She tried to gauge Noah's reaction to that, but it was difficult since she only got a partial side view of Noah's face. "Does that make you afraid of me?"

"Of you?" Noah clarified. "No. Never. You have an incredibly sweet and caring personality, Als, and combined with the fact I *know* you don't want to hurt anyone, I don't think you would ever use your ability to harm if you can help it." Noah hesitated, then braced. "I *am* very afraid of your ability falling into the wrong hands. Or... finding it duplicated in another Faceless."

Aly's eyes widened at the implications of that. "But... Echo Ten burned."

"As did every Ten before them," Noah confirmed. "But what about after? I don't know what happened to Foxtrot and your mother worked on them too."

Aly's mouth went dry and she squeaked in horror. "Oh no."

Noah stared straight ahead. "I don't know what we should do. If Adam's the leader of the renegades, then going to him will just put everyone at risk unless..."

"I'm isolated. Or you go in alone."

"Yeah." Noah heaved a huge sigh. "Starting to think that maybe... Rex had the right idea. Not *his* idea, not his place. But... like... hiding away somewhere. Away from people altogether."

"Run away completely?"

"Yeah."

"Is that what your gut is telling you?" she asked.

Noah puffed out a breath. "No. It's telling me that I

should've interrogated one of the shifters for information. That I need to find somewhere safe to… to leave you so I can go find out what's really going on without putting you in more danger. Which is why the 'run away' sounds so good."

She considered the events of the day and the way she was unabashedly left on the roadside while Noah dealt with those following. "Fletch, am I hobbling you?"

"No. Of course not—"

"You left me on the side of the road."

Noah shot her a confused glance. "I promised you I'd come back, it was just easier to dupe them with—"

She had to tell him how she felt. Even if it hurt him. No more secrets. "You don't know the kind of thoughts running through my head as you drove off. Especially since you already said you wanted to leave me."

Noah spluttered, "Oh. That's why—I… Aly, I don't—I *wouldn't*—I mean, I know I said—but I'm not going to *abandon* you."

Closing her eyes, she muttered, "Yeah. I know. Still hurts."

Noah's shoulders slumped. "You… you're handling everything so wonderfully, I keep forgetting you've never done this before. I've pulled that particular trick so many times, I forgot you hadn't and wouldn't know."

"It's… it's not about the trick. It made sense. It was clever and quick and made sense. It's… I was left out of the trick. I was"—thinking better, she chose a less accusatory way to say how she felt than 'cast out'—"asked to hide so you could deal with things. And I get it!" she hurried before he could protest that. "I'm not much use. I can't change my form. I slow you down and make you consider things you didn't have to before. If I wasn't here, you'd be long gone, and we both know it."

"Aly—"

She curled in on herself. "I hate feeling that you'd be better off without me. It hit home today, that's all."

"I don't want you to feel that way," Noah replied. "That wasn't my intent."

"I know." She sighed deeply. "It's stupid. I know it's stupid to feel this way and I'm trying not to."

"Telling me how you feel isn't stupid," Noah said, and something creaked, but Aly didn't open her eyes to see what it was. "I'm not going to abandon you. If I was actually serious about splitting up instead of talking out of my ass, I wouldn't do it off the back of a chase, we'd have a proper discussion about it."

She didn't reply.

"Cause we're so grown up. Communication and all that."

Aly snorted. "Yeah."

"Here," Noah said and Aly opened her eyes to see a Snickers being held out to her. "I had a feeling this would come in handy."

She laughed and accepted the offering and the implied apology that came with it. "So, now I'm fickle *and* vain."

"It's Snickers," Noah replied with a small shrug. "End of story."

"True."

"I'm serious, though. If it comes to us splitting up, it wouldn't happen on a whim. I promise."

She tore open the wrapping. "I know. I was just trying not to bottle. It's… it's been a fucked-up day."

"Ooh," Noah joked. "A swear. You mean business."

She took a bite and chewed slowly, savoring the taste. "Oh, this really does make me feel better."

"Good."

Sighing, she chewed and let her mind wander. "This war is never going to leave us alone, is it? Not with you being an incredibly powerful shifter and me being some sort of anti-shifter. I bet every side wishes we'd just vanish."

"Probably. Sounds like our best option. *If* they let us go, and I don't think they will."

She idly followed a train of thought. "Unless we took the fight to them. Go on the offensive. End the war so we could live free. We just have to make sure we're picking the right side."

"It's... our lives aren't some sort of movie, Als. There's no easy resolution."

"I don't want to live my life running. Today has just been completely terrifying," she said. "I can't live like this. And I know you don't want to either."

"No."

She stared through the window at the starry night sky. "I want... a degree and a home and a family and a job that I love and someone to share everything with."

"A family?" Noah squeaked. "Kids?"

She shrugged. "Kids. A dog. A hamster named Snickers. I dunno. But I want the *choice*. And I want you to have that choice too, Fletch."

Noah's tone went quiet, "What do you want to do?"

Aly mulled it over. "We're almost certain that Elaine is after us, right? Somehow she and Joseph can preempt us, which means that, most likely, she has some sort of tracking device on us that we haven't seen..."

Noah made a noise of agreement. "It's entirely possible. There's so many different designs and sizes for tracking devices now, or other ways to locate people. It'd be very easy to miss some—" Noah stopped, thought, then laughed. "You know, I wouldn't be surprised if she'd hid a tracker in that flash drive she gave me. Some of the trackers I've seen online are absolutely tiny, with batteries that last for ages because they only need to use charge when they're pinged."

Aly snorted. "That'd be right. Also, remind me to tell you what I found on there. I keep forgetting, and then stuff happens and... it's all a mess right now. I feel so trapped." Frowning, she hit on an idea that filled her with a burst of excitement. "Let's lay a trap for *them* this time."

Noah didn't look convinced. "Maybe."

"It could work!" she insisted. "If we—"

"I don't doubt that. But there's a couple of things I want to do first."

"Like what?"

Noah smiled, "A good night's sleep, for one. Plus, I want to see if we can practice this flame seeing ability."

She narrowed her eyes. "How are we—"

"On me."

That appalled her and her response was instant. Sitting up, she lunged for Noah's arm, clutching tightly. "No."

"Hear me out."

Horrified, she shook her head. "I *won't*—"

"I said *see*, not *touch*. If you can see mine, without any other shifters 'activating' it, then you can see Elaine's and Joseph's too. That means we'd know if you could defend yourself against them. Even if you could just... I dunno... grab their flames? Stop them in their tracks, that'd be something, right?"

"And what if simply *grabbing* their flames removes their abilities? What if—"

"You can... hold a fire, touch it, without snuffing it out," Noah pointed out.

"And get burned. This is a metaphorical flame I see in my head! I don't know what I'm doing with it, at all! I don't know that if I touch the flame a shifter loses their abilities, or what happens. I don't know how this works, and I'm not practicing on you!"

"I trust you," Noah said as though it was the simplest thing in the world.

"Not with this, you shouldn't. I don't know what I'm doing."

"I'd feel so much better if I *knew* you had some sort of defense against Faceless."

She sighed. "I... I don't trust myself with this. I really don't. But I'll think about it."

"Okay." Noah hummed in consideration. "If we're going to lay a trap, we can't get too far ahead, but we also need breathing room. Time to shower and sleep."

"Shower," Aly breathed out the word with an airy sigh, closing her eyes at the thought of it. "Yes please."

"Yeah, me too. So, we'll drive… hmm… till maybe one or two, find a place for breakfast, and then get a room. I'll get us as close to Seth and Solomon as I can, if that's what you still want to do."

"I think it's important."

"Yeah. Me too."

Aly pulled her seatbelt loose to give herself room and leaned through the gap between the seats so she could kiss Noah's cheek. Realizing her intention, Noah tilted so she could reach and Aly thought that only the fact Noah was still in feminine form stopped a turn of the head to kiss her.

Settling back in her chair, Aly let herself smile.

CHAPTER 13

Standing beneath the spray of the shower, Aly let the heat of the water wash over her and loosen travel-tightened muscles. Water trickled down from her hair and across her face and she closed her eyes to enjoy it.

There was still a strong chance they were being followed, but Noah swore he hadn't seen anyone following them. No one behaving erratically. No goose bumps of any kind. And even if there was someone, they'd probably be as tired as Noah and Aly were.

Leaving Elaine's flash drive in the hire car, in case of tracker, they'd parked across the other side of the town they decided to spend the night at, then walked to an out-of-the-way hotel in the hope no one would think to look for them there. They still couldn't be sure if Bonnie had a separate tracker on either of them, or if Ross had more, however Noah had started flagging and found it difficult to shift so they decided to endure it.

He had limits, like anyone, and was fast approaching his, especially after returning to a male form after being in a female one.

After an extraordinarily long day, and broken sleep for several nights in a row due to nightmares or insomnia, she was more than ready to indulge herself in an overly long, hot shower, and then collapse into bed.

The town had a McDonald's, for which they were both grateful, and Noah had bought almost a dozen different breakfast foods to inhale to replace his lost energy. After picking at her food and eating enough to please Noah, she'd had no desire to watch him eat, so went for the bathroom.

Once she was dressed, teeth cleaned and ready for bed, she headed out into the main room. Noah sat at the table, all trash packed neatly into one of the MacDonald's bags and using his cell.

Patting dry her hair with a towel, she said, "I expected you to be in bed already."

He glanced up and smiled. "Just checking a few things. I need to shower or I'll be pretty ripe later."

"And clean your teeth after all that food."

"That too."

"Feel better?" she asked as she sat on the edge of the bed.

"Immensely." He stood and stretched his arms over his head as he yawned. "Won't be long. Did you leave me hot water?"

She grinned at him. "Do I ever?"

It was so nice to sit on the edge of the bed and do something as simple and mundane as stretch her legs. Roll her ankles and wriggle her toes while trying to tame her hair. With its curl, she usually had a full routine of conditioning, combing and straightening before it was manageable, but she hadn't had it short for years. Since she didn't have a straightener or curl crème, it was going to fluff, especially since she was going to bed with it damp.

She'd finished by the time Noah finished in the bathroom. "That was quick," she said as he opened the door.

"Tired," he said, with a yawn to illustrate his point. Switching the light in the bathroom off, he wandered over to the bed and pulled back the covers. "Pillow fort a no-go tonight?"

Draping the towel over the back of a chair to dry, she went around to the other side of the bed. "Nah, it'll give you something to look forward to when you can actually enjoy it."

Noah blinked and hesitated, then gestured his shirt and boxers. "This okay to sleep in? I don't want to—"

"Seen you in less, Fletch," she told him and plopped down on the side of the bed she was going to use. Hoisting the blanket up to her hips, she said, "Just get in here."

With a sheepish smile and one last augment to check outside, he crawled into bed. "Wasn't thinking."

She rolled toward him, tucking both hands under her pillow. She closed her eyes when Noah switched off the light, then opened them back up to give them time to acclimate to the darkness.

Noah sighed, rolling onto his side and shuffling until his head was on the edge of the pillow and he was almost lying in the middle of the bed. She could feel the warmth of his body right beside her and, somehow, he had managed to wriggle there without bumping or touching her at all.

She closed her eyes, hoping that she'd be able to sleep tonight, that her brain would be able to calm itself enough that sleep was even possible. Noah was radiating warmth. Safe and comforting. He was here and that's all that mattered.

A tentative hand on her hip. "Hey, Als?"

Re-opening her eyes, she stared at his lump in the darkness. "Yeah?"

"Um..."

At his awkward silence, she prompted, "Is something wrong?"

"So," he squeaked, then cleared his throat to steady his voice. "This is an overly romantic... um... situation."

Aly blinked. "Does it make you uncomfortable?"

"Lil' bit."

"Pillow fort would make you more comfortable?" She made to sit up and was stalled by slight pressure from his hand on her hip. "I'm sure there's more pillows—"

"No," he blurted, and then laughed. "No. It's not that. It's…"

She waited. When he continued to say nothing, she prompted with, "It's what?"

"It's not a *bad* uncomfortable." He cleared his throat again. "I'd really… um… I'd like to kiss you goodnight, but I… I don't want to… um…"

"Oh," she said, then his predicament dawned on her. Two teens. Two teens in a relationship. Sharing a bed. It was the cliché situation all her favorite fanfictions were made of. Heat flooded her face at how slow she'd been. "Oh! *Duuuh.*"

Noah chuckled. "You're as tired as I am. Could practically hear the *clunk* your brain made as it started then."

"Shuddup," she said, tapping him on the chest, and then left her hand there. "Bumble-butt, you can kiss me for as long or as little as you like. You don't even need to ask me. I am a hundred percent okay with you just laying one on me whenever."

Noah snorted with humor.

"You're in control of that aspect of us, okay?"

"What about you?"

She lifted her shoulder to shrug. "If I wanna kiss you, then I'm going to." She smiled and allowed a single giggle. "Try and stop me."

"Um…" He shuffled. "Aly, I think there'll be days when I—um—would prefer not to."

Gripping his shirt, she tugged on it to make sure he understood and to show she understood him. "I'll keep it to pecks until I can read when they're welcome or not. *You* get to decide how long it's for."

"Oh."

"Neither of us are ready for anything more than kissing. Still very early days."

"Right."

"You know your boundaries better than I do and I'm not going to push you into anything."

"I just..." He sounded so uncertain as he fumbled his words. "I think—"

"You think too much," she said, trying to sound more confident than she was. Propping herself up on her elbow, she slid her hand up to his neck so she could find him in the dark. "Kissing isn't about thinking. It's... intimacy. Feeling." Smiling, she turned cheeky. "Ya feel me?"

He laughed as he propped himself up too, then slipped the hand on her hip across to her back to pull her closer. "I feel you."

It was dark and only one of them could augment to have a form of night vision, so she had to seek his lips with little brushes of hers against his face until she found them. The sudden whoosh of breath he made when their lips touched was a lot more sensual than she had anticipated.

The butterflies in her stomach sighed in delight, fluttering away in a pleasant daze as Noah's lips parted to allow for a little deeper of a kiss. He wasn't hesitant in the way he moved his mouth against hers, but he didn't rush either. It was a big step from the simplicity of pressing their lips together and she was thrilled that he wanted to take his time to learn and discover.

This was... a lingering and a tasting. The sort of kisses that stirred a whirlpool of love and happiness deep inside her. The sort she wanted to savor forever. Uncertain and clumsy and wonderful. They weren't in sync with each other, but it didn't matter. Skill and confidence would come with practice, she was certain of that.

She dusted her fingers along his spine. As eager as she was, she had to let him lead the way at a pace he was comfortable with.

He radiated heat, it seeped into her from every place they touched. She wanted to snuggle down in that warmth and stay there forever. His hand on her back flexed, then moved up to the bottom of her ribs. A soft noise of surprise burst from her as he dragged her closer and tilted his head, nudging forward. Interpreting the gesture, she let her head drop back onto the pillow. Since he supported his weight on his elbow, and her other hand was now free, she slipped it under him so she could use both hands to cuddle him.

Tucked up against him, enveloped in that amazing heat, her head spun from the contact and that seemed silly to her. This was Fletcher, her dorky Fletcher and she'd known him for absolutely forever, so how could he make her feel like she was free-falling? Spinning out of control in a tumble she never wanted to end.

He retreated from her lips and she mourned their loss while he rubbed his nose along hers. There was a hitch to his breath and his voice was husky when he spoke. "That okay?"

She puffed out a giggle, unable to help it. "More than."

"I... ah... I kind of want to keep—ah—" The yawn caught him by surprise and he turned his head to keep from yawning in her face.

She understood. "Today's catching up on you."

"Yeah. I think so."

She clasped his shirt, not ready to let him go. "Can we snuggle?"

"You wouldn't mind?"

"Nope," she said and stifled a yawn of her own. "You're so warm. It's nice."

He settled down, then realized her arm was beneath him and lifted up long enough for her to remove it. Curling up against the side of her body, he rested his head on the pillow next to hers. "Love you," he murmured.

She pressed her lips to whatever part of his face she

could reach. "Night Fletch."

Waking because of a car horn, Aly was surprised to find it almost nine. Almost six hours of sleep and no nightmares. No nightmares, and no dreams that she could remember. Perhaps she was simply too exhausted to dream.

She felt warm and lazy as she stroked her fingers along the arm draped across her belly. He hadn't moved much during the night and was now making cute little Noah breaths against her neck. He looked so innocent and sweet like this. Peaceful.

She looked toward the curtained window, arguing with herself. A large part of her knew she should get up and look outside to make sure they weren't being surrounded. A louder part of her said that it was warm, she was comfortable and safe and should stay.

Sighing, she toyed with Noah's fingers, then slowly lifted his arm so she didn't disturb him and slipped from the bed. There didn't seem to be anyone she could see by peeking through a tiny gap in the window, so she went to the bathroom to freshen up.

Noah was still asleep when she came out and instead of climbing back into bed with him—and give in to the desire to sleep some more—she sat at the table, pulled out her sketch pad and started sketching Noah.

No real reason behind her decision to draw him, other than it occupied her mind and her hands and kept her from thinking too hard about other things.

He wanted her to see the flames. Ideally, she could use the flames in shifters and Faceless to protect herself. Except that she had no real idea of how she saw them to begin with, only that they appeared when there were multiple shifters around. They hadn't been there for Rex at all. Or the shifters she'd seen before that. She really didn't know what she was looking for.

So she sketched the mound of sleeping boyfriend stretched out on the bed. It was interesting to play close attention to this form, instead of Fletcher's, and discover what changes he'd made and how intricate a shift really was. And how similar it was in the ways that mattered to Aly the most.

When she had a basic form, she pulled out a yellow pencil and drew a flame in the center of his chest. Tiny and yellow, a candle lick of flame covered in sparkles.

Nothing happened, which made her laugh at herself. What had she been expecting? To magically be able to feel his flame? It seemed to activate in the presence of the goose bumps, and since she had none, did she even have a hope of seeing it? She picked up her pencil again to add more definition to Noah's body.

Since all this had started—since Rex strolled toward her door and she'd freaked and run—she hadn't had a chance to free-draw. Hadn't really wanted to either, since there hadn't been any point anymore. But the time to herself, doing something that she loved, was relaxing. Therapeutic. She hummed to herself, concentrating on Noah's form.

He rolled onto his stomach and hugged a pillow beneath his head. Smiling, Aly began a new page with his new pose.

"Whatcha doing?"

She glanced up, seeing his eyes open. "Drawing you like one of those French girls."

He laughed, a sleepy yet happy sound, and rubbed his eye. "Do I need to pose?"

"Sure," she chirped in reply. "Can you pull off Deadpool's sexy look?"

"Alas," he lamented, "no one is as sexy as that."

Aly giggled. "Shame."

He yawned and scratched his head, then settled down on the pillow to watch her. "What are you really doing?"

"Doodling your butt."

His head came up and he stared at her. "Really?"

"Did you think I was lying? I'm drawing you."

"Why?"

Aly shrugged. Flipping over another page, she drew a cartoony butt that took up the entire page, then showed it to him. "See?"

He laughed. "You flipped the page."

"Your butt needed an entire page," she quipped. "You're very ass-thetically pleasing."

"You're ridiculous," he said, still laughing.

Giggling, she flipped back the page and continued on the doodle she'd been working on.

A tingle flittered across her skin, like a lover's good morning kiss. Since it felt like an augment, she assumed he was checking on their surroundings, and she didn't bother to look up.

Noah cleared his throat in a way that suggested he wanted her to look.

Aly glanced up and burst into rambunctious laughter. Noah lay there with his rear ballooned to almost three times its size, wearing a shit-eating grin.

"Oh my god!" she crowed, laughing so hard her sketchpad was knocked to the floor. "That's booty-licious!"

"Perks of being a shifter," he said, pleased.

She held out a hand in front of her, mock-shielding her sight from him. "I am too pure," she complained. "Please, do not bestow that disgrace upon innocence such as I."

"Butt-stow," he said with a wink. "And pure? Puh-lease. I've *seen* your 'anatomy practice'."

Aly allowed her eyes to blow wide so she could tease him. "Oooh."

"No," he responded, his cheeks reddening and his eyes everywhere but on her. "Nope. Not happening."

"I could—"

"Nope."

Aly giggled and bent down to pick up her sketchbook from the floor. "Fine, ruin my fun."

Noah watched her and she could see he was trying to

think of a way to ask her about her better mood. She did feel better than she had yesterday, and she hoped that was because of the dreamless sleep and snuggles. That had been awesome, and she hoped he'd want to do it again.

Then, he glanced at the clock and surged upward, scrambling from the bed. "Damn it."

"What?" she asked, startled. "What's wrong?"

He augmented, both returning to normal size and changing his eyesight to scout outside. "It's later than I wanted," he said as he turned in a slow circle. "Can you pack up? We'll head out as soon as possible."

"I forgot," she said, closing up her sketchpad and getting to her feet. "I'm sorry."

He waved his hand, dismissing her apology while he rummaged in the clothing bag. "No. Not your fault. My internal alarm usually works a lot better than that."

"You were pretty exhausted."

He ducked his head, embarrassed. "More… comfortable than exhausted," he admitted.

"Oh," she replied, hopeful. "Really?"

"You're very comfy. Would… would you mind if we did that again?" he asked, looking awkwardly at everything else in the room beside her. "Sharing a bed, I mean."

Since being cuddled had helped her mood improve as well, she chirped happily, "Sure. I'd like that."

"Okay. Good," he said with a sharp nod then escaped into the bathroom.

She stared at the closed door for a moment, then, with a blush dusting her cheeks, she smiled.

By the time he came out again, she'd packed everything up, gotten changed and was sitting on the bed tying her shoes. Noah bounced across the bed and hugged her from behind. "Forgot to say good morning."

Giggling, she touched his arm and curled her back into his chest. "Good morning."

With a smacking kiss on her cheek, he bounded away again. "You ready?"

"Just about. Gotta steal the toiletries," she said and went for the bathroom where she'd left the hair clip Bonnie had given her and her bumblebee necklace.

"You hoarder."

"Absolutely," Aly said, reaching for her jewelry. After putting on her necklace, she fluffed her hair and pinned it back with the clip. As she did so, the blue pentagram gem fell from the clip and into the sink. Aly scrambled for it, catching it right before it fell down the drain. "Dang it."

"What's wrong?" Noah called.

"Broke my…" Aly frowned, then peered closer at the gem. "Hey, Fletcher?"

"Yeah?"

Exiting the bathroom with the gem in the palm of her hand, she extended it out to him. "Is this what I think it is?"

He looked at her, then her hand, then augmented. "Where'd you get that?"

"It was in the hair clip Bonnie gave me."

His eyes darted up to her hair, then back down to the gem.

"Bonnie told me it was a tool. Knife and screwdriver and all that. It sounded like a good idea."

Noah lifted the gem up to the light. "It is. I should've thought of giving you a tool like that. Would've been handy."

She peered closer. "It's so tiny. Seriously, they can be this small?"

"Apparently so," Noah replied, with a frustrated noise. "Dropped the ball on that one, didn't I?" he said, sounding frustrated and angry at himself.

She touched his arm to offer her support. "If she's been tracking us, why hasn't she, like, acted?"

"I don't know," Noah replied.

Aly thought about what Bonnie had said the last time they'd spoken. About how being by Aly's side was one of the most dangerous places right now, but also might be answers. "Do you think maybe she wants to see where we go?"

"Maybe." He stepped back and turned slowly in a circle. "I can't see anyone acting suspiciously. Doesn't mean that we're not being monitored. I just can't see them."

"Means that they're not close. And we'll have warning."

"Yeah." Looking back at her, he smiled. "What's the plan, boss?"

Aly shoved him as she pondered. "We could lay a trap for her too. Go to some hard to reach place and leave Elaine's drive and Bonnie's gem and see what happens... and not Seth's grave. Like..." she snapped her fingers. "We post them! Send them away and take a different route, then watch the address we post them to!"

"Good idea." Noah rubbed his chin, then burst into a grin. "Aaaaand... and... and I think I might have the perfect place." He glanced around again, tingles tickling her skin. "Load up your laptop. We'll plan now while we have a chance. Once we leave this room, we'll be exposed and we want to know where we're going before we have to make a break for it."

CHAPTER 14

Grace trudged along the dirt path. She ran her fingers across the outcropping of rocks beside it so that sandstone dusted the tips, then brushed the dirt clean on her jeans. Glancing at the position of the sun, she wondered how hot it would get. Dawdling behind the other three, she tried to figure out why, exactly, they were hiking in the middle of nowhere.

Joseph had given no explanation for his abrupt departure from the store yesterday and when she returned with her purchases she found him in a heated argument on the phone with someone and Elaine practically glued to her laptop.

Del could offer no explanation either at their behavior beyond suggesting that something had happened. He'd sat in the corner of the room and watched them carefully, offering no clues to his thoughts.

She'd woken in the middle of the night to overhear a muted conversation between Joseph and Elaine, but she hadn't been able to make much sense out of it. Something about a 'loop' and 'back at the beginning' and pondering about 'why was he there?'

'There', Grace supposed, was where they were

currently climbing to. 'He' was most likely Noah, but that's all she could glean. Why they'd waited until nearly midday before coming out here, she didn't know.

She hated all these secrets.

Sighing, she combed her fingers through her long hair, then twisted it up into a knot on the back of her head to keep it off her neck. She wished she had some of her hair clips or pins, but all she had was one tie. Why did they think it was a good idea to walk in the desert, in the summer, in the middle of the day?

Del glanced back at Grace, his face an impassive mask. Pausing in his walk, he waited until she reached him. Offering his hand to help pull her up a larger step in the path, he said, "You okay?"

Grace nodded, taking his much-needed offer of balance. "Are you?" she returned. "You've been so quiet the last few days."

"It's a lot to take in," Del replied.

"Yeah, I hear that."

He snorted out a laugh. "And you said it wasn't like one of my fantasy games."

"Yeah, yeah," she said, waving her hand at him. "I was wrong. But seriously, how do those games end? The protagonist somehow magically obtains powers and bests the villain at their own game. Neither of us are shifters—"

"That you know of," Del replied, trying to give off an air of mysteriousness.

"Which makes us the plucky sidekicks," Grace countered, ignoring him. "And you know what happens to them. We can't just download cheat codes and make ourselves invincible. This is real."

Thrusting his hands into his pockets, Del hunched his shoulders and didn't reply.

"I hate that I didn't realize it wasn't Aly," Grace said softly. The feeling had been burying its way into her stomach for days and now tumbled out. "I hate that I overlooked so much, thinking it was just because of amnesia."

"I hate that I let Noah in so much, so fast," Del replied, acknowledging her feelings with a nod. "We took our cues from that fake Aly and we were wrong. I've never felt so helpless. Or so angry."

"I've been calling her 'Alike' in my head," Grace told him.

Del snorted out a laugh. "Fitting."

"Do you think maybe Aly is here? Maybe that's what we're doing out here? Secret base?" Grace suggested, only half-joking. "Some sort of nefarious underground building? Maybe there's a quest item."

"The possibilities are endless," Del replied with a smile. "But, I mean, logistically, we're in a national park, right? They couldn't build something on here. People would stumble on it all the time."

"Who knows?" Grace said with a shrug. "Bunker or underground base? Maybe they've got people in all forms of government. People in high places, that sort of thing. I mean Area 51 is here in Nevada, who's to say there aren't other secret bunkers scattered around."

"A super-secret society of shifters." He puffed a chuckle. "The S-S-S-S's. Yeah, that sounds about right."

"They sound like a snake."

"Sneaky snakes," Del retorted and Grace was glad he seemed to be in a playful mood. It was a change from the somber, withdrawn mood he'd been in the last few days. "Sneaky snakes in sneakers. Sneaky snake shapeshifters wearing sneakers—"

As one, Joseph and Elaine stopped in the middle of the path and turned to stare at Del.

Halting, Del stared back and lowered his voice, "They're too far away to hear me, right?"

Since the bland, staring expression on Elaine and Joseph's faces were disturbing, Grace whispered, "Maybe 'es' carries?"

"I'm starting to get a 'dig our own grave' vibe," Del

returned and Grace couldn't tell if he was joking or not.

Grace, not really sure what else to do, started walking again. "You have an overactive imagination. They need our help and we need theirs."

"If we're walking to our own grave, I'm coming back to haunt you."

"It was your idea to go with them, Del," Grace retorted.

Del made a huffy noise. "You agreed."

"Only to keep you out of trouble. You're so quick to believe this is all some sort of conspiracy."

"And you don't believe it?"

Grace shrugged. "I don't know what to believe anymore, not when you add shapeshifters into the mix. I just want Aly back."

"When you two are finished chattering," Elaine called waiting impatiently further down the path. "We don't have all day."

"Perhaps it would go faster if you told us why we're here," Del called back and made no effort to increase his walking speed.

Elaine lifted her shoulders in a shrug. "Noah was here yesterday."

"Here?" Del questioned, scathingly. "In the middle of absolutely nowhere? Is this where Aly is being held?"

"We don't know. It's possible it was a drop point somewhere here, or he was meeting someone. Which is why we're looking," Joseph answered. "He's still in the vicinity, which means, if it's a drop point, he might be waiting for an answer."

"Keep your eyes out for something that doesn't belong," Elaine said, waving her hand to gesture the surroundings. "Any sort of trash, or color which doesn't belong or marker or something like that."

Grace and Del exchanged a glance as they continued along the path.

"What gets me," Del muttered as low as he could, "is

why they need our help. We're not part of their world, surely they could do this on their own."

"Probably to convince Aly that it's safe. That they're safe. I imagine she's probably scared out of her mind, not knowing who to trust, 'specially cause, like, *shapeshifters*. Once we prove it's us… and not…" A thought dawned and blood drained from her face. "Oh God, what if she was being tortured? Made to believe some other shifter was us? She could—"

"Now who has an overactive imagination," Del replied as he gripped her shoulder, then slung his arm around her so he could tuck her against him as they walked. "Gracie, she'll be okay."

"She's been gone such a long time," Grace replied and sniffled. "What if—"

"Shh," Del said and pressed his cheek to her head. "If she's not okay, we'll help her *be* okay. Aly's strong and together we're stronger. She'll be okay."

Sighing, she leaned into him for comfort. "I'm glad you're here."

"Wouldn't wanna be anywhere else right now," Del replied. "Do you buy this story about her birth father?"

"Dunno," Grace mumbled. Del hadn't been so talkative in the last few days and Grace had bottled a lot of things she was feeling and wanted to talk to him. Now she had the chance, a lot of her worries had tumbled out, but this one was one of her greatest. "Aly never said anything about him. But, like, I can't see any other reason why she'd be somehow important to them. None of this makes much sense. It feels… it feels like there's holes in their story somehow, but I can't see them."

"True. I've literally been getting that feeling as well."

"Literally?" she asked, feeling relieved. It had been a while since he'd used that word and it made Grace feel like things could be okay again.

A ghost of a grin. "Literally." The smile died as fast as it arrived. "I just… I worry that they're not going to let us take her home."

Grace nodded. "Yeah. Me too."

Studying Elaine and Joseph, Del said, "Do you reckon they can shift more than their skin?"

"What?"

"Think about it. They keep on saying that shifting is literally skin deep, right? But we saw Elaine shift her facial structure and, I dunno, it seemed *more* than skin. Like she shifted her skull shape too. Her nose and her ears, that's cartilage, right? And she changed that so what else can they do? What if they could change their hearing?"

That filled Grace with a sense of dread. "You think they heard you before?"

"Yeah. I do. There might be no limit to what they can change."

Elaine jerked to a stop ahead of them and for a heartbeat, Grace actually believed they'd heard what she and Del were talking about.

"What?" Joseph asked and his demeanor completely changed. He became on high alert, his eyes darting around, passing over Grace and Del like they were invisible, to look at something beyond.

"The first marker," Elaine said and broke into a run. "It's been moved!"

"What?" Joseph blurted and darted after her.

"First marker?" Grace asked as she started running after Elaine.

Del shrugged and gave her an 'I don't know' noise.

The 'marker' turned out to be an oddly shaped rock; sort of curved into the shape of a c, with the top of it having rivets that reminded Grace of a turtle shell. What she didn't understand was how Elaine had seen it at such a distance, as Grace hadn't seen it until she'd gotten a lot closer. Maybe Del was right. Maybe it was more than skin.

Joseph seemed bewildered as he tried to calm the pacing Elaine down. "Why would—"

"How *dare* he?!" Elaine exclaimed. "Did he think we

wouldn't notice?"

"Maybe this is why he looped?" Joseph suggested. "Lead someone away, and came back so he could check out why it was moved?"

"Don't try and explain him," Elaine snapped. "He's different than you remember. He must've moved it."

Scrambling closer, Grace pounced on that bit of information. "You *know* Noah? Like, *know* him, know him? I thought—"

Joseph cast a glance at her over his shoulder, then looked at Elaine, who glowered at the strange, turtle-shell speckled rock and ignored everything else. "We worked together once," Joseph replied. "Not anymore. Now he's rogue and needs to be brought back to face what he's done."

"Worked how?" Del asked. "What is it that shifters do?"

Joseph laughed. "Same thing as everyone else. We try to survive. Earn money. That sort of thing."

"Fine," Del muttered, disgruntled. "But you said you *worked* with Noah. Doing what?"

Joseph sighed. "Noah's a hitman."

A slice of fear chilled Grace. A hitman? And Joseph worked with him? What did that make Joseph?

Del moved so he was half-shielding Grace from view. "And what does that make *you?*" he snarled, echoing Grace's thoughts.

With a growl, Elaine clenched her fists. "I swear, if he's desecrated her grave, I will kill him."

"Grave?" Del asked, his voice cracking in the middle. "There's a *grave* now?" He stepped backward, away from the pair, bumped into Grace and forced her to retreat with him. "What grave? *Who's* grave?"

Grace gripped Del's arm, keeping him close. Her mind whirled straight to the worst possible scenario. What if it was Aly's grave?

Elaine and Joseph exchanged a look and the stone in

Grace's belly sunk even further from their expressions. Elaine tilted her head at Joseph, who nodded.

"It's odd," a voice announced. "How much you all cling to the concept of family, and yet all you do is lie to one another."

Gasping, Grace spun toward the voice.

Sitting on some boulders about twenty feet away, a woman brushed her fingers along the dehydrated branches of a shrub. Her knees were bent up toward her chest, she appeared unassuming and non-threatening, an oddity in itself. In a pale blue shirt and jeans, with her curly brown hair cropped short, her eyes seemed old and tired, and her face looked gaunt, like she hadn't been eating or sleeping right. It took a long moment before Grace recognized her. "Aly?"

Was it really her? Did she escape? Or was it the Not-Aly shifter? Grace didn't know, couldn't tell.

Aly sat up straight, pulled her hand out of her lap and extended a hand toward them. "Stay. Or he'll shoot you."

Grace's eyes widened and Del gulped. "What?" It wasn't her. It wasn't their Aly. It was the imposter.

Alike's head jerked in a shake. "Not you, Grace. Joseph and Elaine. Grace, you and Del, get over here."

Grace gaped at her. "How—" Del grabbed Grace's arms, dragging her out of the line of fire and, as Grace turned her head, both Elaine and Joseph had drawn guns and aimed at Alike. But instead of pulling her toward Alike, Del pulled them both to the side, putting distance between them.

Alike's brow creased. "You guys okay?" she blurted. "Did they hurt you?"

Grace had enough time to nod before Joseph demanded, "Where's Noah?"

"Currently swearing at me," Alike replied with a smile. "He's probably debating whether or not to move from his sniper position and come rescue me."

"I can't hear him," Joseph replied.

"We don't need super hearing to communicate." She turned her head and said mildly, "I'm *fine*, bumble-butt. Promise. If they were gonna kill me, they would've done it already. They need me for something." Raising her head, she fixed her eyes back on Joseph. "Isn't that right?"

Bumble-butt. That was what Aly used to call Fletcher when he was being ridiculous. It was strange to hear it now. The stiffness in Del's shoulders indicated he'd heard it too and felt the same way she did.

Joseph and Elaine said nothing, so Alike pressed on. "I'm so very tired of all this cloak and dagger bullshit, especially when you start threatening my friends to get at me. So," she chirped, looking entirely too happy with the situation. "We're gonna talk."

Elaine started, "What do—"

"Not you," Alike responded, the mild expression slipping to a scowl. "Joseph. You can shut right up, Elaine. I haven't forgotten that I owe you two bullet holes."

Grace's stomach sank. This definitely wasn't Aly. Aly would never joke about guns or shooting someone.

Joseph's face was steel as he stepped forward so he was ahead of Elaine. "What do you want?"

"Answers. Just like you." She waggled her hand at Joseph. "Judging by your reactions, you didn't move the markers."

"No." Joseph frowned. "And you didn't either."

Del and Grace exchanged a worried glance and Del wrapped one arm around Grace's shoulder.

Alike shook her head. "Before you ask, we did go and find their real grave. It's still there, right where it's supposed to be. It's just the markers that have been moved."

"He found the tracker," Elaine muttered to Joseph. "It's the only explanation."

"Yup," Alike chirped in the tone similar to the one Aly used when she one-upped someone in a game. "We did. So, care to share what's really going on?"

"Nothing that concerns you," Joseph said.

"Oh, bullshit," Alike said with a toss of her head. "I'm a *game-changer*. Those were your exact words. So, I'm going to ask you one question and I'd better like the answer or I'm out of here and I'm taking Del and Grace with me."

Elaine rocked her weight from side to side. "I'd like to see you try."

"We'll disappear," Alike snapped with a scowl. "He did it once, he can do it again. So, no more blackmail. No more chasing. You have one chance."

Joseph stepped toward her. "What's the question?"

Alike lifted her chin. "Who do you work for?"

Joseph and Elaine remained silent.

Alike pursed her lips. Hopping from the boulder, she gave a wave. "All you had to do was answer. So, I'm out. Del, Grace, come with me. I'll get—"

"We need your help to infiltrate Welcher's faction," Elaine blurted.

Alike stopped, her arms flopping to her sides before she slowly turned back to face Elaine. "No, you don't. You want the Welcher's faction eliminated. Or Darcy does, cause you work for her."

Grace's stomach churned and her palms dampened. Beside her, Del gulped and his hands tightened on Grace's arms. Eliminate. Like kill. Was Alike a hitman too? Did that mean that Aly was dead? She breathed out Aly's name, a long mournful tone under her breath.

Elaine frowned at Alike. "We don't work for Darcy."

"Uh-huh."

Joseph patted the air in front of Elaine as if to say he'd handle it. "We didn't know you would work that fast. It was supposed to be a slow release. We never expected—"

Alike frowned. "You've seen someone with this... whatever it is... before."

Joseph and Elaine met each other's eyes, then Elaine looked out toward the scrub. "We've never seen a natural at work."

"A natural," Alike echoed, wrinkling her nose, then her eyes blew wide. "A Ten survived?"

Anger in Elaine now. "He *told* you?" She spun on Joseph. "How did he know about the Tens?"

Joseph shook his head, saying nothing.

Staring in utter confusion, Grace wished she knew what they were talking about. She watched a bead of sweat trickle down Del's cheek and knew he felt the same. This could go so wrong in so many ways, they needed to be ready to move.

Alike tilted her head, and then curled a strand of hair back over her ear. It was too short to stay and blew into her face again. "I know a lot more than you think I do," she said and tossed her head. "I can guess the rest. You expected that the Welcher's would take me. You expected that Noah would stay with me, because he's Noah. I was going to infect the Welcher's faction or family or whatever, and then... you'd walk right in and take whatever it was you wanted?"

A twisted conversation which, for all Grace knew, revealed everything and nothing. Names and words and meanings she didn't understand, and yet Alike was getting the answers she desired.

"We expected Noah to run," Elaine said. "Like he always has."

Alike clenched her hands into fists and took a limping step forward. "Except that you *shot* me," she spat. "You knew that if he didn't heal me, I'd die."

"No, I would've—"

Alike laughed scathingly. "Oh, I get it. Shoot me, then rush in and save the day while Noah runs. Perfect way to get me to trust you and be grateful." She scoffed, a harsh sound. "You forced Faceless shifter DNA into a toxin. That's *never* supposed to mix. Do you even know what's going to happen to me?"

Elaine frowned.

"She's lying," Del murmured. "If she was shot so bad

that she would've died, she wouldn't be standing now."

Grace nodded in agreement.

"Even *if* I didn't work so fast," Alike snarled. "The Welchers would still have their resources and numbers, and what would Darcy have to gain by—"

Grace gasped and covered her mouth with her hand as connections appeared in the forefront of her mind. The people in the park. The ones who died. The ones who Joseph and Elaine talked about. 'Slow infection' and 'She worked fast', that's what they'd said.

Alike had killed them. With some sort of toxin. She'd all but admitted it.

"How can you be so blasé about killing all those people?" Grace blurted. "What kind of monster are you?"

Alike jerked as though she'd been slapped and her head swiveled to Grace. "What?"

"You heard me. People *died* because of you and you look like you don't even care!"

"They died?" Alike blurted, her eyes darting from Grace, to Elaine, and off to the wilderness. "I—I—I didn't—you didn't tell"—her gaze flicked back and landed on Grace—"No. No. They lied. They had to lie. Grace, I didn't—"

Grace took a single step toward Alike and clenched her hands into fists. "Where is she? What have you done with her, you *evil* bitch."

Face ashen, Alike took a step back. "What? Who?"

"You know who," Grace snarled. "You *replaced* her."

"You think"—Alike shook her head hard enough to make her hair bounce, then snapped her eyes to Elaine— "You told them I was a shifter? You told them about shifters to begin with—no," she continued, looking back at Grace. "*I'm* Aly!"

Grace scoffed. "Like I'm gonna believe—"

"I swear!" Alike blurted insistently. "Look, I can prove it, we used to—"

"I am not going to believe anything that comes from

your mouth. We know all about you! How you stole our Aly, how you can duplicate her drawing style and fake enough of her memories—did you torture her to get the information?"

"No, I didn't," Alike told her, her hands steepled on her chest while something akin to betrayal flitted across her features. "I'm Aly!"

"We're not going to believe anything you say," Del said, hands clenched into fists. "We know the truth."

"What have you got to gain by turning my friends against me?" Alike demanded of Elaine and Joseph. "This gets you nothing! All it does is make me trust you even less!"

"We're not your friends," Grace snapped. "Where is our Aly? What have you done with her?"

"I haven't done anything to her," Alike all but whined.

"Is she dead?" Del asked.

"What are you trying to do?" Alike asked Elaine and Joseph.

"Did you kill her?" Grace demanded, steeling herself against the fake tears coming from the fake Aly. She wasn't going to let herself be swayed by someone who tried to replace her best friend.

Still talking to Joseph and Elaine, Alike wailed, "Are you hoping to alienate me so much you think I'll have nowhere else to turn? I am *never* going to trust you."

"We don't need your trust," Joseph said. "Just your abilities."

Completely fed up and wanting answers, Grace gathered her voice and demanded as loud as she could, "Where is Alyson Gale?"

Alike snapped her eyes to Grace. "Alyson Gale is dead!"

CHAPTER 15

Grace sucked in a gasp of breath and clutched at her chest as Alike's words hit her like a physical blow. Her head spun and her heart raced.

"What?" Del whispered, his voice cracking.

Alike thrust up a hand and stabbed a finger at Elaine. "*She* killed Aly in a park at Lake Tahoe."

"You can't be serious," Grace said, her chest so tight it was hard to draw breath. "You're lying." She didn't want to believe it, couldn't believe it. Aly wasn't dead. She wasn't. Elaine killed her? *Elaine*? They were in Lake Tahoe a few days ago. Was it possible? What was going on?

Grace clawed at her face, and locked eyes with an equally devastated Del. His hand shaking, Del touched Grace's shoulder, a soft, gentle nudge and Grace turned to envelop him in a hug. Pressing her cheek to his chest, she switched between watching Alike, and Joseph and Elaine, trying to make sense of it all.

"There's nothing for you here. Go home, before you end up dead too." Stiff-shouldered, Alike turned away.

"No, lovely. Don't do that to yourself."

Alike appeared to crumple as a man strode out onto the path a short distance away. With a small, Aly-esque wail, she threw herself at the man and buried her face in his chest. One arm wrapped around her, the other held a short, but deadly-looking shotgun out toward Elaine and Joseph.

"Hello, Noah," Joseph called, sounding unconcerned. "Nice to see you again."

Del's clutch on Grace turned fierce. "You," he growled. "You stole his face."

He didn't look like the Noah she remembered. In fact, he looked more like Fletcher than ever before. Taller and broader shoulders and a lot more muscular, but the face was so startlingly familiar. Different, and yet... not. Unexpected for sure.

"Hello, my darlings," Noah replied with a nod at Elaine and Joseph, although his eyes flicked between the four of them. "That form suits you, Joseph. I'm glad you found one that fit."

Joseph preened and dusted the front of his shirt with his fingers. "Thank you."

Grace frowned at the almost cordial conversation. It sounded like they were catching up, not enemies. Neither Joseph nor Elaine seemed particularly perturbed by the shotgun or the rifle on Noah's back.

"Although, maybe a wrinkle or two, or a blemish would help. We're supposed to hide, not dance around and say 'look at me, I'm so pretty'."

Elaine snickered and relaxed her stance. "He's got you there."

"Ditched Bonnie and Ross already?" Joseph replied, with a mocking shake of his head. "How like you."

Noah lifted one shoulder. "They sold us out. I don't think you can blame us for not sticking around."

Joseph's smirk grew wider. "You just inspire loyalty, don't you?"

"They sold each other out too," Noah replied. "So, yeah. I'm not having a bar of any of you right now. I'll take Del and Grace with me when I go and then we're going to disappear unless you can give me one reason to stay."

Del snarled, "We're not going with—"

"I'm the one with the gun," Noah said, his tone mild. "Yes. You are."

Shocked, Del took a step back, dragging Grace with him.

"Adam needs to talk to you," Elaine said.

"Adam has always had a way to contact me," Noah replied. "And instead, I get news that he *died*. Which *you* confirmed. And then Ross and Bonnie said he was alive. So, forgive me for being skeptical."

Joseph said, "Adam needs you to come in."

"No. If Adam wants me, he can find me himself."

Elaine growled. "You just said you were going to disappear—"

Noah shrugged. "Follow your tracker. In a week, if I feel amenable, I'll pick it up and you'll be able to find me again. If Adam really wants to talk, and this isn't some game of Darcy's, he better be there. Otherwise..." He waved and flashed them a lopsided smile. "Sayonara."

"You'd abandon us again?" Joseph snarled. "Typical."

"I had a great life," Noah snarled back. "Good friends, a home, a family. I was happy, do you have any idea how hard that was to achieve? That was all torn away from me, and both of you are wrapped up in why it was taken. So yes. I'm gone." He nudged Alike and she lifted her head from his chest. "We're gone." Looking toward Del and Grace, Noah gestured with his shotgun. "Let's get moving."

Grace tried defiance and was pleased her voice didn't wobble. "We're not going with you."

Alike stepped away from Noah and wandered over to the rock she'd been sitting on, while Noah leveled the shotgun at Elaine and Joseph with two hands. "I'm not messing around."

Terrified, Grace's eyes were fixated on the gun, and her feet were anchored to the ground, unable to move.

"I told you he was dangerous," Joseph called, smug.

"Oh *please*," Alike snapped, and her voice, while husky from tears, was confident. She reached down and retrieved a hidden backpack. "With three of you playing 'who's a better shifter', I can feel your fl—" her head snapped up and she stared down the path where the four of them had come.

Noah's response was immediate as he spun to face that direction, shotgun at the ready. "How many?"

"Too many," Alike replied and the fear in her voice made Grace shiver. "There's more flaring."

"Shifters?" Elaine asked, stepping forward. "I can't see anything—"

"Aly's gifts don't take things like line of sight into account," Noah replied in a bland tone. "Friends of yours?"

Exchanging a look with Del, Grace frowned. Why did it feel like they'd been dismissed? After being threatened so harshly, they didn't matter anymore. "Maybe we should run for it?" she whispered.

Del nodded.

Joseph countered with a question of his own, "Were you followed?"

Noah holstered the shotgun at his thigh while Alike threw the backpack on her back. "We didn't come from that direction. They're following you." Turning, Noah grabbed Alike's outstretched hand and, in a deft and flowing move, swung her onto his back. Looking at Grace and Del, he said, "If you want answers, I suggest you follow me," he told them.

"We're not going anywhere with you," Del snarled. "You're a liar and a con-artist and—"

Noah clicked his tongue which seemed to irritate Del further. "Your cornrows always were too tight."

"You can go die in a ditch for all I care," Del snarled and spat on the ground to show his discontent.

"Done that. It's not fun."

"You *stole* my best friend's face, tainted his memory. I *never* should have—"

"We're not sticking around. Take your chances with them if you want."

Noah didn't seem concerned, but it was Alike's reaction Grace was drawn to. Pained beyond logical reason and in tears and Grace didn't understand why. "No," Alike said. "Wait."

"We haven't got time for this," Noah told Alike, his tone softening. "But if they don't come, they'll never know *why*." He met Del's gaze and gave him a lopsided smile. "And I know that'll just eat you up inside, won't it, Del?"

Alike stared at them with large, tear-filled eyes, reminding Grace of Aly so much her heart hurt. Grace's brain was doing this push, pull argument with itself. It looked like Aly. Sounded like Aly. Had the same mannerisms as her. But shifters existed, and it couldn't be Aly. Could it?

"Please," Alike begged as Noah broke into a run. "Grace! Please!"

"We're coming with you," Elaine yelled after him. "Wait for us!"

"Run faster!" Noah replied.

Elaine rushed toward Grace and Del, grabbing Del's arm since he was closer and yanked him into a run. "There's no time. Go."

Something whirred overhead, a low buzzing noise hidden in the sun. A drone?

"We're not going with them," Grace blurted, bewildered. "You said—"

"Yeah, well, we changed our mind. Move!"

Joseph fired twice and Grace instinctively ducked. Del, pulled down the slight incline beside the worn path by Elaine, fell over in shock, landing on his rear. Grace's ears rang as she cowered and she glanced up in time to see a drone fall out of the sky.

She barely had time to register that before Joseph took

her upper arm, dragging her into a run behind Elaine and Del. She concentrated on her footfall, unused to running over this sort of uneven terrain, pulled at a speed she had no chance of maintaining. She was one stumble short of being dragged and that was a prospect she didn't want to consider.

How was Noah running so fast? And so strong? Carrying Alike on his back, plus Alike's heavy rucksack. Why were they following Alike and Noah?

She could hear shouting, probably in relation to the drone being destroyed, but she couldn't make out the words. Another whirring sound, farther away this time. Another drone?

Downhill running, while faster than uphill, was fraught with its own set of difficulties, but footing was the least of her worries, not when she was being dragged. Joseph changed his grip on her arm, instead of hoisting her by the upper arm, he gripped her hand instead. Ahead of them, Elaine released Del to sprint ahead.

"I can run," Grace muttered and then embarrassed herself by nearly falling.

Joseph glanced over his shoulder and smirked. "Sure you can."

"Don't patronize me."

"Wouldn't dream of it." That damn smirk grew wider. "Do you want me to carry you?"

"Bite me."

"Sure. Where and how hard?" Joseph winked at her, then laughed at her scandalized expression.

Up ahead, Noah looked back over his shoulder to check on their position, then ducked down behind an outcropping of rock and effectively disappeared from sight.

Joseph made a huffy sound, his lips moving wordlessly.

A hand peeked out from behind the rock and offered up what looked to be a middle finger.

Joseph's snort of laughter didn't make sense, but

nothing was making sense right now. Upon reaching the rocks, Joseph yanked Grace behind them. Pushing her up against the rock face first, he pressed his stomach to her back, presumably to protect her. "What are we doing?"

One arm around Alike, Noah glanced at Joseph. Alike, with her hands tucked into her armpits and her eyes closed, looking like she was trying to hide the fact she was shaking, and not doing a good job of it. "Ross is in that group," Noah said. "They're the same group of people who hounded us yesterday, although some—"

"—A lot," Alike muttered.

"—A lot of the shifters are new. Reinforcements, I guess."

"How can you tell?" Joseph asked and Noah gave Alike a pointed look.

"She can tell that?" Elaine asked, staring at Noah intently.

Noah rolled his eyes. "Elaine, she can tell *us*."

Elaine waved her hand toward the direction they'd come from. "So, walk her back in there to take care of this problem."

Del, meeting Grace's eyes, appeared as worried and confused as she was. Something was definitely going on, but she didn't know what. But there were guns and drones involved, so she was going to stay hunkered down beneath Joseph.

"What?" Noah blurted.

"Any shifter we remove from their factions now is one that we won't be facing later," Elaine said.

Astounded, Noah stared at her. "Do you even hear yourself? We don't—"

"We do now."

Grace was not in a position to see the shots, but the blast echoed in her ears and scared the living daylights out of her. Joseph sucked in a gasp, and curled around Grace, forcing her lower.

With a cry, Noah crumpled. Alike shrieked, dragged

down to the ground by Noah.

Grace tried to see around Joseph, tried to see Del, tried to make sure he was okay, and her eyes fell on Elaine's gun. Elaine stood, legs braced and gun held in both hands as it remained trained on the fallen Noah.

Grace let out an instinctual shriek of horror. Del recoiled, swearing.

Blood. Blood on Noah's shirt. His shoulder. Blood on his jeans. An angry Alike with her hands pressed against his shoulder as she knelt beside him.

What were they going to do? He could die out here! They had to help, she had to do something. Joseph wouldn't move, she was trapped beneath his arms, unable to do anything except stare in horror.

Voices in the distance yelled, and the drone buzzed overhead, and Grace heard the sound of someone returning fire from a distance away. Her heart pounded as she realized she was now in the middle of a gunfight.

Everything her father had taught her thrust its way to the forefront of her mind.

Stay low. Stay hidden. Don't make noise. Assess the situation. Last resort is to fight.

Most of all, if something were to happen, her parents loved her and they were proud of her.

Tears filling her eyes, she wished her father was here right now. He'd make her feel better. She wished she could reach Del, which would make her feel better too.

Noah's voice was full of pain as he snarled, "Was that really necessary?"

Alike raised her head and bared her teeth. "Is this how you greet each other? 'Hey, haven't seen you in years, let's draw lots to see who gets shot this time!' Why does it always have to be *him*?"

Why was she angry instead of panicked like Grace was?

"I need to see you do this," Elaine said without empathy. "Last time you were compromised so we didn't get proper results for the test."

Blood welling between her fingers, Alike raged, "And whose fault was that?!"

"This time you won't be."

Noah shook his head. "You don't even know who's following—"

Joseph interrupted, "They're here for us."

Stance steady and sure, Elaine said, "We watched you do the loop yesterday, so we knew that you hadn't found what it was you wanted to find out here. We knew you'd be back. So we leaked the location and Ross gobbled it up. He will pay for his betrayal, just like you."

Why did none of them seem to care that Noah could be dying! Why were they treating this like a game?

"You want to talk betrayal?" Noah snarled.

"I'm sorry," Alike murmured, hunching over Noah. "This is my fault. I thought—"

"Doesn't matter," Noah said, reaching up to touch her neck. "You know this won't keep me down for—"

Elaine twisted so the gun was pointed at Del. "He's next unless you do exactly what I tell you to. Unlike Noah, he can't regen."

Terrified, Del pressed his back against the boulder. "What the actual fuck?"

Joseph's grip on Grace tightened, turning from protective to confining and fear slithered down her spine. They'd made the wrong decision to trust Joseph and Elaine, she could see that now.

Del snapped, "Don't you point that gun at me!"

"This is why you took them," Alike snapped. "As bait. To get at me." Though he tried to hold onto her, Alike pulled away from Noah and stood, glaring at Elaine. "I am so done with all of this."

"No," Noah blurted and made a grab for her. "No, Aly, *don't*."

"What makes you think I have any sort of control over this? It's not a switch I can just—" Alike's face lost all expression as the shaking in her body increased. "Oh."

Her eyes closed and she curled in on herself, shaking so badly that Grace was surprised she managed to remain standing.

Elaine watched Alike with a sense of predatory anticipation and at that moment, Grace knew things were about to go bad.

Noah struggled to rise. "*Stop!*"

Someone yelled, someone too close for comfort and not part of this group. Although Grace couldn't see anyone, Elaine turned gleeful. "I need to get closer. If all goes to plan—"

"For God's sake, don't let this happen to her!" Noah yelled. He rolled over to prop himself up on his hands and knees, only to be shoved back down by Elaine's foot on his back.

Joseph said, "The drone has a camera. We can steal—"

"Not the same. Jo, keep them contained."

With a heavy sigh, Joseph lifted Grace up by her upper arms with enough force to make her squeak in protest. Trying to wriggle free, she lunged for Del and caught his hand briefly before Joseph pulled her from reach. One arm wrapped around her stomach, he lifted her from the ground, then the cold bite of metal pressed against her temple.

Grace froze, feeling utterly betrayed and more scared than she ever had in her life. A gun. A gun was being held to her head. She could die.

Pressed up against the rock, Del bravely demanded, "Let her go."

"*Joseph*—" Noah insisted, before his attention was inexplicably drawn to Alike.

Alike's eyes were open and fixed on Grace's. Cold as ice, those vacant eyes would haunt Grace into nightmares. Those dead eyes focused on Elaine, then Joseph, and for a heartbeat, nothing happened.

Joseph grunted and doubled over. The gun fell from Joseph's limp fingers as he slumped, then collapsed on the ground, dragging Grace down with him. He went as still as stone, his grip painful against Grace's arms, almost as though every muscle in his body had locked up.

"Aly! *Stop*!"

Del loomed above, reaching down to wrestle Grace free from Joseph's grip. "Let her go, you bastard."

Grace helped as best she could, but Joseph felt odd. His body seemed to be writhing and... gray rolled across the skin of his arms. Diamond patterns, like... scales.

Del recoiled, issuing a long line of expletives before he dove back in to help Grace. She kicked and writhed and clutched at Del as he tried to haul her free. Face screwed up, Del finally hit Joseph in the face hard enough to get his fingers to release so Grace could wriggle free.

Elaine lay face-first in the dirt not far away, suffering some sort of fit. Noah, similarly, was on the ground with Alike lying near him, so very still.

Del heaved Grace to her feet and pulled her into a run even before she'd managed to find her footing. Grace stumbled, ending up on all fours, feeling gravel cut up the palms of her hands. Wincing, she lifted her gaze and her eyes fell on Noah.

The same gray, scaled pattern flowed across his face, faster and in larger patches than it had on Joseph's, but unlike Joseph, he didn't seem to be in pain. More, his face held resignation and acceptance... and there was something going on with his nose.

Del grabbed Grace's waist with both hands and lifted, carrying her several paces forward before she found the strength to run on her own.

They dashed past Alike, lying deathly still, and into the surrounding desert scrub.

There were bodies on the ground up the slope. People writhing and calling out, begging for something to stop. Other people milled in confusion, or darted from person to person in an attempt to help. No one noticed them.

Del faced them down the slope, toward what Grace

knew would eventually link up with a road. Or off a cliff, but she didn't want to think about that prospect.

They came across a prone person about fifty feet down the slope, the scuff marks in the dirt suggested they rolled down the hill. They didn't stop. Didn't help. Barely glanced at the person. Panicked, they ran. They stumbled and helped each other around obstacles in their way. They pressed against rocks and hid while they caught their breath, trying to take in their surroundings before fleeing again.

She couldn't think. Couldn't feel. Two breaths away from complete hysteria, the panic in her didn't ebb. She had to get away, get away from all of this, get away now and find someplace that she felt safe. Was this what Aly endured when she was kidnapped? How did anyone function with this sort of terror surging through their veins? It was a struggle to catch her breath. Del's chest heaved with the effort to keep them at the fast pace.

With a loud *whoomp* sound and a buffet of wind, a shape flew overhead, the shadow on the ground too large and awkward to be a bird. Del skidded to a stop and Grace ran into his back.

"Oh, fuck *me*," Del breathed, staring and Grace gripped his shoulders to peek out from behind him.

Great wings blotted out the sun, spread wide to catch updrafts and allowed a figure to skim across the land. Not feathered like an eagle, but gray and bat-like. An incredibly awkward, floundering sort of bat; its wings didn't want to work in tandem.

Squinting as the figure tipped their wing to circle, Grace could see someone curled in their arms.

Wings. Honest to goodness wings. Real people flying.

What were they going to discover next?

"Del!" the human-bat yelled. "Follow me!"

Del bounced on his toes, ready for a fight that, given the circumstances, he couldn't hope to win. "Nuh-ah!" he bellowed back, his voice cracking in the middle. "No way, man, fuck you!"

The figure circled and now Grace could make out more details. The face seemed strange, but the hair was Noah's as were the clothes and Grace was fairly certain he cradled Alike and her backpack in his arms. "I can get you out of here!"

"Not fooling anyone!" Del yelled back. "You can fuck off!" He turned, keeping his body between Grace and the circling Noah.

Part of Grace wanted to giggle inanely. Del, facing off a great flying being with nothing but words, like he was in one of his games. Honestly, a dragon could swoop down next and Del would brandish a sword and shield and fiercely defend and she'd be okay with that.

"This is a dream," Grace whispered. Maybe someone had slipped something into her drink at the party a few nights ago and everything was a vivid hallucination. "It's gotta be."

With another great *whoomp*, Noah back winged once—twice—then he dropped about ten feet out of the air to land a distance from them. His wings flailed wide as he teetered backward, trying to catch balance, then managed to right himself. "Whoa." He draped his wings on his back, not folded but hanging like he didn't know what to do with them.

Alike's head lolled. It wasn't hard to see she was unconscious. Something inside Grace fluttered in something akin to concern and she didn't understand why.

"Nice landing," Del called. "Ten out of ten, would land again."

With a humorous snort, Noah said, "Bite me. This is the first time I've used Aly's design for reals."

A chill settled in Grace's chest.

Something wrong with his face. Something wrong with his skin. He was shirtless, and bloodied, and somehow still standing there. Wary, he kept his distance. "I know you don't trust me. I don't know what they told you, what truths or what lies, but I can tell you this is the real Aly and she's been eating herself up inside over worry about the both of you. I need to get her out of here and she'll never forgive me if I leave you both behind. Please. My car is just over the rise," he said, gesturing with a shoulder and a head turn. "I swear by the goddamn Snickers, I'm not playing you. Please. I'll tell you everything."

The voice. The way he spoke. The tones and infections. The references to Snickers. It was all so familiar. It was. But she refused to believe it. Grace shook her head. "No. You're lying. That's not the real Aly. Elaine and Joseph, they said—"

Del interrupted, "They just pulled a gun on us, Gracie."

She flung her hand out at Noah and shouted, "So did he!"

"Look," Noah said, shifting his grip on Alike. Somehow, between juggling her prone body and lifting his leg, he managed to withdraw the shotgun from his thigh holster and tossed it awkwardly to the ground. "Take that if it makes you feel better. Just please, come to the car."

With that, he turned and started running. Two massive and clumsy wingbeats before he lifted away.

Grace watched him until he disappeared over the rise. "Del," she admitted in a tiny voice. "I wanna go home."

"Yeah. Me too." With a sigh, Del wandered over toward the shotgun. Bringing it back, he offered the hilt to her. "Let's get this over with."

CHAPTER 16

Noah, when Grace and Del finally reached him, sat against the back tire of his car, with his wings gangly draped on either side of him, a small pile of wrappers by his hip, and several empty cans of energy drink. Still shirtless and bloodied, he appeared surprisingly woundless as he bent one knee and propped his elbow on it to cushion his head in his hand. The back door was open beside him with Alike lain out on the seat, with her backpack in the foot space near her head.

"Sugar rush?" Del asked, gesturing the mess.

Keeping her distance, Grace trained the shotgun on Noah. Why did his skin look so gray? Was he sick? Going into shock from being shot? Why wasn't he still bleeding?

Noah snorted. "Yeah. Shifting requires a lot of energy and I needed a quick boost."

"What's wrong with you?" Del asked with the subtly of a freight train. "Why's your skin like that?"

The humor in Noah's voice died. "I owe you an explanation. What did they tell you about shifters?"

"Obviously not enough." Del gestured his chest, then Noah. "You got shot, dude, and now you look like... what the hell is going on? Wings? Flight? And impervious to bullets?"

"Not impervious. Just able to heal rapidly."

Del asked, "Are you even human? Or some sort of alien hybrid?"

Noah huffed out a laugh. "Human. Pretty sure about that."

Del appeared as though he didn't believe Noah. Grace wasn't sure she did either. "Hmm."

Noah said, "It's a lot like the stories, I guess. People who can change their appearance at whim. It's like... there's different sorts of shifters, different skill levels. Most use it just to change their appearance slightly, enough to fool the normal person, but it takes time to shift. They do basically what's called a skin shift, where they change their appearance just enough that they look like a different person. Different skin tone, markings like freckles, tightness of the skin to give the appearance of a different face shape. It's enough to fool any face recognition software and the regular person, but they can't do things like hair, or body shape or eyes."

"Uh-huh," Del muttered. "Sure. We saw Elaine do it in seconds. Real Mystique level of shapeshifting there."

"Different skill levels," Noah said. "Most take minutes or hours but some of us can do it in seconds."

"And what about adding appendages? Get to the wings, Noah. If that's even your real name."

"Yeah. It is."

"And you're the one who's been befriending us," Del asked, seeking clarification.

"Yes."

"Why?"

"Um... long and complicated answer."

Folding his arms on his chest, Del glared at Noah. "Start explaining."

Noah sighed. "Look... brace yourself. I can't do anything about this right now and I know this part is a shock."

As he dropped his hands and lifted his head, Grace got her first good look at his face. A barely-there nose. The marks on his gray skin almost looked like scales now she was closer. His eyes so pale, they appeared to be only a pinprick of black in the middle. He didn't look human.

Grace froze. Del gurgled.

"Welcome to the world of wonderful shapeshifters," Noah said with a wiry smile on too-thin lips. "You've had an eye-opening first experience."

"Dude," Del breathed. "Reptilian overlords are real?"

Noah snorted.

Grace's hands felt clammy and she didn't like the way they were shaking. Lifting her finger away from the trigger, she asked, "What *are* you?"

Noah tilted his head back as he rolled his shoulders. "My codename is Noah-Echo-Seven. I'm part of a genetically altered shifter group *lovingly* called 'Faceless'. This"—he gestured his face—"the scaly appearance, the whole shebang is basically a brand. We're the monsters of the shifter world, the dark secret which lurks under their bed. They don't want to acknowledge us, or in most cases, think we're even human, yet they all want to get their hands on our specific skill set." He laughed and it sounded hollow.

"What's so funny?" Del asked.

"I'm just so tired," Noah replied. His arms slipped from his legs and he collapsed back against the car. "Tired of the running and the hiding and the lies. I just wanted to keep her safe. Keep her happy. Play games. Do homework. Listen to music. Be *normal*." He lifted a hand in front of his eyes and studied it. "But I don't get that. And now, I've dragged the two of you into my world as well and... I wanted to tell you, so many times, Del. But I couldn't. It would've put you in so much danger. Aly can't escape it and you both have been sucked in too and there's no longer any choice for any of us."

Del spared Grace a glance to share his confusion with

her. "You're not making sense."

"Get out now, Del. Go home while there's still time. If you know any more, then you'll know too much and you'll never be able to live out your dreams."

Del shook his head. "Not without Aly. The real one."

Noah laughed mirthlessly. "This is the real Aly. And she *can't* go home."

"That is not Aly," Grace proclaimed. "Elaine said Aly was being held captive and had been since she was abducted. That one is a shifter masquerading as her."

"And Joseph and Elaine are so, *so* trustworthy," Noah said with a roll of his eyes. "That *is* Aly. Think about it. What would a shapeshifter do if they're hunted? If they wanted to hide?"

After a moment, Del answered, "Change form."

"And the form I'm in—*was* in, it's different from the one I used in Bellhollow," Noah pointed out.

"Barely," Grace said. "The resemblance is uncanny."

Del added, "The eyes, though. You literally copied Fletcher's eyes. I got proof."

Noah conceded with a nod. "That was more for Aly's benefit than a need to hide. Aly's still in the same form she was in Bellhollow. The best she could do was cut her hair, which is what she did. If she was a shapeshifter, she wouldn't be running around in that form."

"Unless she wanted to be found," Del muttered.

"Which we don't."

"Joseph and Elaine had no reason to lie to us!" Grace snapped.

Noah fixed his eyes on her. "They had no reason to tell you the truth either. You were bait, Grace, to lure Aly to somewhere they could get their hands on her. They wanted to make sure you wouldn't run off on them the second you saw her."

"I don't believe you. They wouldn't—"

"They totally would." Noah shrugged. "The thing about shapeshifting is that it's an approximate guess on how people appear. It's a copy and a shifter can't do an *exact* replica. Look at her. There's a scar on her knee when she sliced it at the lake." He glanced at Alike. "Okay, she's in jeans, that won't help." He sighed, then brightened, flicking his pale gaze to Grace. "There's a birthmark I *know* you've seen."

"Aly has a birthmark?" Del asked, curious.

Grace pressed her lips together, not wanting to betray Aly as to the location. Or give Alike a chance to change to match.

Noah snickered. "It's on her butt, Del."

"Oh," Del chirped, taken aback before he frowned. "Wait. How have *you* seen it?"

Noah ignored that. "You're free to check if you want, Grace. And, if you think I'm giving her clues onto what kind of birthmark it is so she can shift, I haven't said a word about which side, color or size."

Grace didn't move. He'd been sitting there a while. He could've told her before they got here.

Noah seemed to guess. "She's really unconscious if you're worried about an attack. What she did takes a lot out of her."

"What *did* she do?" Del asked and swung his arm to gesture behind him. "What was that back there?"

"I'm not entirely sure," Noah answered with a speculative look at Alike. "Something unexpected." With a sigh, Noah turned his attention back to Del. "Aly has the ability to sense shifters. She doesn't even need to see them, she just reacts to their presence. The closer they are, the worse the reaction and… if they get too close, she has a defensive mechanism that basically strips the shapeshifting ability from them."

Del eyed him skeptically. "This all sounds like bullshit."

Noah dropped his eyes. "Look. I don't care if you believe me or not," he said and wearily got to his feet. He teetered beneath the weight of the wings and rested his hand on the top of the car to keep his balance. "But I need to leave. Not all of the shifters were taken out and some of them will probably find us soon. I need to get Aly out of here. You're welcome to catch a ride into the closest town."

"We're not going anywhere with you."

"Suit yourself." Turning his back to them, he braced himself against the car. The wings spread wide, then Noah grunted and the wings shuddered. Grace could hear bones creaking and skin rippling as the wings were sucked into Noah's back. "Huh," he said as the wings stopped decreasing in size and remained about arm's length. "Interesting."

"I thought you said she took away shapeshifting abilities," Del accused.

"I'm not a normal shapeshifter," Noah replied and sighed, tucking the wings flush against his back. "One more part of this dance you need to know." He reached down into the car and pulled out a red flannel shirt to put on over the top of the wings. "The reason why it was so easy to well.... 'infiltrate' your friendship. Why you both felt like you knew me but couldn't understand why. Why Aly seemed so at ease with me from the beginning. Why I have those eyes. The reason why you're still here, listening, rather than shooting me."

"We're not murderers," Grace snarled.

"Why you called me Fletcher at the pool," Noah continued and turned around to face them. A lot of the gray scales on his face had returned to normal, natural skin tone, but there were still patches of gray, especially on the half-formed nose. His chest from the neck down was still all scaly gray. One eye was pale gray, but the other was a warm chocolate brown.

Grace sucked in a breath in recognition. Close. Close and not close, not with all the gray remaining. But there was enough that her brain immediately conjured a name.

"No," Del breathed, then grew angry. "No. Don't you dare—"

Grace grew angry right along with him. After all they'd been through, Noah was not going to use their love for Fletcher against them. "You're a complete bastard if you think—"

"It's because—"

Del jabbed a finger at Noah. "I swear, if you spoil his memory I will punch you in the face."

Noah snorted and smiled. "Search your feelings. You know it to be true."

Del scowled and slashed the air with his hand. "Nope. No. You are not going to Vader me. Fuck off with that."

"Don't tell me you believe him," Grace said. "He's a shapeshifter! He can—"

"I didn't have a choice," Noah said.

Anger radiated from Del as he balled his hands into fists and stepped toward Noah. "You let us believe you were dead!"

His eyes fixed on Del's, Noah told him, "I was discovered and—"

"Selfish prick, that's what you are. Don't you care—"

Yelling in each other's faces, their bodies stiff and the accusations raw, the anger between them was palpable and Grace could think of nothing that would calm them down.

"Do you think I wanted this?" Noah asked. "Someone tried to assassinate me! I went over the bridge. By the time I'd hauled myself from the river, Jonathan had been told. *Penelope* had been told. Aly was waking up from her meds. I just had news my *brother* was murdered. You remember how off I was that day! I was terrified, and then someone came after me and confirmed my worst fears! What was I supposed to think? I had to leave to protect you! If I'd revealed myself then, there would've been questions I can't answer."

"You told Aly!" Del accused, throwing his hands around. "Why didn't you tell us?!"

"Aly had no clue until they abducted her! What would you have me do? They tried to kill me! I couldn't—"

"*But you came back*!" Del roared.

Grace jerked her head to Del. Did he *believe* Noah?

"You told her!" Del continued. "You didn't trust us—"

"*I couldn't risk you too*!" Noah shoved a hand through his hair and growled. "You guys were my *one* chance at normal and I lost that. Don't you get it? I was *never* going to tell her. I was never going to tell anyone. I was going to wait for you all to finish school and then fade. Fond memories, nothing more. I never intended to *die*. But I can't take that back. Then they took her. Then she... she can *feel* them, Del. She can sense shifters. She can sense me, she just never knew what it was. They were *always* going to come for her, but I got in the way. If I hadn't been there, she'd probably be dead by now. She didn't know anything about shifters and she still knew me. She *knew* me and it scared me so much! She knew who I was, knew to trust her heart instead of her eyes. Could you have done the same?" Noah accused. "I bet you didn't even believe there were shifters until Elaine showed you."

"You didn't give me a chance," Del snarled, his breath whistling through his teeth as he tried to calm down.

"Yeah," Noah said, his expression softening as he cast a fond glance at the woman lying in the car. "She said that too."

"Don't accuse us of not believing in you," Del snarled. "You didn't trust us."

Noah returned anger with frustration. "We weren't even sure if me coming back was going to work! We were playing this all by ear and—they could've come back at any moment and we'd have to go and—"

"You really believe him?" Grace asked. If Del believed—if Noah was really Fletcher, then that would mean...

That would mean that was the real Aly. Lying there, deathly pale, having done something that clearly put her life at risk to save Grace and Del. And Grace had said horrible things to her best friend.

The hand holding the shotgun lost all its strength, falling limp to her side, while she covered her mouth with her free hand and made a dismayed noise.

"Do you think I liked lying to you guys?" Noah yelled. "Do you think I enjoyed watching—"

That was Aly. *Her* Aly. Not some imposter pretending, infiltrating, lying. Her Aly.

Grace had called her a monster.

"Yes, I do," Del snapped. Angry beyond reasoning, he reached forward and grabbed the lapels of Noah's unbuttoned shirt, yanking him forward.

She hadn't known! How could *anyone* have guessed that truth? It was so far beyond what Grace had ever been able to fathom. Fletcher, alive and a shifter. Grace had been so quick to believe Joseph and Elaine. So quick to believe that there had been something wrong with the way Fletcher had died and wanting a truth she could cling to. So quick to believe there was a simple explanation as to why Aly had been so weird.

She'd been played.

And she'd betrayed her best friend in the process.

Dropping the gun, Grace staggered forward, intent on Aly and barely aware of the boys and their argument.

Noah curled his hands around Del's wrists. "Don't do this."

"I think you had a grand old time watching us grieve, laughing behind our backs as you tried to worm your way back in. We trusted you and you. Broke. *That.*"

Being too focused on Aly, Grace didn't see the first punch being thrown, but the resounding smack of Del's fist hitting Noah's face startled her.

The pair of them fell away from the car, wrestling and fighting. The sound of punches and grunts thrummed in her ears.

She didn't care about them. Let them get their aggression out, she had bigger concerns. Stumbling forward, she only had eyes for Aly. She had to know the truth.

The birthmark. That would tell her for sure. It would tell her everything.

Aly lay in a recovery position on her side, which made things slightly easier. Grace scrambled into the car, squeezing into the small footrest space around the backpack. While it was an invasion of privacy, Grace also knew that Aly would understand. Hopefully.

It was there. The brown splotch of skin against Aly's pale flesh.

Grace sat back and stared, then reached out to brush the hair away from Aly's face. "Oh, Aly." Lifting one of Aly's hands, she pressed her lips to Aly's fingers. "I'm so sorry. I didn't know. How could I have known?"

Hurt beyond comprehension, Grace bowed forward until her forehead was against Aly's arm. "I'm so sorry. I didn't know." Wrapping her arms around Aly, she sobbed. "Please wake up."

The car shuddered as the wrestling pair thumped against it and Grace poked her head out, set to berate them, only to find Del pressing Noah up against the car, arms around his neck as they hugged each other.

"Oh."

Del felt as Grace did. Overwhelmed and hurt and with no real way to process what was going on. He jerked his head toward her, then immediately looked away so she couldn't see the tears streaking down his face. Not releasing Noah, Del held out his arm for her in an invitation to join.

She didn't hesitate. Pressing up against her boys, Grace wept.

The three-way hug didn't last long. Tears from the release lingered, but there is only so long someone could cry before other emotions surged and demanded to be acknowledged. Grace pulled back enough to whack *Fletcher* upside the head. "You ass!"

Fletcher ducked and cringed away while Del snickered.

"Ow, Grace. What'd I do?"

"Don't you play that game with me! Do you know how much heartbreak you could've avoided if you'd told us? We could've helped! We could've—"

"No. You couldn't. You have nothing to protect yourselves," Fletcher stated. "Aly can sense them at least. Look how easily Joseph and Elaine fooled you."

"And they wouldn't have fooled us at all if we'd known," Grace snapped. "We could've been prepared. Instead, we were thrown in the deep end and—"

"So was Aly," Fletcher pointed out. "There was no predicting any of this."

"Doesn't matter about predicting," Del said, frowning. "A little trust goes a long way."

Fletcher ducked his head. "I've... I've never trusted anyone with this. It was always too risky."

"Well, we know now," Grace said, waving her hand. "We can go home and berate you for a dozen years and—"

Staring at the ground, Fletcher shook his head and interrupted her, "You don't get it. Aly can't go home. She can't go back to her life."

"What?" Grace breathed.

Fletcher flicked her a glance, then raised his head, looking beyond them. "Get behind the car."

Del grabbed Grace and had her moving around the car before she was even aware that Fletcher had said anything. Pushing the car door closed, Fletcher strode for the shotgun Grace had left on the ground.

"Okay. That's far enough," Fletcher called, leveling the shotgun. "What do you want?"

Elaine crept out from the surrounding scrub, her hands raised and the only reason Grace knew it was Elaine were the clothes and hair. The rest of her was similar to Fletcher's appearance before he managed to change most of it back; gray and scaly and a barely-there nose. "What the absolute hell, Noah? What was that? We can't shift back, why can you—"

"That is what happens when you push Aly after she tells you not to." Fletcher shrugged. "As for the shifting, it may come back, it may not. I find it hard to care anymore."

"Who *is* she?" Elaine demanded. "We *know* she's not Rex's daughter, she doesn't match. Why does she affect us?"

"Like I'm going to tell you," Fletcher said. "I don't trust you."

Elaine said, "This is why you were assigned to her, wasn't it? She's why you betrayed us."

Fletcher's shoulders tensed. "What?"

"How did you do it? We don't even recognize you anymore, you've changed so much. What possibly could have been worth forgetting all we've been—"

He huffed. "God dang it, not the fucking brain shift stuff again."

A woman appeared behind Elaine, sporting Joseph's clothes—which hung loose on her smaller frame—and his haircut. "You didn't brain shift?"

Grace pressed herself against the car. "Is that Joseph? They can change their gender?"

"No idea," Del murmured.

"Nope," Fletcher said to Elaine. "And I'm guessing neither did you. Why are you working for Darcy?"

"We infiltrated her to get information on this new batch of Faceless," Joseph said. "Adam got intel which concerned us, we were confirming it." Sharing an awkward glance with Elaine, Joseph shrugged. "That's all we can share, right now."

Fletcher accepted that with a nod.

Elaine said, "Before the split, Rex believed that you... had..."

Fletcher supplied, "Brain shifted."

Elaine nodded and continued, "And were working for some unknown client. Adam said you weren't, but he never… he didn't say why. Wouldn't say. When… I saw you with Belinda Bell, I was *sure* I had proof you were and wanted to prove that to Adam."

"Because Belinda works for Welcher's Purist front. And so do you. And *I* can't be given the benefit of the doubt? Fuck that."

Elaine blinked at him. "Ross told you about the Purist front?"

"They've been a wealth of information." Fletcher sighed and scrubbed a hand over his face. "Look, Elijah, I know you don't trust me, and I don't trust you. I think we can agree that *Rex* is a liar who is playing all sides. He told me *you'd* brain shifted, so I think it's only fair that I tell you—"

"I can't brain shift."

Fletcher replied, "Neither can I."

"But you're so different," Elaine blurted, bewildered. "We can't predict how you'll react anymore. Why—"

Fletcher held up his hand in a demand for silence. "Just stop." He sighed and pinched the bridge of his nose. "I said it to Rex and I'll say it to you. I don't want to be part of this war, but if you keep coming after me, if you keep coming after her, I will join and I will *end* it. Do you hear me?"

Elaine drew back. "You… you've *seen* Rex? Recently?"

"A few days ago." Fletcher sighed. He relaxed his stance, leaning his shotgun against his shoulder and shoving his other hand into his pocket. "Just after the park shooting, which I still owe you for."

Elaine went pale. "Noah, we—"

Fletcher pressed on without listening to Elaine. "He told Aly he's her father. Neither of us is sure we believe it because, as you said, she doesn't match. But that's because Rex *isn't* his natural form."

Elaine's jaw dropped and Joseph rocked back in surprise.

"He can't hide from Aly. She sees the truth."

"But… how?"

"When Aly reached for you, did you let her or did you fight her?"

Exchanging a troubled glance with each other, Elaine and Joseph didn't answer.

Fletcher continued, in the same smug tone Grace had heard Fletcher use when he one-upped someone. "It's rather intimate, isn't it? Having someone touch your abilities like that. So you fought."

Elaine seemed bewildered. "I don't understand."

Fletcher smirked, then glanced at Del and Grace and indicated the car with his eyes. "We're leaving. It's too risky to stay right now and I want to hear all of the lies you've been telling Del and Grace before I make any decisions."

For the first time, Elaine looked nervous. "Noah, we didn't know—"

Nodding, Del opened the back passenger door for Grace. "Time to jet."

"Please!" Elaine begged. "Noah, we need her! She's important!"

"I don't care what you need."

Carefully lifting up Aly's head, Grace slipped beneath it to allow Aly's head to be pillowed on her lap.

With one last instruction to Elaine and Joseph, Fletcher went for the driver's seat. "Your tracker's going to Minnesota. Bring Adam. Then we'll talk."

Bonnie picked her way through the scrub, checking each body she came across. Some faces were frozen in one last moment of panic, but many more faces openly wept from being unable to touch their gifts.

Checking her cell again, she switched it off and put it away. He was close. Her idiot. He should've waited for her. He should've been in his room when she'd gone to tell him about Aly's proclamation that Rex Braddock and Alistair Welcher were the same person, instead of selling them all out.

Then Aly and Fletcher would still trust them. Then Bonnie would still trust him. Right now, all she wanted to do was break his nose again.

Spotting a familiar jacket, she rushed over to Ross' side and grabbed his shoulder.

Ross woke with a snap, rolling to protect himself. "Shit," he said when he saw her.

Bonnie recoiled. His natural face. Scaly and gray. Aly could affect them too? Unexpected.

Flopping back, Ross moaned and covered his face with his hands. "I hurt."

Frowning Bonnie smacked his chest. "You dickhead," she signed when he looked at her.

"Yeah, I—" Catching sight of his hands, Ross swore. "What happened?"

"Aly," Bonnie signed.

He flipped them over, inspecting his palms, before he turned them again. "But I can't shift. I *can't* and—"

Bonnie reached down to grab Ross' hand and hoist him to his feet. Grunting, she scowled at him, then tossed him over her shoulder to carry him.

"I did it for you," Ross said as Bonnie turned to make her way back down the path. "Darcy said she could help you get your voice back and—"

She punched the back of his leg to show her disgust. There was nothing wrong with her. She had a voice, if the dumbass would listen. They didn't need Darcy. They couldn't trust her, and Bonnie knew Darcy would exploit them.

Knowing her brother, he wouldn't have done it just for Bonnie's sake. As much as they loved each other, he always put himself first.

"Tango said she could help me too," Ross admitted. "I'm sorry. I just wanted—"

Nodding, Bonnie grunted. She'd always suspected that Darcy would talk one day through the clones she sent.

Either to them, or to Adam, it didn't matter. Echo group were still among the living and the clones died. Bonnie didn't understand what made Echo so special, but she knew Darcy would want that.

After this second display of power, against Darcy's paid shifters no less, Darcy would want Aly too. And even though Bonnie had told Aly that there was no place better—and more dangerous—than at her side, all Bonnie wanted to do was run. Take her stupid brother and leave this all behind.

Her car wasn't far, but she knew with Ross' appearance, he couldn't remain here undiscovered for long. At least with him hanging over her shoulder, his face was hidden from view.

Hoisting him into the car, she let him flop on the backseat, then extended her arms above her head to stretch muscles stiff from exertion.

"Hello, Bonnie."

Knowing the voice, Bonnie froze and lowered her arms. One hand resting on the door and covering the opening with her body, she turned.

Belinda Bell. How had she found this location? Was she mixed up with Darcy too? And who was that with her? There were two men, one she recognized as Jonathan Locklear, the father of Aly's friend Grace, the other Bonnie didn't recognize at all.

"He looks pretty bad," Belinda said, her voice all sunshine and false cheer. "I've seen those sorts of skin flaws before." She reached around behind her and pulled a gun from her belt. "I always wondered if there were human-looking Faceless abominations. Now I know."

CHAPTER 17

A low whistle. "Damn, man. That's some story," Del murmured.

Grace stared at the back of Fletcher's head, unable to truly comprehend what he'd told them. Both Aly and Fletcher were tangled up in something beyond what she had conceived possible. Fletcher's past and upbringing, Aly's abilities, the kidnappings, and factions. Elaine had sugar-coated the truth so much.

Surely in this day and age, things like this wouldn't happen. "No wonder Aly was so weird. It must've been hard to deal with."

Fletcher adjusted his seat. "She wanted to tell you both, she really did. She hated lying."

"Can see why she lied, though," Grace replied. She would've had trouble believing if she hadn't seen it all happen.

"If I'd told you, if we'd sat down and talked, things would've been different."

"Maybe, dude," Del said as he stuck his feet up on the dash. "But, like, it's not the sort of thing you can tell. Where would you even begin?"

Fletcher swatted at Del's feet to make him remove

them. "Perhaps, but Penelope knew about shifters, which I only found out about recently. I wonder how much would've been different if I'd told her, or Aly, right from the beginning."

Pulling a disgruntled face, Del instead stretched his legs out as far as they could go ahead of him. "I know what being persecuted for the way you look is like. Like literally. It had to be hard to... yeah. I get why you kept it a secret. Hindsight one-oh-one, shit never works out the way you want it to."

"True."

"So," Del chirped and lightened his tone. "What else can you augment?"

A burst of laughter, brief and welcome. "Aly said you'd ask that. Right down to the eyebrow wiggle."

"Aly-cat knows us so well," Del replied with a laugh of his own before he sobered and peered over his shoulder at Grace, then down at Aly's unconscious form. "She is gonna be okay, right?"

"Yeah."

Grace looked down at the girl sleeping on her lap and brushed her fingers along Aly's forehead. While she could ignore the bruising, she couldn't ignore how pale Aly looked. "She looks gaunt."

"She's... she's okay."

"Fletcher," Grace scolded.

"Okay, *mom*," Fletcher said, exasperated. "She's not eating and she's not sleeping much. We've had a very stressful time and her body is trying to heal from gunshot wounds. We're doing our best here."

She could understand that. She didn't like it, but from what he'd said, they'd both had a horrific time, and they didn't need her scolding them to eat and sleep better. "Yeah. Okay."

Del glanced over his shoulder at Aly and Grace. "It's so trippy that you can heal from that type of shit. She honest-to-God got shot?"

"I am well aware. And I wouldn't lie to you about that."

Another low whistle from Del. "Wow. *Wow*. She's so lucky."

Desperate to have the conversation turn to something lighter, Grace smiled at the back of Fletcher. "So, what *is* going on between you and Aly?"

His shoulders stiffened and he made a pained noise. "*Graaaaace.*"

A part of her was concerned about several things Fletcher had said, especially concerning his age and mentality, but the gossipy part of her wanted details first. To know where they stood, or if that 'just friends' barrier was still in play. "I saw you two on Grad night. Dancing and all up on each other. You can't hide."

"Who said I was hiding?" Fletcher stalled, then muttered, "Okay, there's something there and *maybe* we're talking about exploring it."

Grace smiled, triumphantly. "I *knew* you were bi. Like can sense like."

Fletcher frowned at her in the rearview mirror. "Thanks."

"Sexuality is so hard to figure out, but I'm glad you got there in the end. I swear, I thought one of you would explode before you figured it out."

Fletcher muttered, "Seems everyone knew but me."

"C'mon, bro," Del said and reached over to shake Fletcher's shoulder. "You could at least make it seem like you're happy about it."

"I am," Fletcher said, his voice rough. "Honest."

"You sound exhausted too," Grace replied softly.

"We spent all day yesterday running and then that today. Exhausted is an understatement."

Grace switched on her 'mom' voice. "You need a good night's sleep and food. We're here now. Del can drive if you want to catch some z's."

"Thanks for the offer. And maybe when Aly wakes up

I'll take you up on it. Right now, though, I need to feel like I'm in control of something. If I stop… it'll be bad."

"I hear that," Del said.

"It's been a rough few days."

"For everyone."

"So, what now?" Grace asked. "You said Minnesota."

Shooting her a cautious glance, Fletcher replied, "For Aly and I, that's the plan."

"Couldn't we come with you?" Del asked.

Fletcher wriggled in his seat, arching his back and then relaxing and Grace wondered if the wings were bothering him. "I don't think that's a good idea. It's dangerous and… no. It's better if you go home. You can claim… I dunno. Fun weekend away or something. Your mom's a pain in the butt and you had to get away. Something."

A snort from Del. "Understatement of the year. We had a massive argument."

"YouTube?" Fletcher questioned.

"Yeah," Del muttered and sulked. "She's got this notion in her head that she can treat me like an adult, right up until I make a decision she doesn't like. Then I'm a child."

"That sucks."

"Big time. So I'm definitely for a trip away."

Fletcher sighed. "You can't. If this was just a normal trip, I'd say let's go. But it's not. Once people know you're tangled up in this, it's hard to get free."

Grace leaned forward as much as she could to touch Fletcher's shoulder. "Would we see you again?"

"Of course."

Del shuffled. "I don't want to call liar, but you don't sound too certain."

"Maybe not in person, but there's always the internet. Email. Phone calls. I can contact you the same way we contact Penelope if we're really careful. But people can't know Aly's alive. That'll put you in danger."

With a sad nod, Del said, "And her."

"She can't go to college," Grace lamented and swallowed the lump in her throat. "She can't be an animator." Poor Aly. She must be so heartbroken. Everything she'd gone through, and then on top to have to deal with her accusation that Aly wasn't the real one. Tears pricked her eyes as she wished she could take those words back.

"Alyson Gale can't be an animator," Fletcher replied. "But I'm pretty good at forging Ids, so I'm hoping that, maybe, once this all settles down, we can get her into another animation college. If not, like, there's a huge market online at the moment for animators. There's a way," he assured Grace. "There has to be. I want her to have as normal of a life as she can."

"Normal?" Grace queried. "Normal. With shifters and factions and whatever she can do. She's never going to have normal again."

Del nodded. "This whole situation is literally fucked up."

"Yeah," Fletcher sighed, resigned. "I know."

Flame in the dark. Soft and yellow. Tiny stars. So pretty. And hers. She held it in the palm of her hand and watched it flicker. So full of love and trust.

Noah's flame. She'd held Noah's flame.

She'd been pulled toward the red flares and trying to ignore the yellows when Grace had been threatened. A sharp twist of pain and a blind grab. She hadn't meant to grab his flame! The others had fought against her, writhed and burned in her grip, but his flame had come to her willingly. Had let her hold it close to her chest and use it as an anchor.

She hadn't wanted to let it go, but as the other flames had winked out, so too had her connection with Noah and his flame faded until it was gone.

Gone. Because she'd taken his abilities from him!

Momentum slowed dramatically, almost causing her to

roll from the soft pillow she rested on. The momentum continued to slow, accompanied the sound of tires hitting gravel and brush.

"Dude?"

"She's waking up."

Fletcher's voice. Del's voice too. Their words came from a great distance. Were they taken? Where they in trouble? It was so hard to think, to remember.

"She's still out," Grace said. "She hasn't made a sound."

"Trust me."

She tried to contain the panic that swelled in her chest. She'd felt the flames winking out, so much faster than last time. So much easier. Gone without a thought or a care. She didn't like it. She wanted it to stop. Hadn't been able to.

Movement ceased with a screech and car doors opened. Fingers against her face. Hands over hers. A pulse checked. Her name was called. A hand shook her shoulder and the movement was enough to jostle her eyes open.

Faces. All around her. Faces and people and blotting dark combined with blinding light and she couldn't think, couldn't see.

She panicked and flailed, throwing up her arms.

People cried her name and hands clamped her wrists. "Aly! It's us!"

Scaled hands. An upside down face covered in patches of gray scales. They crept over his sunken, half-formed nose and down his neck. One eye was as pale as ice while the other was warm chocolate. Half-formed. Terrifying.

Aly screeched.

The hands around her wrists snatched back as the figure above her recoiled in shock and horror. Aly surged upright and scampered away, pressing herself up against the opposite door. Hands clawed the door handle to try to escape, but in her panic, she couldn't get purchase.

Someone gripped her arm. "Aly!"

With a squawk, Aly spun so she could lash out at her restrainer and came face-to-face with Grace. Grace. Her best friend. With no hint that it was a shapeshifter. No goose bumps, no warning. Aly stared at her, trying to comprehend, before tentatively asking, "Grace?"

Grace smiled in relief. "It's us."

"You're okay, Aly-cat," Del said with an equally relieved grin.

"Del? You're here too?"

No goose bumps. They were real. They were real and they were here and they were safe.

A weight lifted off her chest, setting her free and making her giddy with happiness. She sagged against the door for a moment before she flung herself at Grace, buried her face in Grace's neck and hugged her close. "I've been so worried about you!"

Clutching, Grace stroked Aly's hair. "I'm so sorry about the things I said. I was so awful to you. I didn't know. Elaine lied to us about everything—"

"I don't care. You're safe. You're here." Aly pulled away and made a futile effort to blink back tears. "Everything's been such a mess and I missed you so much"—she stretched out her hand to grab onto Del's arm as he watched from the front seat—"both of you and I've been so scared and alone and you're here and safe and I've been so terrified for you both since Joseph said he'd gotten you—"

The car door behind Grace clicked shut and Fletcher moved away.

Aly froze. Fletcher. It'd been *Fletcher* who'd woken her. Fletcher who was stuck in half form because she'd used her abilities on him. "Fletcher!" she blurted and crawled over Grace to get to the door. She and Grace tangled, and Aly fell headfirst out of the car. She wriggled, crawling forward so she could writhe free. "Fletcher!"

"What are you—Aly, get off the ground."

She scrambled up, lunging for him so she could hug

him, only to be confused when he danced away from her, and turned his face away. She stared at him, stunned as she took in the appearance of his skin. Her fault. The scales creeping up his neck and along his arms. His face. The hunch in his back. It was all her fault.

He must hate her.

She burst into tears at that thought. She'd taken his abilities from him and hadn't been able to stop herself. He was doomed into one form for the rest of his life, and an incomplete one at that. "I'm sorry!" she wailed as she shook her head and squeezed shut her eyes. "I couldn't let go! I tried so hard and—"

"Aly—"

She hugged herself and doubled over. "I felt flames go out. I held yours in my hand. I didn't mean to!"

"You didn't take anything. It's still there."

She didn't want to believe him. Couldn't trust that he wasn't concealing the truth in order to keep her from getting hurt. "I know what I felt." She wiped her face furiously but the tears kept coming. "You have scales," she wailed. "That's my fault. You have every right to hate me."

"Als, c'mon, I don't hate—"

"I'm *so* sorry, I—"

"—didn't want you to see me like this if you weren't ready."

Aly's eyes snapped open as the feeling of his tingles flickered over her skin, weak and jittery. The tears stopped from the shock of feeling them, and she looked up to gape at him. Tingles. Somehow different than before, but still there.

He'd half-turned toward her but still hid his features. "I know I look horrific right now. I don't want to scare you."

Wiping the tears on her hand on her pants, she offered it to him and used her other hand to dash away the streaks on her cheeks. "No. You don't."

He hesitated. Shuffled and looked away, uncertain. His hand rubbed his scaled fingers against his thumb like he wanted to extend his hand, but couldn't.

She wriggled her fingers. "It's still you. That's all that matters to me."

He toed the ground, sighed, then extended his hand to her. "I haven't had a chance to fix it all yet," he mumbled as she curled her hand around his. "I'm a little burned out. I will. I promise, and it's okay if you don't want to look at me."

"I'm so sorry. I really didn't mean to—"

He turned his head, still not looking at her, but sort at the ground by her feet. "It's not your fault."

Scales still extended over his right cheek and down his neck, but both eyes were now the clear brown she loved so much. Fascinated, she reached out to lightly touch his throat, drifting her fingers down his chest to trace the lines and patterns of his scales. Soft. So soft and wonderfully warm, they felt both delicate and strong against her touch. Enraptured, she could stand there for hours admiring them.

He didn't understand what she saw. Didn't see his scales as a thing of beauty, but as a brand. Giving his fingers a comforting squeeze, she pressed her other hand against his heart.

His expression twisted and he looked away. "Don't force yourself."

"I'm not."

"We both know you're keyed into visual," he mumbled.

"It's you," she insisted. "I'm keyed into you."

Fletcher blinked and dared to sneak a peek back at her. "Als…"

Tilting her head, she glanced back down at her hand on his chest. His bare chest. "Why is your shirt open?" she asked, having only just looked beyond his scaled appearance to see the oddities with his clothes. His unbuttoned shirt hung strangely tight on his frame and his back seemed larger than normal. "What's going on with your back?"

Fletcher cringed. "Er…"

"Dude can grow wings!" Del announced, leaning out the window from the front seat and waving his hands around. "Sprouted from his back and made him flounder like some sort of demented potoo, all flopping and flapping."

Offended, Fletcher retorted, "I'd like to see you make wings on the fly!"

Del snickered. "That *is* the idea of wings, man."

"They worked?" Aly blurted.

"Can you like transform into other animals?" Del asked, getting louder as he became more excited. "Can you do like a Chupacabra? We could do one of those stupid hunter videos and pretend to freak out. Oh *oh*, what about Bigfoot?"

"Really, Del?" Grace asked with an exasperated noise as she climbed out of the car and leaned on the panel beside the door.

Del opened his door and bounced out. "It could work! We'd get my drone and fly overhead and Fletcher could be all *rar* and you could do a fake scream and literally make a killing on YouTube."

"He's already trying to make money off me," Fletcher muttered, the teasing smile betraying the grumpy tone.

"You know Bigfoot is normally naked, don't you, Del?" Grace asked, smirking. "I don't think he wants to walk around displaying his goods."

Del refused to be deterred. "What about Roswell? Aliens, Gracie, we could pretend—"

Aly's face flamed while Fletcher shuffled uncomfortably. Gripping Fletcher's shirt and desperate to change the subject, she tugged to get his attention. "They worked?"

"They worked," Fletcher replied, smiling. "To a degree. Del's not wrong about the flopping around. I need to practice."

She was so excited for him and she bounced on her

toes. She wanted to know everything! "Can I see?"

"Later," he said. "Right now, we need to move."

"Oh. Right." The excitement took a nose dive straight back into fear. Swallowing, she asked, "Those shifters... did I kill them?"

"No."

She screwed up her face, not believing him.

He touched her chin, lifting up her face but she refused to open her eyes. "I didn't have time to check everyone, but the ones I checked were alive. I swear by the Snickers. In pain but alive. They were too far away from you."

"So, the ones in the park?" Some of them had been touching her. Was that close enough? Or were people lying? Fletcher never said she'd killed them. Rex said she'd taken away their powers, he'd never said she'd killed them either. The news had said eleven people died and Grace believed that. So what was the truth?

A soft noise and she waited for the denial. "I... I don't know. Honest, I don't. I was... I had to get you out of there."

"You didn't stop to check?"

"No."

She didn't really blame him for that. "So, I could've—"

"Elaine lied," Grace interjected, having stopped teasing Del to listen. "Aly, I *never* meant to infer that you—we didn't know what we know now. There's no way you'd hurt people if you can help it."

Aly didn't want to let it go. Not knowing haunted her. "But—"

Fletcher slipped his arm around her. "We'll talk. There's a lot to tell you and we have some decisions to make, after we get someplace safe, okay?"

Nodding, Aly allowed him to settle her back in the car, where Grace reached for her hand. "I'm so sorry," Grace told her and tears welled in her eyes. "Elaine told us so many things and I didn't know what to believe. She told us that—"

Aly squeezed Grace's hand. "I know what Elaine's like. It's okay, Grace."

"But I called you—"

"It doesn't matter," Aly insisted, with a sharp shake of her head. "It really doesn't. I've been where you are. It's information overload."

Grace swallowed what sounded like a hysterical giggle and leaned over the gap to embrace Aly. "Yeah. It really is."

Fletcher flopped into the driver's seat and wriggled until he was comfortable, which required manual readjustments of his back several times.

"There's just so much going on," Aly continued. "I don't know what, or who, to believe anymore. So many people deliberately lying or giving just enough truth for it to be believable…"

Grace nodded. "It's so hard to keep everything straight. Most of what Fletcher's told us is so confusing at times."

Aly smiled. "I've been living it and I still don't know what's going on half the time."

"Tell me about it," Fletcher muttered. "So many different stories."

Aly smiled at Grace. "I know you'd never have said those things if you had all the information."

"I can drive for a while," Del offered, as he looked at Fletcher with a frown.

"I'm good," Fletcher replied, pulling the car back onto the road.

"Did they hurt you?" Aly asked Grace, her eyes roaming across her friend and expecting some sort of injury. "Joseph said that he would if I didn't do what he said, I was so afraid that—"

"They were nice," Grace said, lifting her shoulders to shrug. "They told us a lot of things which turned out mostly true, according to Fletcher, as well as some pretty big whoppers about you."

"Lies built on a foundation of truth often work better,"

Fletcher mentioned. "It's easier to keep straight."

"I get that." Leaning close, Grace murmured in confidence, "Joseph was kind of cute, though."

Aly blinked, then narrowed her eyes at Grace. "Really?"

"Sure," Grace said with a smile. "I mean, he built his body to be gorgeous, didn't he?"

"Didn't notice," Aly replied, relieved that she could talk to Grace without censoring herself or worrying Grace would see through the lies.

"Well, I did. That kind of form deserves to be noticed. I mean, I don't get the whole gender switchy stuff yet, but I admit I'm intrigued."

Aly was torn between wanting to tease Grace and trying to warn her about Joseph. "But... I mean—Grace, Joseph's—he's—we don't know—"

"I can appreciate a fine specimen without wanting to get involved," Grace said, waving her hand at Aly's spluttering. "But what about you? Spill all the deets on you and Fletcher."

Aly tried not to blush and failed. Deliberately avoiding Fletcher's gaze in the rear vision mirror, she said, "It's new."

"It's *old*," Grace said with a proud smile. "Very old. A long time coming."

"It's like you said." Hunching her shoulders, she ducked her head, then locked eyes with Fletcher. "Fortify and no regrets."

"I knew it," Grace laughed and clapped her hands in glee. "I was right!"

"You don't always have to be right," Del said, shaking his head at them. "Just let them get it on without us being in their face about it."

"No one's getting anything on," Aly protested.

Leaning forward, Grace clutched the back of Del's seat. "You and Lloyd made bets."

He spun around in his seat to shush her. "We did not!"

"You so did!" Grace replied, sounding jubilant. "Lloyd

even bet that something would happen prom night, remember?"

"Wait, what?" Aly blurted.

"Girl, you're so obvious," Grace said with a wink and a hand flop. "We all knew, we were just waiting for Fletcher to figure himself out. So, tell me. Since Fletcher was back as Noah, *did* something happen prom night?"

"So!" Fletcher announced, clearly trying to change the subject. "The plan."

"Oh," Aly said, picking up his cue. "What are we doing?"

Del scoffed, "Subtle, dude. Real subtle."

Fletcher shot Del a look. "When have I ever appreciated talking about my love life?"

"Or lack thereof," Grace chirped.

"Do you really have to tease us?" Aly complained and resisted the urge to sulk.

Del's mischievous smile dropped from his face. "We might not get another chance to. That's the plan, right? Aka, 'how to get me 'n Gracie home'."

The smile and happiness drained from Aly as Fletcher nodded. "You can't come with us, Del."

"So, we have one last hurrah, and then you ship us back? And we have to live life normally? That ain't gonna fly. We *know*."

"There are plenty of people who know who live normal lives," Fletcher said.

"Name one," Del demanded.

"Penelope," Fletcher responded. "She lived with this knowledge for eighteen years."

"Until it all came crashing down," Aly muttered.

"Because of Rex, not anything Penelope did—"

"Because of me."

Fletcher cleared his throat and pressed onward. "Beyond Elaine and Joseph, no one knows you know about shifters. There's no paper trail for people to follow. They might follow Aly's life and find you, but there's no reason to think that you know anything—"

"Belinda Bell," Aly said. "I called Lan, remember, and Belinda answered. You said she could track that."

Fletcher made a disgruntled noise. "It's just one thing. She can be—"

"Belinda Bell was at my house?" Grace blurted. "That FBI agent?"

"She seems to work for a Purist front operation for one of the larger factions of shifters, but she could very well be an FBI agent for all I know. I don't think she's a danger to your family," Fletcher replied. "She believes she's protecting mankind and—"

"Yeah, but," Grace coughed and smiled weakly. "I might've accidentally-on-purpose used a credit card to let my dad know where I was."

Fletcher groaned.

"Well!" Grace replied, affronted. "Joseph wouldn't let me call him, and I just wanted them to know I was okay! I didn't know any of this and—"

"I'm not blaming you," Fletcher replied and drummed his fingers against the steering wheel. "So, it's possible that now Jonathan and Belinda are together in this. If he thinks she's an FBI agent, and his daughter is missing... yeah, he'd bring in all the help he could get. Knowing your dad, he'll probably be somewhere... close."

"Definitely on his way," Grace agreed, hopeful and worried at the same time.

"Which is why you did it," Aly said with a nod of her own. She would've done the same thing had she been given the chance, and hadn't known the depth of this rabbit hole.

"Mom worries," Grace said with an apologetic shrug. "I... well... with the news you might be... I didn't want her to worry about me as well."

Fletcher sighed. "We could leave a trail and have him pick you up. You could make up some story about getting away from Del's mom and..." he frowned and stopped.

"That wouldn't... no, that won't work. You would've taken Aly with you."

"Last we heard, she was on a trip with her mom," Grace said.

"It's not like Grace to act out though," Aly said.

"First time for everything," Del chirped, then brayed, "I'm a *baaaaaad* influence."

Fletcher snorted. "I don't think you can pull the wool over your mom's eyes that easy."

Del grinned. "No, it's far better to tell her we're on the 'lamb'."

Fletcher laughed.

"Oh, here we go," Grace said, rolling her eyes.

The laughter died, then Fletcher cleared his throat, refusing to be lulled into further jokes. "If Jonathan is with Belinda, and that's a pretty big *if*, then it's possible he knows about shifters. Let's hope he doesn't absorb too much of Belinda's prejudice."

"If he knows about shifters, he might not believe it's us," Del said. "I mean... I didn't believe it was really Aly. We'd have to prove ourselves... well, Grace would."

Grace looked thoughtful, then brightened. "Fletcher, can tattoos be duplicated?"

With a frown, Fletcher said, "To a degree. Not with any finesse though. It'll look like a tattoo from a distance, but up close it'll look like discolored skin. And we definitely can't do color."

"So, a tattoo could, conceivably, be used as a kind of identification."

The frown deepened. "I suppose... I never really thought about it before... I think some of Rex's faction did have tattoos that they kept through their various shifts." He rubbed his chin in thought. "Huh. That would be an interesting way of tracking someone. I wonder if it's something that they do, if all the factions have identifiers like that. I know they have code words." He wrinkled his nose. "There's pros and cons for it, Grace. A tattoo is permanent, and that makes it dangerous, especially if an opposite faction can identify you by it. Makes the ability to shift pretty moot if you're trying to hide. You can paint them on, I suppose… maybe if it's small enough… and in a place no one can see easily…" He shook his head to clear it. "Why are you asking?"

Grace wriggled in excitement and Aly's eyes widened. "You didn't."

"I did!" Grace exclaimed. "Just after my last exam, Dad took me."

Aly's face lit up. "Did you use my phoenix design?" She and Grace had spent ages talking about tattoo designs and she'd even done a few cutesy little firebird tattoos for Grace. Simple and elegant, a phoenix with its wings spread wide and orange flames for a tail.

Grace winked at her. "I told you I would!"

"You have a tattoo, Grace?" Del blurted. "Where?"

"It's on my hip," she said. "Been itchy as fuck. I wanted to wait until it was healed before I showed you guys. But that could work, right, Fletch? I show my dad, he's seen it and its bright red ink. There's no mistaking it. That could be proof."

Del grew excited. "And—and—and, like, if we all get secret tattoos, we could use them to identify each other."

"You could get your bee, Aly," Grace said.

"I could!" Aly beamed.

"I want Bigfoot," Del declared. "On my foot."

Fletcher choked on his laughter. "What? Why?"

"Who's gonna expect that?" Del chortled. "Bigfoot, with his big foot, on my foot. Besides, if the girls get mythical beasts, you're a supernatural being, then I want a cryptid."

Aly giggled. "A bee is not a mythical anything, Del."

"It's either that or an alien on my butt. Your choice."

"And you'd have to pull down your pants each time to 'prove' you're you?" Grace replied and pulled a face. "I'll take the Bigfoot over butt-aliens any day."

"Can we please circle back to what we're going to do?" Fletcher complained. "And not talk about Bigfoot kicking alien ass."

Del guffawed. Reaching out, he gripped Fletcher's shoulder to shake as he laughed. "That is a *perfect* tattoo!"

"Hey! Driving!"

"Serious, dude, you get the alien and I'll get the Bigfoot."

Fletcher shook his head and lost his smile. "I can't, Del. I can't mark myself like that."

Del's face fell. "Aww what? But how will we be able to tell it's you?"

"Aly will know it's me. And if you can tell her, you'll be able to tell me. I could always—"

"That completely falls apart if something happens to Aly," Grace said.

Fletcher's expression turned fierce. "Nothing is going to happen to Aly."

Del pressed, "That's all well and good, but dude, she's been shot already."

"Del," Aly began. "I can take care of myself—"

"Nah, man, the real reason you don't want to get one is that you don't want to be tied to us. You're already planning on dumping us and vanishing and—"

"What, the absolute fuck, Del?" Fletcher snapped. "I'm not planning on dumping you. Whatever gave you that idea? A tattoo is dangerous for a shifter. We were discussing an idea, not an absolute! If push comes to shove, I could just show you my scales and—"

Del wasn't having it. "Deny it. Deny that you would leave us on the side of the road. Go on. I dare you."

"Stop it," Aly snapped. "I want you to go home, too."

Swiveling his head, Del stared at her in shock. "Aly-cat?"

"I am *scared*, Del. I have never been more terrified. I am wound so tight I can't sleep. I can't eat. I can't do anything but breathe and try to keep up and there's no *end*. We are living from moment to moment. I don't know who's after us. I have no concept of what's safe and I do not want either of you tangled up in this either!"

Fletcher met her eyes in the rearview mirror and she could see her own pain and turmoil echoed on his face.

"Aly," Grace breathed, horrified.

"We don't know what's going on," Fletcher added. "We don't know who's involved. We don't know if you go back home you'll be safe. I don't know if I can keep the three of you safe if you come, because I can barely keep Aly safe right now. We're facing impossible choices and I don't have any answers. If we lost one of you..." Fletcher choked on the word and stopped talking.

Aly spoke, slowly and carefully, "You need to go home. Where it's safe. Where you can live your lives and not have to be scared every moment. And you need to let us go."

Jonathan Locklear hadn't been able to take his eyes off Ross. The unending stare of someone who couldn't believe what he saw, and couldn't figure out the 'whys' and 'hows' and had settled on a 'what'.

It reminded Bonnie of the faction who had taken her and Ross in after she'd been shot in the head. It made her feel nonhuman and that fostered an instant dislike for the man.

Half a day's travel and she sensed that somehow they weren't far from where they'd been originally. Belinda was following some lead and she wasn't sharing her information, not even with her companions. Constantly texting on her cell while the other man drove.

Bonnie smiled to herself. They were captured in the loosest sense of the word. She was biding her time. The knots in the ropes Belinda had used to subdue Bonnie were practically useless against someone of her training and could be easily escaped from. Especially since Belinda seemed to have forgotten that Bonnie spoke only through sign language, and would need her hands released if

Belinda wanted to interrogate her.

She had to wait for Ross to recover enough to make an escape worthwhile. There was no reason she couldn't do a little recon while she waited. If the opportunity arose, she could certainly take them all out and steal the car, but she wanted to know more.

Belinda had called the other man 'Gomez', but her interactions with him and been snappish and controlling and Gomez had followed her instructions meekly. Gomez, the name was familiar even if the face wasn't. There was a Gomez in Welcher's Purist front, a shifter sent as a decoy and used to sniff out non-conforming shifters. The same Gomez who had been with Belinda in the park where Aly had done whatever she'd done. So if this Gomez was that Gomez, then, while he was lucky to be alive, he was no longer a shifter.

Bonnie glanced at Ross' unresponsive form and pondered the scales replacing his skin. It was unnerving to see them again, especially after all this time believing he was unable to shift. And then to be within Aly's vicinity when she did whatever she does. Was he still a shifter? Or was he stuck like this, like he'd been stuck in that other form? Why was he still so out of it? Why had he even been affected when last time it had only been the naturals? She didn't have any answers, but it had taken Aly a while to recover from releasing, so maybe it took those affected a while too.

Bonnie twisted her wrists to test the bonds which held her and alleviate some of the discomfort before she returned to glaring at Jonathan.

Belinda's cell rang and she answered, "Hello, this is Belinda Bell." Straightening, Belinda broke into a grin. "What a pleasure! I was hoping you would... yes... yes, that's correct. I have two of them."

Bonnie scowled at the back of Belinda's head.

"The pictures I posted are authentic," Belinda continued. "And although only one of them is currently displaying scales, the other is his sister, so I don't doubt she's hiding them as well. I'm concerned about how long the one with scales will live. I was led to believe the scales imply breakdown of cells, so we'll need to do this quickly."

Bonnie snarled and lashed out, kicking the back of Belinda's chair.

Without looking back, Belinda pointed her gun at Ross in order to placate Bonnie. "Yes, certainly. I'll await your location." Hanging up, Belinda twisted around in her chair and told Bonnie, "I don't need you alive."

Bonnie bared her teeth at Belinda and snarled.

Belinda smirked. "Soon, your kind will be nothing but a distant memory. A shadow on America's greatness, quickly forgotten as your kind is eradicated."

"Why?" Jonathan piped up. "What did they do to deserve eradication?"

With a frown, Belinda looked at Jonathan. "They're not human. They hide and they lurk and they prey like the animals they are." With a huff, she turned back. "They don't deserve to live."

Bonnie watched a shadow flitting over Jonathan's face before it was carefully schooled to be neutral and wondered if she had an ally in all this.

CHAPTER 18

Holding open the door for her friends, Aly looked at the hotel room, then at Fletcher. It was barely four in the afternoon, plenty of light left in the day to travel, and they were already stopping. They weren't even out of Nevada yet.

Not that she blamed him. Fletcher was still sporting a hunchback, which they'd managed to hide beneath the backpack as they booked in. His shifts all day had felt stuttered and strange, but at least the scales on his face were gone. Watching him move across the room, Aly could see he was exhausted.

So was she. Bone tired, of everything. Running, the constant fear and the unknown. While she didn't want to add to his worries, as inevitable as it would be, there were still things they needed to talk about without Del and Grace hearing.

It must've been a difficult decision for him, weighing up exhaustion and the possibility of Jonathan being close enough to rescue Grace and Del, and the need to keep running.

Del flopped down on the closest double bed and spread out.

"You've been in a car for hours," Grace complained and pushed his feet to force him to remove them from her way. "And the first thing you do is lie down?"

Aly wandered through the room to the window and peeked through the curtain.

"It's not like we have gear to unpack," Del complained. "And we're underage, which means we can't even enjoy the wonderful entertainment available at the casino downstairs at all." He sat up and eyed Fletcher. "Unless my man wants to age up and—"

"No," Fletcher said. "But there's still enough time for you two to go shopping and get a change of clothes. There's a mall across the street."

A burst of nerves in Aly's chest. "Is that wise?"

"No one will be looking for them," Fletcher replied, pulling out his wallet. Thumbing out several bills, he handed them to Grace along with the door card. "If you're careful, you should be fine. Buy a change of clothes, whatever you need for the night, okay? Maybe a carry bag, I don't know, we can worry about particulars tomorrow. I need sleep. Brain's dead."

"And then what?" Grace asked.

"Then, you come back here—oh and make sure you're alone in the corridor when you enter the room—wake me up, and we go for dinner. Or have room service. Watch a movie."

"One last hurrah?" Del asked, voicing the concern everyone felt.

Fletcher stared at the floor and nodded. "You can go with them too, Aly," he suggested. "I'm sure there's things you want to get."

She wanted to hide. Stay out of sight and feel safe, just for a moment, but she didn't know how to voice that without appearing weak. "I'll stay here and nap too."

Stifling a yawn, Fletcher nodded. "'kay."

Del snickered. "Nap. Sure. Right."

"Mind out of gutter, Del," Fletcher responded and

pulled a face at him. To Grace, he said, "Don't use your card, okay? We'll do that tomorrow and get Jonathan's attention."

"Alright," Grace said and pocketed the cash. "You guys want anything? Crisps? Snickers? Other goodies?" She peered at Aly. "A piece of fruit or two?"

"I'm fine," Fletcher replied.

"An apple?" Aly suggested, trying to be good.

"And you will be here when we get back?" Grace said in a demanding tone while pointing at the floor as though her action could cement them to it. "You're not going to leave us?"

"No," Fletcher promised.

"We'll be here, Grace," Aly said. With Fletcher looking as exhausted as he was, there was no doubt in her mind he'd be asleep in moments, and she wasn't going anywhere without him.

Fletcher fished the car keys out of his pocket. "If it makes you feel better, you can take these."

"Hmm," Grace said, and gave them both a stern look. "Okay, fine. C'mon, Del. A walk will do you good."

Del flopped back again and sprawled out. "Awww, I don't wanna."

Grace grabbed his ankle and gave it a yank. "Move."

Aly stayed by the window while Fletcher saw Del and Grace to the door. "It's gonna be hard for you to sleep with wings," she mentioned as he shut the door behind their friends.

"Yeah, but I knew you'd want to see them before I got rid of them," Fletcher replied, reaching for the buttons on his overstretched shirt. "And I'm too tired to regrow them. Removing them will be okay though. Extra energy to burn."

Aly tried to push back a sudden overwhelming need to cry. "Oh. I…"

Fletcher paused to peer at her. "Are you okay?"

Pressing her lips together, Aly shook her head. "I tried

to let go," she said and hugged herself. "I tried so hard, but I don't know how this thing works. You said you were okay, but I can feel you're not."

With a tilt of his head, Fletcher frowned. "You can feel?"

"Your shifts have been all... wobbly."

He smiled at her fondly. "Lovely, I'm *exhausted.*"

She felt miserable and had since she'd woken up, as much as she could hide it in Grace and Del's presence. "I shouldn't have tried to talk to Elaine, I should've remained hidden like you told me to. Every time I improvise, we end up worse for it and—"

"Hey, no," he said, walking over to her. Rubbing his hands over her upper arms, he continued, "Every time you improvise, something amazing happens. Look at what happened this time. You rescued Del and Grace, we learned a lot about what Elaine and Joseph were up to, and I learned something about your abilities. Yes, we might be tired and sore now, but—"

"You did?"

Fletcher smiled and tapped the side of his nose. Quickly unbuttoning the rest of his shirt, he turned around to take it off, then stretched his wings wide so she could study them.

The gray scales still covered most of his back from the neck down. Below his natural shoulder blades, he'd grown what looked to be a second pair around the point the wings sprouted. "You went with the finger approach," she said with a nod of approval. Skin stretched out between long, thin finger-like bones, similar to the anatomy of a bat's wing, and the skin of the wings attached to his back in two long strips on either side of his spine, all the way down to the small of his back. She'd made several mock designs as a break while studying for her finals and they both agreed the bat wing model looked to be the easiest to shift into. "Although, they're a lot smaller than I would've thought necessary."

"I shrunk them. Travel-sized. I wasn't adept at flying, but now I've grown them once, I can do it again. When I'm not so tired."

Her fingertips brushed the diamond scales on his wings and she watched in awe as he extended and bent them for her so she could see how they moved. "You're amazing."

"You're the amazing one," he told her. "I couldn't have done this without you."

Pleased, she smiled. "I suppose we both improvise pretty well. But... I still don't like that I take people's abilities away and I don't like that—I grabbed your flame and look what it did to you!"

"Okay, stop. Yes, you pushed me into my natural form, but my exhaustion is entirely my fault. I had to create these, and heal bullet wounds and get us out of there, on top of all the shifting I did yesterday. Besides, I don't think that..." Fletcher hesitated, then his shoulders and wings hunched. Turning back around, he smiled sheepishly at her. "Okay, you're gonna be angry with me about this one."

Feeling his tingle skip over her as he absorbed the wings, Aly narrowed her eyes at him. "Why?"

"You know when Rex was explaining your abilities, did any of it sound odd?"

Aly shrugged, not knowing what answer he was looking for. "All of this is odd."

Fletcher floundered for a bit. "Yeah, okay, that's true. Here's the thing; I'm not sure I believe him. Rex isn't his natural form, right? But it still *feels* like his natural form to me. And Elaine too; I asked her about it. I always wondered how he could know so much about your never-seen-before abilities without having felt it. How he *knew* for sure that three or more shifters would be a danger to you. The only way that he could be that specific was if he'd seen you in action."

Aly's stomach flopped. "You think he... ran tests? Or Maddie ran tests?"

Fletcher shook his head. "I think you have actually released on him."

That didn't make sense. "But he can still shift."

Fletcher swallowed. "According to Rex, Maddie said 'enhance'. I don't think she lied. I think *he* did. To deter you from releasing again, at least until he got you away from me. You don't 'infect' anyone. You're not a toxin. You're an... well, the best way I can put it is that you're an activator. Basically, you 'activate' their abilities. Switch it on. You control it, to a degree, and give them... something akin to what I can do. Rapid shifting ability, which, as a side effect, I guess, forces them into their natural forms. Except they can't handle the rapid shift, so they either...shift wrong and have a heart attack or something, or... manage to control it long enough for your activation to stop. In which case, because they're controlling it instead of allowing it to happen, it hurts. And probably damages their abilities."

She tried to make sense of that. "Oh..."

"If they let it happen, if they let themselves be pushed into their natural form, what if it makes their abilities *better* somehow? If you've released on Rex, and made his abilities better, it could explain why I couldn't tell Rex wasn't in natural form."

"Or maybe that's only for you. After all, we're supposed to have been built to be compatible. A weapon and her guards. Makes sense I wouldn't be able to do anything to you unless I target you." Aly blinked, then took a step back, shocked and horrified. "Wait. *Wait.* You *let* me touch your flame?"

Reaching out, he ran both hands up and down her upper arms and held her gaze. In a resolute yet gentle voice, he said, "Yeah. I did. I've felt your flame grabby thing before."

The room span uncontrollably leaving her lightheaded. "*What?* No. I—"

"Remember when you sliced your knee? Del had

recently moved to town and the four of us went swimming at the lake. The two of you were always trying to one-up each other and you did the stupid thing of jumping from one of the over-hanging trees, even though I begged you not to, and landed on an underwater log."

Aly groaned. "Please don't remind me." At the time, she'd been afraid Del would replace her as Fletcher's best friend because she hadn't been spending much time with him since Grace had come to town. It was an adjustment period for all of them, but they'd managed, especially since they had a stupid adventure story to share. "What does that have to do with it?"

"That night, you were... well, you were high on painkillers."

Color flooding her cheeks, Aly nodded. Del had loved that part of the story too. "Potato sacks and unicorns."

His smile was meek and he ducked his head. "You scared the crap out of me. That's the first time you'd gotten badly hurt and... I don't think I really got the concept of 'fragile' before that."

Her heart went out to him and she lifted her hand to touch his elbow. "Oh, Fletch."

"Penelope, bless her, knew how upset I was. She set me up a mattress on your floor. And... that night, you had a nightmare. You were ranting about flames chasing you, and I tried waking you up and... well... you opened your eyes and I felt something grab me. It felt like I was burning and I was forced into natural form. At the time, I didn't think it was you at all, just... maybe my body was finally breaking down. The more I fought it, the worse it became, so... I stopped fighting and let it happen."

Aly swallowed hard at the implications of that. Reaching up, she rested her hand on his chest.

"It went away. You went to sleep. I stayed up all night watching over you. And that was it. By morning, I was able to shift again and you didn't seem to recall anything at all, and I never thought about it again, right up until you mentioned seeing flames and I felt that feeling of being grabbed again."

So few words for what must've been a harrowing experience for him. "And you thought the best thing to do was to *let* me?"

Fletcher shrugged. "It worked last time. Sometimes you have to go with the flow. I knew you didn't want to hurt me. I trust you and in shifting, intent matters. So, yes. I let you touch it."

"You shouldn't. Not with this." She hesitated, then asked, "Did it work?"

"The enhance part?" He shrugged. "No clue. Last time, shifting was different—easier maybe but it's always been easy for me. But again, I didn't equate it with anything you'd done. This time... I did create some awesome wings."

She didn't know if that made it better. "You should've told me," she scolded.

He cringed and ducked her mock swat at his head. "I didn't really know! Not for sure. Not until I felt it again and it made sense."

Dropping her hands, she rested them on his hips, hoping for a cuddle and checking to see if that was okay, as well as wanting to continue the conversation. "Were you shifting at the time?" At his frown, she elaborated, "The first time."

He stepped closer to her and wrapped his arms around her shoulders, drawing her in. "No."

"Huh." She didn't know what that meant. Was there a time she could use her ability without being surrounded by shifters? Did she lose it? Or did she grow beyond it?

She didn't know.

Turning her head, she rested it on his chest and slipped her hands around his waist and clasped them behind him. "So, you think I enhanced all those other shifters?"

"It's an educated guess at best. I... I didn't have time to check, but... I mean, it's possible you do both? Take away powers of those who fight you, and enhance those that don't. Maybe there's some subconscious intent involved. Or maybe, since you're… if Rex is to be believed that is…"

She understood what he was inferring. "I work differently on Faceless because I am one?"

"It's a possibility."

"Or I kill shifters and we didn't check."

"I don't know, Aly. I really don't. Maybe distance is a factor. I just don't know. There's so many people lying to us and each other, I can't tell what's true anymore." He ran his hands up and down her back. "But I don't think you should fear your abilities. Don't try and hold them so close anymore."

She closed her eyes and listened to his heartbeat. "I don't want to be responsible for killing someone unintentionally."

"Lovely—" Fletcher began.

She raised her head to look in his eyes. "Seriously, it's already hard enough that I faint after every time. That puts us both at risk."

With a smile, he cupped her cheek. "And maybe you faint every time because you're trying so hard to hold them in. Maybe if you embrace them—"

Sighing, she dropped her head until the top of it rested against his chest. "I'm too tired to think. I feel like I should be reacting badly to this, but… Meh. There's only so much I can take."

"Nap time?" he suggested and made no move to release her.

Drifting her hand along his chest and stomach she traced the scales that remained there. "You are such a bullet magnet. Every time you're hit, it feels like my heart is going to burst."

"Better me than you."

"Don't say that," she whispered.

Fletcher touched her chin, lifting her head away from

his chest. "I would take a hundred bullets so you didn't have to," he murmured and bent down to kiss her.

"We're seriously not going to stay here and watch the door, are we?" Grace asked. Arms folded on her chest, she propped herself up against the wall with her shoulder.

Del leaned with his back against the wall beside her. "Until we know for sure they're not going to just... run."

"I have his car keys."

"He's got money to hire another one. I saw it in his wallet."

"Del—"

"They *want* us to go home, Grace," Del said, and his voice rose in pitch and passion. "Forget about all of this. Go and be normal. There is no normal anymore, not with all this out there."

She looked down the hallway toward the hotel room Aly and Fletcher were in. "You believe everything he's said?"

Del scrunched his face. "I believe he believes it. I believe she believes. And... I don't know what happened back there, but, like, it's literally obvious they've seen that sort of thing before. Even Elaine and Joseph, they just *reacted.*"

Grace hummed her agreement.

"A secret underground war? There's so many games and stories and even actual history with that premise. Adding shapeshifters to the mix, yeah, I believe all that. I mean, seriously. Cloned, reptilian-branded shapeshifters, all with biblical names. Let's think about how wrong that is to start with."

Grace nodded solemnly. "Yeah. Sounds like someone bought that overlord conspiracy theory."

"Or *started* it," Del muttered. "Not to mention human cloning. How many UN accords does that go against?"

"A lot."

"Do we even have the technology to do that?" Del

asked.

"We have nanobots killing cancer cells in mice. We have trackers the size of peas and body cameras with streaming capabilities that are smaller than the palm of your hand. Technology is ever-changing and adapting."

"*Now*," Del replied, elongating the word. "But eighteen years ago?"

"Dolly the sheep."

He conceded that with a grunt. "What about creating a full-blown adult human?"

Grace shuffled uncomfortably. "He met Aly at eight. After being an adult. Sooo…" When Fletcher'd dropped that piece of information on her, Grace hadn't known how to react. She hadn't known how to react to a lot of what he'd said. Having time to process it, she wasn't sure she liked it.

Del nodded to show he understood her concerns. "There's that 'born yesterday' trope thing. He said he's got sixteen years of memories, which, literally makes his brain younger than us, even if he's got an older body. It's like… we are what we experience, right? We spend all our lives growing up and changing into the people we become, making mistakes along the way, he didn't get that chance, just went straight adult. Probably didn't even realize how creepy that might be at the time he did it."

That didn't make her feel any better. "Maybe."

"He knew we'd have a problem with it and wanted to make sure we understood. I've never, *ever*, seen Fletcher do anything to make Aly uncomfortable. I've seen him be a dumbass, I've seen him be thoughtless, but never make her uncomfortable."

"Yeah, that's true. Still, I don't know how I feel about it."

"Not up to us, I guess. She's eighteen, can make her own decisions and such. She seems happy." Del pulled a face. "With him and them, I mean. She seems pretty distraught otherwise."

"Poor Aly. I can't help but feel she might be clinging because he's the only thing that's constant right now. And that it might not be good for her in the long run."

Del nodded in agreement and said, "Dude, like, it's Fletcher. The relationship part would totally be Aly's choice."

"Very true."

"That said, one of us should check that she's okay with it."

Grace nodded. "I'll do it."

"Before he leaves us behind."

Grace swallowed hard. "He could change into anyone and be gone. He could walk right past us and we'd never know."

"Exactly. So, yes, I'm gonna stand right here and watch the door."

"Hotel security will get suspicious."

With a noisy huff, Del dragged his hands out of his pockets and folded them over his chest. "Let them. It's not even just Fletcher. Aly doesn't want us here. She's just got more tact than he does."

"She might be right, though," Grace said. "Look at what happened today?" She lowered her voice to a hushed whisper. "We saw him shot, Del. Shot, right in front of us, and I don't know about you, but that freaked me out. We saw things we were never supposed to see. Maybe we should go home. We're in way over our heads here."

"Can you really go home knowing what we know?"

Grace tried to think about this logically. "We have no proof of any of this. Neither of us can shift. We can't help out. We can't fight. Elaine shot Fletcher, for *fun*. If that's the kind of world he really lives in, do we really want to be a part of it?"

Del stared at the floor in thought and Grace wondered what he was thinking about. After a moment, Del said, "We can take Aly with us. We take them both back. Fletcher pretends to be someone else again, with the three of us having his back. We all move to LA and you guys go to college, I do YouTube and Fletch does whatever. Everything goes back to normal."

Grace wanted that scenario badly. "Do you think people were really told she was dead back home?"

"No idea. But Fletcher and Elaine both told us the same story. So… probably. Maybe we should see if there's a library close so we can check the internet? Get on social media. Maybe talk to Aly's mom."

Grace's heart sank. "Oh God. Do you think Penelope even knows?"

Del looked up, aghast. "That would be horrible."

"I don't even want to imagine." Pushing away from the wall, she said, "What pant size are you?"

Del grinned at her. "Looking for a way to get into—"

"You stay lookout," Grace said, cutting off his tease with a roll of her eyes. "I'll shop. Can't be suspicious, you know. We need to actually get a change of clothes. And toothbrushes." She teased and waved her hand in front of her mouth as though to ward away air. "Cause that breath is *rank*."

He shoved her shoulder. "Don't make me breathe on you. One person hanging around in a hallway is more suspicious than two."

"So come with me. Faster with two and then we can come back and stalk the door again."

Del pressed his lips together, then pushed away from the wall. "Yeah, okay. There's something I want to buy."

CHAPTER 19

"Are you sure you're okay, honey?" Penelope asked.

"You look so tired," Roger included. "Your hair looks lovely though."

"I'm fine," Aly said, drinking in the sight of them through the laptop screen. She sat on the balcony of the hotel room, curled up in one of the wicker chairs. She'd tried to sleep, but, as seemed to be the norm as of late, her brain kept churning. Instead of tossing and turning and disturbing Fletcher, she'd decided to call her parents. Fletcher had said that would be okay before he'd fallen asleep, as long as she followed the process he'd outlined. And with Del and Grace still out, she had time to spare. "Honest. It's just... it's a lot, that's all. I wasn't ready for how hard it would all be."

"Running the risk of sounding like an old man," Roger said with a smile. "Make sure you eat properly."

"And take supplements," Penelope added. "Drink lots of water."

"You might laugh at us," Roger said, smiling lovingly at his wife, "but honestly, getting sleep and eating while you can will really help."

Aly nodded. "Fletcher's making sure we do that. But...

ahh… Dad, I need to ask you a medical question."

Roger smiled. "I'm pretty sure you're well versed on the birds and the bees, but we can do a refresher course if you—"

"No!" Aly blurted, completely embarrassed that *that* was his first thought. "No, it was something else."

Roger raised his eyebrows and waited for her to elaborate.

Chewing on her lip, she wondered how much to tell him. "Say… someone was hurt and… say, like a shapeshifter was able to replicate exactly the… um… area that was hurt and… what complications or side effects could they expect?"

"Honey, what happened?" Roger asked, concerned. "Because I can tell when you're making things up on the fly."

Clearly, being vague wouldn't work and she was too tired to think of anything else. "I… I don't want you to panic."

"We've been in a state of panic since this all began," Penelope said. "There's nothing you can say that will add to that."

Aly gave her a wiry smile. "I got shot."

Penelope rocked away from the screen. Her hand slapped down on Roger's arm, gripping it like her life depended on it, while her other covered her mouth. "What?"

"I'm okay. Really I am," she babbled and her talking speed increased the longer she spoke. "Now, this next part's gonna sound weird, but Fletch regenerated me. He said the bullet went into my liver, but he was able to replace the damaged sections, and feed me blood and— well—it's badly bruised and still hurts, and I'm wondering if that's bad and—like, I need to know what I should watch for. Complications and such. Cause, it's sort of like a transplant? I guess? With extenuating circumstances because it's an exact match to me and…" Noticing her parents' statuesque posture, she paused. "Um? Mom?"

"He... did what now?" Roger garbled.

She forced herself to slow down and speak clearly. "Some shifters can regenerate. Like regrow parts of their body. Skin. Organs. That sort of thing. Not all of them, in fact, most of them can't, but Fletcher can. He fixed me."

Pale, Roger looked over at Penelope, who sat rigid in shock. "In your liver, did I hear that right?" Roger asked.

"Yes. It was really weird how he did it."

"Well," Roger said and swallowed hard. "Liver. So. Um... jaundice... changes in—he fixed you?"

Aly nodded. "He rebuilt it. He said he's never done it to a non-shifter before, but it's worked on shifters, so... I mean, he's keeping an eye on it, I just think I need to know what could happen too."

Roger flopped back on his chair. "Bloody hell."

Aly resisted the urge to giggle-snort as Roger's English upbringing made itself apparent.

Roger rubbed his neck as he tried to regroup his thoughts. "It's... well... it's obviously possible, or you wouldn't be here right now."

Aly nodded.

"And... he matched you exactly, you say?"

"Yes."

"And... he knows how to match you exactly?"

"Yes," Aly said, as patiently as possible. She could understand Roger's hesitance and confusion, since what Fletcher did went against every medical procedure Roger knew. "He does."

"Okay... can I talk to Fletcher?"

Aly glanced over her shoulder and back into the hotel room. "He's asleep." Like she should be, but she found it difficult and she wanted reassurance from her parents. "But I'll get him to call you."

Roger nodded and cleared his throat several times as he worked through what she'd said. "Alright. So. Jaundice. Changes in appetite, although that might not be helped given the circumstances. Changes in urine or stool, especially the appearance of blood. Chronic nausea or vomiting. Um… I assume there's some residual bruising?"

Aly nodded.

"Take a picture of it at the same time every day. If it gets worse or doesn't fade, let me know. There will be some bruise spread, but if there's more than you think there should be, then tell me."

"Okay."

"Supplements. Especially Iron and Vitamin C."

"That's your advice?" Penelope blurted. "Take pictures and vitamins and—No. No. No," she announced, each no firmer and harder than its predecessor. "We're coming to you, wherever you are. Roger will be on the next flight and—"

The temptation to let her mother swoop in and save the day was immense. She wanted to be safe and warm and her family always brought her that. But if Penelope came, then Tim would too and that would put her baby brother in the line of fire. Given how many times she'd been shot at, and how many times Fletcher had taken a bullet in order to shield her, she couldn't do that. "Mom, you can't."

Roger looked skeptical. "Poppy—"

"You need to protect Tim," Aly protested. "We're still running. I won't put him in danger—"

"You're in danger!" Penelope shrilled.

"Exactly!" Aly replied, her voice rising. "I can't risk you!"

"I am not going to let you go through this on your own! You're just children and you're alone! You need—"

Aly shook her head. "Del and Grace were dragged into this mess and I can't risk—"

"Del and Grace?" Roger asked, bewildered. "How did—?"

"All the more reason you need us!" Penelope announced. "We'll be on the next flight. Tell us where you are."

"No."

The 'Mom' tone and the stern finger waggle arrived and with it the swift use of Aly's full name. "Alyson Rose Gale, you will tell us where you are so we can come and help you!"

In the past, Aly would have backed down and deferred to Penelope, but recent events had forced her to strap steel to her spine and take control of things. In this instance, she knew more about what was going on than her mother did, and she was sure of her decision. "Mom, I need to know that some of the people I love are safe and free of this mess! I won't risk you, and I won't tell you where we are. I called because I needed to hear your voices and ask you about Madeline."

Penelope's face fell and Roger reached over to squeeze her hand. "Maddie."

The anger receded. "There are things I need to know. Things only you can tell me."

"I'll go see what Tim's doing," Roger said, patting Penelope's hand before he stood.

Penelope nodded, turning to watch him leave. "What did Rex tell you?"

"Not a lot," Aly replied. "She was a talented geneticist. He used her."

"Or she used him. One of the things I have learned from Rex over the years is that he does, in his own way, love you." Penelope sighed. "That doesn't mean Maddie didn't love you either. I just... I never knew her, Aly. Maddie was fifteen years older than me. She left for college when I was three, and I didn't hear from her again. My mother disowned her... like she disowned me when I took you in."

Aly blinked and tilted her head. "She did?"

With a tight-lipped smile, Penelope shrugged. "Unwed, with a baby I'd apparently hid. She saw what she wanted to see."

Aly was astounded at that. "I never knew."

"I never told you," Penelope said and sat back in her chair. "While I can guess why Maddie was disowned, I can't say if you have other siblings out there. If Maddie has other children, I don't know about them. The only reason you had any contact with my mother was that she had Alzheimer's and couldn't remember that Roger wasn't your birth father."

As mundane and common as this family secret was, it still surprised her that there was someone in her family who felt that way. "Oh."

"I have only a few memories of Maddie."

Saddened, Aly bowed her head. "Really?"

Penelope leaned forward to rest her elbow on the table her laptop sat on and cupped her chin in a hand as she smiled at Aly. "I know you look a lot like her. You have her freckles and dimples."

"I do?"

Penelope nodded. "Maddie showed up once when I was fifteen. She was a doctor, working in a lab, and was completing her Ph.D. and she wanted to show our parents how she'd made it without their support. My mother thought—well, it doesn't matter what she thought. She wouldn't let Maddie in the house, but I snuck out to see her. We had a short time before my father reluctantly came to separate us. I wish I'd had more time to spend with her but... I see her in you."

Aly swallowed hard, not knowing what to say to that.

"I looked for her when I left for college. Sent a few emails, posted on message boards, even hired a detective, but I didn't get anywhere. She didn't want to be found. I never knew what happened to her until Rex and Maddie showed up on my doorstep holding you."

Aly lifted her head. "Rex *and* Maddie?" Rex lying was nothing new, but knowledge of specific lies could help her untangle a truth.

Penelope smiled. "They explained that they had to go

into hiding and that it was dangerous for a newborn. Maddie wanted her to be with family and that, because she was estranged, the people she was hiding from wouldn't know about me. Rex promised he'd be able to support me financially while I cared for their daughter. You were family so I took you in. Weeks turned into months, and then years and then…" Penelope sighed. "After I met Roger, Rex came back. I thought he was going to take you away, and I was prepared to fight for you, but he revealed Maddie was dead and the woman I saw was a shifter designed to gain my trust. He told me about shifters and about the war he was in, and how he was important to it. He told me that you weren't a shifter, and that, because of his importance, he was a danger to you, which is why he had to leave. He wanted you to have a normal life. He was just there to make sure Roger was who he said he was… and to give his blessing for formal adoption. To further hide you, he said."

Aly nodded and her mouth twisted bitterly. That sounded more like Rex. "Weren't you angry with him?"

"Of course I was. The timing of it was so convenient. But he's your birth father and he's provided for you over the years. He bought our house. Paid for your trust fund. Paid off my college fees. He did his best with the hand he was dealt."

Even though Fletcher had said that Aly was Penelope's niece, she was compelled to say, "You don't even know for sure that Maddie's my mother."

"I married a doctor, sweetie. I know." She leaned closer to the screen. "Aly, you're my daughter. Even if I didn't give birth to you, you're *my* daughter, and you're Roger's daughter. That is never going to change."

A weight lifted from her shoulders. A simple, unwavering truth was exactly what she needed to hear and Aly blinked back tears. Sniffling, she wiped her eyes. "Thanks, Mom."

"Have you talked to him?"

Aly nodded, knowing which 'him' Penelope was referring to.

"Do you want to talk about it?"

Aly lifted her legs onto the chair so she could hug them to her chest. "Can't."

Penelope's face showed she understood. "Did you get answers?"

"They only spawned more questions." Aly sighed and rested her chin on her knees. "And, I don't know how much of it was the truth, or half-truths because Fletcher was there and Rex doesn't trust him." Shuffling, she changed the subject. "Mom, did you name me? Or did he?"

Penelope frowned. "That's an odd question."

"Just asking," Aly replied with a shrug, trying to pretend she was less interested in the answer than she was. "Because reasons."

"He named you." Penelope smiled. "Rose was Maddie's middle name."

That made her feel better. "And Alyson?"

"Rex never said," Penelope replied. "But he's never liked that I shortened it to Aly. You always seemed more of an Aly than an Alyson."

She smiled at that. "Yeah."

Penelope peered at her. "How are you and Fletcher?"

Aly looked over her shoulder at the darkened room behind her. "We're fine."

"We're fine, fine? Or he's *fiine*," she crooned.

Aly blinked, then swiveled her head back to her mother. "Mom!"

Penelope giggled. "Oh, let me tease, I've been waiting years. Did he tell you what happened? I am insanely curious."

Aly nodded. "Someone tried to kill him, thinking that he was my bodyguard and if he wasn't here, Rex would come out of hiding."

Penelope stared at her, then slowly shook her head.

"Why didn't he just come back?"

"He originally thought they were after him, and that I'd be safer."

Penelope nodded to show she understood that line of thinking. "It must have been very hard on him."

Aly hunched her shoulders. "We're the only family he's ever known. It destroyed him to stay away."

"He'll always have a place with us. Make sure he knows that."

A door at Penelope's location banged open. "Mom! My turn to talk to Aly!"

Aly beamed as Tim, Aly's six-year-old brother, rushed over to the screen. "Hey, squirt!"

"Sorry!" Roger called from off-screen. "He got away from me."

"It's fine," Penelope said, moving to the side to make room for the ball of energy fast approaching. "We're finished."

Tim bounced. "Aly! Hi! Where are you? We're going to England! I've never been to England before."

"Yes, you have," Aly laughed lightly and her smile grew brighter. England. Of course. Where else would Roger take his family to protect them? His affluent parents owned several holiday cottages where they could hide.

"Oh, yeah," Tim sang and was picked up by Roger to sit on his knee to help keep him still. "I was just too little to 'member."

"Three years is a long time," Roger said. "You were half the age you are now."

"I bet Nan and Pa are so excited that you're coming," Aly said, tucking her hair behind her ear as she drank in the images of her family. "Make sure you give them loads of kisses for me."

Tim nodded furiously. "You're gonna meet us there, right Aly?" he implored.

The smile dropped from her face as her eyes darted between her parents. She didn't know what he'd been told regarding what had happened. If anything at all. "I…"

"Tim," Penelope said gently. "We talked about this. Aly has to do her own thing right now."

"Yeah, but Aly promised me she'd take me to a castle. She said there would be dragons."

"Tim," Roger said. "You know how we said that Aly's going to college soon and wouldn't live with us anymore. This is just like that."

"But it's *England*," Tim protested. "She's got to come."

"I'll try my best," Aly said, hoping to give Tim something to cling to. It might be a long time before she could see him again face-to-face. "I can't promise you, but if there's any chance I can get there, I will."

After ending the call with her family, Aly slipped back into the hotel room and quietly put her laptop away. Glancing around the room, she sighed and then stretched out on the bed beside Fletcher. While she knew she probably wouldn't sleep, she could rest.

Fletcher snuffled, then shuffled closer to her until his chest aligned with her back. His breath tickled her shoulder as he mumbled, "How's Mom?"

"She's good," Aly replied, reaching for his hand so she could hug it to her chest. "Ready to jump on a plane to defend us."

"Hmm," he returned, his voice thick with sleep. "Sounds like her. Nap?"

"Yeah. I'll try."

He didn't reply and, as Aly glanced over her shoulder, she saw he was asleep again. Smiling, Aly adjusted her head on the pillow and closed her eyes.

CHAPTER 20

Aly didn't think she'd ever experienced a more violent wake up than to be unceremoniously shoved from the bed and forced across the room. Tingles shuttered along her spine in waves and before she was even completely aware, she was squashed between the wall closest to the balcony and Fletcher's back. Cowering, she ducked as low as she could, while keeping one hand on him. She didn't know what was going on, but for Fletcher to react like that, it must've been bad.

"Whoa! Shit, dude, it's us!"

It was several heartbeats before Fletcher relaxed enough that Aly could peek out from behind him. "Damn it."

Del, frozen mid-stride with his hands raised as he stared at Fletcher stood at the end of the entrance hallway, while Grace had pressed herself against the wall behind him. Del blurted, "That was a freaky move."

Another long moment before Fletcher answered, "I'm a little on edge."

"A little?" Aly whispered. He barely acknowledged her moving around the room, and climbing into bed with him, but Del entering the room put him into instant attack mode.

"Seriously, that was literally like Superman." Del mimed the action. "*Whoosh*. How'd you move that fast?"

"Well, you barged in, yelling," Fletcher replied. "I just reacted."

"I warned you to knock first," Grace chided, swatting at Del.

"Bare-chested Superman," Del noted, ignoring Grace as he smirked at them. "Did we walk in on something raunchy?"

"If you consider sleeping raunchy, then yeah," Fletcher replied. Glancing over his shoulder, he saw Aly's squashed state and budged forward to give her room but not far enough that he'd stop shielding her. "You okay?"

"You scared the crap out of me," Aly told Fletcher and peered around his torso to look at Del. "You were so loud. Is something wrong?"

Grace shook her head and, with a dramatic roll of her eyes, said, "Del bought electronics and wants to impress you."

Aly smothered a giggle and Fletcher muffled an exasperated groan. "Now is really not the time for a new gadget, Del."

"But it's really cool!" Del proclaimed and lifted the plastic bag he held. "Grace and I were playing with it earlier and it's awesome. Wait 'til you see!" He dropped the bag on the bed closest to the door and opened it.

"It's nearly seven," Grace said as she moved away from the wall. "There's a buffet downstairs. Signs in the foyer said there was some sort of live band on later, so maybe we should eat before it gets busy."

Fletcher nodded and went to put on a shirt and his long sleeved plaid. "Great idea, Grace," he announced in a jovial, over-the-top tone. "I'm absolutely famished."

Smiling, Aly followed along with the game. "I hope they have pasta. I think I need some carbs."

"I think we all do," Fletcher said and grabbed his wallet

from the counter, then picked up the valuables bag. "Get some greens into you too."

Del pouted. "Hey, c'mon, don't you wanna see—?"

"Pretty sure there was an all-you-can-eat dessert bar," Grace announced.

"We can see it after, can't we, Del?" Aly patted Del on the shoulder as she moved past him toward the bathroom door. "Be right back."

With a long-suffering and completely put-on sigh, Del left the bag on the bed. "Fine. Whatever. I guess dessert wins this round!"

"Hey, Als," Fletcher called before she could close the bathroom door, and Aly poked her head back out. With a smile, Fletcher gestured. "Del and I will go get a table, meet you down there. I'll signal when it's safe, okay?"

"Not safe?" Del asked. "Why wouldn't it be safe? We checked the corridor before entering."

Aly sighed and closed the door, preventing herself from hearing Fletcher's answer. Still feeling groggy from the hasty wake-up and the little amount of sleep, she washed her face and ran her fingers through her hair. Remembering the conversation with Roger, she lifted her shirt to look at the bruise on her stomach where the bullet went in and a chill ran down her spine.

Gray scales had replaced the Fletcher-grown skin. Aly swallowed heavily as she ran her fingers over them. They felt like his scales did, soft and silky.

Aly lowered her shirt and stared at her reflection. Then she lifted her shirt again to check the spot again, certain she'd been imagining it. She hadn't. A jagged circular pattern of complete scales. About twenty in total, as beautiful and perfect as his, on skin that they didn't belong to.

Fumbling for the buttons on her jeans, she pulled them down to inspect her leg. The same circular pattern of scales, spread across a smaller area. Since her leg was less tender than her stomach, she poked the scales with her finger.

She could feel them like they belonged to her. Pressure against her finger, pressure against her leg. Scratching them caused a lingering sensation on her leg when she lifted her fingers away.

What did all this mean? Was her body rejecting Fletcher's healing? Had her toxin release reverted the parts of him in her back to their original coding? Would they change back once she'd gotten some decent sleep? What if her liver was compromised now?

Panic brimming, she opened her mouth to call Fletcher, then hesitated. He and Del were headed downstairs and the last thing she wanted to do was cause an upset. It didn't hurt, she didn't feel sick. She probably wouldn't even have noticed for a while. She could wait to tell him at a more appropriate time.

Plus, there was Del and Grace to contend with. If they didn't believe she was fine, they might not go home where they'd be safe. They'd join her and be subjected to the same constant danger, and Aly wouldn't do that to them.

Aly screwed up her face. She couldn't lie to Fletcher. She'd lied to him and kept things from him too much recently. She hadn't listened to instructions and gotten them into trouble. And maybe things had worked out better for it, but their relationship was based on trust and understanding. He'd asked her to tell her if there was any change, she couldn't delay that.

Scrubbing a hand through her hair, she turned away from the mirror. She'd have to find a way to be subtle about it.

Fletcher's tingles were a mere whisper across her flesh, softer and gentler than she'd ever sensed them, and she noted they were going down and away. Probably in the elevator. They were clearer too, since he'd gotten some sleep and she wondered at the delicateness of his shifting now. Was he right in his hypothesis? Did she enhance as well?

She should tell him about the changes in his tingles too. They should talk about it.

Taking a deep breath, she tucked her shirt into her jeans as she did them up, then checked the rest of her appearance. Presentable, if pale. She hoped Grace would see the paleness as exhaustion.

Plastering a smile on her face, Aly left the bathroom. "Ready for dinner?" she asked Grace, who had sat on the bed. "I'm starved."

Grace patted the bed beside her in invitation. "Can we talk?"

Aly tilted her head. It sounded serious, so Aly went to sit by her. "Sure. What's up?"

With an uneasy look, Grace bit her bottom lip which gave Aly a large clue about what she wanted to talk about, so Aly smiled.

"Let me guess," she said in as cheerful a tone as she could manage. "You're concerned about Fletcher and whether or not that really is him."

"Wouldn't you be?" Grace asked. "I mean, shapeshifters. That's so far out there we never would have believed if we hadn't seen it. And then to believe he really is Fletcher?"

"You don't think he is?"

Grace's shoulders slumped and she wrung her hands together. "I honestly don't know. I really don't. So much has happened. I *want* to believe we've got him back. Looks like him, sounds like him, it's got to be, right? So why am I confused?"

"Because we also grieved for him," Aly replied, trying to be reassuring. "I quizzed him thoroughly before I believed him, even though I can feel that he is. He knows things only Fletch could've known."

"Really?"

Aly nodded. "It was really weird, my heart was telling me one thing, my eyes another, it took a while for it to sink in."

Grace squared her shoulders. "You met him when you were eight. He already had experience as an adult and—"

"Ahh." She couldn't fault Grace for this. She'd had her doubts too. Plus, her birth father had also raised the issue. "You think he's been brainwashing me."

"No," Grace assured her, shaking her head. "It's... it's Fletcher. He wouldn't..." She pulled a face as she tried to figure out what she wanted to say. "I just... I'm allowed to be concerned. I want to make sure you thought about this part. It's... it's *weird*, Aly."

"For the majority of our friendship, I thought he was gay. He was never going to tell me he wasn't until he had to fake his death." Aly touched Grace's shoulder. "This is something Fletcher and I have discussed. In length. When I met him at eight, he only had about six years of memories, and most of those were *bad* memories. He never got a true childhood. He's never done anything inappropriate. Our entire relationship has been my choice, friendship or something more, it didn't matter. He was absolutely content to be my friend and stay that way." She snorted. "I wasn't."

"What I'm getting out of this is: we're older than him."

Aly smiled at the cheekiness in Grace's voice. "He's a widdle baby."

"We can tease him *so* much with that. He lorded his age over us, the first to turn eighteen and now, he's younger."

"We can definitely tease him! Cut up his meat so he doesn't hurt himself."

"Blow on his food. Tie his shoelaces."

"All the good stuff."

Grace nodded. "Okay. I just... I promised myself I'd make sure. At the moment, you don't even know where you'll be tomorrow."

"True," Aly said, accepting that with a nod. "But I'll be with him."

"I wouldn't be a good friend if I didn't have some concerns."

"And I appreciate that. Really I do. I'd be lying if I said you had nothing to worry about, but I feel I can say you have nothing to worry about Fletcher's intentions."

Grace snorted. "Mom *never* let me out of her sight at eight, and Fletcher somehow managed to travel alone without being detected. Is it a boy thing?"

Aly laughed as well. "White privilege thing. White eight-year-old boy, obviously there's got to be a parent close. As long as he didn't look scared and looked like he knew what he was doing, who would question?"

"True."

"Plus..." Aly shrugged. "I mean, he is a shifter. It wouldn't be hard to add a few years if people started looking at him funny. I met him at eight, but that didn't mean he was traveling representing that age, he might've aged down so he could talk to me."

Grace latched onto that and pressed, "Why did he talk to you in the first place? I mean, who does that?"

Aly turned her head and stared at the floor. "He was tired and lonely and I was interesting. Sometimes connections with people just happen. It wasn't just *me* he connected with. It was Mom too. And then later with you, Del, Tim, and Roger too. We gave him a home and family."

Grace nodded and then grinned sheepishly. "I suppose I'm one to talk, with my Twilight phase."

"What we want in our stories is different than what we'll accept in life. But I agree," Aly said with a wink and a nudge. "You hypocrite."

Grace's smile died and she asked in a small voice, "You really can't come home?"

Aly shook her head. "My 'biological' father was coming to take me away before people found out about me, so I think my supposed death would've happened regardless. I can't come home. It's not safe."

"But you think it'll be safe for us? We're connected to you, Aly."

"No one knows about you," Aly said. "You could—"

"Elaine and Joseph do."

Aly pressed her lips together. "Grace, everything I've worked hard for years for, I have to give up. I can't go to college. I can't do the things I dreamed of doing, not if I want to stay alive. You can. I'm not going to let you give it all up."

"You really expect us to be able to go back to our lives? Knowing all this?" Grace waved her hands around. "You expect me to go back there and *pretend*?"

Aly stared at her. "Do you *want* to come with us?"

Grace rocked back and looked away.

"Grace, you have to think about your mom and dad. They can't lose you. You need to go home. You have a life to live, we can't take that away."

"Sure," Grace said scathingly. "We'll just wander off home an act like none of this ever happened."

Aly pressed, "Fletcher was shot in front of you. You were threatened at gunpoint by people you thought were helping you. That's a constant thing for me right now. People with guns and running for our lives. You don't want this. I don't want this and I don't have a choice. You do."

"What if you both die for real? We'd *never* know."

"Fletcher *will* find a way to keep in contact with you," Aly promised.

Grace held up her hand. "I get it. I do. This whole situation is terrifying and the threat of death is very real. But, like, I feel like I'd be a bad friend if I left you to deal with this on your own."

Reaching out, Aly wove her fingers through Grace's upheld hand. "You're not." With a squeeze, she continued, "I'm not on my own. I'm with Fletcher. We'll be okay."

"I wish I had your confidence."

Fletcher double tapped her, and Aly turned her head toward the door. Before Grace could reply, Aly stood. "Look, the boys are waiting and I think this is a conversation the four of us should have."

Grace sighed. "Yeah. You're right."

Glancing around the room out of habit, Aly asked, "Did Del leave his electronics in the bag?"

"I think he's got it on him," Grace said with a light shrug.

"Did you get clothes for tonight?"

Grace gestured the bag. "In the bag, along with a backpack. Fletch said to buy one. Why?"

Aly nodded. Moving to the clothes bag that Fletcher had left on the bed, she said, "We should pack them and take the bag with us."

Grace tilted her head. "Why?"

"In case we need to leave in a hurry," she said. Grace's expression asked for elaboration, so Aly complied, "We've had to up and run several times. I'd rather not leave anything in the room. Fletcher's already got the valuables bag, so this one isn't essential, but...but it helps me feel safe."

The confusion on Grace's face cleared and she nodded to show she understood. Pulling out the newly bought backpack, she said, "And that's important right now."

It didn't take long before the pair were heading downstairs to join the boys for dinner. Walking into the elevator, they both stood in opposite corners. Aly leaned her shoulder against the wall, the backpack of clothes on her back while Grace carried the one with Del's and her clothing in it.

"You look tired," Grace said. "Did you get any sleep?"

"Lil bit," Aly replied. "Then Del barged in and woke up the building."

Grace sighed. "He just doesn't think sometimes."

Aly's smile felt sad on her face. "It was nice to have a bit of normalcy."

It came as no surprise that Fletcher had chosen a table that was both well away from the door of the restaurant, and with a direct line of sight to it, and close enough to the buffet that Del didn't complain. They cleared themselves with the staff member on the door, and headed toward the boys.

Fletcher had a full plate, laden with meat and vegetables in front of him and was busy eating as fast as he could without it looking like he was stuffing his face. Del, with his plate in front of him, was showing Fletcher something on what looked to be a brand new phone. In the place setting on the other side of Fletcher, there was another plate filled with chicken, roast potatoes and some spaghetti, which he gestured at when he saw her.

"Oh, he'll feed *you*," Grace teased, and headed for the buffet to get herself a plate. "Perks of finally getting together, I suppose."

Smiling, Aly wandered over to sit beside him, tucking the clothes back against her chair. "Thanks."

Fletcher winked at her. "Totally being selfish. If you took much longer, I was gonna eat it."

"Of course," she said and reached for one of the bread rolls piled on a plate in the middle of the table. "What do you have there, Del?"

"New phone! Check it out," he proclaimed and in a single breath, rattled off all the details he could about it. He waved the cell around, swiping to show Aly features as she feigned polite interest.

Leaning sideways, she whispered to Fletcher, "I see why you called me."

"Save me," he told her with a smile while Del didn't seem to notice.

"Nice," Aly said when Del finished the spiel. "Sounds like you got a good one."

"They had a special on, so I paypal'ed some of my YouTube income to get it. I'm literally stoked to have an uncracked screen, and it can play so many more games than my last one and—"

Plunking her plate on the table, Grace flopped into the chair between Del and Aly. "Has he finished talking about his phone yet?"

"Just done," Aly replied.

"Good timing."

Del's voice lost its happy tone, "I figured, like, we'll still get to stay in contact then. Fletcher's gonna show me how to make it untraceable. If I don't give anyone this number or tell anyone about it, it'll be a safe way you can contact me."

Tears pricked Aly's eyes and she ducked her head to stare at the food. "Yeah."

"If there's a way to come back, we'll find it," Fletcher told Del. "College is a place of change and rediscovery, and you're right; LA is huge, we could hide among the sheer number of people. If we get free of this…" His hand closed over the top of Aly's wrist. "We can try. But I can't promise."

A brief smile burst on Del's face before it was gone. "That's all we're asking. I don't want to lose you again, man."

"I know. And you won't. We'll keep in touch."

"So that's it?" Grace asked, staring at Fletcher. "Del and I go home?"

"That's it," Fletcher said with regret. "After this, we'll get hold of Jonathan and you go home. You'll have to be extra vigilant for a while and we can work out some code words so that when we call, you'll know it's us. It's not ideal," Fletcher continued, "but it's all we can do." He squeezed Aly's wrist and returned to his meal.

Aly took a bite of her food and it felt thick in her throat.

"Are you sure we'll be safe?" Del asked.

"No," Fletcher answered with a mournful shake of his head. "But it'll be safer than coming with us. I think people will be more interested in us, and as long as you don't say you were in Nevada openly, the people chasing us won't connect the dots. There's no going back if you come with us, I'd have to ask you to give up everything in your life, all the friends, all the contacts, your YouTube channel, your parents, everything."

Aly frowned. The logic in that was slightly flawed, since Fletcher wasn't asking Aly to give up contact with Del and Grace anymore, but she understood why he was painting the 'no hope' picture. Plus, if she had to, she knew she would've allowed her friends to continue to believe she was dead if it guaranteed their safety.

"I wish it was different," Fletcher said. "But we need to run. Far and as fast as we can, outrun whatever's coming for us. When we're safe, we'll let you know."

"We'd better make the most of tonight then," Grace said.

"Everything ends," Del said. "We were splitting up when you girls went to college anyway, and probably would again after you graduated. Mom said it's rare that high school friendships last a lifetime. Like the internet's not a thing."

"Change might've been coming, but I never expected this sort of split," Grace said.

"I did," Fletcher murmured. Without looking at any of them, he stared at his food. "I've always known my time with you was finite. I was lucky to last as long as I did."

"Must've been hard with that hanging over your head," Del commented.

Fletcher nodded. "Which is why I'm glad I get to keep being friends with you, even if it's over the internet. Our friendship is going to change, but it doesn't have to end anymore. And that's something I can live with."

"Me too," Aly said.

Del looked at Grace. "We'll have to come up with something pretty compelling to make people believe us, especially if Aly's 'died'."

Grace snorted and waved her hand. "Nah. You had a fight with your mom, and we went on an impromptu road trip since we'd thought Aly had gone away with her mom. Car broke down out of cell range and it took us a while to get back to civilization. We might both get grounded, especially since… Elaine made me leave my car in Sac. Although, I suppose it's still there."

Fletcher nodded. "Probably. Claim battery trouble, and say you hired a car. I'll modify one of our car hire receipts with Del's name, since your dad has access to your bank account, he'll know you didn't hire anything with your money."

Grace asked, "What if Belinda told him about shifters or something like that?"

Fletcher shook his head and raised his hands, palms up. "No clue. Judgment call on you. If you want to tell him what really happened, that's up to you."

"Can't we jazz it up?" Del asked. "Sounds pretty mundane. What if—"

"Nah," Fletcher said. "People know you. A temper tantrum is perfect."

Del whacked Fletcher's arm while Fletcher laughed. "You dick. That's mean."

"Simple is better," Aly said. "Less likely that you'll be caught in a lie."

Grace nodded. "We'll be suitably devastated that we weren't around, but honestly… people never really talked to us about you when you died, Fletcher. They all sort of talked among themselves and never really bought it up. Maybe that'll keep going with you, Aly. Maybe they'll assume we found out and took some time together to grieve. I mean, we just lost Fletcher, losing another friend so close is enough to make anyone mental."

Aly nodded in agreement. "Hope so."

"That might be what you tell everyone else," Fletcher said. "But it might not fly with your dad."

"True…" Grace conceded, and tapped her lips in thought. "But! Maybe we can say finding out made us crazy with grief and we just had to get away. I mean, your mom knows you're not dead, right, Aly? She could say she told us."

Fletcher said, "That could work."

Aly shook her head. "Mom, Roger, and Tim are... well... fleeing the country right now, so they won't be around to confirm that. It'd appear even more suspicious."

"They are?" Fletcher asked.

Aly nodded and poked at her potatoes with her fork. "But we can't tell anyone."

"Where are they going?" Del asked, staring at her.

"I can't know," Aly told them with a one-shoulder shrug. A small untruth, since she knew they were going to England. "It's safer that way."

"Do you think people are going to go after them?" Grace asked.

"We don't know. We don't think so, like we don't think people will go for you, but we don't know. Because shifters do know about Mom. Which is why you need to be vigilant, especially when you talk about us."

"Secret handshake time," Del told Grace, nudging her with his elbow. "We'll stick with the 'temper tantrum' slash improv road trip. That should be an easy lie."

Stabbing a piece of chicken, Aly tore it away from the bone and forced herself to eat a bite. Fletcher's foot nudged against hers and, because she knew he was worried about her, she ate another bite.

Del, pausing in his meal to have a drink, eyed Fletcher's plate. "Man, that's a lot of food."

"Need the energy," Fletcher replied, nonchalant.

The walking stomachs that were Del and Fletcher quickly polished off their meals and went for refills, while Grace took her time to eat.

Distracted, Aly stared at her plate. The food wasn't sitting well, settling heavy in her stomach. She fingered the shirt above where she'd been shot and could feel the scales through the fabric. It worried her in more ways than one. If the skin had changed, that meant parts of her liver might have reverted too, and that could be a world of trouble coming. Or, maybe it would change back later and she wouldn't have to worry about it at all.

As Del went back for thirds and Grace decided to tease him by heading for the dessert table, Aly touched Fletcher's wrist to stall him from getting more food.

Lowering the plate onto the table, he sat. "You okay?"

"Not really," she mumbled, glancing at Del and Grace. Seeing them a distance away, she leaned over to whisper, "Fletcher, I have scales."

He sucked in a breath. "What?"

"Where you healed me," she rushed. "The skin is scales."

The burst of tingles across her told her he was checking and she moved her torso so he could get a clearer look. "That shouldn't be possible."

"I don't feel sick. I feel anxious, but not sick. I don't feel itchy or sore or anything else. I'm not displaying any signs of rejection and I asked my dad about that when I called. I just... I know it's not the right time at all, but I promised to tell you if anything changes."

He touched her face with a hand. "Really no pain?"

She cringed and wobbled her head. "I mean, it's still sore and achy because of the bruise, but there's no difference in pain."

"Ahh."

"There's some on my leg too."

"It... takes a while for a body to accept new parts," he said, sounding like he was reaching for an explanation. "Maybe it wasn't long enough for your body to recognize that area as you." He made a hum of consideration. "I wonder if this ever happened to Jonah or Adam."

"You think it could be a normal side effect?"

He lifted his eyes from her torso and, as he checked on Del and Grace, the tingles stopped. "Maybe. I can't see anything. Everything's still connected perfectly. No inflammation that I can tell... yet, I suppose." Reaching out, he rested his hand on her shoulder. "Seems like with you, anything goes."

"But you gave me blood. What if the rest of what you gave me has reverted—?"

"I'm pretty much a universal donor in my natural form, Als. I don't think we need to worry about that."

She puffed out a breath. While she was relieved she'd told him, it didn't do much to alleviate the anxiety she endured. "So, we keep an eye on the scales."

He leaned closer and pressed their heads together to offer comfort. "That's really all we can do."

A click echoed as Del took a photo with his phone, then flopped into the seat beside Fletcher. "Aww, how sweet."

Fletcher pulled back with an apologetic smile and turned to Del. "You need to delete that."

"Not happening," Del replied with a shrug. "Need something to remember you by. Look at them, Gracie. We should totally do that too."

"No, thanks," Grace replied as she slid into her seat. "I'm good. I love you, but I'm not into you."

His frown deepening, Fletcher insisted, "Del, I'm serious."

Del wasn't having it. "Relax, dude. I won't be uploading it anywhere. It'll stay on the phone and it'll literally be passworded to high heaven."

Grace picked up her spoon and cut into her cake. "After he sends a copy to me, of course."

"Of course," Del agreed nonchalantly. "Besides, we can just say we took it before you died. Right?"

Fletcher grumbled. "Del—"

"Tough," Del replied and stabbed his fork into the pasta. "I need it. I want to remember you both, together. Give us that."

Aly rested her hand on Fletcher's wrist. "We should take some of the four of us. It was one of the things I regretted we didn't do more."

"Me too," Grace said. "Fletch, memory is important, as well as having keepsakes for that. Do you know how really rare the pictures we have of you are? We had to hunt them down for..." she gasped and covered her mouth with her hands. "Oh my god, the Seniors tribute."

Fletcher laughed, his rising-in-increments belly laugh that Aly loved to hear. "That was a wonderful tribute." He pressed a hand to his chest and bowed his head in reverence. "I'm so touched."

"You ass," Grace said fondly, while Del groaned.

Still smiling, Fletcher said, "Alright. Let's make a night of it."

Their last night together was bittersweet. They talked, laughed and took silly photos together. They talked late into the night, reminiscing about their past, speaking about their future. To Aly, it felt like the last night they might have before separating to head to different colleges. Fun and sad at the same time, a finality no one could avoid. Scattered tears and long, spontaneous hugs all around.

More importantly, they rehearsed their story together, over and over again, until the lies were so smooth they were truth.

Early on in the night Grace called her father from the hotel room and explained their story. Del had a fight with his mom, and had to get away, so Grace went with him to stop him from being stupid. They'd left her car in Sacramento, because they'd decided to hire a car to go visit Del's brother in Denver via the scenic route and didn't think hers would make it, had broken down, lost her phone and needed some help and she was really, really sorry she didn't tell them her plans it would never happen again. She'd acted sufficiently surprised when Jonathan said he was close and would pick her up in the morning.

Not once did he mention Aly, and Aly suspected that was because he wanted to break the news to Grace in person. Grace also said Jonathan mentioned 'they' were close and the way he phrased it did not sound like he meant him and Lan, so they assumed he meant Belinda.

It lurked at the back of her head for the rest of the

night. Belinda Bell. She was the person who started all of this. All the running and hiding and uncertainty. She took Fletcher's life away. She kidnapped Aly. It was all her fault.

Now she was close. What's more, she didn't know Aly and Fletcher were here.

If they were very, very careful, they could probably take Belinda for questioning. Aly didn't want to think 'hostage'.

Scenarios kept cropping up in her mind during the course of the night, 'what ifs' anxiety made her solve. Again and again, a hundred variations of tomorrow. It kept her awake, long after the others had gone to sleep. Del gurgled, Fletcher slept on his side, facing away from Del the snorer, and Grace was curled up in the bed beside Aly. Rather than tossing and turning, and disturbing Grace, she rose and snuck out to the balcony.

One of the beautiful things about an isolated desert town was that there wasn't enough lights to drown out the brilliance of the night sky. The wind held a slight chill native to such an environment. Gripping the railing with both hands, Aly stretched up on her toes and breathed in the night air, before relaxing to lean on the railing with her elbows.

"Can't sleep?"

She smiled over her shoulder at Fletcher as he closed the balcony door. "Neither could you, I see."

"The mouth breather next to me makes it hard. Plus, I'm somewhat of a light sleeper right now." He hesitated, then shyly suggested, "It would've been better if we could've shared a bed."

Cheeks turning pink, she laughed. "And that would've meant Del and Grace in bed together, and that would never happen."

"God forbid. The world would end." He leaned on the balcony railing beside her. "Are you worried about tomorrow? They'll be fine. We're going to make sure of that."

"No," she said and tilted sideways until her head rested

on his shoulder. "I know they'll be fine. I was thinking about Belinda."

"I'm not going to let her get you," Fletcher promised. "I know you're scared but—"

"You're dangerous."

A noise ripped from the back of his throat. "*What*?"

"You could make her talk, right?"

He drew away from her, taking several steps back. "What the actual fuck?"

Aly blinked and stood up straight as she heard the hurt in his voice. "No. No, Fletch," she rushed and spun around to face him. "I worded that wrong. I'm really sorry. I mean, you're not dangerous to *me*. I know that. But you *are* dangerous. You're a highly trained ex-soldier. You know how to get people to talk. Shifters are scared of you. Your siblings are scared of you. Even if it's not warranted, they are."

Eyes wide, and visibly pale in the moonlight, he stared at her. He turned his face away and thrust his hands into the pockets of his sweatpants. "That doesn't make me feel better."

"Fletch, I didn't mean—"

He shook his head. "Tell me why you said that."

She swallowed hard. "Belinda has been one step ahead of us this whole time. Now, we're ahead of her. She doesn't know we're here. We could question *her* this time."

"Why would we want to?"

"She started all this. She killed you. She took me. She knew Rex had a daughter. She had his name; she had Maddie's name. I want to know how. I want to know why."

Fletcher was sullen. "I suspect Welcher's Purist front had something to do with that."

"But we don't know for sure. It would be confirmation. We don't have a lot of that."

"Like we could trust anything she said."

"The more information we have, even if it's

contradictory, the better. We've got more chance of figuring out the truth."

"It's kidnapping. Interrogation. It's illegal."

She frowned at his tone. "It's a request for a civil conversation and it's not our fault if she escalates the situation."

He narrowed his eyes at something in the distance, refusing to look at her. "And that's a distinction you're okay with?"

"Yes. We talk. We get answers. We leave. Simple."

"We'll be exposed. She'll see our car and follow."

Her brain had already conjured up this possibility, as well as solved it, so it was easy for her to answer. "So we park somewhere else. Slash her tires so she can't."

"Let's just commit murder too," he muttered. "Since you're so keen on breaking the law."

Her jaw dropped at the ire in his voice. "What's with you?"

He ignored that. "She can follow on foot and get our number plate."

"So we hire two cars. Get in one, drive to the other. Switch and go in the opposite direction."

"I can't believe you're even considering this."

"I can't believe you're not. Why are you being so obtuse? You taught me this!"

His expression was shy of a full-blown pout. "You called me dangerous."

She'd feel sorry for him if she wasn't so exasperated. "That *is* how others perceive you. I'm dangerous, too." She took several steps towards him and touched his chest. "Bumble-butt, you're not a danger to me. You're not a danger to our friends. Those people who find you dangerous don't know you, not like I do. I'm not scared of you and I know how to kick your ass. All I was trying to say is that Belinda is going to be flat-footed. I feel we should use that."

He remained standoffish. "Hmm."

"You said before you wished you'd interrogated those shifters."

"Hmm."

She poked him in the belly. "Stop pouting. Talk to me."

"Hmm," he said, and this one was laced with humor. The kind of 'hmm' he knew would get a rise out of her.

"Fletcher!" she scolded.

He dragged his hand out of his pocket to catch her hand before she could poke him again. "What if she hurts you?"

"She tried to intimidate me so many times, then claimed on the phone she could help me. She, like everyone else, wants me for something. We play on that."

"What if she's just as clueless as we are?"

"That's an answer too, then."

"Are you sure you want to do this?"

"I've been thinking about it all night. We might not get another chance. She has answers. I want them."

Fletcher sighed and closed his eyes in resignation. "We'd have to plan carefully."

Aly burst into a smile. "Of course."

"You'd have to do what I say and not be impulsive."

"When am I ever?" she teased.

"Don't make me list all the times lately," he replied. "More importantly, any information we might gain isn't more important than our lives or the lives of Del and Grace. If I say we abandon it, we abandon it."

She nodded and pressed her hand to her heart. "I promise."

"Okay then," he said and took her hand to lead her over to the small table and chairs on the balcony. "Let's talk this through."

CHAPTER 21

With her hair hidden beneath a pink cloche and her eyes behind a large pair of bug-eyed sunglasses, Aly sat on a bench, sipping a strawberry milkshake and doing her best to look nonchalant and inconspicuous. Del and Grace loitered across the street chatting to each other as they waited for Jonathan, but Aly could see their constant glances in her direction. Noah was nearby—positioned halfway between Del and Grace, and where Aly waited—leaning against the wall of a store and holding his phone like he was reading from it.

It was risky, her being out in the open like this, especially if Belinda was coming, but she couldn't remain hidden in the car. She had to see for herself that Del and Grace were safe. She had to be there to react as necessary.

They'd said their goodbyes. Cried and grieved and told jokes to ease the pain and now it was time to let go. In her heart, she wished for more time, as much as she knew that was impossible, it had been nice to have even a few hours where she wasn't running and hiding and could relax with friends.

A car pulled into the parking lot behind her, parking in the space several spots over from where she was. Aly turned her face away when Jonathan got out, his eyes fixed on Grace. She wasn't close enough to hear what Belinda said to Jonathan when she got out of the car, but it didn't seem to her like Jonathan took much notice as he hurried across the road toward his daughter.

Her heart twanged as Jonathan swept Grace up in a tight hug. As happy as she was for Grace, she missed her parents. She missed feeling safe. Sighing, she checked on Noah, then took a sip of her drink as she tried to be invisible. An extra in this movie scene, the focus should be on Del and Grace.

Belinda leaned down to speak to someone in the backseat of the car, before she followed Jonathan across the road.

The oddity made Aly curious. "There's someone else in the car," she told the air, knowing Noah was listening. "I'll wander past and have a look. There's a trash can I can use as an excuse."

Noah gave her a double tingle-tap acknowledgment.

She slurped hard on her drink to finish it off and jumped up from her seat. Hidden behind dark glasses and hat, she was confident she could look where she wanted to as long as she didn't turn her head.

At first glance, she didn't see anything out of the ordinary. The front two seats were empty, and there were people in the back, but her quick flick didn't really give her much chance to look. As she walked past the front of the car, she looked again, startled when she saw Bonnie staring at her. Bonnie lifted her bound hands and scratched her cheek, then turned her face away.

Aly's step hitched, but she kept going and tried to play off the misstep as a catch on the sidewalk. She'd thought her disguise had been good. Had Bonnie recognized her? Or had she seen Noah in the distance? Probably one, possibly both. The lifting of her bound hands was a signal, Aly was certain of that. "Belinda has Bonnie captured," she whispered as she dropped her empty milkshake container in the trash. "There were two other figures in the car."

Bonnie. Bound and captured. There was no way she could leave Bonnie in the hands of someone like Belinda Bell. Not ever. It was bad enough Jonathan had been taken in by the woman. It didn't matter that Bonnie may have betrayed them. She was Noah's sister and no one deserved Belinda.

"Now we have no choice," she said as she turned around to head back to her seat. As she moved adjacent to the car, one of its doors opened and a man got out.

The hair on the back of Aly's neck rose. Noah's tingle raced through her in warning.

She'd seen him before, not in this form, but she knew him in the same way she would always know Noah. She'd seen him before, in the diner back in Bellhollow, in the alleyway, and then again in the abandoned mall and he'd been with Belinda then too. Last time, he had been a shifter. Now he *wasn't*.

It was true. All true. She took away a natural shifter's abilities. She'd hoped Rex had lied. She'd hoped Noah had been mistaken. Now, she was confronted with concrete evidence and it sliced her up inside.

But it was also an *answer*.

The man stared at her in a way that unnerved her. Was the sense still there, even if he couldn't shift? "Hey," the man called and pointed a thick finger at her. "You."

Cover blown, there was no choice now but to act.

Aly charged him. The door was between them and she hit it with all her strength, squashing him between the door and the car. He cried out in pain at the action. She slipped between the cars and the door and grabbed the stunned man, hauling him from the car and tossed him out into the open parking lot. A gun clattered out of his hand and hit the gravel and Aly scooped it up as protection.

Peeking into the car to prepare to take care of the other person capturing Bonnie, she was surprised to see Ross staring at her. Ross and his clearly unbroken nose and his hands bound like Bonnie's. The unbroken nose gave her pause, but his appearance made her recall the prickly thorns against her skin back at the mountain. He'd been there, so she'd held his flame too. Had his abilities returned?

"Aly!" Ross blurted, frantic as he tried to lean around Bonnie to get to her. "Aly, what are you doing, you need to get out of here—"

She squinted at him, perturbed by his concern. Before, he couldn't have cared less about her. What had changed? Was it because he could shift again? Too little, too late. Ignoring him, she asked Bonnie, "Can you get out of those?"

Bonnie nodded, staring at Aly with wide eyes.

"Then run," she replied as she straightened. She checked the safety on the gun, then tucked it into the back of her pants and advanced on the man. She kept her distance as she instructed him to stay where he was and moved into a position where she could watch him, and keep an eye on Belinda as she approached.

Across the street, Grace, Del, and Jonathan were watching, with Jonathan standing protectively in front of the other two. She had hoped that they'd be gone before she and Noah acted, but it had been out of her hands. Del and Grace had been let in on their plans first thing this morning and had been given their own instructions to find out if Jonathan knew about shifters, and, if he did, explain to him what was going on or get him out of there. She'd hoped they'd had a chance to, or this could go bad.

Because she was watching, she saw the moment Belinda recognized her. It was the same moment that Noah, pretending to be a pedestrian on his phone and unaware of his surroundings, stepped into her path. They collided, Belinda manhandling herself past Noah without even looking at him, while Noah stammered half-hearted apologies.

"Wait!" Belinda called. "Please!"

Aly wrinkled her nose and took a step back.

"I can help you!" Belinda promised, quickening her pace.

"Yeah, right," Aly said and skipped back a few more steps. She thrust up her hand, palm toward Belinda. "That's close enough," she snapped and waited for Belinda to pull up. "Like I'd trust you."

Belinda smiled and it held that slight sinister vibe Aly always received when she was around the woman. "There's nowhere else for you to go. No one else for you to turn to. Everyone thinks you're dead, you're alone."

Aly laughed. "Bold of you to assume that."

"Stay away from her," Ross snarled. He leaped from the car, racing to stand between Aly and Belinda protectively. "Get out of here, Aly, we'll protect you!"

Bonnie, having followed Ross from the car, grabbed Aly's arm and tried to coax her away. Aly frowned at Ross' declaration. "Since when do you care what happens to me?"

"You know each other?" Belinda asked, that smile getting wider. "Interesting."

"Ross, back up," Aly snapped, then softened her voice to speak to Bonnie, "Just wait." To Belinda, she said, "I have questions."

The man Aly had thrown moaned, "Please," and Aly flicked him a worried glance. Had she hurt him more than she'd meant to?

Belinda commanded attention by planting her hands on her hips to look menacing. "As do I. Starting with—"

Knowing she had to remain in control of the conversation, Aly interrupted, "I'm doing the talking. How did you know about me?"

Belinda laughed. "That's your question?"

She wasn't going to be deterred. "Someone must have told you about me. Who?"

"And I'll answer that, but first we have to get you somewhere safe and—"

"I was safe!" Aly snarled and clenched her hands into fists. "I was safe and so well hidden I didn't even know about any of this, and you ruined that! I demand to know why!"

Belinda scoffed. "You can't demand anything."

"Give it back," the man moaned.

Giving up on trying to move Aly away, Bonnie snatched the gun from where Aly had stashed it and threw it to Ross. He caught it and brandished it at Belinda, holding it in such a way that it was invisible to passersby, yet Belinda could see it.

In the scant seconds it took for Ross to receive the gun, Belinda groped for her weapon to defend herself. The bewilderment on her face when she came up empty was laughable. "What the—?"

Ross crowed in absolute delight. "Now who has the upper hand, bitch?"

"Please!" the man yelped, the word tearing from his chest. He stared at Aly with feverish eyes, sweat dotting his face. His expression was this creepy combination of hunger and desperation and she took a tiny step back. He didn't like that, as he scrambled forward and lunged at Aly. "Please, you have to give it back."

She reacted with a startled yelp and a skip backward. Shifting her weight onto her back foot, she braced and raised her fists.

Bonnie moved to shield Aly, slamming her fist into the man's stomach. He doubled over and she grabbed the back of the man's head and smashed his face into her lifted knee. The man dropped to the ground, bleeding from the nose and groaning in pain. Bonnie gripped the back of his shirt and dragged him away from Aly.

"Gomez!" Belinda cried out in alarm. "What did you do to him?"

"How about we all calm down?" Noah suggested, and Aly swung to face him. He'd doubled back around, sauntering in and Aly smiled in greeting. She'd been aware of his position by the gentle, reassuring tingle, and was glad he'd decided to add himself to the conversation.

Taken aback, Belinda stared at him. "Will Ward, I presume?" she said as she found her voice. "Why am I not surprised?"

"You shouldn't be," he said, tossing Belinda's gun from hand to hand. "I mean, I was very obvious about walking into you. Last time we spoke, I told you to look into the Welchers. I'm curious to know if you did or not."

Belinda frowned at him, then sneered, "I am under no obligation to tell you anything. And I'm certainly not going to tell an abomination."

Noah stopped beside Aly, offering her a reassuring smile and said to Belinda in a sickeningly sweet tone, "And I'm under no obligation to stop Ross from shooting you in the face."

Ross' smile was sinister. "Oh, please. It would be my pleasure. Getting very sick of being called an abomination."

Belinda seemed unfazed by that as she pointed out, "Here, in broad daylight?" Her light laugh was scornful. "I don't think so."

Noah laughed. "We can change our shape. You'll only catch us when we want to be caught."

"She can't," Belinda said, in triumph and jabbed her finger at Aly. "She's not one of you. We'll always be able to find her."

Aly glared at Belinda and refused to be quelled by her. United front. Noah had drummed that into her. No matter what happened, she couldn't show fear or frustration, no cracks in the facade, only confidence and unity.

Noah turned his back on Belinda so that he could sign to Bonnie without Belinda seeing, and talk at the same time, "Willing to bet your life? I don't know if you've noticed, but this area is conveniently free of CCTV and I took the liberty of informing the local sheriffs that they wouldn't be needed. You're a dangerous kidnapper, after all, and it's my job as an FBI agent to ensure you're brought to justice."

Bonnie replied to Noah, something long and complicated, while he was busy talking to Belinda and Aly assumed she was probably informing Noah of why they were with Belinda. With a nod, Bonnie put her foot on Gomez's back to hold him in place and waited.

Belinda's eyes searched the area as she frowned. "That's a lie. You're not——"

Smirking, Noah turned back and said, "You've been faking being an FBI agent. For shame. The local law were most unimpressed you'd managed to dupe a fellow deputy."

She protested, "He asked me for help! He'll back me up."

"Are you sure?" Noah replied.

"You're a serial kidnapper, too, don't forget," Aly pointed out. "And a stalker, on someone who died in the park several days ago. Where *you* were. There's evidence and a paper trail. The sheriffs were *very* interested in that."

Belinda went pale. "What?"

Seeing Belinda finally rattled was empowering. All the times she had Aly running or scared was twisted back on her. They had the upper hand, answers would be next. "How many people died at the park?" Aly asked, ignoring Noah's sharp look. "I'm sure the sheriffs would love to know you were involved."

"Aly——"

"Me?" Belinda said, incredulous and pressed her hand to her chest as though they had physically threatened her. "The only creatures who died were abominations."

Aly's heart sank and she felt sick to her stomach. Some shifters had died. Not all of them, not with Gomez lying face down and unable to access his abilities. But the ones that were too close were the ones she guessed where gone. The ones who bore the brunt of it all. They might have had families. Friends. People who depended on them.

She had blood on her hands. As much as Noah had tried to keep her from finding out for certain, now she knew.

"She doesn't believe we're people," Ross snarled. "How callous can you be?"

"I assume you had something to do with it," Belinda said at Ross. "Some sort of airborne toxin? Poison?"

Her. She did it. She was the toxin that killed those people.

There was a strange sort of disconnect in Aly's head. She did it. It was because of her people had died. But it didn't feel real. She hadn't meant to. It wasn't her fault. It hadn't been anyone she'd known and all she'd done was snuffed out their flames.

"Not your fault," Noah told her in a quiet voice and touched her arm. "Don't blame yourself."

She looked at him with tear-bright eyes, then to Gomez and decided Noah was right. It hadn't been her fault. She hadn't known, couldn't have known because her supposed father had kept it from her. If she'd known the truth, if Rex had told her everything, right from the beginning, it wouldn't have happened.

Now that she did know, she could flare early, before killing shifters, thus ensuring she only stole their abilities and not their lives, assuming it could even work that way. She'd tried to do that before, on the mountains, but she hadn't been certain it worked. Ross might know.

This was something she was going to have to live with and figure out how she could be okay with it. Later. Right now there were other answers she wanted and this was the only opportunity she might get.

Meeting Noah's concerned gaze, she nodded. "I'm okay," she lied.

Thumb stroking against her arm, he held her gaze and she wondered if the lie was enough, or if he knew she was pretending.

He probably did. He knew her best. But he seemed to

accept her ruse as he turned to Belinda. "Cooperate, and we'll drive you to the next town and leave you. Don't and we'll hand you over to the local law enforcement and you can sort out that mess."

"Or, we could drive her out of town and shoot her," Ross said. "Problem solved."

"We'll put a pin in that option," Noah said, then raised his chin. "Tell me what you found out about Welcher."

"Not much," Belinda replied, feigning a nonchalant tone. "For example, how do you even spell that?"

Noah raised an eyebrow at her, unimpressed.

"I'm not a research agent," Belinda snapped, folding her arms on her chest defensively. "I'm a field agent. Other people do the research, I act on it. You gave me a name, that's all. How am I supposed to find info on that?"

"You aren't very good at lying," Noah replied after a brief study and pulled out a phone with a black case. "No matter. I can look for myself."

"Hey!" Belinda complained. She stepped forward as if to retrieve her phone, only to be stopped by a sharp noise from Ross as he reminded her of his gun. "That's mine!"

A smile at Aly accompanied Noah's brief tingle. "She has a fingerprint scanner. A shifter hunter, with a fingerprint scanner."

She wanted to play and tease along, but all she could offer was a ghost of a smile.

Belinda scoffed. "You can't shift your fingerprints—"

Noah laughed. "And a pattern lock. You know the natural grease on your fingers makes that easy. Let's see here…" He thumb-scrolled through her recent calls. "Who's 'Tegan'? That name rings a bell."

"Hey!" Belinda complained. She eyed the gun Ross held and didn't move even as she protested. "You can't do that!"

"Welcher's head of communications," Ross supplied, his body language suggesting he was itching for Belinda to give him an excuse to use the weapon. "She's the contact in the Purist front."

"She's the one who got to Mom," Aly said under her breath.

"Ahh," Noah said and clicked his tongue. "Mimic Identification and Prevention Unit? Really? What do you think they're trying to prevent?"

Belinda loftily announced, "The world from suffering your kind."

"Fanatic." Noah rolled his eyes, then frowned at the phone. "So you found info on the Welchers, and yet you were still going to give Ross and Bonnie to them. Nice."

"I was not—"

"Oh, bitch, don't lie," Ross scoffed. "You were going to sell us to the highest bidder. The highest bidders would've been them."

"Human trafficking to add to your list of crimes," Noah said and thumbed the call button. "Well. Let's see what she says."

Belinda held out her hand. "You'll never get her to talk to you," she insisted bravely.

With a grin and a tingle, he lifted the phone. "Hello, Tegan," he said in Belinda's voice. "It's Belinda Bell."

The jaw drop on Belinda was impressive before she drew herself up. "You'll never get the code."

Noah shrugged. "Yes, of course," he said, with a smile at Belinda. "Everything is ready for the transfer. Absolutely. I can... no, I had no intention of selling..." he frowned and tilted his head and his tingle told Aly he was augmenting. There was a long pause, then abruptly, Noah laughed. "I really shouldn't be surprised it's you," he said in his normal voice. "But I am. You really have your fingers in everyone's baskets... Yup, it's me... I could hear him in the background, be more careful... ... why do you care? ..." He rolled his eyes. "Yes, she's fine... them, too. Worse for wear, but we got them. Your girl here was indeed planning on betraying you, there's evidence all over her phone."

Aly tilted her head at him in confusion, and he turned his back on Belinda to hide as he mouthed, "It's Elaine." With a sigh, he started to wander as he often did when he spoke on the phone. Tight little circles that went nowhere and everywhere and Aly watched in silence.

His tingle was still gentle against her skin, so Aly closed her eyes and focused on the flames, trying to see his. If she could do that, she could see if Ross' flame changed. Or if that man's, Gomez, if he even had one remaining.

Since Noah was the only one shifting, the flames didn't want to form and she couldn't make them appear. She could feel something there, flickering just beyond her reach, but she couldn't bring it to the forefront. There was an invisible wall, one that she could press herself against and feel the lingering warmth of his flame.

Couldn't see, couldn't manipulate but could feel. Feel two other flames as well. Ross's thorny presence, a feeling that rubbed her the wrong way. Bonnie, an itch between her shoulder blades. Would Ross' have sparkles now? Like Noah's did? Is that what the sparkles meant?

The man's flame was absent. No sense of it at all. It didn't mean much, maybe she couldn't see flames under normal circumstances. Maybe she was trying too hard. Maybe there was simply not enough active shifters around for her to see the flames, even though she could still feel the Faceless.

"If I feel inclined... Well, I don't particularly care what they do, they're certainly not coming with us... and why should I trust you? You've not given me any reason to yet, especially if you're the one who sent Belinda after Aly in the first place. You started—I see... mmm... no, she's not cooperating... hmm... I'll try that, thank"—Noah huffed out an exaggerated sigh "—you want to discuss that now? ... I'll take it into consideration. No. Follow your drive, that's all," he said and hung up, stuffing the phone into his pocket. "Well, that was enlightening."

"Sounded like it," Ross said mildly without removing

his eyes from Belinda. "Going to share?"

"Nope. Ms. Bell, you need to answer Aly's question. Who told you about her?"

Belinda looked between them all, probably trying to out-think them. "So, Tegan is a shifter? I suspected, but I never had proof. Do all shifters know each other?"

"It's an exclusive club," Noah chirped. "Stalling for more time isn't going to help you. Tegan said to tell you her people are mightily upset by your actions and 'Glenn's at risk'."

Belinda's eyes flew wide and she swayed, making a gurgling sound like she couldn't breathe, so Aly guessed that Glenn was someone important. Her husband, probably, since Aly remembered Belinda mentioning one.

"So," Noah said conversationally. "Give us what we want, so we can go and you can run off and save Glenn."

With a hard swallow, she looked between all of them before she squared her shoulders. "I was given it."

"No shit," Noah said. "By whom?"

"Her mother," Belinda said, then addressed Aly. "She asked me to find you."

Aly frowned. "My biological mother did not ask you to find me. Madeline Spenser is dead."

"Madeline Spenser is the one who stole you," Belinda rushed as though desperate for Aly to believe her. "She and Rex tried to pass you off as their child. Your real mother's name is Lorelai—"

Aly shook her head. Maddie was her mother, Noah confirmed a genetic link to Penelope.

"—Darcy."

Noah tensed. Bonnie made a sound and Ross turned his head to stare at Aly.

Aly hesitated as the name registered. "Lorelai Darcy?" Lorelai? As in the Welcher cousin? And Darcy as in Noah's Darcy? She swung her gaze to Noah, seeing him rigid with shock, a shock that was echoed in Bonnie and Ross. "It's a coincidence, right? It's got to be."

Noah looked at her with an unreadable expression.

"Oh, come on," Aly blurted. "This is ridiculous."

"In the shifter world? No. Names are important."

"But... you knew her first name."

An unreadable look in his eyes. "We've never known her by any other name than Darcy."

Desperate, she turned to Bonnie. "You know Lorelai's surname?"

Bonnie shook her head and signed and Noah translated, "She said 'they're too secretive. We only found out there was a cousin by accident.'" Turning away from Bonnie, he continued, "It fits, Aly. In the grand scheme... she *knows*. And she knew before we did. She could be miles ahead and..." He sighed and ran his hand through his hair until he could grab a fistful. "Fuck, what do we do now?"

"Darcy and Welcher are in bed together?" Ross forced out. "Oh, that's just *perfect*. We need to get her away from here. And hidden. Fast. If Darcy knows..." Ross adjusted his stance, rocking away from Belinda in a sudden case of nerves. "Noah, we need to go to you-know-who."

"If Darcy knows what?" Belinda asked and was ignored. "Who do you need?"

"Agreed," Noah replied and groped for Aly's hand. "We need to go."

Aly didn't need to ask who they were talking about. She turned her eyes toward Del and Grace, swallowing the hard lump that formed as she forced herself not to cry. There wouldn't be time. Noah wanted to run. Run far and fast. She could feel that need vibrating through him.

But there was something more important she had to do first. "What info did Darcy give you?"

"Aly, we need to go."

Taking a step forward, she urged, "My name? My age? What info did you have?"

Confused, Belinda answered, "I had a list of possible names and ages. You were the seventh I checked and the only one with an abomination bodyguard."

Aly's brain worked furiously. Darcy hadn't come after her. If she'd had Aly's name, she would've come after her in the last few months after Belinda first took her. Unless, Darcy was also trying to coax Rex out of hiding, but that didn't make sense if Rex was Alistair, because Lorelai Darcy was his cousin and she'd sided with him over the younger brother? Or had she? Could Rex be the younger brother? What was his name? If that was the case why was she named after Alistair? Had everything she'd theorized been wrong or was this all some sort of coincidence? "Does she know about me now?"

Belinda shrugged and held up her hands. "I haven't been in contact with her."

Did that mean Del and Grace were safe from Darcy? If Darcy didn't know who she was for sure, would she leave their friends alone? Could they take the risk?

She was going to come out of this with more questions than answers.

"We'll take care of this," Ross said. "You really need to go. Where can we meet you?"

Del and Grace looked back at them, expressions torn and hearts aching and Aly had to turn away. She wanted one last moment, one more goodbye. Their goodbyes had already been said and any more lingering would make their absence in her chest hurt even more. She raised her hand, then let it drop, turning away from the pair, her heart breaking. She was going to have to trust they'd be safe.

Noah had been watching her as she'd had her internal crisis, and now he turned his gaze to Ross. "No."

Aghast, Ross protested, "You need us! To protect her!"

"Funny how you only want to now." He released Aly's hand and wrapped an arm around her shoulders to lead her to the car. They'd parked a distance away to better hide. "Hand her over to the sheriff or take her to the next town and dump her, I don't care which. Just don't kill her. Prove you can be trusted."

"Not if you don't give me a way to contact you," Ross returned.

"Bonnie has one," Noah replied and Aly guessed he told her about the tracker mail they'd sent. "And her trust is what matters." To Aly, he asked. "Did you get the answers you need?"

She nodded. "They only spawned more questions. But if you're asking if it was worth it? Then, yes. I think it was."

"Will, you can't do this, I can help you!" Belinda protested, calling after them. "I can help her! She doesn't belong with you, she belongs with her own kind and—"

With his arm around Aly, Noah pulled her close so he could shield her as they hurried away, his tingles leaving trails across her skin. Behind them, Belinda yelled denials.

Across the road from them, they kept their eyes on Del and Grace for as long as they could without it being seen as suspicious. "Can we?"

"We can't."

"I want…"

"I want to, too, but—"

She planted her feet. "She knows about me. Even if she didn't know for sure, it wouldn't take much to look at each of those girls and see I'm the one who stands out. Joseph and Elaine came after them because of me. What if Darcy uses them against us too? They can't go home."

"That's why they have to," Noah said and rested his hands on her shoulders. "If we take them with us, your 'death' turns from unfortunate to damning proof. Darcy will come after everyone we love and everyone Del and Grace love. This is plausible deniability. They *can't* possibly know anything, because we would never leave anyone behind who did. As long as they stick to the story, they'll be okay."

She wanted to believe him. She really did. But it seemed impossible. "Fletch…"

"I'm sorry, lovely," he murmured, stepping closer as if

to hug her. "I really am. If there was any other way—"

She broke away from him, racing across the deserted street to throw herself in Grace's arms. Noah could've caught her if he wanted to, she knew that, and the fact that she made it to Grace meant that Noah wanted this as badly as she did. She barely had time to look over before Fletcher was hugging Del just as hard.

"You have to be careful," she told Grace as she was squeezed so tightly the words came out more of a gasp than a warning. "Don't trust anyone."

"Keep each other safe," Grace responded, weepy. "Call every other day."

"Aly," Jonathan said and rested his hand on her upper arm. "I'm glad you're okay."

"He knows," Grace said. "He knows everything. He'll help."

She spared Jonathan a smile and closed her eyes, burying her face in Grace's shoulder. "I love you," she sobbed. "So much."

Someone tugged on the back of her shirt and she was swapped to Del while Fletcher smothered Grace.

"I'm so afraid for you," Del told her as he wrapped his arms around her and crushed her to his chest. She pressed her cheek against his heart and listened to its steady beat.

"And Fletcher," Jonathan murmured. "My God. I'm so glad to see you."

"Did Grace tell you everything?"

"She did. I'll protect them."

"Thank you."

The words didn't want to come, but Aly forced them. "We'll be okay," she said, desperately wanting to believe that herself. "We have each other. We'll find a way back."

"You better."

Fletcher cleared his throat, ducking his head to kiss Grace's cheek as he released her. "We need to go."

Aly released Del, only to find herself trapped in Del's arms as he tightened his grip. "Del—"

Del's voice cracked with effort. "Let me come with you."

"You can't," Fletcher replied as he gently pried Aly from Del's embrace.

"I can help you."

"I know you can, but Grace needs you," Fletcher said, drawing Aly to his chest as though Del could steal her. "Her story doesn't work if you don't go home. You need to keep each other safe. We need to go."

Del followed them to the edge of the street. "I could take recordings. Do an exposé on the bastards. We could livestream you shifting. Let the world know."

"If I thought that could help, I'd do it in a heartbeat," Fletcher replied. "But until then, it's safer if you continue your lives. Pretend we're dead."

"Belinda's gonna know that we know," Del said, desperately searching for anything that would keep them there and Aly understood that. She'd tried it too.

"And you'll be able to tell her how full of shit she really is," Fletcher responded with his lopsided smile. "Be loud and obnoxious about it."

Del's lips crinkled up in a ghost of a smile.

"We gotta go, Del," Aly said, tears leaking from her eyes.

Del swallowed hard, but he straightened his back and squared his shoulders. "You call us."

Coming to the edge of the road too, Grace leaned her shoulder against Del's arm. "Every day. Promise us."

"We'll try," Aly said.

Fighting back a torrent of tears, Aly allowed Fletcher to rush her across the road. She glanced over at Bonnie and Ross, seeing the pair securing Belinda in the car. "Somehow, I expected that to go different."

"Don't assume she's going to let this go, just because we beat her this once."

"You're worried," she murmured. Fletcher's fear was contagious and she could feel it spreading.

"I'm terrified. Darcy's known about you all along, even if she doesn't know where you are now. Minnesota may not be far enough. I don't know if anywhere is safe anymore."

Aly swallowed and had to concentrate to keep moving.

"Maybe it's time to call Rex. He might have information."

"Or more lies," Aly muttered. "But I don't have anything better."

"It always comes down to her," Fletcher murmured, talking to himself. "I'm never really going to be free as long as she's out there."

"Fletch?"

He spoke as if he were voicing thoughts as they came to him. "I always knew it would come to this. I always ran, but now I think it's time."

Fear dug its claws into her chest. Was he thinking of going after Darcy? "Are you—?"

Ignoring the unspoken question, Fletcher declared, "We should get fortified. Follow through with the plan and see who shows up."

Aly nodded.

Wordlessly they hurried, their pace shy of a run and Aly wished they hadn't parked so far away. Fletcher yanked open the car door for her when they reached it. His tingles were still strong, he was constantly changing augments in an attempt to waylay any sort of direct attack on them. After making sure she was settled in her seat, he rushed for the driver's door and slid in.

The tears she'd been holding back flooded her eyes. "They're gonna be okay, right, Fletch?"

Fletcher reached over and took her hand. Lifting it to his mouth, he kissed the back and said, "They're safe. We need to worry about us. It's a long drive to Minnesota and we have a lot to do."

Beep.

"Hi Uncle Lee, it's Fletcher. Monthly check-in, as promised. About the same. Enjoying life. Aly keeps quizzing me about colleges, I'm running out of excuses... oh you'll like this, her last suggestion was 'pest control'. Ahh, she's so wonderful. Surely it wouldn't be bad if I kept this life, would it?"

Beep.

"Hi Uncle Lee, it's Fletcher. It's not true, right? It can't be true."

Beep.

"Hi Uncle Lee, it's Fletcher. I-I- someone came after me. I had to—I had to abandon. Everything. Her. My life. I hate this. When will it stop?"

Beep.

"They came for her, too. Because of me. Fucking Purists and their ideals. She's safe. I kept her safe... Plus, get this, E was there, but it's... These new—gah what do I call them?—'cousins'. Something's... it's horrible. It's horrible and wrong and how could she do that? What's going on? I wish I could talk to you."

Beep.

"Hi Uncle Lee. I've decided to fuck it all and stay with this life. It's mine and I'm not giving her up for anyone."

Beep.

"Hi Uncle Lee, it's Fletcher. The rebel has resurfaced. I don't know what to do. Aly got scared and ran and... then this thing happened to her. And it's scared the shit out of me. I don't know what to do. I wish I could talk to you. I found R and B, and they said you were... well... holding out hope, I guess."

Beep.

"Hi Uncle Lee, it's Fletcher. I was using this as a touchstone. You know. A way to keep in contact even if the messages were unanswered. And they helped. But now I'm getting conflicting information about your demise. Memorials have been moved. Siblings are betraying. Aly is wrapped up in all of this and I need confirmation. Listening to me babble has gone on long enough."

Beep.

"Uncle Lee. Aly is Ten. Mom knows. I'm not running from this *anymore.* "

Beep.

"Fletcher, it's Uncle Lee. I'm coming."

To be concluded in '*Flare*'.

ABOUT THE AUTHOR

Rikkaine Thompson lives in the Northern Territory of Australia with her wonderful husband, one boisterous child, and two grumpy teenagers, and a puppers named Toby.

Eldest of three, she was born and raised in Darwin to teacher parents who fostered a love of reading. Her early years were filled with love, light and the written word, a love that has followed her all through life.

In high school, her family moved to Katherine, where she met her now-husband and they fell in love. At band camp. Before the movie was popular.

After graduating high school, she and her husband moved back to Darwin. Having children put a dampener on writing for a time, but as they started school, she found herself with a lot more free time to pursue the things she loved which didn't run away on stubby little legs giggling like crazy when she caught them.

Her parents taught her how to read, then how to turn the written word into pictures in her head, and she taught herself how to put them on paper. Or a post-it note. Or on the inside of her wrist in permanent marker at two in the morning.

Tangle is her third novel and she's currently working hard on the fourth and final book of the series *Flare*.

THE FACELESS SERIES

- Shift
- Twist
- Tangle
- Flare – coming soon

CONNECT WITH RIKKAINE

Follow me on Facebook
    https://www.facebook.com/rikkainethompson/
Follow me on twitter
    https://twitter.com/rikkaine
Visit my website
    https://rikkainethompson.com